# *Immortal*

Nick M. Lloyd

First Edition

Published in 2019

*Be kind to yourself — preferably without physically, or emotionally, burgling your neighbours.*

# ACKNOWLEDGEMENTS

For the third book in a row, top billing of acknowledgments goes to Therese my amazingly supportive wife. Without her forbearance and love, I could not have finished this story.

And much love and appreciation to my kids, who have continued to support me emotionally even when I've been a little … needy.

Heartfelt thanks also to my friends who have stepped-up and given their time and sage advice: Sally B, Richard C, Khosro E-N, Cecilia E-N, George M, Noel C, Rosa J, Michael E, Dougy M, Ella C, Arne W, Tom L, Ashley R, Bruce L, David L

And to the unnamed cast of thousands who gave 'ad hoc' opinions on blurbs, book covers, etc.

And finally, thank-you to the professionals who got involved. John & George at wearewhitefox, Sidonie Beresford-Browne who did an awesome book cover, Alison Birch at rewrite, Helen Baggott, Andy Mosley, and Chris at Writersservices.

I have been very well supported.

I hope that you enjoy reading the book.

# PROLOGUE

**London, Friday 4th August**

When Imperial College's students had been ordered to vacate the main campus for the whole of Friday evening the rumour-mill had gone into overdrive, settling on the view that an extremely influential investor was being given a private tour.

Coming a close second was the supposition that the entire place was being fumigated for rats.

The students were wrong on both counts.

The chancellor of Imperial College was hosting a presentation, but precious few of the invitees knew any more than the temporarily disenfranchised students.

The attending academics, press reporters, and politicians had been told nothing more than to expect something era-defining.

As Tim Boston was patted down for recording devices at the third and final security gate, he smiled; he was one of the select few to know the truth.

Tim opened the door to the lecture theatre for his colleague, Samantha Turner, who wheeled herself through.

Normally dressed entirely for utility, Sam was looking rather glamorous this evening. Her blonde hair, usually stuffed under a beanie hat, was now an asymmetric bob with electric purple streaks.

'Cool haircut,' said Tim as he followed her in. 'I didn't see it in the taxi.'

'Thanks for noticing,' said Sam. 'I thought I'd try for once.'

Tim chuckled. Sam didn't need to try – as evidenced by the many eyes following her as she entered the auditorium. His smile slipped, though, as he noted the initially approving eyes now looking for a plaster cast or other acceptable reason for her to be in a wheelchair.

*Superficial arseholes.*

Tim put it out of his mind, knowing Sam was accepting of it. It was she who'd pointed out that particular behaviour to him in the first place.

Looking around the lecture theatre, Tim reflected that it hadn't physically changed much in the fifteen years since he'd left the place.

The atmosphere was very different today, however. Along with the sheer number of people packed in, the nervous anticipation was palpable.

'A full house,' said Sam, glancing around the room. 'They're probably not even here.'

'They may be.'

'You know what MacKenzie's like,' said Sam.

Tim shrugged. 'We're here …'

Today was launch day for Francis MacKenzie's new MedOp service. As the core members of the MIDAS (Massive Integrated Data Analysis System) delivery team, Tim and Sam had been invited. From what Tim had managed to get out of Charlie Taylor, MacKenzie's right-hand man, there were at least nine other teams working – in strict silos – on other aspects of MedOp. Tim would have liked to meet someone from the quant algorithm team but whether any of them had been invited was unclear.

Charlie had said many times in the run up that MedOp team attendance was strictly limited. He'd gone on to say, in great detail and with notable deference to MacKenzie, that Tim and Sam had been very lucky to be invited at all and that they were absolutely not allowed to network at the event.

Tim looked across the room. Charlie was talking with Max Greening, the chancellor of Imperial College.

*He's networking …*

Sam leant over. 'The chancellor has won the lottery tonight.'

Tim nodded. It would be amazing publicity for Imperial College.

'I imagine Chancellor Greening has had full unrestricted briefings,' said Sam.

The tone of her voice made Tim turn.

Sam, her eyes wide and innocent, smiled sweetly.

'Charlie should have told you,' said Tim. 'But you know what MacKenzie's like.'

'Don't worry, I've practised my surprised smile,' said Sam, winking.

Tim smiled back.

Charlie had been in a relationship with Sam for almost six months – during which, he'd consistently refused to tell her anything about his own work with MacKenzie. It was not a high point in their relationship dynamic, and was possibly made worse by the fact that Tim had told Sam everything he knew. Which wasn't that much about wider MedOp activities, but it was more than nothing.

'Why would MacKenzie think we'd have leaked anything anyway?' asked Sam.

'It would have added to the general distrust of MacKenzie if we'd told anyone our role,' said Tim. The public was increasingly conscious of data privacy and how third parties used personal data. MIDAS was the most advanced data aggregation and analysis system ever developed; data privacy was the clear victim of its capability … but within a few hours everyone would be begging Francis MacKenzie to harvest their data.

'But … can people distrust him any more than they already do?' asked Sam with a raised eyebrow.

Movement towards them drew Tim's attention before he could answer. Charlie was walking over with a big smile on his face.

'Don't wind him up,' said Tim.

Charlie shook Tim's hand, then bent down and kissed Sam on the cheek. 'Almost time,' he said. 'Ready for the most momentous scientific proclamation of the century?'

'I'd enjoy it more if I knew more about it,' said Sam, point-scoring.

'You soon will,' said Charlie, the smile fixed on his face but now looking a little forced. 'I got you the best seats. Sorry, I'd better get back.'

As he departed, Sam turned to Tim. 'Front row … and that's just one of the benefits of the crippling pain and lack of mobility,' she said, tapping the arm of her wheelchair.

Tim winced. Almost five years after the accident, he still couldn't handle Sam's flippancy about her condition even though he knew it was an important coping mechanism for her.

Again, Tim craned his neck and looked around. Did any of these people look like mathematics geniuses, capable of writing a ground-breaking data analysis algorithm?

Sam nudged Tim. 'Over there,' she whispered. 'Behind Chancellor Greening, I recognise her …'

Tim looked. In the low lighting of the auditorium he could make out only the vaguest details of the woman's face but she did look a little familiar. 'Not sure.'

Moments later, Chancellor Greening took to the stage, to brief applause. As it subsided, he spoke. 'Government ministers, benefactors, academics, friends, and ladies and gentlemen of the press, welcome. Tonight, I'd like to introduce you to Francis MacKenzie, the father of entrepreneurial science advancement.'

The lights dimmed further, and Chancellor Greening stepped to the side.

An enormous screen which filled the middle of the stage slowly lit up. Gradually an image became clear. It was the head and shoulders of Francis MacKenzie: trademark thick black-rimmed glasses, a close-cut beard, and chin resting on the tips of his fingers, pressed together as if in prayer.

He slowly blinked and a took a breath, seemingly preparing himself.

Then, looking straight into the camera, he spoke.

'Good evening. It is my pleasure to address you tonight,' said MacKenzie.

Tim looked across at Sam to see her produce a mock yawn with accompanying eye-rolling.

'Many of you will have heard of me for my work on SpaceOp,' said MacKenzie. 'Some of you with longer memories will recall my corporate raider days.'

Tim knew this. He'd performed a detailed background investigation of MacKenzie before he'd taken the role at MedOp. Francis MacKenzie was ruthless and not particularly well liked.

'Today, in these brief minutes, I shall be telling you about my new venture MedOp.' MacKenzie paused. 'Looking back over human history, it is clear to see that for most of the time, life has been regarded as a very cheap commodity. The pharaohs, the robber barons, the various dictators, have all spent human capital without much thought. In the last fifty years, however – an eye-blink relative to human existence – social and medical advancements have made life valuable … treasured … precious.'

The screen faded out.

Total darkness and utter silence lasted for a few seconds.

When the screen lit again, it was filled with the image of a single fern-shaped leaf.

Tim looked closer. It wasn't a biological leaf, the shape had been created by a mathematical model.

'The fabled fractal leaf,' whispered Sam. It was the secret MedOp emblem.

The word 'MedOp' appeared superimposed over the leaf.

Just as a murmur started to build around the auditorium, a spotlight appeared at the side of the stage.

Francis MacKenzie stepped into it.

The murmuring stopped.

'I do not intend to make life cheap again. I intend to make it free.'

It was not clear whether MacKenzie expected applause or cheers, but the auditorium remained silent.

MacKenzie did not miss a beat. 'Nine years ago, I set up a corporation focused on life improvement via genetic engineering. The early work suffered from accusations of eugenics and sustaining the global elite.'

He paused for a moment to take off his glasses, clean them, and replace them. Then he walked to the front of the stage.

'But that was just politics, which frankly does not bother me at all.'

A polite chuckle filtered around the room.

'What did bother me, very much, was that it never really worked.' MacKenzie paused. 'Biological life is complex. I won't insult the mathematicians here by saying *infinitely complex*. But, as we hit unintended consequence after unintended consequence, I realised that solving the equations of life from first principles was beyond humanity's ability.

'For instance, my teams spent years trying to work out which genes controlled the development of arterial plaque, which enzymes and proteins were involved, and how they could be turned off. Every time a lead was found, months later, it would be shown that those same enzymes and proteins were also critical for eyesight, or balance, or liver function.

'So … here and now, I am formally surrendering to theory. I won't fight it. From now on … it's all about practical application.' MacKenzie scanned the crowd. 'So where am I going?'

The image on the screen changed from the fractal leaf to a spider-shaped robot.

'Health. Affordable and available.' MacKenzie looked up at the screen. 'This robot is my firstborn. Invisible to the human eye, it operates for up to four hours without recharging.' He paused. 'But what does it do?'

After waiting a few seconds, he continued. 'Injected directly into the blood stream, with special human antigens on its surface to ensure it is not rejected by the immune system … it eats arterial plaque.'

He pointed at a simple graphic that had just appeared on the screen. 'It doesn't care how the plaque is formed.' MacKenzie paused. 'Or why the plaque is formed.' He paused again. 'It simply demolishes it.'

Low background conversations sprung up around the auditorium.

MacKenzie talked over them. 'Within three years, MedOp will provide free arterial cleaning to whoever wants it.'

Tim had gone into the presentation knowing that MedOp would be providing the arterial cleaning, having been told himself six months previously. He had also known that MacKenzie intended to provide it as a free service for everyone. Paying for the service was a key aspect of the MIDAS application.

Chancellor Greening walked back onto the stage. 'Thank you very much, Francis. I believe you are prepared to take a few questions?'

Smiling in assent, MacKenzie turned to the audience. 'Questions. Please state your name and then your question.'

The house lights came up and a couple of the administrative staff handed out microphones to questioners.

'Professor Steven Johnson, Biomedical Engineering, UCL. Have you started human trials? And if so, where?'

Talk about a pointed question. Human trials with tiny spider robots injected into someone's bloodstream. Tim could feel MacKenzie's lawyers all holding their breath. If they'd run those tests without enormous levels of approval from government agencies, then MacKenzie would be complicit in a myriad of crimes.

Silence.

The image on the screen changed back to the fractal leaf.

'We have not yet *completed* human trials.'

A ripple passed around the crowd.

MacKenzie was being deliberately antagonistic. The word completed could be interpreted in many ways.

Sam laughed quietly. 'Showman.'

'Show *off,* more like,' replied Tim.

MacKenzie turned back to the screen. 'But to wind in my own innate desire for shock and awe, I will clarify. No, we have not yet started human trials. Next question?'

'Mary Cleaves, Harefield Hospital,' said a voice towards the back. 'How does the immunosuppression work?'

'I will not be sharing the underlying science,' replied MacKenzie with a slight shake of his head. 'But at the end of the evening, a data sheet will be distributed with facts about rejection rates and suchlike. I am sure you will understand, some information will be kept confidential.'

Chancellor Greening stepped forward and raised his own microphone. 'If I may. How will people apply for the treatment?'

MacKenzie addressed his answer to the audience. 'Taking the arterial cleaning will be one hundred percent elective. From tomorrow, any UK resident will be able to apply to join a waiting list. Once all tests and approvals are completed, we will start working through that list.'

'Simple as that, Francis?' asked the chancellor.

Again, MacKenzie shook his head. 'Not quite. People who sign up will commit to participating in a series of anonymous surveys across any subject matter chosen by MedOp. They will also provide detailed personal data along with a DNA swab.'

'But they will not have to pay anything?'

'Nothing.' MacKenzie paused. 'Just fill out the surveys anonymously and accurately.'

Historically, the weakness of online survey tools had always been convincing people to fill them in; response percentages were usually in the low single digits. MedOp applicants would have a very compelling incentive.

MIDAS would create, disseminate, and analyse the responses to those surveys, correlating them where required with the participants' DNA readings and all manner of other personal data.

Sam leant in close and whispered, 'I'm going to ask him about certifying the data privacy.'

As Sam raised her hand, Tim grabbed it and pushed it down. 'Please, not now.'

Sam looked for a moment as if she would overrule Tim, but she relented. 'Later.'

Back on the stage, MacKenzie continued to speak. 'I can assure everyone that all data received will be treated confidentially, and all applications will be treated fairly.'

'What political fallout are you preparing for?' asked the chancellor.

'The next three years are not going to be easy. I am in close discussions with the prime minister to ensure that although the service remains a private enterprise, MedOp enjoys the full backing of the British government, which will be examining the implications for international relations, tax, the retirement age… the list goes on.'

'Are you signing up for it yourself?' someone shouted from the back corner of the auditorium.

'I expect to need it, to remain healthy to fight all the upcoming battles.'

MacKenzie turned away from the audience towards the chancellor, but the heckler had a follow-up.

'Will you make immortality available to everyone once you crack it?'

From his own research of MacKenzie, Tim understood the basis of the question. MacKenzie had given generously to cryogenic research and stem cell research long before he'd started MedOp.

MacKenzie ignored the question. 'Free arterial cleaning for everyone within three years.'

After briefly shaking the chancellor's hand, he walked off the stage.

--------

After waiting ten minutes for the auditorium to clear, Tim and Sam headed for the post-talk drinks reception.

Again, Tim scanned the room. He hadn't given up all hope of meeting the mathematician who was responsible for the underlying data analysis algorithm. It was only two percent of the overall MIDAS code – Tim and Sam had written almost all the rest – but that algorithm was one of the most devilishly clever bits.

In fact, Charlie had helped with some of the coding logic too. Charlie's own background in behavioural modelling had supported their work on dynamic meme linking.

*Speak of the devil …*

Charlie had broken away from talking to the familiar-looking woman they'd seen earlier in the lecture theatre and walked over to join them.

'Are there other team leaders here?' Tim asked Charlie as he arrived.

'Nope,' said Charlie, reaching down and taking Sam's hand. 'You two are special cases.'

'You said there was a chance I'd meet a few,' said Tim, aware that he was sounding a little needy.

Sam came to his defence. 'Come on, Charlie.'

'I never promised that,' said Charlie, his eyes darting to the corner of the room where MacKenzie was speaking to Chancellor Greening. 'You know what Francis is like.'

'Who was the lady you were speaking to before?' asked Sam. 'I saw her in the lecture theatre behind Chancellor Greening.'

For a moment it looked like Charlie wouldn't answer, but then he relented. 'Xandra Kusr.'

*Ah…*

Tim knew her name. Dr Xandra Kusr was a neurosurgeon – a *struck-off* neurosurgeon.

'She's formally working with MedOp?' asked Tim.

'Almost,' said Charlie. 'I know that you know her background. It's complicated.'

'Can I talk to her?' asked Sam.

'No,' said Tim, aware the question had been for Charlie. 'We mustn't risk annoying MacKenzie. You know his views on compartmentalisation.'

Tim really didn't want to annoy MacKenzie. Their ability to earn significant money developing MIDAS was entirely reliant on the final discretionary bonus that MacKenzie would decide independently. MacKenzie was not known to be generous at all, but even less so with people he felt had crossed him in any way. The previous year, Tim had found an editorial in a business journal detailing a company MacKenzie had bought. The factory workers were rumoured to have been 'off' with him on his first site visit. So, MacKenzie had shelved his turn-around plans, stripped the assets, sacked the workers, and sold off the real estate – all within three days. The editorial stated that MacKenzie had been entirely upfront about his change of heart, simply stating that the original rescue plans had assumed a certain level of employee buy-in and motivation. When it became clear to MacKenzie that part of the equation did not exist, he'd implemented Plan B.

'I want to know what Kusr has been up to,' said Sam.

Charlie shook his head. 'Sorry.'

Sam's face registered disappointment. For a moment it looked as if she would wheel herself over to the woman in question, but then a voice interrupted the conversation.

'Mr Boston. Miss Turner.' The voice of Francis MacKenzie.

Tim turned.

'Is MIDAS ready to send surveys to applicants?' asked MacKenzie.

Tim took a breath before answering. MacKenzie knew it was. They'd been testing it hard for the last two months. 'We're ready,' he said.

'It's critical,' said MacKenzie. 'I need to track public opinion and keep ahead of any growing concerns. The information I get from that survey data is gold dust.'

MacKenzie was correct about the data being valuable. As well as using it for early identification, and validation, of negative public perception – which could then be countered with focused interventions – MedOp also needed the financial security it would bring. Participants very explicitly agreed, in their contracts, for the data to be sold to third parties.

'It's ready,' Tim repeated. He always felt uncomfortable when the commercial element came up. MacKenzie always stated that data tranches would be anonymised and individuals' privacy protected, but Tim knew that Sam seriously doubted the anonymisation would be enough. The available tools providing smart data triangulation were simply too strong. Sam should know; she'd designed the module used in MIDAS for just that purpose.

Tim looked at Sam, willing her not to bring the subject up.

She seemed to be considering it, but luckily Charlie – perhaps sensing the moment too –intervened.

'We think that at least five million people will sign up,' said Charlie. 'And they will commit to answering surveys every week to keep their allotted spaces.'

'Blackmail,' said Sam lightly.

MacKenzie smiled, appearing to take the comment in the intended manner. 'I think, Samantha, they're getting the better end of the deal. They tell me which butter they prefer, and I cure their heart disease.' He paused. 'Anyway, don't book yourself on any holidays. It's going to be non-stop.'

'We're on top of the next set of enhancements,' said Tim.

'Improved anonymisation …' said Sam quietly.

MacKenzie affected not to have heard Sam, but the tone of his voice indicated his mood had soured. 'I hope so. Your bonus depends on it.'

With a disapproving glance at Tim, MacKenzie walked away with Charlie hurrying after him.

'Not great,' said Tim.

'Sorry,' said Sam quietly.

They both watched as Charlie was waved away.

'I wasn't the only one who annoyed him this evening,' said Sam. 'There was the guy with the immortality question.'

'You can see how MedOp looks at first sight. There's some big ethical questions,' said Tim. 'Who wouldn't want to live forever?'

'Me,' said Sam with a tiny gesture at her wheelchair. 'Not like this, anyway.'

Tim took a sip of his drink and scanned the crowd.

The silence stretched.

'Sorry,' said Sam. 'You know I don't mean …'

Charlie slunk back. 'Dinner for three?'

Tim considered the invitation very briefly. 'Not for me, thanks. I'll soak up the atmosphere here for a bit.'

'Maybe find an algorithm writer?' asked Sam.

'Please don't,' said Charlie, with an admonishing look.

Sam gave Tim a final smile, before turning and wheeling away with Charlie. 'See you Monday,' she called over her shoulder.

'See you Monday,' said Tim quietly, to her retreating back.

Alone now, Tim watched the crowd ebb and flow whilst he finished his drink.

It should have been him taking Sam for dinner, but somewhere along the way, he'd missed his chance.

# CHAPTER 1

**MIDAS Butler Street Offices, East London, Monday 8th April**
Climbing the stairs to the company offices in Butler Street, Tim entered the password into the door and then swiped his smart card. The light flashed green.

Inside the main office area, he typed the daily encryption key-code into his phone and the room registered his presence by adding his name to a smart screen on the wall.

Sam was already at her desk. This was not unusual; a combination of poor sleep patterns, desire to leave at a sensible time, and the fact she preferred not to be watched during her arrival routine meant that she was normally in the office first.

Sam's hair appeared to have been heavily re-bleached over the weekend, and the tiny blue tattoo of the Greek letter psi stood out even more prominently on her neck. Her desk, ostensibly subject to the same overnight cleanliness policy as Tim's, was already piled high with junk: two soft drinks cans, a bowl of muesli, a raincoat, and a Virtual Reality headset.

'Does the extra colour mean you won?' asked Tim.

'Yep,' said Sam, gingerly leaning back in her chair. 'The Triple-Bs fragged their way to another trophy.' She made a gun from her pointed finger and blew imaginary smoke off the top of it.

'Has Charlie said anything about the exact dates of the next code delivery?'

'He was working on special projects for *Francis* all weekend.' Sam rolled her eyes. 'I didn't see him.'

'Fair enough,' said Tim, aware that Sam and Charlie were going through some relationship tension.

*Just don't dump him before we get paid.*

The thought jumped unbidden from some dark place within Tim's psyche. Luckily, his filter stopped him verbalising it. Charlie had been instrumental in them getting the contract for MIDAS, and his ongoing goodwill was critical.

'OrcLore?' asked Tim, nodding at the Virtual Reality headset on Sam's desk. OrcLore was an online role-playing game that had first interested Sam purely as a pastime but had recently become enmeshed in her work, as a potential source of data. It had tens of thousands of subscribers all running around a make-believe world interacting with each other, mostly fighting but sometimes having conversations.

'Yep. I finished the scripts last night. I'll give you an update later.'

'Great,' said Tim, moving over to his desk. He booted up his computer and checked the overnight runs. 'I look forward to seeing if your gamebots can extract information from other players whilst they're hunting wolf pelts.'

Sam sniffed in response, and then narrowed her eyes. 'You'll see.'

Tim turned back to his own screen and checked the status.

*Odd...*

One of the security logs was showing a data anomaly.

'Have you picked up the overnight server room prints?' Tim asked Sam.

'Sorry, no.' Sam dug around on her desk for a few moments, and then passed over a few A4 printouts. 'These are the office ones.'

Given that MIDAS was constantly connecting into millions of external data sources, MacKenzie had been obsessive about having intricate checks to protect against hacking. They used highly specialised passive sniffing modules clamped around the various ethernet cables within the main office and server room. The modules measured the tiny changes in electromagnetic radiation when signals passed to MIDAS from the office workstations. Separate programs monitored the various processes on every computer. By triangulation, and big data analysis, a security protocol raised alerts if there was a chance that data had been stolen, moved, or created without appropriate permissions.

The security log anomaly implied something had happened.

Tim looked up at the smart screens and then across to Sam. 'Have you noticed any data leakage?'

Sam shook her head. 'My stuff is all secure. Why?'

'One of my logs is showing a blip,' said Tim. 'I'd better report it.'

'Let's track it down first. Send me the log file.'

*Wise words ...*

MacKenzie's obsession with secrecy meant that Tim and his development team had no access to the MIDAS production systems installed in Anglesey. Just because their development system was showing a blip didn't automatically mean that MacKenzie's MIDAS production had been impacted.

*But if there was a risk...*

Quickly, Tim dropped an email to MacKenzie stating a possible hack had been registered and they were investigating.

The response came back in five seconds.

`Full report by tomorrow lunchtime.`

Toby – the third and final member of the MIDAS development team – arrived. Walking over to the wall where a sheet of paper was stuck on the corner of a smart screen, he scrawled '40 million' on the sheet. 'I changed my mind over the weekend. Immortality over freedom. Everyone of the right age who can read, write, and has internet access.'

It was their ongoing team bet as to who could guess the eventual number of UK MedOp applications by the time initial registration was frozen at the end of the year.

'So, you don't think anyone is put off by the data suck requirements?' asked Sam.

'Personal medical data, like the DNA swab, is a bit sensitive,' said Toby. 'But the surveys are just market research.'

'We don't actually know what is asked day-to-day,' said Sam, raising her eyebrows. 'Do we?'

Tim suppressed a groan. Sam was needling Toby. MacKenzie had forbidden anyone professionally involved in MedOp from applying for registration. Their families were forbidden also, but Sam was positive that Toby's father, having applied with a fake name and address, was getting surveys. In fact, Sam had always said she wouldn't apply as she didn't want MacKenzie accessing all her personal data.

*As if he couldn't have swabbed the desks in here for her DNA a hundred times if he wanted it …*

'Let's not go there again,' said Tim.

'Do you really not think it's worth it?' asked Toby, looking at Sam as he set his coffee down on the desk. 'This is an amazing step towards proper technology augmentation for humans. Surely it's reasonable if MacKenzie needs to pay for the research using marketing data?'

Sam looked uncertain for a moment, but then her eyes narrowed and face hardened. 'I get the maths, yes. Give me your data and I will give you good health.'

'So, you just don't want MedOp to tell the corporations what your favourite pizza topping is?' asked Toby.

'It's not that,' said Sam. 'I don't have a problem with selling the data as long as it's not attributable back to a single individual.'

'Agreed,' said Tim. A few months previously, MacKenzie had sold the first tranche of MIDAS data to a large pharmaceutical firm. Tim and Sam had triangulated searches around the company and its employees to see what they could discern about the contents of the data. It had all appeared clean. MacKenzie seemed to have adhered to his data privacy commitments.

'When can you get the real number?' asked Toby.

MedOp registration included severe preconditions that applicants were not allowed in any circumstances to discuss or broadcast anything related to MedOp. It was impossible to get the real number of applicants from public sources, but newspapers – with God knew what sources – had estimated that in the eighteen months since the Imperial College launch, five million people had signed up.

Tim, due in Anglesey later in the month, would have access to the production systems and had undertaken to try to get the real number. Of course, he would not attempt it if there was even a tiny chance of being caught, but he had some ideas. 'I'm not promising anything.'

'I accept that fear of a heart attack is a strong driver,' said Sam, 'but I'll stick with six million.'

'Why so low?' asked Tim, whose own guess was nine million. 'Is it really data privacy? Or do you think people are just waiting to see if the first candidates get eaten alive from the inside?'

Sam smiled warmly at Tim, causing a small buzz of satisfaction to flow through him.

The feeling ended abruptly as an alarm sounded and five of the smart screens on the office wall flashed.

Each of them displaying an identical message.

*We are the Ankor*
*We are 'Aliens'*
*You must obey us in full*
*to survive*
*There will be no dialogue*
*We will send critical*
*directives*
*A Gamma Ray Burst will*
*arrive in 164 Earth days*
*Three concurrent defences*
*are necessary*
*Deflector shield*
*Survival units*
*Community bunkers*
*Individual instructions*
*will follow*

'What's that?' said Sam.

'Some type of practical joke?' said Toby. 'An Eastern European hack?'

'Maybe a viral advert for a new online game,' said Tim, wondering if the earlier data anomaly was related.

'It's on my phone too,' said Sam, holding up her mobile.

'And mine,' said Toby.

Tim looked at his own. He had it too.

'Aliens,' said Toby. 'My mother is going to freak out.'

'She freaked out when they changed the shape of the one-pound coin,' said Sam. 'Didn't she go to bed for three days?'

'Yep,' said Toby, already dialling.

Sam dialled hers, too.

Tim considered calling his own father but decided to simply send a text checking everything was okay. He stood and looked out of one of the main windows onto the street below. Two floors up, and shielded by reinforced secure windows, Tim couldn't hear any sound from the street. As he looked closer, however, he could see groups of men and women clumping together and staring at mobile phone screens.

A few cars pulled over onto the pavement; people got out and congregated.

Back in the room, Toby was whispering urgently into his phone, whilst Sam had obviously completed her call and was now launching a series of searches within MIDAS and feeding them to the main smart screens.

Tim closed the window blinds and returned to his desk.

The central smart screen showed MIDAS in action: newsfeeds, social media feeds, and real-time automated surveys flooded the screen with text and information. The far right-hand screen simply showed a summary, whilst other screens displayed maps, video streams, and other information.

After twenty minutes of information bedlam, some relevant items appeared on the smart screen. This was data that MIDAS had determined to have the most validity, consequence, and relevance.

*Multiple governmental agencies across the globe have validated that the messages are coming from somewhere just outside the current orbit of Neptune. An elaborate hoax has not been ruled out but there are very few Earth craft out there*

\*\*\*

*Gamma Ray Burst arrival 164 days. Source unknown. Damage unknown. Large Gamma Ray Burst associated with previous Earth extinction event*

\*\*\*

On a new screen, Sam typed in 'alien invasion'. Within moments, MIDAS came back with:

**Alien Invasion largely rejected by data feeds. Trending words: pointless, unlikely, conspiracy**

There were also links to the most read and most recently published articles about alien invasion. Tim created a duplicate of the search results on his own desktop and started reading.

'I'd quite like to get a sense of the atmosphere out there,' said Sam, reaching for her emergency crutches. 'Coffee?'

'Are you sure?' asked Tim. 'We'll be able to monitor more from in here.'

'But we'll *feel* more out there.'

'Okay,' said Tim.

Knowing from experience that Sam could only function on crutches for twenty minutes before serious discomfort set in, Tim stood and retrieved her wheelchair.

Spinal injuries were bastards to manage, with crippling pain being the constantly lurking enemy. Once the final bonus payment from MacKenzie came through, Tim hoped he could convince Sam to try ground-breaking neural pathway regrowth treatment.

'I'll stay in and monitor the news,' said Toby.

Five minutes later, they were out on the pavement, Sam wheeling herself, as usual. Her chair did have detachable handles stored under the seat – *for emergency purposes only*. She was very clear on that. Tim had had his thigh punched on more than one occasion for trying to give unsolicited assistance.

Up and down the road, the pavements were filling up with other people who had decided to go outside too: mothers with babies, old people, and youths who should have been at school all gathered on the pavement.

The nervous energy was palpable.

Suddenly, being outside didn't seem like quite such a good idea. 'Maybe we should go back?'

'We're not going to suddenly be attacked by our neighbours,' said Sam, pointing towards a large group of middle-aged men and women congregating outside an electronics store a few doors down. 'Let's see what's going on over there.'

As they got closer, the crowd resolved into a collection of worried individuals. Newsfeeds showing on televisions in a shop window showed various governmental agencies asking for calm. All the programmes had a ticker along the bottom of the picture saying the prime minister would address the nation at two o'clock.

Tim reached for his phone to check the latest on the internet.

`Unable to connect`

'It's the start of an invasion,' someone said.

'Judgement Day,' said another woman.

Each phrase triggered part of Tim's brain to run a little simulation and determine both the likelihood, and the severity of the consequences.

*Not good!*

'You okay?' asked Sam, obviously seeing his face registering fear.

'Yeah, let's get that coffee,' said Tim, burying his fear.

Two minutes later, they entered their favourite coffee shop Bean Ground Down?

The proprietor was switching off the lights. 'Sorry. All my staff wanted to get home and check in with their families.'

'No problem,' said Tim, suddenly wondering whether he should have done the same. He turned to Sam. 'Do you want to go home?'

'I'm fine,' said Sam.

Tim called Toby and gave the same message. His sense was that Toby had left the building before Tim had hung up.

'I'd better check that Toby locked up properly,' said Tim.

'I've got to come back to collect my stuff.'

They returned to the office where they found Toby had locked up, and set all the alarms, correctly.

Tim opened his workstation while Sam gathered her belongings.

'Do you want me to come with you?' asked Tim, when it was clear Sam was ready to go.

'Nah,' said Sam. 'I'll be fine.'

'You sure?'

'I'm sure,' said Sam, wheeling herself out.

Tim turned his attention to MIDAS. The primary information had not changed. As far as he could see, the Ankor had sent just the one message, although rumours were emerging that certain world leaders had also received personal messages.

Tim just surfed. The benefit of staying in the office was that MacKenzie had paid for their development site to have incredibly fast internet access.

Several government agencies were reportedly sending a radar pulse back along the trajectory of the incoming message to confirm if something was there. They'd all been at pains to say that the Ankor would not interpret it as an attack – the power of the pulse was carefully set to be only just sufficient to make the eight-hour round trip.

*Let's hope the Ankor feel the same way*

At two o'clock, the prime minister, Joshua Timbers, addressed the nation. He looked older than Tim remembered.

*This is an unprecedented event in the history of humanity. We are working tirelessly across all government agencies to validate the message. Please continue with your lives as*

*usual. **My next update will be in six hours, or
sooner if new pertinent information presents
itself.***

For a statement that said nothing much at all, it hadn't
been a bad one. Reassurance had been given, and a clear
timetable for the next update as well.

Tim headed home and continued to browse.

Already the internet was awash with disaster theories –
the most pertinent being that historical precedent set a grim
picture for junior species, or societies, when the big boys
came calling. Even if the senior species was altruistic, which
was not always the case, it rarely ended well for the little guy.

The prime minister's evening update added more detail.
The various governmental agencies across the globe were
sharing information concerning the radio pulses they'd sent
towards the Ankor. Unfortunately, atmospheric interference
and signal scattering meant that no meaningful information
could be gleaned about the size or nature of the alien craft.
However, a craft did exist, it was currently somewhere near
Neptune, and it was approaching Earth under its own power
at a speed unattainable by any human technology.

The Ankor were less than three weeks away.

# CHAPTER 2

**10 Downing Street, Tuesday 9th April**

Colonel Ben Martel hunched his shoulders and stepped out of the side alley. Ahead of him a mass of at least three hundred chanting protestors swarmed around the gates of Downing Street.

The protest outside was indicative of raised tensions everywhere. Although full scale rioting still seemed some way off, the whole country was already on a knife edge as the oxygen of social media commentary fanned its flames of outrage.

*Is it simply fear of the unknown?*

Entering via a secret underground back route to Number 10, Martel was ushered into Cabinet Office Briefing Room A – COBRA.

'Thank you for joining us, Colonel,' said the prime minster. 'We're just about to start.' Timbers gestured towards an empty chair.

Martel scanned the room. He knew most of the faces present from the briefing materials. They were top tier Cabinet members with several high-ranking civil servants mixed in.

*And, of course, Francis MacKenzie*

Whereas other spacefaring nations had kept their launch capabilities under governmental control, the UK had licensed Francis MacKenzie to lead the ongoing British space programme. And – coincidence or not? – it had been Francis MacKenzie who, according the prime minister, had provided early warning of the approaching Ankor. A few hours before the Ankor's message had come through, MacKenzie had apparently intercepted a signal from their craft on one of his radio telescope arrays.

'We are all familiar with the content of the message,' said the prime minister. 'This group must achieve consensus on how the British government will respond to it. Firstly, let's assess the GRB threat. Colonel Martel is the MOD lead on the threat assessment and mitigation.'

Martel stood. 'The MOD believes the message is genuine. The GRB threat is not yet established. Theoretically, a gamma ray burst coming from an exploding star close to Earth would be fatal, but the Ankor have not given us coordinates.'

Questions erupted from every angle.

**How can you tell it's genuine?**
**Surely a hoax?**
**What else have they said?**

Of the fifteen people in the room, only two – the prime minister and Francis MacKenzie – remained silent.

Martel could see that most of the participants were still in denial of the fact that there was something utterly uncontrollable coming their way.

The prime minister raised his hands for silence and then indicated for Nadia Peterson, the deputy prime minister, to speak.

'Can't we check every nearby star to see if any are candidates to explode?' she asked.

'Every large star within three hundred light years has been assessed over the years,' said Martel. 'There are no obvious candidates.' He paused. 'Further out than that it is less likely the explosion would be critical to Earth.'

'But you've checked every possible candidate?' asked Peterson. 'Even those further away?'

Martel noticed MacKenzie roll his eyes dramatically. Peterson noticed too and returned MacKenzie an icy stare.

'There are one hundred billion stars in our galaxy alone,' said Martel. 'It is impossible to check every candidate.'

'But surely we can check the big ones …' said Peterson.

Francis MacKenzie cut in. 'Unfortunately, when it comes to stellar explosions, some of the most viable candidates are binary pairs. They are almost impossible to see unless they collapse into each other and produce a supernova. By the time you see it … it is too late.'

Peterson opened her mouth to respond, but the prime minister interrupted. 'We have the relevant experts digging for evidence, working across the international community.'

Peterson accepted the point and then turned back to Martel. 'What damage would an explosion like this cause?'

'The explosion emits very high intensity gamma rays which would strip away the ozone from our atmosphere,' said Martel. 'This would leave the Earth vulnerable to the full force of the Sun's ultraviolet radiation. Earth would very quickly become uninhabitable.'

'What does the MOD recommend?' asked the prime minister.

'The MOD recommends that the threat is assumed to be real. In one hundred and sixty-three days the Earth will be hit by a catastrophic gamma ray burst.'

Seated next to the prime minister was Molly Oakley, the home secretary. She now leant forward. 'Assuming it is real, what are our options?'

'We can't get out of its way. It will hit us. A shield is the only option.' said Martel, noticing the satisfied expression on Francis MacKenzie's face.

'This should be our public position,' said Peterson. 'But how do we establish whether the threat is real?'

'The Ankor have to provide us with the exact location of the supernova,' said Martel. 'And, even then, we may not be able to tell until weeks before the gamma rays hit.'

'Why wouldn't they tell us now?' asked Oakley.

The prime minister cut in again. 'We don't know for certain. That question is part of the wider investigation.'

'So, for now, we have to take whatever they say on trust?' asked Oakley.

'Yes,' replied Timbers. 'However, there is a little more to it. I received a personal message from them – along with a number of other world leaders, as I understand it – a message telling the UK to prepare to send materials into space for the shield.'

'Do we know what they actually want sent up?' asked the home secretary.

'Not yet,' said the prime minister.

'We must nationalise SpaceOp,' said Peterson. 'Take it under direct government control.'

MacKenzie put on an outraged face and started to protest.

The prime minister waved him down. 'No. We leave ownership and management as is.'

Nadia Peterson leant forward in her chair and slapped her hand on the table. 'This is unacceptable.'

'The MOD will be putting people into Mr MacKenzie's SpaceOp facility in Anglesey, but day-to-day operations will not be changing. There is too much at risk,' said the prime minister. 'That leads us nicely into Francis giving us a quick summary of SpaceOp's capability. I depend on you all to know this, so you can individually defend the government's position.'

MacKenzie didn't stand. 'Thank you, Prime Minister. As you know, SpaceOp has been active as a company for over ten years. My team has overseen launches both from Anglesey and by renting launch time from other platforms. We have rockets that can comfortably achieve low Earth orbits. Depending on the payload, we can get closer to medium Earth orbits. We are ready.'

'Short and sweet,' said Peterson. 'What have the Ankor said to you?'

'Nothing,' said MacKenzie. 'My facility captured the original ping that told us of their approach. It was just a ping, not a message. Since then, we have not received anything … other than the same message everyone got.'

A few murmurs around the table seemed to indicate that MacKenzie was perhaps not one hundred percent believed.

Peterson turned to the home secretary. 'How did the broadcast message work?'

'I have Scotland Yard's Cyber Security team working on it,' said Molly Oakley. 'We don't have anything concrete to share yet.'

Peterson turned to Martel.

Of course, Martel had a few of his own MOD team looking into it. Even with investigations underway for only twenty-four hours, they had already ruled out a few options. The Ankor couldn't have broadcast the message in real-time from Neptune. They must have already had some technological foothold on Earth. Martel's team had also identified an internet spike a few hours before the message came through but, when followed, the trail ran cold. 'I will report back the moment I have anything definite.'

The prime minister addressed the room. 'The predominant view of the other heads of state is that we treat the message at face value whilst continuing to assess the possible threats.' He paused. 'Obviously there are millions of conjectures, but our efforts need to be spent keeping the country calm and preparing to respond when the Ankor communicate further.'

Now Timbers passed out some annotated paper copies of the broadcast. 'We must stay together. Please review my own speaker notes regarding the Ankor message.'

**We are the Ankor**
*this is their name*

**You must obey us in full to survive**
*there is an external threat, as yet*
*unconfirmed, but assumed to be real*

**There will be no dialogue**
*they won't talk to us, they have their*
*reasons, we are investigating why this may be*

**We will send critical directives**
*they will tell us what to do, we will review*
*orders case-by-case*

**Gamma Ray Burst Arrival in 164 Earth days**
*these can be dangerous if close, but we assume*
*164 days is enough time to respond with*
*support from the Ankor*

**Three concurrent defences necessary: Deflector**
**shield, Survival units, Community bunkers**
*it is unclear and what any of these mean, but*
*we expect further information*

'Are other launch sites acting similarly?' asked Peterson.

Martel wondered if he'd imagined MacKenzie flinching at the question; he was now nonchalantly stroking his beard.

'Yes, it is a coordinated global response' said the prime minister, looking around the room for further questions.

Peterson continued. 'Colonel Martel, do we know how the Ankor got here?'

'Assuming we accept the GRB story as fact, the only way the Ankor could get here ahead of the gamma rays would be to perform faster-than-light travel – FTL. This is beyond our scientific understanding. If the GRB is true, then FTL is likely true, and that puts the Ankor way ahead of us technologically.'

'And if the GRB story is not true?' asked Peterson.

'Then,' said Martel, 'we know absolutely nothing.'

Again, the prime minister pushed the formal position. 'We will prepare as if we believe them. The alternative would be too great a risk. If we argue and procrastinate, and miss our chance to complete a shield, and then the GRB comes …'

The prime minister left this hanging, then turned to Molly Oakley. 'How are your national security plans, home secretary?'

'The police are reporting heightened tensions on the streets,' she said. 'We are having daily briefings to monitor and put additional controls in place.'

Timbers nodded. 'My intention is to continue to broadcast public updates, open and clear, each day. Hopefully that will help.'

Francis MacKenzie spoke up. 'As you are all probably aware from your own pre-briefings, my interest in alien contact goes back well over twenty years. Everything I have read, both factual and fictional, leads me to believe that our only option is to assume the Ankor are benevolent.'

Around the table people leant in to their neighbours and shared whispered conversations. Martel noted to himself that he would have made people speak more openly, but the prime minister seemed content to allow people their own private discussions.

After a few minutes, Timbers cleared his throat. 'To be clear: the speaker notes I have distributed represent the position this leadership team should be defending in day-to-day conversations with the media and other agencies. Any further points?'

There were none.

'Okay.' The prime minister wrapped up the meeting. 'We'll have these meetings daily until further notice. Thank you for your support.'

MacKenzie stood immediately and headed for the door.

Spotting the imminent escape, Martel interposed himself smoothly between MacKenzie and the exit.

'Mr MacKenzie,' said Martel.

'How may I help you, Colonel Martel?' asked MacKenzie.

'I'd like to finalise the arrangements for the permanent MOD inspection team to be established in Anglesey. Who should I liaise with?'

'I'm not sure that a permanent team has been agreed,' said MacKenzie.

Martel held MacKenzie's stare without responding for a moment before replying. 'I understand your position; however, a team will be established immediately in the national interest. Its permanence, or otherwise, can be decided at a later date.'

Martel waited a few seconds, interested to see if MacKenzie would try to regain the upper hand, but MacKenzie simply nodded, stepped around him, and walked out of the door.

--------

**Later that evening**

In a concrete bunker four storeys below the rioters in Whitehall, Martel relinquished all his electronics to a waiting soldier. Then, after being scanned, he entered the 'quiet zone'. Down here in the bowels of the government building, there was no electricity, no communications technology; just a series of concrete rooms shielded from any electromagnetic radiation.

'Welcome, Ben,' said the prime minister, shaking Martel's hand. 'Well done up there.'

'Thank you, Prime Minister,' replied Martel, with a deferential nod.

Timbers sat down at the bare table and indicated a seat for Martel. It was just the two of them. As far as Martel was aware, even Nadia Peterson didn't know about these briefings.

'What can you tell me about the Ankor?' asked the prime minister.

'Not much yet,' said Martel, 'but we've bounced radar beams off them. There is one roughly cubic shaped craft, somewhere between one and ten miles wide, coming our way.' Martel paused. 'It's fast but slowing. Probable arrival within three weeks. We cannot be sure it's alone.'

'Any evidence to suggest other alien ships?' asked the prime minister.

'None, but …'

'If we're measuring these things then others will be too,' said Timbers. 'I will front-run the information about the size of the craft in this evening's public address.'

'Understood.' It wasn't Martel's gut instinct to share that type of information widely, but he had no logical reason to convince the prime minister otherwise.

Timbers drew a short breath. 'How are the military preparations going?'

'Given the Ankor overwhelmed the Earth's entire communication network, it's hard to see anything technological hurting them. So we need to be ready to deploy conventional weapons in space.' Martel paused. 'Fortunately, as the Ankor asked us to prepare space launch infrastructure, we can focus work on rockets and payloads without drawing attention to ourselves.'

'Understood. Quietly, I hope.'

'Of course, Prime Minister,' replied Martel. 'My team is carrying out all aspects of military preparation in a deep underground facility like this at Porton Down,' said Martel.

'Are they invading?'

'There's no easy way to reconcile the facts: they gave fair warning of their arrival, they haven't done anything aggressive, but they have an uncorroborated cover story and are making demands for us to send them materials.'

Most of the scenarios Martel had developed over the years at the MOD had included aliens arriving with their own weaponry or remotely subverting Earth's own military facilities.

'We don't know what they want us to launch yet,' said the prime minister. 'What type of materials could they ask for that would worry you?'

'Assuming they ask for large volumes of metal, then they could be dropped back onto us,' said Martel. 'However, given the size of their craft, if they need orbital bombardment weapons, they could simply scoop up asteroids between Jupiter and Mars.'

The prime minister summarised. 'So, nothing obvious?'

'The most likely explanation is that they need the materials for the shield, or the materials are a pure red herring. We will have a better idea when the required payloads are communicated to us.'

'What's your take on their refusal to respond to questions?' asked Timbers.

'We have to assume they have a good reason,' said Martel. 'If the gamma ray burst is real, then it probably happened between one to three hundred light years away and has been travelling for one to three hundred years towards us. They could have been studying us for a few centuries and, based on those studies, taken the view that the authoritarian approach is best.'

'A lot of assumptions,' said Timbers.

'Were the messages you mentioned in COBRA new ones?'

'Each of the world leaders I've spoken to has only admitted to receiving one message, which came at the same time as the original broadcast,' replied the prime minister. 'They were all variations on the same *trust us* routine. Although, some, like my own, had specific people of interest mentioned.'

*Exhibit A – Francis MacKenzie.*

Martel had already met Timbers in a similar secret briefing the previous day, just hours after the Ankor had broadcast. One of the reasons he was focusing half his efforts on investigating Francis MacKenzie was that MacKenzie been singled out by the Ankor.

'I know about his business ventures,' said the prime minister. 'What can you tell me about MacKenzie as an individual?'

'Only a handful of non-business interviews exist,' said Martel. 'Of a personal nature, I mean. He's assiduously single, mildly asthmatic, and reads a lot of history books.'

'That's all we have on his personal background?'

'There is an entirely uncorroborated interview claiming he lived in an orphanage in his early years. Certainly, there are no records of living parents. It didn't seem prudent to drag his friends in for interview – not that he has many friends.' Martel paused. 'Everything on the internet is about his business ventures.'

'Does that include the SETI material?' asked the prime minister.

SETI was the American-led Search for Extraterrestrial Intelligence.

'He acquired his own radio telescope fifteen years ago when the Americans refused to entirely open their SETI data to him,' said Martel. 'We're still digging there.'

'I assumed you'd have found more,' said the prime minister.

'He's a powerful businessman with wide-ranging interests,' said Martel. 'But there isn't much out there about MacKenzie the man.'

'Next steps?'

'Paper-based research,' said Martel. 'Plus, we're still trying to get to people on the inside of SpaceOp and MedOp without raising alarms. GCHQ are on the case.'

Timbers remained quiet.

'I strongly suggest the MOD takes over the entire UK space response, Prime Minister,' said Martel. 'I understand you've received a direct request from the Ankor to keep MacKenzie in place, but the removal of one man cannot possibly be a deal breaker for them.'

'On what basis?' asked the prime minister.

'Controlling the unknowns,' said Martel. 'Plus overseeing the general security of the response.'

'I understand he has a large private security force in SpaceOp.'

'He has a large *private* security force,' said Martel. 'We need the British army on the ground there.'

'Sorry, Ben, but three-quarters of our prisons are run by private security agencies – and the Ankor explicitly told me to keep him.'

'He's outside the direct line of command,' said Martel, trying to soften his tone – he was used to giving orders. 'It feels like an unnecessary risk.'

'His attendance at COBRA is already all over the news and it is trending positively,' said the prime minister. 'He enjoys wide public support thanks to MedOp. I can't risk annoying the public as well as the Ankor. In any case, I spoke to him an hour ago. He will accept on-site supervision.'

Martel nodded; stationing trusted soldiers in SpaceOp would allay some of his concerns and give him more opportunity to investigate.

'A safe pair of hands, is what the public are saying,' said Timbers. 'You wouldn't want to have him for dinner, but you would want him to clean out your drains – thorough, meticulous, not afraid to get his hands dirty. Of course, he could be in league with the Ankor for nefarious reasons, which is why you need to keep digging.'

'I will keep looking.'

'And, meanwhile, I'll be telling everyone how wonderful he is.'

# CHAPTER 3

**Butler Street, Tuesday 9th April**

It quickly became apparent to Tim that he was the only person on the whole planet to have decided to go to work. As he left the house, his phone alerted him to the fact that the Underground trains weren't running. He decided to take a bus, but after waiting for an hour he gave up on that too. In the end, he walked. It took two hours – plenty of time to wonder if people really expected not to work for the next one hundred and sixty-three days … if that was the case, humanity would starve long before the gamma rays hit.

As it was, when he arrived at the office, Sam was already there.

'Hi Sam,' he said as he came through the door. 'How's it going?'

Sam raised her hand to acknowledge she'd heard him but did not take off her VR headset.

'Three mins,' said Sam distractedly, still clearly focusing on whatever she was up to.

'Okay,' said Tim, booting up his workstation.

As he absentmindedly watched the opening screens on his computer, Tim's thoughts drifted back to the radio call-in he'd listened to as he'd walked in.

*Can we trust the Ankor?*

Everything revolved around that question.

'Fuck you, Charles Tiberius Taylor!' screamed Sam, before pulling off her headset and throwing it onto the desk.

Tim didn't flinch. Sam screaming her boyfriend's name during a gaming session was slightly disturbing, but not unusual. 'City guards?'

Sam smiled, and ran a hand through her hair. 'I was hiding in the palace cellar … obviously testing the survey scripting. The city guard found me.'

Tim smiled, raising an eyebrow. '*Before* you finished the test.'

'Obviously not,' said Sam. 'The guard did find me in the cellar, but not until after I had ensured the scripts work. We now have twenty automated characters running around the OrcLore world. They will ask questions to player characters, and never ask anyone the same question twice. Plus, most players will think they're interacting with another real player – maybe just one whose first language isn't English.'

'Very cool,' said Tim. With tens of millions of people logged onto computer games at any one time, the automated extraction of information from gamers was going to be big. Assuming, that was, that the Ankor didn't kill everyone and that MacKenzie gave them a licence to reuse MIDAS once MedOp was up and running.

The advertising revenue would be enormous, although to appease Sam on data privacy matters, they'd need to sell it in aggregate with zero chance of database purchasers being able to identify individuals.

'Are you sure you want to be here today?' asked Tim.

'You're here,' said Sam.

'Fair point,' said Tim. 'But my dentist cancelled my check-up. So …'

'Anyway,' said Sam, indicating all the screens. 'Can you think of a better place to see exactly what's going on?'

Tim noticed one of the smart screens.

*MacKenzie: MedOp, Ankor, SpaceOp,
Transhumanism, Immortality*

'Are you spying on MacKenzie?'

'What's the issue?' asked Sam. 'We've got the greatest search engine the world has ever seen. He expects it.'

'You know he receives records of every search we do,' said Tim. 'He went mad at me last year when someone submitted the search, *Is Francis MacKenzie a sociopath?*'

'That was Toby,' said Sam.

'What's behind the Transhumanism link?' asked Tim.

'It's the standard stuff about MedOp and what it could lead to. Merging technology and biology, and all that,' said Sam.

'And Immortality? Physical, right?' asked Tim. They'd had the discussion many times before. There were three main varieties of immortality: spiritual, legacy, or the genuine live-forever physical version.

'I don't think he's given up on spiritual and legacy,' said Sam. 'But, you're right, most recent comment is on the physical one … entirely linked to the Transhumanism and MedOp.'

'Not the Ankor?'

'Nope,' said Sam. 'Have your views changed since the alien invasion?'

'Physical immortality … Unchanged.'

Six months ago, Sam had defended the right for people like MacKenzie to search for physical immortality on the basis that the world was already rife with inequalities. Life expectancies of people in the poorest areas of the world were well under half of those in the richest. Life-saving medical procedures, such as kidney transplants, were simply not available to the bottom tiers, and so new longevity treatments would not be any more unfair. Ruling out these treatments to one group of people would not save the others.

Tim had not outright disagreed with her – because eventually the technology would trickle down – but he'd taken a slightly dimmer view about the long-term damage of physical immortality from a cultural and happiness perspective. Without death, population controls would become fundamentally necessary. What about the billions of new lives not created? What about the loss of purpose for individuals? Death would become a curse that only happened to unlucky people.

'Anything new relating to the Ankor?' asked Tim, pointing at the smart screen.

'Nothing more than he owns SpaceOp and is currently a valued member of COBRA,' said Sam.

'Has Charlie said anything to you about the COBRA meeting?'

'Nope,' said Sam. 'He doesn't talk about Francis.'

'I suspect it's all covered by the Official Secrets Act,' said Tim, sighing inwardly. Having been best friends with Charlie during their doctorate studies, after a few years of Charlie working for MacKenzie, the two of them had drifted apart and the juiciest gossip had dried up. A few years after that, Charlie had started dating Sam and pretty much all non-work contact had stopped.

Tim's phone buzzed. A text from Francis MacKenzie.

**Update?**

Knowing that replying with, '*I stopped thinking about the possible security breach when the aliens invaded*' would not be taken as a joke, Tim replied that he had dug into the issue and it was highly likely to be linked to the Ankor broadcast, but that he was continuing to investigate.

'Shit!' exclaimed Sam. 'Just got a text from Charlie. Any second now …'

'What?' Tim looked up from his screen.

'Any second …' Sam typed something into her computer and then looked intently at a blank part of the office wall.

A smart screen opened showing an apparently static image. Although blurred, it appeared to be an infrared of the alien craft. Details were lacking – all that could be seen was a grid of hot spots joined by slightly cooler sticks. The image had a scale superimposed; the craft was five miles high, five miles wide. As the craft was facing directly towards Earth, its depth was harder to determine.

A stream of text under the image indicated the pictures were taken from an orbital telescope that had been swung around to point towards the alien craft. The timer countdown indicated that another picture was due in just under three hours.

'A pile of red ping-pong balls stuck together with drinking straws,' said Sam.

'I suspect the technology is a little more advanced,' said Tim. 'But you're not wrong.'

'Why didn't they bring a shield with them?' asked Sam, continuing to look at the image. 'Why didn't they simply appear in orbit above us?'

'I guess announcing their presence near Neptune gives us a few weeks to adjust,' replied Tim. Of course, he was suspicious about the Ankor, but not for the same reasons as Sam. There were plausible reasons for where the Ankor had appeared and for them not building the shield, which was going to have to be truly enormous – thousands of miles wide.

The issue for Tim, and the one bubbling on the internet, was *why haven't the Ankor given the location of the GRB?*

The positive identification of a star likely to produce an Earth-shattering gamma ray burst would help to corroborate the Ankor story.

A screen at the far end of the room buzzed. 'What's new?' asked Tim.

'More alien predictions,' said Sam, clicking through items covering alien abduction, invasion, and nuclear fallout. A lot of it was social media junk, interspersed with bland technical commentary from genuine scientists trying not to be dragged into wild speculation.

There were also many less scrupulous scientists diving straight in. Over five thousand separate and unique assertions, each one claiming to have predicted the Ankor's arrival. Just under a hundred were from professional scientists with multiple citations in peer-reviewed journals.

Sam flicked across to a screen showing a graphic representation of the solar system with the alien craft's expected track and predicted timings. The Ankor were decelerating hard, although still doing fifteen million kilometres an hour – over one hundred times faster than Earth's fastest space probe.

A little while later, another alarm went off on the smart screens. There was live video footage showing MacKenzie arriving at Number 10. They all watched as he was greeted at the front door by the prime minister before being ushered inside.

Tim smiled to himself. At least MacKenzie wouldn't be phoning him in the next few hours.

Two seconds later, his phone buzzed with a text.

**Come and reinstall the security encryption in Anglesey on Friday.**

'I got the call,' said Tim to Sam. 'Security reinstall.'

The production MIDAS hardware ran in Anglesey, but the Butler Street offices hosted the security servers. Tim had to physically go to Anglesey and then coordinate with Sam back in London. MacKenzie had so much technology security that it took a full day to reboot the encryption.

Sam wheeled herself over to Tim's desk. 'In a way, I'm jealous … I'd quite like to get a look at the preparations in Anglesey. SpaceOp is bound to be involved if we're sending shield material into space.'

# CHAPTER 4

**Sam's Flat, East London, Wednesday 10th April**

Reading an actual newspaper! The sheer retro nature of it made Sam smile as she put the paper on her lap and wheeled herself out of the lift towards her top floor flat. Even though the block was an ex-council building, and therefore had had to be built with strict economies in place, it had been designed and constructed well – it was bright, airy, and the lift only very occasionally broke down. The last time the lift had broken Sam had levered herself up the stairs on her emergency crutches, all six floors.

*Two hours of character-building fun …*

Having watched the prime minister's afternoon briefing to the country only an hour earlier, Sam hadn't expected to read anything new in the evening paper and, although Ankor-related items dominated the first four pages, she'd been correct. It was just more of the same. For the past few days, the Ankor had travelled at almost unimaginable speeds from Neptune to Uranus. During that time, they had not broadcast any more messages. It was still not clear what they required humanity to do.

In non-Ankor news, the police had confirmed a small uptick in violent crimes being reported, however they had explicitly ruled out any coordinated activity. It was simply a result of increased stress.

*Appeasement …*

That was the word that MIDAS had picked up on. Still only trending in small volumes, but growing daily.

'Hi Sam,' called Charlie, coming through from the kitchen and planting a kiss on her mouth.

After lingering on the kiss for what she hoped was an appropriate time, Sam pulled gently away. 'All okay with you?'

'Fine.' Charlie smiled warmly and returned to the kitchen.

'The prime minister is doing well,' said Sam.

'He's steady, not spectacular,' said Charlie. 'How's work?'

'All good thanks. My OrcLore data collation is going well. MIDAS is auto-generating questions based on in-game user responses,' said Sam. 'Have you heard anything more about the Ankor?'

'Nothing.'

'Really?' asked Sam. The fact that MacKenzie was in the COBRA meetings and Charlie was his right-hand man suggested this was improbable.

Charlie's head twitched. 'What do you mean?'

'Well …' said Sam, levering herself out of her wheelchair. 'Shit!'

A jolt of pain temporarily stopped her movement. She always forgot to take it slowly after being in the chair for over an hour. Her muscles had locked up.

Charlie put down the wooden spoon and walked over to help her.

'I can manage,' she said, shooing him away. Sam pushed herself more tentatively up and out of her wheelchair.

*Fucking prison …*

Then, with a small painful shuffle, she moved across to a kitchen chair and sat down. 'I mean the Ankor. What they are doing and saying to the government?'

'I've been told nothing,' said Charlie. 'That shouldn't surprise you. You know how Francis is about compartmentalisation.'

'Fair enough,' said Sam. 'What about MedOp? The rumour that MedOp is ranking application forms doesn't seem to be going away.'

'People are being treated fairly,' said Charlie.

'And their data still isn't being packaged individually?' asked Sam – it was her stock question to Charlie. Her eyes were drawn to a framed letter she kept behind the kettle.

The letter was from an insurance company stating that they were taking her to court for fraud over her injury claim. The police had been involved and hadn't been very supportive, even when the fraud was traced back to a nurse who'd worked on the ward where Sam had spent months in traction. The nurse had stolen Sam's private data from the hospital database but, critically, had also got useful information from Sam's social media pages. If it hadn't been for Tim's private sleuthing – he'd used a prototype of MIDAS to find unusual spending patterns, linking Sam, the nurse and some outrageous holiday photos posted on Instagram – then it might have gone badly for her.

The real victory for Sam was that it fully opened her eyes with regard to misuse of data. She and Tim had an ongoing ideological argument about whether data theft – a crime – and people willingly giving away their data – not a crime – were comparable.

'All the participants agreed to sell their data for the treatment,' said Charlie – his stock answer.

Sam felt very strongly about how the data was used. She'd designed and coded a large part of the anonymisation routine – the so-called 'n greater than 5' module – that lay on top of the aggregation logic. The module allowed MacKenzie to tell regulators, or other government officials, that a complex algorithm facilitated mining data for commercially useful information whilst also protecting individuals.

So far, MIDAS had only operated with Sam's routine active … as far as she knew. MacKenzie had made Sam add override flags such that data could be presented on an individual basis – for emergency purposes.

'How's tension in the office?' asked Charlie, bringing Sam back to the present.

'Toby has spent the last two days close to tears,' said Sam. 'Tim's more stoic, but he does occasionally lapse into analysis of *what would happen if the aliens attack.*'

'And?'

'Typically, he extends the timeframe of his simulation until he finds a positive outcome.' Sam paused. 'He said it would be good for the icecaps and the rhinos, but the Ankor are probably too late to save the pandas.'

Sam chuckled. She loved Tim's irreverent humour.

Charlie didn't acknowledge the joke.

'Charlie?'

'They're not invading,' he said.

Carefully reaching over, Sam grabbed her rucksack off the back of her wheelchair and emptied it onto the table. She laid out her top-of-the-range gaming mouse and keyboard. 'I've got a tournament at the weekend. The Bitches need to win three of four games to reclaim top spot. Do you want to play later?'

'Probably not,' said Charlie, taking a break from stirring the saucepan to flex his wrist and hand muscles. 'You go ahead though.'

Early in their relationship – as friends, and subsequently as a couple – they'd played a lot, and Charlie had been very good. Over the last year, they'd played much less.

*Rather like our sex life …*

Not that the lack of sex really bothered Sam; full intercourse was tricky with her medical condition, and basically relied on her lying very still.

But gaming she could still do. The *Bruised and Broken Bitches* was Sam's team, all female, all wheelchair bound, and a force to be reckoned with. They were good, frequently winning regional tournaments … when the fourteen-year-old

Jappers weren't around. Not that she called them that to their faces; she was politically correct when on the record.

'Is it a big tournament?'

'Not really. The Den is hosting a series of local games. Do you want to come?'

She was just asking out of politeness. In just over two years of their relationship, Charlie had only met her teammates a few times. Captain of the Triple-Bs was Sam's alter-ego, her escape. Her approach wasn't unusual; nobody on the team wanted to associate her gaming life with her daily routine.

Of course, her teammates knew all about Charlie. He represented big kudos for Sam at the gaming lair. It was nothing to do with him being Francis MacKenzie's right-hand man, either – in fact, that counted against him. No, Charles Taylor was well respected in the world of computer game development. As part of his post-doctorate, he'd worked at Imperial College on behaviour simulations, designing code that had made amazing leaps in the behavioural patterns of NPCs – non-player characters. It was the reason Sam cursed Charlie's name when the city guards found her hiding behind the food barrels – without Charlie's code, those guards would have never 'thought' to look for people hiding.

It had also earned Charlie a nickname in the gaming industry – 'Father of NPCs'.

Sam pulled out her laptop and booted up. She couldn't get a network connection. The internet providers were restricting logons.

Charlie indicated towards his phone on the kitchen table. 'You can hot spot off my mobile.'

'You've got internet?'

'One of the few benefits of my relationship with Francis MacKenzie.'

'What's he focusing on today?' asked Sam.

'He's going to Anglesey to accelerate the launch programme,' said Charlie.

'You too?' Sam noticed the tiny burst of hope that accompanied the question.

'Yes,' said Charlie, carrying two plates of pasta over to the table.

As he put down the plates, his shirt sleeve rode up. A bandage was clearly visible, almost entirely covering his right forearm.

'Are you okay?' asked Sam, pointing at his arm.

He shrugged. 'It's nothing.'

Sam hadn't seen Charlie for a few days, but the bandage looked recent. Involuntarily, she thought back to the last time she'd seen Charlie with his clothes off.

*Months ago.*

She'd seen a long thin scar on his leg on that occasion – too straight and regular to have been the bramble scratch he'd claimed.

*Is Charlie self-harming?*

She couldn't rule it out, although she noted other reasons for the injury were more likely.

If it was self-harm, then perhaps it was an act of devotion. Sam certainly didn't want to ask that; the conversation would undoubtedly circle back to his faith and she didn't want to go there. That was one area of Charlie's life she couldn't fathom. He had deep spiritual beliefs, not that he ever discussed them – and neither did Sam ever ask. For her, the concept of an all-powerful god – who'd decided to cripple her and make her shit into a bag for two years – just felt impossible to stomach.

*He may be doing it out of solidarity?*

That wasn't it either … probably.

Sam looked at Charlie appraisingly. Her feelings for him had been cooling for some time now. She should have left him a year ago when they'd stopped playing together on a regular basis: gaming and sex.

*Except that he adores you.*

Sam ignored the small voice. It was just a perverse area of her subconscious stirring things up. There was a myriad of reasons to work on the relationship, and concerns about her ability to find someone else didn't even make the top five. Sam shook her head to clear it. It could be that the slow spiral she found herself in with Charlie would improve. In any case, she couldn't dump Charlie: Tim would shit kittens, as it could impact their financial settlement from MacKenzie.

After the accident, Tim had spent all his energies investigating treatments for Sam's injuries. When Sam had asked him not to, he'd said he would rein it in. Then she found out he'd simply done it behind her back instead: reviewing clinical cases in journals, speaking to surgeons, and generally becoming an expert in lower spinal injuries. Now Tim wanted the maximum financial reward from MacKenzie so that they could afford to pay for a ground-breaking neural treatment provided by Dr Hung in South Korea. It would be a two-month residential stay with nerve-splicing operations every four days, for a cool three hundred grand.

*Just the money and the two-year waiting list to get through.*

Sam didn't want to get her hopes up. She had already undergone three surgeries in the UK. Her bowels now worked almost normally, and she could sleep lying on her back. However, the operations had not materially improved her mobility, and she still suffered from periodic crippling pain.

Dr Hung was not the only option. Against Tim's wishes – on the basis that it was definitely not his body – Sam had done her own research into a new pain management approach that comprised irreversible nerve removal. That operation would sort the pain – but would consign Sam to a wheelchair forever.

*Swings and roundabouts …*

Aware that she hadn't spoken for a while, Sam looked over towards Charlie. He was deep in concentration, so she used his phone to connect her laptop to MIDAS and kicked off a search on *latest news*.

```
Ankor invasion: nothing new
***
Ankor saviours: nothing new
***
Ankor this: nothing new
***
Ankor that: nothing new
***
Violence Uptick
Australia: Reports of heroin addicts killed
with poisoned methadone
Brazil: Churches burned
```

Nothing new since she'd left the office.

Sam entered a more specific search.

```
MacKenzie Anglesey
```

The returns confirmed it was now common knowledge that launch sites worldwide had been told to be ready to send materials up into near Earth orbit. 'Charlie, do you have any idea what materials the Ankor are asking for?'

'None,' said Charlie, clearly closing down the conversation.

Sam's phone buzzed. A text from Tim.

```
All okay?
```

Sam texted an 'all fine' message back to Tim, kicking herself a little. She'd promised to text Tim to let him know when she was safely home.

Normally, if he'd asked her to do something so patronising, she'd have told him to sod off, but the atmosphere on the streets was strained. He'd walked her to the end of her road but refused her invite to come up for an evening drink.

Her eyes drifted over to Charlie.

*I wonder why.*

# CHAPTER 5

**Whitehall, Thursday 11th April**

Frustratingly, Colonel Martel found himself in London on the day he was supposed to be leading an inspection of SpaceOp in Anglesey. It wasn't a major problem – his second-in-command, Captain Whaller, was entirely capable of performing a thorough initial review – but it rankled.

On his journey to Whitehall, he'd seen cars stuffed full, inching along the roads – people heading for somewhere less inviting for an alien invasion fleet than London.

*Would the Ankor really give humanity a two-week warning of invasion? Or is it a double bluff?*

Heading down into the bowels of Whitehall, Martel reflected on the latest COBRA meeting. It had also gone around in circles, mostly focused on mundane issues such as the various crashed websites as people tried to move money, or get holiday bookings refunded.

On the actual subject of alien arrival, the politicians had all felt a need to represent their views, but – critically – none of them had any relevant expertise.

*Do we send the materials up?*

In public, the prime minister only ever gave the impression that the British government would comply fully with the Ankor's requests. But it was more complicated than that, and the Ankor broadcast had ruled out meaningful interaction on the subject.

*Which, in itself, is suspicious.*

Inside the secure room Joshua Timbers, already seated, was talking to someone Martel had not met. He looked American: Caucasian, mid-40s, tanned, perfect teeth, smartly dressed, and manicured.

The prime minister indicated for Martel to take a seat. 'This is James Piper. He arrived this morning from Washington. We're sharing information. Full clearance.'

Piper leant forward in his seat and held out his hand. Martel shook it.

The prime minister kicked off the discussion. 'Our radar returns now indicate the craft is almost certainly cubic, and five miles long on each side.'

'Agreed,' said Piper.

'There is the faintest hint of an aura around it,' added Martel, 'as if something far less dense extends beyond the main structure.'

'Ideas?' asked the prime minister.

'Our current best guess,' said Martel. 'A communications network … a giant mesh of interconnected antennae.'

Timbers turned to the American and raised his eyebrows.

'Feasible,' said Piper. 'We certainly don't have a better idea.'

*Ah …*

Not good news. Martel had hoped for more. 'Have the US been asked for plutonium?'

Piper shook his head. 'No. Just scraps of metal and glass.'

'Why haven't the US government broadcast this to other launch sites?' asked Martel.

'The whole US programme is being run by the military,' said Piper. 'You're lucky that I'm even allowed to be here.'

'What's your take on the plutonium?' the prime minister asked him.

'Plutonium has a large fear factor,' said Piper. 'Which isotopes have you been asked for?'

'Not specified; we are assuming they can manipulate it as they wish,' replied Martel: plutonium-238 was useful for generating electric power, plutonium-240 was fission bomb material, others were simply radioactive poisons. It was hard to second-guess the Ankor motives without more detail. 'Do you have any weaponised satellites?'

'That's a pointed question,' said Piper, smiling. 'You did hear me say I'm lucky to be here.'

The prime minister cut in. 'I am pretty sure I agreed full disclosure with your President.'

'We have some conventional satellite busters. Nothing that can travel even one percent as fast as the Ankor. But, if they settled into a steady orbit, we have options.' Piper paused. 'Unfortunately, all our weapons are controlled by radio transmissions.'

'Highly encrypted, though?' asked Timbers.

'Just as highly encrypted as the channels the Ankor have already swept through.'

'How do you think they overwhelmed Earth's communication network?' asked the prime minister.

'Sorry,' said Piper. 'The theories at the Pentagon are manifold: artificial intelligence hidden in our internet, self-replicating virus, or an inside job.' Piper paused. 'We're looking at all of the options.'

'We doubt the existence of an Earth-based Ankor artificial intelligence,' said Martel. 'We have not ruled out that they are working with someone on Earth. Our current assumption is along the lines of your self-replicating virus idea – programmed to act, and then self-erase. We've found no traces of it.'

'The home secretary,' said the prime minister, 'told me that the internet network feeds linked into MacKenzie's SpaceOp base in Anglesey are showing incredible volumes of data heading that way.'

'There's nothing unusual about internet activity surrounding any of his known installations,' said Martel. 'It's been extremely high ever since MedOp was launched.'

'I will ask MacKenzie about the data volumes,' said Timbers. 'He knows we're keeping an eye on him and that his leadership of the UK response is predicated on my goodwill.'

Martel nodded his approval; even though the Ankor had explicitly asked Timbers to keep MacKenzie in charge, it wouldn't hurt to remind MacKenzie that he was under close observation.

'Is Francis MacKenzie a suspect?' asked Piper.

'We've no evidence of wrongdoing,' said Martel. Doubts about MacKenzie's loyalties were purely circumstantial. He happened to: have a strong interest in space and aliens, a rocket launch capability, and a history of ruthless pursuit of his goals. 'Do you have anything?'

Piper shrugged. 'Before MedOp, he invested money into longevity research and cryogenics. But … nothing more than the average billionaire looking for an out.'

'What about the liaison team in SpaceOp?' asked the prime minister, changing the subject.

'Our on-site inspection team landed in Anglesey a few hours ago. Captain Whaller hasn't made a substantial report yet.'

'For tomorrow's briefing,' continued Timbers, 'I'm going to openly state that no decision can be made on the subject of plutonium until we have quantified the risks from the gamma ray burst.'

'Quantify is a good word,' said Martel. 'It doesn't imply we don't believe the Ankor, but it puts pressure on them to tell us where the supernova is.'

Piper leant forward. 'My guys think it's very possible the Ankor have withheld the exact location so that everyone on Earth will be equally incentivised to support the shield development?'

'How so?' asked Timbers.

Piper continued. 'I understand the peak pulse will only last a few minutes. If we knew the exact location and exact time of the explosion, then we could estimate where on Earth the most intense radiation will fall.'

The prime minister looked at Martel. 'Colonel?'

'I understand the concept,' said Martel. 'But most scientists agree a strong gamma ray blast would render the entire Earth sterile. I'm not sure the epicentre of that initial pulse will be meaningful overall.'

Piper accepted the point with a nod and then turned to Timbers. 'Are you getting much civil unrest?'

From the television reports Martel had seen, the US was suffering hourly riots.

The prime minister answered Piper directly. 'We have a two-pronged attack. My daily briefings are getting good feedback; the UK population seem to believe that people and government are in it together. Secondly, we have put a lot more police onto the streets, with clear instructions to calm and reassure.'

*Calm and reassure …*

Martel suspected that reasonable words were only going to soothe the population for so long.

--------

**Butler Street Offices, Wednesday 17th April**
Approaching the MIDAS offices, Martel rechecked the transcripts of the most recent mobile phone conversations that Tim Boston and Samantha Turner had had. There was nothing remotely suspicious about their behaviour, which was entirely consistent with almost every other adult in London.

Ringing the buzzer, he waited.

'Hello.' It was Tim Boston's voice.

58

'Colonel Martel. I believe you're expecting me,' said Martel, holding his ID up to the video entry lens.

'Ah yes,' said Tim. 'SpaceOp background checks?'

The door buzzed, and Martel found his way upstairs, where he was met at the second security door by Tim and Sam.

'I'd assumed we were going to be summoned,' said Tim.

Martel smiled. 'You'd be surprised how many diary clashes I'm informed about when I try to arrange meetings in advance. I find that doorstepping is the most efficient method.'

As Martel was led through the main office, his eyes swept the room. Most of the screens were switched off, but there was one showing new information.

*Binding resolution ES-15/1, the United Nations General Assembly by majority vote has disbanded the Security Council. Discussions concerning the alien arrival will only be held in full sessions*

'The USA will go mental,' said Sam, noticing the direction of Martel's gaze.

'I suspect some smaller countries are worried the big players may cut a deal,' added Tim.

'A reasonable assumption,' said Martel, allowing himself to be ushered into a meeting room and sitting down on the proffered chair.

'How can we help?' asked Tim.

For the next twenty minutes, Tim talked him through the previous few years' work. He and his colleague Sam had written most of the code for the MedOp data aggregation tool, MIDAS, but MacKenzie had a separate 'quant' team to provide the complex algorithms underlying its natural language processing. Tim and Sam also provided periodic installs of the main MIDAS system which was held in

Anglesey but, as far as they knew, none of the MIDAS processing was used for SpaceOp.

'So, you focus on data analysis for MedOp?' asked Martel. 'But you've never met this quant team who write the more complex analysis routines?'

Tim smiled. 'Not quite how I would put it. The quant team provided some very specific natural language processing code. Most of the analysis routines were written by Sam and me.'

'So, MacKenzie is using MIDAS to analyse and sell survey data that he gets as payment from MedOp applicants?'

'Not just survey data,' said Tim. 'MIDAS pulls relevant public information from the internet and can be pointed at any database to do the same.'

Sam spoke. 'It's not just MedOp applicants. MacKenzie has deals with all sorts of survey companies. They all send him data.'

'Can I see a MedOp survey?'

'Unfortunately, not from here. You'd have to be in MacKenzie's Park Royal office,' said Tim. 'We're just the development site.'

'So none of the live data is produced in Butler Street?'

'None,' said Tim. 'The production system is split between Park Royal and Anglesey.'

'Well ...' said Sam. 'Currently, we do have the production encryption servers here.'

'So,' said Martel. 'Francis MacKenzie sets up his data search categories in Park Royal, they are encrypted using some technology here, and then they are sent to Anglesey for execution.'

'Correct,' said Tim.

'Do you keep any data here at all?' asked Martel.

'Nothing sensitive,' said Tim. 'We create BinCubes as part of the test runs. It's all public data and we don't keep them.'

'Are his systems in Anglesey entirely secure?' asked Martel.

Tim nodded. 'As good as I have ever seen. Obviously anything networked has some level of vulnerability, but all his systems have constant key encryption changes, passive data intrusion monitoring, hard-wiring, and lock-down circuit breakers. Everything possible to stop an inbound attack that could result in data loss.'

'Okay,' said Martel, deciding to switch subjects. 'What do you know about MacKenzie's work in Colombia?'

'Only what I've read in the newspapers. It was before our time working for him,' said Tim. 'He was angry that the US government appeared to be throttling SETI data and so bought his own radio array.'

'You weren't involved in any of the technology there?'

'No,' said Tim.

'When did you start working for MacKenzie?' Martel asked.

'We started here June 2016,' said Sam.

'You worked together before that?' asked Martel.

'Since 2011,' said Tim. 'We worked at DataFact together.'

'Okay,' said Martel, making a note. 'Can I now ask you about Charles Taylor?'

'He and I are currently … an item,' said Sam. 'He does all sorts for Francis MacKenzie but tends not to speak about it.'

'Not even to you?' asked Martel.

Sam smiled. 'Especially not to me.'

'Do you know what he did for MacKenzie in Chile?'

'I know he went there,' Sam frowned. 'But he hasn't talked about it to me.'

'Apologies,' said Martel. 'Investigations usually involve asking multiple people the same questions.'

Tim glanced at Sam. 'Charlie was in Chile from late 2012 through to early 2014. Working for Francis MacKenzie, he was doing low energy physics experiments down a salt mine – hidden from cosmic rays and other electromagnetic disturbances.'

*During which time, Mr Boston, you were involved in a car crash that crippled your colleague Samantha Turner.*

Obviously, Martel wouldn't mention that. 'Has he been to Chile recently?'

Tim took a deep breath. 'No. As far as I know, Charlie's work has been entirely in the UK. A mixture of MedOp and SpaceOp.'

'Understood, thank you,' said Martel. It was clear that they were not able to add anything further regarding MacKenzie's activities in Anglesey.

Martel stood up and shook hands with them both. 'Many thanks. I will let you know if I have follow-ups and if you think of anything just call, or email.'

'Thank you, Colonel. I'll show you out,' said Tim.

# CHAPTER 6

**Leicester, Thursday 11th April**

It was beyond comprehension to Xandra Kusr that they would demand she kept to the terms of the original agreement.

'What are they thinking of?' she asked the blank wall of the clinic's bedroom as she stuffed clothes into her suitcase.

The clinic, in an industrial park on the outskirts of Leicester, had been Kusr's home for the previous six months ... and she'd signed up for six more.

*Signed up to what ...?*

The contract had been for an exorbitant amount of money – and offered a route back to respectability – but had severely restricted her movements. She'd been allowed to use internet video-calls to keep in touch daily with her husband and children, but had only been allowed to visit them once a month.

Neither was she allowed to discuss any of her responsibilities at the clinic.

*The MedOp Revolution*

That was how Charlie Taylor continually described it, but he never gave any more details than were required for each immediate task.

Some of the work Kusr had done was revolutionary – the ongoing neural grafting work, creating stable links between mammalian brains and computers with silver wires, had never been done to the level of complexity she'd achieved at MedOp. The cataract operation for Francis MacKenzie himself and the series of immune response tests on Charles

Taylor, were less ground-breaking, but at least showed that her two bosses had skin in the game.

The real work was due to start the following week, as far Kusr knew. Taylor had explained that a research team in Seoul would be providing the specifications for a new mix of enzymes and proteins that would allow stable interfaces. All the ones she'd used so far had decayed after a few minutes.

It would be revolutionary.

However, with the Ankor arrival, Kusr felt she simply couldn't stay to fulfil her part of the bargain. They would have to understand – and either find a replacement surgeon or delay their plans. After all, the rest of the world had put its plans on hold. Why shouldn't MedOp?

Amber and Jada, her darling daughters, needed their mother in this time of turmoil.

Footsteps down the corridor drew Kusr's attention.

'Dr Kusr,' said one of the clinic's orderlies, 'your car is ready. However, I have this for you.'

Since yesterday, when she'd informed Taylor of her final decision to leave, it had been Taylor trying to make Kusr change her mind. She had not been moved.

Now the big guns were out. A handwritten note from Francis MacKenzie himself, assuming the signature – which looked like something a seismograph might produce – was genuine.

> *Xandra*
> *Please reconsider your decision*
> *Work at MedOp cannot stop at this point*
> *The research team have discovered some potentially paradigm-changing behaviours in nerve regrowth. I need to test them within the week. We have patients in urgent need of treatment.*
> *I am happy to double your remuneration and allow extended family visits.*
> *Francis*

*Tempting.*

If MacKenzie's research claims were true, this story would be a wonderful one to be part of. Although MacKenzie was not well known for sharing the credit for his achievements, and most people's short-term priorities were fairly fluid at the moment.

Her duty was to be with her family.

'Lead me to the car,' said Kusr to the orderly, folding the letter and putting it in her pocket.

The orderly nodded and, picking up Kusr's bag, started walking through the maze of corridors.

*I may regret this ...*

There was no doubt in her mind that MacKenzie would not forgive the slight, and that she would now be excluded from all further research.

She ground her teeth. She'd been excluded before. Her previous job at the Royal Mary Institute for Neural Repair had not ended well. A lawsuit citing surgical malpractice had forced her into a 'leave of absence' which had quietly turned into a voluntary redundancy. To make it worse, she had been forbidden to re-examine the patient who'd supposedly been in so much pain after the procedure she'd performed.

*It had been a simple trapped nerve in the neck, nothing more.*

A few minutes later, after signing out at reception, Kusr followed the orderly into the underground car park – the same one she used for her monthly visits home.

A heavy-duty SUV with blacked-out windows was waiting.

The back seats were piled high with blankets and junk, so Kusr climbed into the front passenger seat. She didn't recognise the driver. Certainly, it was not the usual one, or any of the orderlies multitasking.

'Hello,' said Kusr, strapping into her seatbelt.

The driver grunted a response and they set off.

Waiting for the first of two barriers to rise, Kusr thought back over her time at the clinic. She would miss it. She'd miss the cutting-edge technology and the responsive nature of the team. In fairness, she had been treated like royalty whilst she'd been there.

*Perhaps I should stay?*

But as the steel gate rolled up – the final barrier to the outside world – Kusr saw the blue sky and her resolve hardened.

'An hour?' asked Kusr.

The driver half-turned. 'A little longer,' he said. 'Traffic conditions.'

Kusr struggled to place the accent.

They pulled out into the traffic, which was light despite what the driver had said. The journey home, to a small village outside Cambridge, really couldn't take more than an hour.

*And then I will see my jewels.*

Kusr pulled out her purse and looked at her favourite family photo of the four of them eating ice-creams on a windy beach in Cornwall.

*They will be surprised to see me.*

She hadn't called ahead. Right up to the last moment, she hadn't been sure if she would change her mind.

As they headed east, the roads were even quieter.

Kusr was surprised when the driver took a turning for Corby. 'You know where we're going?' she asked.

The driver nodded. 'Traffic issue.'

Instinctively Kusr wanted to argue, but she let it go. There would be no benefit in annoying the drive unnecessarily, and in any case, they were still heading towards her home – just not taking the most direct route.

They drove on, Kusr looking out the window, imagining the look of glee of her daughter's face when she gave her the pocketful of boiled sweets she'd been saving from the clinic's canteen.

*Margrot?*

She knew Margrot, of course; it was an old air force base on the banks of the largest reservoir in Northamptonshire. It wasn't the right direction.

Kusr turned to the driver. 'Hey!'

The car stopped. Kusr felt movement behind her.

Hands grabbed her from behind and the driver leant over, a hypodermic needle clearly visible in his hand.

Kusr's eyes met those of the driver. There was no surprise in the driver's eyes, only resolve.

*What?*

Kusr tried to raise her hands to fight off the needle, but the person behind her had pinned her arms.

She looked left, wondering if she could throw herself out. The passenger door didn't seem to have a handle.

A sharp prick in her neck indicated she'd been injected.

*Fight!*

But suddenly there was no fight in her. A cool feeling spread down her right side and up into her face. Kusr's eyes, feeling heavy, started to close. The last thing she saw was a sign for the reservoir.

# CHAPTER 7

**Butler Street Offices, Friday 12ᵗʰ April**

Waiting in the Butler Street server room for Tim to call, Sam double-checked she had all the encryption keys ready. She did. In fact, it wasn't a hard job to reset the security software and if MacKenzie had allowed them to have an automated process it would have only taken five or six seconds. MacKenzie, however, did not allow the automation and in order to ensure there was absolute protection for the MIDAS Production system in Anglesey Tim had to physically be there to perform the reset.

In the background, the Radio Juice talk show was trawling through the bad news from the last twenty-four hours.

> '*So you don't think the heroin addict deaths a tragedy?*'
> '*Nah. They're a drain on society. We're better off without them.*'
> '*Well, caller, I disagree. Those addicts have a chance to … heal?*'
> '*Bollocks!*'

*Heroin Addicts?*

No stranger to pain killers – Sam continued to have a constant fight with the opiate lure – Sam kicked off a MIDAS search.

Moments later it came back. The police had released a statement saying that an ex-serviceman had been linked to a series of suspected murders. Twenty heroin addicts had been killed with contaminated heroin from the same supplier.

The next caller drew Sam's attention back to the radio.

> '*Hi, Andy, this is Marcus from Sunderland. It's appeasement …*'

There was the word again. Appeasement. Over the last weeks there'd been a growing number of commentators talking about preparation for the Ankor arrival and how some groups were thinking that some sort of cleansing activity was required to prove humanity's worthiness.

*For fuck's sake …*

The phone rang. Tim.

'Hey buddy, how was the trip?' asked Sam.

'Bumper to bumper, replied Tim. 'You'd not believe the amount of traffic heading into SpaceOp.'

'What's new?' asked Sam. She had been there once the previous year for a large MIDAS install, and she knew the basic layout. There were five zones: Control, Storage, Assembly, Launch, and Harbour; lots of warehouses, fences, roads …

'New temporary buildings going up all over the place,' said Tim. 'And Tosh sends his regards.'

Sam liked Tosh; he ran security for SpaceOp. 'Cool. Send them right back at him. What else is new?'

'I'm not sure if I should say this but they do seem to be preparing for plutonium. There's a place here they're calling the Hot Zone – massive razor wire fences and security guards in hazmat suits.'

'Has any arrived yet?'

'Everyone here says no,' replied Tim. 'And the official position is that it may never arrive … hold on.'

Sam waited on the end of the phone.

A minute ticked by.

Tim was back. 'Sorry Sam, MacKenzie's personal bodyguard Juan just arrived to tell me they're ready for the encryption reset. I have to go up to MacKenzie's desk to run the workstation piece. You set your end running.'

Sam hung up and kicked off the data encryption scripts.

Two minutes later, Tim texted.

*Starting my end now.*

Tim initiated the scripts to link MacKenzie's workstation with the existing MIDAS Production system, and then pointed them both at the Butler Street encryption servers.

At the right time, Sam keyed in her authorisation key from Butler Street.

It was all over in a few minutes.

'All good with you?' asked Tim.

'Sure,' said Sam. 'You?'

'Fine here,' said Tim.

'Come back safe,' said Sam. 'Come back soon.'

'I'll visit my dad later today,' said Tim. 'And then Sunday I'll be back in London.'

'Butler Street gossip at five-ish Sunday afternoon?' asked Sam.

'It's a date,' said Tim.

'Well, if it is,' said Sam, trying to keep her voice light, 'I won't tell Charlie about it.'

*Naughty girl…*

Sam hung up and turned back to … the encryption logs … there was an issue.

--------

**Sam's Flat, Later that Evening**

Sam returned to her flat with a predicament. The timestamps returned with the encryption key exchange indicated trouble.

There was no problem with the actual reset – MacKenzie now had a fully cleaned MIDAS system in Anglesey, just as he wanted. The issue was the exact values of the timestamps.

```
05:32:12.347349
05:32:12.461463
```

The millisecond-microsecond elements of each timestamp had been replaced with three-digit twin primes. The chances of that happening randomly were astronomically high.

*My code ...*

Unbeknown to Tim, Sam had hacked in guerrilla code to the MIDAS application. It checked the value of the flag that prohibited data aggregation for single individuals – the 'n greater than 5' setting. As it had to be a tiny amount of code, it didn't review when the settings changed, or what individuals were targeted.

It just identified the crime.

Obviously, given the Ankor situation, Sam could come up with hundreds of scenarios in which MacKenzie was targeting individuals for politically and morally positive reasons.

*Should I tell Tim?*

She looked around at the flat, searching for inspiration. She couldn't tell Tim. He'd remove the code to protect their investment.

No. This was a red line. However well-intentioned MacKenzie's reasons may be – if they were well-intentioned at all – they led to data privacy oblivion where people's deepest secrets were identified and sold.

Her mobile rang.

*Fuck!*

She'd left it on the kitchen table when she'd dumped her stuff.

She stood up a little too fast. A jolt of pain deep in her left side punished her.

Taking a deep breath to stabilise the pain, Sam hobbled to the table.

**Francis MacKenzie**

*Double fuck!*

For a moment, she considered not answering.

Then she thought better of it. 'Hello, Mr MacKenzie.'

'Sam. Are you well?'

'Passable, thank you. Today appears to be a good day.'
Sam never complained about her pain, but she liked people
to understand that all was not always sweetness and light.
'What can I do to help?'

MacKenzie paused. 'I wanted to call you to thank you for
doing the security reset.'

*Really?*

Although MacKenzie did sometimes thank people for
their efforts, this did not feel like one of those occasions.

'That's kind of you,' said Sam, seeing an opening. 'Are
you able to use MIDAS to help the Ankor effort?'

'It's useful in all sorts of ways, Sam,' said MacKenzie.
*No immediate confession then …*

She waited. There would be another reason for the call. It
was not unprecedented. MacKenzie checked up on her from
time to time.

In the first pseudo-personal call she'd got from him,
twelve months ago, MacKenzie had asked her opinion about
all sorts of aspects of MIDAS development … and
specifically asked her not to mention it to Tim. At the time,
thinking it was a one-off, she hadn't said anything to Tim. A
few months later she'd got another call … and she hadn't
told Tim about that one, either. Another call followed a
month after that.

Now, she couldn't tell Tim.

More pertinently, most of the questions in the last few
months had not been about MIDAS – they'd been about
Tim. Sam got the impression that MacKenzie couldn't quite
read him. In all cases, Sam simply ensured MacKenzie got
rosy views whilst occasionally slipping in a tiny criticism for
the sake of balance.

She also used the call to promote her own agenda, trying to cement MacKenzie's support for enhanced data privacy. He'd always been very receptive about cyber security to avoid data loss … but was notably less forthcoming on protecting individuals' identities.

Thinking for a few seconds to frame a question, Sam reran it in her head a few times to ensure it was light enough to avoid drawing suspicion. 'With the Ankor arrival imminent,' she said, 'are you going to change the focus and format of the data aggregation?'

A suitably open-ended question. MacKenzie knew how important 'n>5' was to Sam, and so if he had changed the flag and wanted to explain it to her then she'd given him the opening.

'Given my role in SpaceOp, I am asking respondents about the Ankor,' said MacKenzie. 'Data aggregation remains at group levels.'

Sam knew he was lying, but was no closer to determining why, and she couldn't dig any further without causing suspicion.

'How's Charlie doing?' asked MacKenzie. 'Not too stressed?'

*Charlie?*

Normally, MacKenzie asked about Tim.

'I haven't noticed any significant difference,' said Sam. Not quite true. Charlie's meditation – and chanting – sessions were now lasting an hour, up from twenty minutes a few months previously. 'He's excited.'

'I suspect he is,' said MacKenzie, with a tone in his voice Sam couldn't place.

'What do you think of the Ankor?' asked Sam. The prime minister's twice-daily briefings were always careful not to be critical of the Ankor – to the extent of being apologetic about their dogmatic communications approach.

'I trust them absolutely.'

'What are the surveys saying?'

'The wisdom of crowds … that's classified information, Sam,' said MacKenzie. 'But I can say that people are not as worried as the press make out.'

'Understood,' said Sam.

'With regards to Charlie, I would feel responsible if he cracked. I know I'm putting him under some strain,' said MacKenzie. 'Please text me if you see anything unusual.'

Sam agreed and they both hung up.

*Unusual about Charlie?*

Returning to the sofa, she thought about it. He was still attentive and loving when he put his mind to it. But he had been very distracted over the previous six months, and that had led to a drop off in physical intimacy … but that seemed to suit them both fine.

--------

**Sam's Flat, Sunday 21st April**

'So, what's up?' asked Sam, as Charlie entered the flat with a bag full of groceries.

'How do you mean?' he said, loading up the fridge with the food he'd brought: salmon fillets, Brazil nuts, and brown rice.

'I don't know,' said Sam. 'You seem tense.'

'Sorry.' Charlie took a breath and his face cleared. 'I'm fine. I haven't done my meditation today, that's all.'

Sam smiled. 'What's the latest with MacKenzie? When's he launching?'

'I haven't seen anything of Francis for a few days,' said Charlie. 'He's been in Anglesey since Thursday. I hope to catch him tomorrow, before the meeting with the prime minister. Tim will know the latest.'

'Tim's visiting his dad,' said Sam. 'Is MedOp still pushing forward?'

'It's being slowed,' said Charlie, 'but Francis is adamant it's not stopping.'

'Fancy a little OrcLore?' asked Sam, nodding towards the games console.

'You go ahead,' said Charlie. 'I'll make lunch.'

Levering herself up from the kitchen table and reaching for her crutches, Sam hobbled over to her gaming chair in the living room. Every third day was a crutches day and the pain was significant, but it was important to keep fully vertical periodically.

Launching OrcLore, Sam selected her dwarven pit-fighter. 'Is it too easy for you now you've learnt from the best?'

In the year after they'd started seeing each other, Charlie had played with her quite a lot. In the last few months he hadn't played once.

Well, not with her, anyway. Sam opened the OrcLore Guild screen and checked Charlie's main character: Edward Mariner the Half-Elven Pathfinder. It was fortieth level and had awesome gear. Charlie was obviously still playing.

'Maybe you're embarrassed the guards are too dangerous,' she said.

'Kind of you to say,' said Charlie, with a smile. 'OrcLore does use some of my code.'

In fact, the NPCs in OrcLore were not the most complex in the gaming world. OrcLore guards obeyed clear rules. If you shot at them, they hid, or shot back, or both. They used physical cover – mostly walls and trees – but their choices were effectively hard coded based on their health status and their weapon.

'You know,' said Charlie taking a few steps from the kitchen. 'My most recent NPCs play dead and they can choose to pretend to swap sides.'

'Very cool,' said Sam, working through the opening screens of the game.

'In a few years, I'm sure a wounded guard could start begging for mercy, or telling you he or she had children.'

Sam paused the game. 'Maybe even to the extent the guard didn't know it wasn't a real person? Maybe it would become aware of us out here?'

Again, Charlie stepped into the doorway between the living room and the kitchen. 'Maybe if we spoke to them, they'd say they were the real ones and we're the simulation.'

'Zhuangzi,' said Sam, 'the Chinese philosopher ...'

'Zhuang Zhou,' said Charlie, using the more formal name. 'He said that one night he dreamt of being a butterfly, but it was so real that in the morning he wondered if—'

Sam cut him off. 'He was a butterfly dreaming of being a man.'

'A valid line of investigation.'

Sam switched subjects, hoping Charlie's defences were down. 'Is MacKenzie still doing the individual data protection?'

Charlie didn't look around. 'As far as I know. Why?'

'I worry that he'll use the Ankor emergency as a reason to go back on his promise not to sell individual data.'

'He didn't promise,' said Charlie. 'MedOp costs money.'

'Isn't he making enough with the aggregated data?'

'Plenty,' said Charlie.

*A lie? Or is Charlie also deceived?*

She returned to her game.

Charlie brought the food through to the living room. 'When is your Triple-Bs game?'

'A couple of hours,' said Sam, putting her gaming controller aside. 'I'll go after lunch.'

Just as Charlie put the plates of food down, his phone rang. Indicating for Sam to start eating, Charlie went back to the kitchen.

Sam watched through the doorway. The conversation looked terse. Charlie spoke in hushed whispers and absentmindedly rubbed the bandage on his lower arm, now visible as his sleeve had ridden up. It had to be MacKenzie.

Sam had queried it at the time and been brushed away.

*A scratch, nothing more ...*

Sam ate as Charlie's phone conversation dragged on.

Eventually Charlie hung up. He grabbed his coat immediately and headed for the door. 'I have to go. Sorry.'

'That's fine,' said Sam, used to Charlie's sudden departures.

Five minutes later, lunch eaten and cleared away, Sam left the flat herself – off to her Triple-Bs gaming match.

Her mind racing as she entered The Den, Sam winked at Barney, the owner.

'You're on in twenty minutes, Sam,' said Barney. 'The others are already set up.'

*Maybe just a quick look then ...*

'I just need to cover a few things,' said Sam, finding an empty booth. 'Please tell them I'll be right over.'

'Okay.'

As she settled in, Sam reviewed her hastily made plan. She wasn't being stupid. She could do this quickly. Perhaps not as easily as Tim, but it wasn't a difficult hack and she was responsible for monitoring how MacKenzie was using MIDAS.

*Our technology!*

The Den was a good choice; it had IP scramblers that routed via the Baltic states. Any intrusion would never be traced back here.

*Time to hack.*

The computer had a separate webcam. Sam turned it to face the wall.

Sam knew the IP address of the MIDAS encryption server by heart – 1.32.256.14. She opened a command window and logged in using dummy admin credentials she'd created earlier in the year for just such an eventuality.

The encryption server believed it was talking to the real MIDAS Production Anglesey system and assigned Sam a valid key to access MacKenzie's workstation in Park Royal.

Next, mimicking a system package loss, Sam tricked the workstation into resending the last set of BinCube creation parameters.

MIDAS was being instructed to create files indexed on individual names.

*Bastard.*

Unfortunately, all Sam could see were the current system parameters for the BinCube creation; she couldn't tell how long the individual setting had been active.

*It could be months … or it could be the first one.*

Sam checked additional parameters. She would have been mollified if they had shown MacKenzie was only creating individual information packs for the top fifty most influential people.

Not the case – it was tens of thousands of individuals.

*Strange…*

A different set of parameters appeared to be altering the standard output file structure. Sam was too smart to write it down, but she memorised the settings.

Next, she sent a command instructing the workstation to resend the latest survey questions; she wanted to know what people were being coerced into telling MacKenzie.

A few seconds ticked by.

Extreme secrecy surrounded the contents of the surveys. Every MedOp participant signed a punitive non-disclosure agreement, and the internet was constantly monitored for anyone transgressing. Immediately after the MedOp launch, with the prevailing open data-sharing environment, it had been impossible to stop survey questions leaking onto the web: photo images, blogs, allusions in opinion pieces.

MacKenzie had come down hard. Within a week, executives and board members of internet service providers were being removed from MedOp patient waiting lists.

Within a month of that, survey questions were nowhere to be seen; neither posted, nor discussed. The ISPs and physical network companies had initiated significant additional security features including monitoring, and blocking, transmissions from the so-called Dark Web rather than letting them cross their infrastructure.

Sam breathed out. Her screen filled with free text. Triple checking no-one could see over her shoulder, Sam started to read.

It was a survey sent out in the last twelve hours.

*Do you think Ankor are friendly?*
*Do you trust the Ankor to defend us from the gamma ray burst?*
*Do you accept the Ankor travelled here faster than the speed of light?*
*Do you trust Francis MacKenzie to succeed at SpaceOp?*
*Do you expect to contribute materials and effort to Earth's defence?*
*Were the deaths of the poisoned heroin addicts tragic or acceptable?*

Her eyes returned to the list. There were many more survey questions, but all covered aspects of the Ankor or humanity's expected response to the situation.

A chair scraped across the floor bchind her.

She turned.

It was simply a kid moving a chair.

Nothing more.

*Bastard.*

With a long list of actions in her head, Sam joined her gaming team.

# CHAPTER 8

**Park Royal Estates, West London, Monday 15th April**

Sitting down at his desk, having just arrived back from yet another COBRA session, MacKenzie was content. When he'd told the COBRA meeting that the Ankor had given explicit orders to prepare for plutonium – *and he'd started already* – Nadia Peterson had tried to make him squirm, saying that he was mindlessly obeying the Ankor and that Britain would never send plutonium into space. The prime minister had not backed her up and agreed MacKenzie could continue to prepare Anglesey to process plutonium.

*Subject to an overriding condition that the British army will oversee any physical plutonium.*

It did not go entirely his way; the prime minister had challenged him on the data volumes being sent into Anglesey.

MacKenzie had attempted to look confused, and told them it was normal MedOp business that was continuing as before. Furthermore, he'd told them that out of public duty, he'd set up the most recent surveys to focus on the country's perception of the Ankor; and that he had every intention of sharing the results with COBRA.

Peterson had asked for the raw data, not the interpretation. She'd gone on to challenge him: could the data be stolen by the Ankor, given they'd shown themselves to be capable of subverting Earth's systems? In reply, MacKenzie had said they couldn't and that he'd take Colonel Martel's team through the security once they were on site – but if anyone had doubts then he was prepared to simply switch off the systems.

At that point, the prime minister had stepped in and diffused the tension by accepting MacKenzie's offer of the data and the walkthrough.

MacKenzie tapped his desk, gathering his thoughts. Of course, on arrival, the Ankor would likely be able to subvert his own systems in Anglesey and take anything they wanted. Currently, with the Ankor in the outer solar system, and given his security processes, the four-hour time lag on transmissions was far too great a distance for them to hack him. They got what he sent them and nothing more … as they had done now for fifteen years.

*Fifteen years.*

MacKenzie smiled to himself. The initial deal negotiations had taken four years; he'd held out for rewards that justified the risks. And to ensure the Ankor delivered those rewards, he had to ensure they continually needed him for this, the final month of the plan.

Eventually, of course, the balance would switch and MacKenzie would put himself entirely in their power.

Fundamentally, they would always need him for the physical elements of the plan.

*Although … not necessarily me.*

The risk remained that another Earth-based space agency was also secretly working with the Ankor.

*Am I the only game in town?*

MacKenzie looked over to a series of network ports embedded in one of the concrete walls. Port B3 was a simple access point to the internet. He only ever plugged in a unique computer tablet that he used for browsing social media sites across the world. The internet access point had dynamic IP scrambling; the computer tablet had no wireless capability and was locked in a safe when he was not using it. Each time he used it there was a complex set of checks to ensure the tablet had not been tampered with. It was as secure as it could be given that it had to connect to the internet to function.

Every day, often more than once, MacKenzie browsed photos from a seemingly arbitrary selection of his three hundred favourite nature bloggers.

His moles.

Each of them had a different background and different job. There were cleaners, cooks, security guards and even a few conservationists. Many of them thought they were working for a foreign government. Certainly, none of them were traceable to MacKenzie in any way. Their job was to post photos – incongruous photos – every day or so.

The photos were of birds, landscapes, and trees.

*All totally innocent. An interest in nature and nothing more.*

Even if someone looked closely, that was all they would think. Every single photographer had a different set of targets and unique codes. None of them had received instructions electronically. Eighty percent of them were decoys, photographing areas of no interest to MacKenzie.

The current information he was getting from his moles indicated greatly increased military presence close to each of Earth's space launch facilities.

Not surprising, and not worrying.

It was, however, something to keep an eye on.

Rather than putting the tablet back into the safe, he transferred it to the secure crate he'd been gradually filling for the transfer of his most critical belongings to Anglesey. Having been in Anglesey for much of the weekend it was clear that his place was there.

MacKenzie looked around the room, considering what else he would take.

His walls were mostly bare concrete but there was a painting he'd decided to take: a Scottish Highland scene with a stag crouched down amongst the heather. It was clearly exhausted and had gone to ground. In the distance, a pack of hunting dogs, slavering wildly, was closing in. The painter had left it open to interpretation whether the stag – only moments away from a densely wooded copse – had one more burst of energy left to take it to safety.

MacKenzie knew what he thought. The deer should never have sat down. That was the motivation he took from the painting – fight to the very last, standing.

*Which reminds me …*

MacKenzie initiated the primary video link into Xandra Kusr's new laboratory. Simultaneously, he switched on the data security analysis module and initiated a second hidden camera in the corner of the laboratory. An image of her side profile appeared on the split screen. In tandem, the security module returned a green status, satisfying MacKenzie it was a real-time feed of Kusr and not a simulation.

The kidnap had gone as well as expected – in that Kusr had been secretly transferred into the depths of SpaceOp without any serious physical damage.

Since then, it had not been so good. MacKenzie had expected to explain her choices to her in a reasonable way: continue with the experimentation and be paid handsomely, or suffer daily physical and emotional abuse until she changed her mind.

She'd feigned acceptance … and then smashed up the first laboratory.

MacKenzie had been a little impressed.

That feeling had quickly faded when she smashed up the second one too.

*So, we're doing it the hard way.*

The real-time video feed showed Kusr sitting on the floor of her laboratory looking directly at the camera. With one eye lightly bruised and a shallow weeping cut on her cheek, Kusr's stare did not waver.

In the background, the laboratory equipment appeared to be intact. Movement in the cages on her right indicated that her experimental subjects had survived her two rebellions.

*And the nerve-grafting experiments need to be complete.*

Xandra Kusr was one of the world's preeminent neural experts, both surgical and theoretical. She'd been working on various elements of MedOp for a few years, all related to harmonisation of biological and non-biological technology.

For the first eighteen months MacKenzie had allowed her to progress all her own bespoke investigations, but once the Ankor had provided initial TechMeld data earlier that year, MacKenzie had brought her full-time into secure MedOp facilities. He'd passed the data on, telling her it came from a highly sensitive national programme, whilst implying it had been stolen from the Chinese.

A few months earlier, Kusr had successfully created a stable two-way interface between a group of nerves and a simple computer. Before the kidnap, she'd been trying to replicate it on live mammalian brains – thus the need for the extreme dexterity of a world-class neurosurgeon.

Apart from Kusr's current impromptu sit-in, the main obstacle for MacKenzie was that the Ankor were still withholding two pieces of critical information: the exact concentration of the enzymes required to control the reaction pace in a live working brain, and the protein distribution on the cellular membrane that controlled the flow of ions across it.

The buzzer on MacKenzie's desk sounded.

Charles Taylor had arrived.

MacKenzie switched on the relevant CCTV screen.

Taylor looked pensive.

Deciding to make him wait – Taylor was susceptible to a little bullying – MacKenzie returned his attention to his workstation.

There were two items waiting for him.

**FTL Refutations**
**Professor Trent**

MacKenzie clicked through on FTL. To his satisfaction, the reports indicated that the universal feeling, sourced from news articles, academic papers, and social media, was that the Ankor did have faster-than-light travel available to themselves.

'The masses believe, and the physicists want to believe,' he said to himself. The 'masses' simply sucked up the twenty-four-hour news cycle, and the physicists had had precious little new to believe in during the last few decades. They were fertile.

*Trent* …

Professor Trent had been the resident alien communication expert at his Colombian Radar Array – the site MacKenzie had used to communicate to the Ankor during the early years. He'd been a showpiece. He'd been employed based on his alcohol addiction and his generally poor scientific capability. He'd never been allowed anywhere near anything even potentially related to the Ankor.

After the Radar Array had been destroyed in 2011, on MacKenzie's orders, Professor Trent had tried, and failed, to salvage his own *precious* data from the site. Surprised by Trent's tenacity, MacKenzie investigated and found that Trent did harbour a feeling that Colombia had received some interesting signals. MacKenzie had wanted to have him killed immediately but Charles Taylor, on behalf of elements within the Ankor, had pleaded for clemency: no-one would believe a scientist as discredited as Trent, especially if he had no data. So Trent had been framed and imprisoned. Now, MacKenzie simply kept a watchful eye on him. For as long as he said nothing inflammatory, he would be left to serve out his jail sentence. His full sentence. Through backchannels,

MacKenzie had ensured the Colombians only agreed on extradition based on the strict condition that there would be at least eight years before parole was considered. Almost everyone had considered it entirely reasonable to honour that – after all if the UK government gave Trent early release, it would be a slap in the face to the Colombian government and then the UK would struggle to repatriate other criminals with more sympathetic backstories … like eighteen-year-old backpackers tricked into being drug mules.

MacKenzie clicked on 'Professor Trent'.

Nothing new.

*Luckily for him.*

MacKenzie turned to his head security guard, Juan, who was standing silently in the corner of the room, carefully placed so he could not see any of MacKenzie's workstation screens.

'Please bring Taylor in.'

As Taylor came into the office, MacKenzie saw old bandages sticking out from under his right sleeve. 'I wouldn't let Kusr anywhere near you with a knife for a little while.'

Taylor nodded. 'No improvement?'

MacKenzie showed Taylor the feed of Kusr, still sitting resolutely on the floor of the laboratory, staring into the camera.

'I can live without the final procedures.'

MacKenzie snorted in derision. 'But I can't.'

Irrespective of Taylor's piety and submission to the Ankor, unless Kusr completed all the tests to MacKenzie's satisfaction the deal would be off.

'Her family are making noises about the last missed appointment,' said Taylor. 'I told them she'd moved to Anglesey for security reasons and there were communication issues but she would call them by the end of the week.'

'She will. Assuming she starts to cooperate. If she doesn't, then she'll be seeing them even sooner,' said MacKenzie staring hard at Taylor. Of course – in reality – he'd be unlikely to order the slaughter of the entire Kusr family, but it didn't hurt to have Taylor think there was a chance of that happening. Taylor needed to be more supportive of encouraging Kusr's participation in meeting MacKenzie's goals.

In fact, the kidnap had been rushed. They'd brought it forward a few days because they'd found out that Colonel Martel had been about to shakedown the MedOp buildings.

'Assuming she comes round,' said MacKenzie, moving on to the next subject, 'she'll need the final TechMeld specifications.'

Taylor squirmed. 'They're not due for a few weeks; the original—'

'They're due now,' insisted MacKenzie. 'Kusr needs them to finish the tests before I authorise the first release.'

Taylor remained silent.

MacKenzie knew he'd only been promised the data on Ankor arrival day – four days away. However, it didn't hurt to turn the screws a little.

The information the Ankor had promised concerning TechMeld was a critical factor. It would feed into MacKenzie's final choice: betray Earth and join the Ankor, or throw away fifteen years of planning and reverse the deal.

Given the amount of evidence the authorities would undoubtedly find following an Ankor betrayal, MacKenzie was under no illusions. He would be going on the run forever, and the later he left his escape, the more chance there would be of being found.

He'd planned for that too. From his earliest considerations, MacKenzie knew that in the event of a reversal it would be impossible to return to his previous life on Earth. He'd put in back-up plans to ensure a life of anonymous comfort.

Of course, until a final decision was made, the Ankor would never be given reason to doubt his loyalty. And his preferred option, by a wide margin, was to stick with the main plan.

MacKenzie continued. 'Also, as predicted, Colonel Martel is installing people on-site. I want you in Anglesey as the point liaison.'

Martel's observation team would be a distraction but, given they would all be tagged and tracked around Anglesey, there was limited risk. There were already three thousand people in Anglesey who had no idea what was really going on.

'I'd like you to prepare an accident for one of them,' said MacKenzie. 'Just to keep them unsettled.'

Taylor's face fell. 'I don't … Juan usually …'

'We're all in this together,' said MacKenzie. A tightness in his chest betrayed his rising anger. Taylor was too quick to use Juan for his dirty work. 'It's time for you to step up.'

'I'll have to think,' said Taylor, clearly struggling to process the request. He shared a complex set of ethical beliefs with the Ankor. Some truly violent decisions came easily, whilst others appeared to be anathema to them. The Ankor also perceived an enormous moral difference between torturous suffering, physical sacrificing, and simple killing. Theoretically, MacKenzie could see there may be distinctions, but in practice the last two came down to the same thing for him personally.

*Dead is dead.*

'Just get it prepared. We can all discuss whether to trigger it later,' said MacKenzie. He recognised that, whilst he wanted Taylor's hands bloodied, there was little point pushing him far enough to break him at the moment.

'They won't approve of sacrilegious waste.'

MacKenzie knew that, for all the Ankor's efforts in presenting a united view, not all of them felt similarly.

'Let's just wait and see what they approve,' he said.

Taylor took a few breaths and mumbled a meditative devotion under his breath. Then his face cleared of all stress.

Not for the first time, MacKenzie wished he had the level of faith that allowed Taylor to dispense with his worldly concerns so easily.

# CHAPTER 9

**Butler Street, Monday 15th April**

Aware that any emails could be routinely read by 'authorities', Tim had a series of coded messages that would be triggered if MIDAS was compromised. When an email entitled *free coffee for deep thinkers* popped into his spam folder on Saturday night, he knew someone had been tampering with the encryption servers. A few checks assured him the hacker was Sam – it was not her first offence.

Arriving at the office, Tim caught the tail-end of an exchange between Sam and Toby on video conference, Toby having dialled from his house.

'I give a shit!' Toby shouted out of Sam's monitor, clearly quite agitated, before killing the connection.

'A what?' said Tim, looking quizzically at Sam.

'I said: Mrs Fowler, living at 124, Okal Road, has an ant farm … it may be one of them is the leader … she doesn't give a shit.' Sam pointed to the smart screen covering the 'alien invasion' meme. The percentage was still low, but rising – twenty percent now believed the Ankor meant some type of harm to Earth.

'Who's Mrs Fowler?' asked Tim, scanning the other feeds on the wall. One was constantly searching the internet for new images of the alien craft – it was still just a blurry lattice of red ping-pong balls due to arrive in a few days.

*A five-mile-wide blur …*

'I made her up,' said Sam. 'I was making the point that the Ankor probably think of us in the same way. We're bugs to be stood upon.'

Tim pointed at the blank screen. 'And Toby disagrees?'

'Actually, I think he agrees,' said Sam. 'But he doesn't like to think about it.'

'He's unlikely to come back to the office any time soon.,' said Tim. 'His dad's been listening to some of the judgement day doomsayers and Toby's worried he's going to set fire to the house.'

'He told me,' said Sam, smiling. 'I asked him if there was any chance he could be inside when it happens.'

'What are you up to?' asked Tim, looking at Sam's other screen.

'Watch,' said Sam. She typed briefly on her keyboard, the window blinds closed, and the office wall came to life. Three smart screens showed live feeds of data provided by MIDAS. The central one was focused on the 'alien arrival' search criteria.

On the left of the 'arrival' screen was a series of graphs of constantly fluctuating red, green, and blue. 'Is that your improved media hype section?' asked Tim, remembering that a few weeks previously, Sam had told him it was one of her development projects.

'It's the *all-new* media hype truth-meter,' said Sam. 'MIDAS picks up data on stories that are receiving serious media coverage and produces a graph for the major subjects. The red shows intensity of coverage. Next, it cross-references on that subject with expert commentary. This can be sourced from many sites, but they must be certified as experts.'

'Not all opinions are equal,' said Tim. 'So, experts are represented in the green?'

'Yes,' said Sam. 'Although *experts* is a pretty loose term.'

'And the blue?' Tim asked.

'The blue is primary evidence. Much harder to source, requiring seriously intense data validation calculations,' said Sam, typing on her keyboard. 'Here's an example I've got saved.'

### Digging nuclear fallout shelters

A graph of three columns appeared on the screen. A tall red block showed that the traditional news media were implying everyone was digging in their back gardens. The blue and the green blocks were universally low.

'Where do you get green and blue data?' Tim asked.

'The online self-chronicling obsession means that people who are digging, or have neighbours that are digging, are also telling everyone they know. So, MIDAS gets green data from social media feeds.'

'You count that as expert opinion?' asked Tim.

'Yes, I do,' said Sam, raising her eyebrows – challenging Tim to argue. 'I told you it was a loose definition.'

Tim remained silent.

*I guess they're experts about what they're currently doing …*

'For the blues,' continued Sam, MIDAS checks hard data points: hit rates on websites that give instructions about digging shelters, shovel and spade reserves at big retailers …'

Tim cut her off. 'Spade reserves?'

'MIDAS puts in an electronic reservation for a spade – click and collect – from every online retailer in the country. The order processes often give the number of items in stock. Then MIDAS cancels all the orders and repeats an hour later.'

'How do you know if the levels are unusual?'

'MIDAS hacked some historic sales data from annual reports, and compares it with the current numbers.' Sam frowned. 'I know it's not perfect.'

'It's cool.' Tim's smile faded as he remembered his first task for the day. 'Can we grab the breakout room for a few moments please, Sam?'

'Sure,' said Sam. 'Will you wheel me?'

For a moment, Tim was thrown. Sam never allowed people to push her. Nodding, he steered her into the meeting room, before closing the door.

Tim's demeanour must have registered.

'Yes, I hacked,' Sam said.

'Why?'

'I was curious. I wondered if MacKenzie was creating BinCubes of data indexed on individuals … n less than five.'

'That's all you've got?' asked Tim. 'You'd risk our whole set-up because you were curious? I know that data privacy is your big thing. I also know that MacKenzie often behaves poorly. But … did you have any evidence?'

'Tim …' Sam's eyes were plaintive now. 'I was careful.'

'I found out in seconds,' said Tim. 'Data will have been transmitted from the source disk in MacKenzie's building to your screen. It can be traced and reconstructed. We'd be ruined. Irrespective of any criminal charges, we'd not get a penny for MIDAS.'

Sam remained silent.

It was unlike her. She usually fought over every statement.

'We need the money,' said Tim.

Sam pulled herself around the corner until she was inches away from Tim.

'Maybe I don't care about the money,' said Sam. 'Maybe … it's you that needs the money, so you can give what's left of my knackered body to fucking Dr Hung.'

Now Tim was silent.

She gripped his arm. 'I don't enjoy living with hope. I just want to get on with what I've got.'

Tim hadn't imagined it would escalate so fast. He knew he mustn't say the word *sorry*. 'It's not *all* about you.'

*It is mostly about you …*

Although Charlie hinted that MedOp could one day provide nerve regrowth technologies, Sam was unlikely to wait for it. Would she try the South Korean, Dr Hung, or was she still considering nerve cauterisation? In terms of pain management, it was a much simpler routine for a surgeon to take out all the relevant nerves, but she'd never walk again. Tim felt a phantom abdominal spasm.

Sam would lose all feeling below the waist. But she'd be able to sleep for more than two hours without resorting to horse tranquilisers.

'If not me, then what?' asked Sam, her eyes still narrowed.

Tim continued. 'If MacKenzie lets us have a copy of MIDAS … it could be used for worthy purposes. A global database to track stateless people, a repository for vaccination information, supply-chain management for disaster relief.'

Sam released Tim's arm and let her hand fall. She wheeled herself a little backwards.

'Any idea how long he's been packaging individual data?'

'None, all I saw was the most recent settings,' said Sam. She told him about the survey questions: Are they friendly? Are they lying? Is MacKenzie reliable?

'Any other questions?' asked Tim.

'A few on appeasement-type activity, particularly the poisoned heroin addicts,' said Sam.

'Poor bastards,' said Tim.

Sam shrugged.

'Sam … most of them have unlucky circumstances,' said Tim, knowing he was on dangerous ground – Sam's accident and near-constant back pain for the previous five years meant she had little sympathy for people who 'brought it upon themselves.'

'Heroin poisoning is not the only one.' Sam pulled her tablet onto her lap and launched a smart screen on the wall of the meeting room.

**Ankor, Appeasement.**

Moments later, MIDAS returned the search results: murders, supposed murders, and pages of blogosphere commentary indicating vigilante action against all sorts of suspected undesirables. Although there was no evidence of any actual global coordination, it was spreading.

'Like a cat bringing home a half-dead bird,' said Sam.

It was a good analogy. How could the vigilantes of Earth possibly know what moral structures the Ankor had?

'He could be doing it for the government,' said Tim, returning to the subject of MacKenzie's surveys. 'Providing them with information on how people feel about the situation.'

'Certainly, none of the survey questions appeared to have any commercial focus,' said Sam. 'There was one other strange thing. The BinCube settings were using an odd file structure.'

'How so?'

Sam described it.

'Those are data compression variables,' said Tim. 'Used for sending data via satellite burst transmission.'

'So,' said Sam, her eyes widening. 'He could be sending it to the Ankor.'

Tim wasn't wholly convinced. 'Or another government, via satellite. It's more secure than routing via ground-based internet cables.'

'How easy would it be for him to send a whole BinCube up to the Ankor?' she asked.

'Easy with these compression settings,' said Tim. 'In Anglesey, MacKenzie can pump one hundred megabytes a second, straight up to them. A BinCube would be three hours of transmission time.'

'What should we do?' asked Sam. 'Tell Martel?'

'Let's not be hasty,' said Tim, immediately worrying that MacKenzie finding out would mean oblivion for them both whether, or not, MacKenzie was sending data to the Ankor. 'He could easily be doing this for the UK government.'

'But he could be sending data to the Ankor,' said Sam.

'And… if he is, it still would most likely be with the UK government's blessing.'

'Okay,' said Sam. 'But, perhaps, you could you see if you can get anything out of Charlie? If he knows and it is legit then he may let something slip.'

'My relationship with Charlie has changed,' said Tim. 'We're not that close any more.'

*Did she just blush?*

'Since Chile?' she asked.

*No, since you started seeing him!*

Tim's well-conditioned internal filter stopped his thought being said out aloud.

Unfortunately, Sam took Tim's silence as a calculated evasion and she followed up. 'What happened in Chile, exactly?'

Sam had asked before and Tim had dodged the question. He'd been instructed by both Charlie and MacKenzie not to talk to anyone about it. 'I am sworn to secrecy.'

'I think we're in the world of extenuating circumstances now.'

Tim took a breath. Sam was right.

'Remember this was years ago. Charlie was in Chile down an abandoned salt mine for two years. He was doing experiments for MacKenzie.' Tim paused. 'Transhumanism.'

'Transhumanism. The head-freezing brigade,' said Sam.

Tim nodded. 'There's many different varieties, of which cryogenics is now considered main-stream … for Transhumanism.'

'So …'

'Transhumanism starts with technology augmenting biological systems. The main issue being convincing the body not to reject whatever gizmo is being integrated.'

Involuntarily, Tim's memory reverted to an image of Sam under the harsh white strip lights of a hospital bedroom, tubes and wires running in and out of her, dosed up on industrial-strength immunosuppressants to stop her body rejecting the lot.

Tim pushed the thoughts away and continued. 'Pacemakers are the standard example, implanting small transistor chips under the skin to open security doors is a little more out-there.'

'I know all that,' said Sam. 'Skip to the new bit.'

'Well,' said Tim. 'The next step is having technology replace biological systems … a mechanical heart, for instance … but the logical *extremis* extension is having software replacing physical technology. That's what Charlie was investigating.'

'What exactly?' asked Sam.

'Charlie was running complex energy grid experiments to test whether it could be possible that our whole reality is a program running on an extremely powerful computer from another universe.'

'Really?' Sam was quiet for a moment. 'For two years?'

'They're difficult tests,' said Tim. 'And, to clarify, we're not talking a computer in another galaxy; we mean a whole different universe. It's called Simulation Theory. It states that everything existing here – stars, planets, life itself – is all a simulation for someone else's benefit.'

'Charlie occasionally mentions characters in computer games written so intricately that they don't know they're just characters in a computer game.'

'As far as I know,' said Tim. 'he didn't find any proof.'

'So, what do we do?'

'There are so many plausible explanations that it makes no sense confronting him, or Charlie, directly,' said Tim. 'But, we can have a think about how we could see what is happening to that data.'

An alarm sounded – another broadcast from the Ankor.

**10,000 anti-gravity units assigned**
**A-Grav allocation to be confirmed case-by-case**
**Do not tamper**
**We will remove after use**

The news cycle exploded. *What was an anti-gravity unit? What did it do?*

# CHAPTER 10

It appeared to Martel on arrival that MacKenzie had hung around the back of the meeting room waiting for Martel to choose a seat before sitting down as far away as possible. Martel tried to catch MacKenzie's eye, but failed.

'Prime Minister,' Nadia Peterson said, opening the question and answer part of the meeting, 'do we know anything more about these A-Gravs?'

'Yes, Nadia, we do.' The prime minister paused for a moment. 'None of this can be repeated outside these four walls.'

Martel watched Nadia Peterson's eyes brighten a fraction. Martel suspected that Joshua Timbers had never held such sway over his ministers and civil servants. Not that some of them wouldn't still be averse to taking shots at him if they saw weakness and opportunity.

'A-Gravs are the survival units, mentioned in the initial broadcast,' said the prime minister. 'They will create barriers to protect people from the gamma ray burst.'

'How big will these barriers be?' asked Peterson. 'Have you been told how they work?'

'I have not received any information about their workings,' said Timbers. 'But I have asked our science teams to come up with theories.'

*Forcefield? Bend space-time? A big metal box?*

Martel grimaced. They were being expected to take a lot on blind faith by the Ankor.

'But, Prime Minister, are these A-Gravs capable of protecting everyone?' asked Peterson.

'No,' said Timbers. 'The UK will get about one hundred A-Grav units which I am told will house less than one percent of the population. I have also been given a list of locations where they are to be installed.'

From his place at the far corner, MacKenzie spoke. 'Our only option is to support the Ankor to develop the shield.'

'It's not our only option,' said Peterson.

'Yes, it fucking is,' replied MacKenzie, his face contorting in rage for a microsecond before smoothing back out to his standard smirk of all-knowing disdain.

As one, all members of the meeting turned to face Francis MacKenzie. Now, with everyone's attention, he addressed the table. 'I was not aware of the A-Grav function, number, or distribution. However, it makes no difference. Even if these A-Gravs save half the population, the GRB will still make Earth uninhabitable by stripping away the ozone. Supporting the shield development is my only focus. We are on target for a test launch in two weeks, with formal launches soon after.' He paused and looked directly at Martel. 'None of which is helped by ongoing investigations of the SpaceOp capability which somehow includes looking at my MedOp laboratories in Leicester.'

Martel met MacKenzie's eyes with a steady stare. He had ordered a team to give MacKenzie's MedOp buildings a 'once over', outwardly to gauge MacKenzie's organisational structures. But, internally, Martel wanted to give MacKenzie a little shove to see how he reacted. Martel's whole investigation was based on assuming the Ankor, and any close Earth associates, were guilty. If the prime minister felt Martel was going too hard then the approach would be reviewed.

MacKenzie looked back at the prime minister. 'We need to agree payloads.'

*Plutonium.*

Sending plutonium into space in large quantities was a serious proposition – and the Ankor were requesting large quantities.

'The policy has not changed,' said the prime minister. 'You should continue to prepare as you see fit but no decision to supply plutonium has yet been made.'

MacKenzie smiled and made a small gesture of acquiescence with his hands.

*He took that well.*

Any decision to launch plutonium into space depended on what it would be used for and the relative dangers presented by the GRB – whose location was still unknown.

'Have other countries been asked for plutonium?' asked Peterson.

'Yes,' said the prime minister. 'Some. China has confirmed a similar request.'

Martel, listening to Timbers, but still surreptitiously watching Francis MacKenzie, saw MacKenzie flinch at the mention of China.

*Something to file for further consideration.*

Nadia Peterson looked directly towards Martel. 'Are we sure the A-Gravs are not bombs, or some other type of weapon?'

'It can't be ruled out,' said Martel, immediately noticing a disapproving glance from the prime minister. 'The army will take all precautions available.'

Of course, her next question would be – *how can you take precautions if you don't know what they do?*

Timbers intervened. 'Nadia, none of us can be sure,' he said. 'Speculation about the A-Gravs could go on forever. Additionally, I have been told to bring together engineers capable of developing materials for radiation shields and vacuum proofing, apparently to fit out the A-Gravs.'

*Vacuum proofing?*

Martel had not heard that mentioned before. He looked around the table; others appeared to have had their curiosity piqued as well, but the prime minister continued to talk.

'My decision is to take the Ankor requests at face value,' said the prime minister. 'The alternative is that we add to the risk that the Earth will be sterilised by the GRB.' He paused. 'Let's move on. Constant reassessment of everything we don't know doesn't move us forward.'

One of the senior civil servants raised his hand. 'With regards locations, are A-Gravs linked to the prison moves I recently read about?'

'Yes,' said the prime minister. 'We are in the process of emptying ten prisons through early releases and transfers.'

A murmur built in the room. This time, the prime minister allowed it to continue for a few seconds before talking over the noise. 'Home Secretary, what's the status of prison moves?'

'We're under a little pressure,' said the home secretary. 'There's rife absenteeism: people are staying home, and those that are parents, are keeping their children home too.'

'What about the basics … like food in the supermarkets?' asked Peterson.

The prime minister answered on behalf of the home secretary. 'At the moment, we're not at critical risk there. I'm ready to mobilise the army if things deteriorate.'

--------

**Later that day**
Deep below Whitehall, having passed through all the security filters and electronic checks, Martel stood with Joshua Timbers and James Piper, the USA representative.

'Nothing new on the Ankor,' said Martel. 'My team is now on-site in Anglesey. It all looks like MacKenzie is

103

running it effectively. However, three people is not enough to cover over three thousand employees. I'd like to send an additional twenty.'

'Sorry,' replied Timbers. 'This is a delicate balancing act and, although you have my full support, I cannot move against MacKenzie without evidence of wrongdoing or severe risks.'

Martel nodded, noting to himself that things might have changed in the five hours since his last report. Their assumption that the Ankor had total control of all electronic communication meant that moving messages was much more manual and took time. His team was looking assiduously for a reason to move.

'There's very little hard data about him, but we did find some new information,' said Piper, stepping forward and placing two pieces of paper on the table between them.

The first was a series of covert photos, undated but apparently recent. Someone had clearly been shadowing MacKenzie. The images showed him taking pills; a zoomed-in image showed a common brand used widely for treating anxiety.

*Not the public image he portrays.*

The second piece of paper was a transcript purportedly from many years previously. It was an interview MacKenzie had taken to be accepted into CryoGenInfinite – a company specialising in near-death cryogenic suspension where, close to death, the subject's head would be removed and stored at temperatures low enough to stop cell degeneration.

There was a page of interview questions and responses. Almost all of it was factual discussion about MacKenzie's circumstances: middle-aged, healthy, and rich. However, one short section gave an insight into his outlook.

*'Your top five favourite books are history books. We usually get people with a passion for the sciences.'*

*'I don't like the feeling of missing out.'*

*'And that's your motivation for applying to CryoGenInfinite?'*

*'I want to see everything.'*

Martel was sure that the sentiment applied to most humans on the planet.

'This is all you have?' asked Martel.

'We'll keep looking,' said Piper. 'But he's never been a person of interest to the United States.'

Disappointed – he'd been hoping for some more seedy information about MacKenzie – Martel turned his attention back to the prime minister.

'Thank you, Mr Piper,' said Timbers. 'On a different matter, why hasn't the US government shared payload information with us?'

'The response team is in lockdown,' said Piper, shaking his head. 'We're almost, although not quite, treating this as a negotiation with a hostile invading force. There is a large contingent of senior people in the White House who are convinced the Ankor don't have faster-than-light travel and have been studying us for years.'

'Studying us?' asked Timbers.

'Using an enormous radar array to suck up all the electromagnetic waves we've been pumping into space during the last hundred years.' Piper looked a little ashamed of the position he was defending. 'There's not a lot of defensible science in their arguments.'

Martel knew that even at a distance of a single light year away – closer than any star – there would be no watchable Earth TV signal, unless the alien planet had a receiving radio array the size of a solar system. If the Ankor were a hostile invasion force and did not have faster-than-light travel, then their selection of Earth as an invasion target would have been based on spectral analysis: the presence of oxygen in the atmosphere would be a key indicator of possible life. The Ankor could do that from five hundred light years away. Their invasion would be based on a guess.

'Whereas our official line is that they are benevolent,' said the prime minister. 'Although Ben's job is to prepare for the scenario where that proves to be false.'

'Let's hope it doesn't come to that,' said Piper. 'We're at the bottom of a gravity well, they can drop rocks on us all day.'

Martel agreed. His own team had run wargame scenarios. There was little upside for Earth, with the exception that if, and only if, the Ankor couldn't land – an assumption highly dependent on them not having faster-than-light travel capability – then a stalemate could be achieved. Humanity would simply be hiding down deep holes eating mushrooms for a long, long time.

'And we have two more days?' asked the prime minister.

'Yes. They're not coming straight at us.' Martel took out a piece of paper with a sketch of the current approach path of the Ankor. 'This analysis was provided by the Chinese National Space Agency, and my team have confirmed it. The Ankor are moving in an energy-inefficient manner. They are constantly keeping Earth between their own craft and the Sun.'

Piper chipped in, 'We've come to the same conclusion.'

'Do we have anything more on what the craft looks like?' Timbers said.

Martel answered. 'Just about every telescope based on Earth is pointing at it. Unfortunately, it's tiny – relative to the size of planets, that is. Most of them either can't see it, or see it as a single dot. The scientific telescopes in orbit around the Earth are struggling to track it. They're only designed to look at things hundreds of trillions of miles away, or a few thousand miles away on Earth.'

However, there was a special case. Martel turned to Piper. 'Is the Persephone preparation on plan?'

'Persephone is being repointed at the Earth,' Piper addressed the prime minister. 'She's at L2 and usually points into deep space. She's not easy to move around.'

Martel drew the equivalent location onto his sketch. Relative to solar system distances, even though outside the orbit of the moon, Persephone was almost touching Earth.

'L2?' asked the prime minister, clearly not remembering what Martel had told him a few days earlier.

'The L2 is the Lagrange Point 2, it's a gravitationally stable point relative to the Sun and the Earth. It's about one and a half million kilometres from Earth, directly away from the Sun – in constant shadow.' Piper paused. 'The Ankor should fly straight past Persephone heading for Earth.'

*Two days.*

# CHAPTER 11

**Butler Street, Thursday 18th April**

Sitting at his desk in Butler Street, having simply watched the news come in for the whole day, Tim struggled to push down the growing sense of dread. Reports throughout the morning had focused equally on the Ankor's imminent arrival, and on the recent death in custody of a church's groundskeeper who had confronted a vigilante gang as they'd been trying to set fire to his church.

*The appeasement brigade …*

A group of ten people – mixed ages, genders, and races – had stormed a church in the leafy suburbs of Guildford. The groundskeeper had confronted them. A scuffle had ensued. The police had arrived quickly, and the groundskeeper had been taken into custody. None of the reports were clear about why he was the one arrested. However, the next thing anyone knew was that the groundskeeper had died in the police station.

The event, over in a matter of hours, had triggered a wave of anti-Ankor sentiment, with the protestors accusing the 'establishment' of being in league with the church-burning Ankor.

Tim opened a new smart screen on the wall and entered a search.

`London UK riot masses unrest`

'It's everywhere,' Sam said, indicating her own feed on the wall which was showing angry crowds congregating outside Westminster.

'Those are protestors, not rioters,' said Tim.

'I'm not sure you'd make the distinction if you were amongst them,' said Sam.

'What does the hype truth-meter say?'

'It says … ' said Sam. A new screen sprang to life, red and green blocks high, indicating the media and experts agreed that meltdown was imminent. The blue bar, showing primary evidence, remained slightly lower … but not by a comfortable amount.

'What are the primary evidence sources?' Tim asked Sam.

'Twitter feeds, live footage analysis,' replied Sam. 'Plus, there's a few pirate sites that claim to hack police radio … and MIDAS analyses background noises of most public live streams for sirens.'

'Nearly time for the prime minister's evening briefing,' said Tim, looking up at the main wall. The latest MIDAS summary analysis showed a split decision fifty-fifty.

**Alien intentions**
**Trending words: saviours, invaders**

'They're not helping, and they should be,' said Sam, wheeling herself over to the window. 'The silence is making it worse.'

'Agreed,' said Tim. 'We're being blinkered … and unlike horses, we don't seem to like it.'

A smart screen burst to life. The live video feed showed Joshua Timbers standing behind a forest of microphones, immediately outside Number 10.

'Brave of him doing it outside,' said Sam without a trace of sarcasm.

In the background, the noise from a large crowd could be heard.

'I do not want to mobilise the army,' said the prime minister. 'But if the current tensions continue to escalate, I will have no choice. I must repeat to the nation: there is no need to be alarmed. The Ankor have done nothing aggressive. On the contrary, they have alerted us to a danger and are coming to support Earth's defences against the gamma ray burst.'

The prime minister continued. 'The Ankor have not explained the workings, or purpose, of the A-Gravs.'

Sam mouthed the word '*explained*' to Tim.

She was right – it was ambiguous use of language.

'All our efforts,' said the prime minister, 'must be focused on the production of the gamma ray shield.'

'MacKenzie will like that,' said Sam, looking over.

Internally, Tim winced.

*MacKenzie … Maybe I should have told Colonel Martel about the data …*

On the screen the prime minister continued with his address. 'I have asked the home secretary to put additional police onto the streets to help reassure the population. Please do not regard this as an escalation. I will provide another briefing tomorrow morning.'

'We should get some rest,' said Tim. 'Tomorrow is going to be massive. We can't stay here for the next twenty-four hours.'

'Actually, I *was* thinking about staying here,' said Sam.

Tim searched Sam's face for the hint of a joke. There was none. Knowing that Sam's pain management routine each day included a long bath and specialised physiotherapy equipment in her flat, Tim got a sense Sam was more nervous than she'd been letting on.

'I'm happy to escort you home,' said Tim, reaching for his keyboard. 'Let's just check for any reported trouble in the area.'

Sam nodded, studying her screen intently. 'You could stay at mine.'

'It doesn't look too bad,' said Tim. 'I think …'

'Tim, I will rephrase. Would you please stay at mine?' Sam turned abruptly in her chair. 'Late-night wings challenge?'

Over the years of working late together, the late-night wings challenge had become a custom. They'd compete to see who could eat the hottest. Sam always won. She had a pain tolerance Tim couldn't match.

'Sure,' said Tim. It suited him fine: no Tube journey, quick walk, some company. 'Assuming you don't take Tramadol to cheat.'

--------

**Butler Street, Friday 19th April**

Eight o'clock in the morning and, having spent a quiet night on Sam's sofa, Tim walked with her through mostly deserted streets back to the office.

'Looters are late starters,' said Sam.

Tim smiled but kept a watchful eye on every doorway and window as they walked. It did seem quieter, but whether the prime minister had achieved some of this with his personal addresses, or whether it was just primeval instinct to hunker down, Tim was not sure.

*Arrival day.*

The calculations indicated that, unless the Ankor varied their course significantly, they'd arrive in orbit some time during the afternoon. It depended on what altitude they selected.

Tim and Sam entered the offices, carefully ensuring doors were closed and locked behind them.

Tim went to make coffee in the breakout area to give Sam a little privacy as she struggled out of her wheelchair and into her office chair – not that he'd ever admit it was the reason.

*And perhaps guilt plays a part too.*

As had been the case for the last few days, every wall of the Butler Street main office was covered with smart screens, and the floor was criss-crossed with cabling – kept as discreet as possible so not to interfere with Sam's wheelchair.

Tim took another look around the room. 'No images projected onto the window blinds, Sam. You missed a trick.'

Sam smiled. 'We're going to need to look through the blinds now and then … to check for mushroom clouds.'

Tim smiled; a little gallows humour didn't hurt.

'Is that a real-time image from ground-based telescopes?' asked Tim, pointing at the Chinese National Space Agency image. The Ankor craft was a rotating blob. 'Poor resolution due to atmospheric interference?'

Sam typed on her workstation. 'Actually, it's a computer amalgamation,' she said. 'The CNSA are building it up from over twenty near-infrared feeds around the world. Most Earth-based telescopes are getting about eight hours of decent exposure before they lose sight of it.'

'And the next big item,' said Tim. 'NASA's Persephone images.' He checked the time. 'They should fly past Persephone in just under an hour.'

'That one,' said Sam, pointing to a blank screen. 'That's the NASA feed.'

Tim continued to scan. Three screens showed constant updates on the alien craft: heading, real-time image, and speed with arrival countdown. Another wall showed MIDAS summarised newsfeeds, and raw newsfeeds from the most cited ones.

In the corner of the room, a series of six screens showed live feeds from launch sites. Some launch sites had close-up feeds that included countdown clocks. A few launch sites, including Anglesey, USA and France, only provided long-distance shots.

Like the rest of the world, Tim and Sam simply waited and watched.

Just after noon, the NASA feed came to life with a simple text message.

> **Initial images expected to be poor quality as Persephone needs a separation distance of greater than five hundred thousand kilometres to focus. Camera online from 08:00**

'That's US local time,' said Sam.

Tim did the maths. Assuming the Ankor continued their constant deceleration, it would be thirty-four minutes between the alien craft passing Persephone and it reaching five hundred thousand kilometres of separation.

'You've not heard anything from Charlie?' asked Tim.

'Nothing. It doesn't matter. We've got better data here anyway,' said Sam, indicating all the feeds: the aliens were invading, the aliens were going to bring us eternal life, the aliens were going to judge us individually, they had lied about FTL … the list went on and on.

Tim's eyes tracked back to the NASA screen showing a graphical representation of the Ankor's approach. 'I wonder why they're hiding from the Sun?'

'Maybe they're an intersolar species,' said Sam. 'Born in deep space, and constantly travelling between the stars.'

A beep from the central server was accompanied by a new screen opening. An algorithm monitoring traffic had found a news feed passing a critical trending threshold and displayed an old but familiar image on a newly opened screen.

It was a NASA Space Shuttle. Although Tim recognised it as the *Atlantis*, the shuttle that had performed the programme's last flight, in 2011, it had been renamed.

*Lincoln*.

The shuttle was being wheeled to the launch pad at Kennedy Space Center.

'It takes about six hours to wheel it out,' said Tim. 'But soon, Persephone is going to show us everything.'

A few minutes later the NASA feed beeped. The screen came to life, showing images from the Persephone telescope. The feed was almost real-time, with NASA providing an image enhancement feed alongside the raw data.

Sam flicked a few switches on her workstation. The office lights dimmed, as did the luminosity of all the other screens.

This was it.

They'd had more complex radar images before, but this would be the first time a truly visual image would be more than a single blob.

Initially the image provided by NASA was a simply a blurred cubic shape – something they already knew from the radar returns.

They waited as details were added.

Within a few minutes, a series of vertical stripes appeared on the splodge of red on the screen. A few minutes after that, horizontal stripes appeared too.

The NASA image continued to resolve, becoming more and more fine-grained.

Soon it was showing a very regular cubic shape made up of individual pods, separated by what seemed to be rods protruding from each one at ninety-degree angles. The whole cube was rotating about a single axis.

There were hundreds of pods. But the NASA feed indicated that none of the structure was hotter than a hundred degrees Celsius.

No obvious engines.

No front pointy end.

No wings.

Just a big cube, slowly rotating and heading directly for Earth at half a million kilometres an hour.

'An hour to go,' said Sam. 'Then we'll see if they do the alien equivalent of a skid, before taking off their motorbike helmet and snogging your sister.'

'I don't have a sister.'

The image now showed the craft was made up of spherical pods joined by thin filaments, and more detail had become clear. It was seven pods wide, seven pods deep, and seven pods high.

'Three hundred and forty-three pods,' said Sam.

The NASA feed was excellent and provided significant image processing and commentary. Each pod appeared to be a sphere one hundred metres in diameter, and each was joined by either three, four, five, or six connections to its neighbours, dependent on where it fitted in the cube. The separation between pods was just over one thousand metres.

'There are gaps in the heat patterns,' said Sam.

Tim saw them. 'Some of the pods are either missing, or not generating heat.'

They watched with the rest of the world as, over the period of an hour, the Ankor craft set its orbit at about twenty thousand kilometres above the surface of Earth. Technically, it was a solar orbit not an Earth orbit: the Ankor continued to move such that the Earth was directly between themselves and the Sun; because of the Earth's gravity, the Ankor would have to expend significant energy to remain in that orbit.

'Twenty thousand is fairly high,' said Tim.

'Fewer satellites to hit?' said Sam.

'Out of reach of our rockets,' said Tim, looking to see how humanity was reacting. Were they all getting the same tight feeling in their chests that he was?

One of the screens was a composite grid of sixteen live video streams from public areas across London. After mostly remaining at home for the morning, crowds were now gathering at key public locations.

'They're back again,' said Tim. It seemed to him that fundamentally people were on edge rather than panicky. Whether that was simply the product of his hope overriding his logic, he was not sure.

The MIDAS summary status continued to display significant anxiety.

```
Alien orbit imminent
Population scared
Trending words: invasion, support, saviour,
murder
```

Not long afterwards, improved images of the craft from ground-based telescopes started to filter through MIDAS. The craft was not lit up in any way, so normal optical telescopes were almost useless. On top of that, the moon, which might have provided a little reflected light, was on the wrong side of the Earth for another few weeks. So, again, it was left almost exclusively to infrared telescopes to perform the observation work. Unfortunately, they were not numerous, or well suited for the job. They required their lenses to be cryogenically cooled and shielded from ambient heat sources, and were designed to look at effectively stationary galaxies and nebulae thousands of light years away. On the plus side, the temperature gradients across the Ankor craft appeared to be the most interesting thing to observe, and the infrared telescopes were ideal for that purpose.

By seven o'clock that evening, a high definition image of the Ankor's craft was being streamed directly from the CNSA who continued to create an amalgamated image from all the best Earth sources.

The now-familiar lattice cube of seven by seven by seven, just under five miles high, wide, and long.

There were no missing pods. Each of the three hundred and forty-three pods was shown with some indicating different levels of temperature. The units were 'K', Kelvin, with 0K being absolute zero, 273K being roughly the freezing point of water, and 310K being the average operating temperature of humans.

One MIDAS aggregator feed overlaid the CNSA image with data.

```
343 Pods
213 Operating at an average 305K
78  Operating at an average 220K
52  Operating at an average 4K
Questions as to function of different pods
have been sent.
No responses received.
```

'What do you think that means?' asked Sam.

'I'm not sure,' said Tim. 'All the pods appear to be the same size. There's no obvious correlation between the location of the pod in the lattice and the temperature.'

'Maybe they have different function,' said Sam.

Tim kicked off a search to look for hypotheses. 'Let's see what's being postulated.'

'I need to take a break,' said Sam, wheeling herself towards the breakout room which had a sofa. 'Call me if something big happens.'

'Okay,' said Tim, knowing that physical exhaustion and back pain were her constant companions. 'Shall I bring you a glass of water?'

Likely, Sam would be taking painkillers.

'I've got a bottle in my utility wheelchair,' said Sam. 'But thanks.'

Tim returned his attention to his own workstation.

An hour passed.

'Expert' opinion started to appear on the internet. People broadly agreed that the 305K temperature reading probably meant the Ankor had a biological component, something the Ankor had not communicated to anyone on Earth – as far as Tim was aware.

There was little agreement on why the pods didn't include more insulation, or indeed whether each pod had a different internal temperature.

Even more perplexing than the pod temperature differentials was the fact the craft didn't appear to have any engines.

The evident vast gulf in technology between the Ankor and the Earth should have calmed humanity – after all, the Ankor were there to help. This, however, was not how humanity reacted. The overwhelming immensity of the situation could not so simply be absorbed.

Smart screens burst to life as demonstrations picked up all over the globe: masses of people demanding answers, accusing their governments of cover-ups, and begging for protection.

Tim monitored the demonstrations, some of which were degenerating into riots. Although a lot of 'alt' groups – whether left or right – were grabbing the chance to peddle their own messages, most of the demos showed a genuine upsurge of public fear.

Images of an overturned police car in West London started appearing and being reused.

About to wake Sam and tell her about the new developments, Tim received an email from Francis MacKenzie.

*I want you to move the encryption servers on-site to me from your offices and entirely disable Park Royal. Report to Anglesey by Tuesday.*

Clearly MacKenzie wanted as far as possible to isolate the MIDAS Production system. Although, given most of the data came from the internet, MIDAS could not be entirely isolated. However, with the various data breakers and passive system sniffers, if the whole system was in Anglesey, any intrusions could be more easily intercepted. Sam had already proved that things weren't secure with the encryption servers in Butler Street.

*Tuesday?*

It was doable. Deciding to ask Sam her opinion, Tim walked over to the breakout room.

Inside, on the sofa, Sam was dozing in front of a smart screen showing the Ankor craft.

As he put his head into the room, Sam looked up. 'I couldn't switch it off. Join me?'

'I wonder if anyone isn't watching it?' asked Tim, grabbing a blanket, easing off his shoes and settling himself down on the sofa with her.

'Is it quiet in the street?' she asked through half-closed eyes.

'Last time I looked,' said Tim, hypnotised by the image of the slowly rotating Ankor craft. 'What do they want?'

'No idea … Save our lives …' Sam was clearly exhausted. As she shifted to get comfortable, a flicker of pain registered on her face.

Tim looked back at the image on the screen. Would the Ankor provide anything more than the shield? Could they help injuries like Sam's? Their current approach of minimal communication made it seem unlikely, but … maybe.

'I will support whichever decision you make about further treatment,' said Tim. 'I'm not trying to heal you for my conscience.'

'I know.' Sam smiled, keeping her eyes closed. 'Just remember it's my body, my decision.'

'When this Ankor stuff is over, and arterial cleaning is running,' said Tim. 'I'm sure MacKenzie will focus MedOp on neural repair.'

'We did see Xandra Kusr at the launch,' said Sam. 'Before she was struck off, she'd been doing pioneering nerve regrowth work.'

'I know.' After the accident, Tim had spent every night for over a year researching nerve damage regrowth.

With her eyes still closed, Sam elbowed Tim gently, slightly slurring. 'I don't know why she didn't fight to clear her name. Why did she simply take MacKenzie's gold?'

'Yeah, free healthcare for the masses,' said Tim. 'What a selfish bitch!'

Sam chuckled and opened one eye. 'I have enough upper body strength to push you onto the floor.'

Tim smiled.

Warm silence descended, and Tim drowsed.

*Barp! Barp! Barp! Barp! Barp! Barp!*

His brain whirred to life. It wasn't a burglar alarm. It was a critical MIDAS alert.

The image on the smart screen did not appear to have changed. The Ankor were still slowly rotating in perpetual night twenty thousand kilometres above the equator.

Tim looked more closely.

The Ankor cube had altered – it was no longer perfectly cubic. A set of numbers in the bottom right corner of the screen seemed to confirm the picture of the Ankor craft was still a live feed from the CNSA.

'Sam!' Tim nudged Sam, deeply asleep next to him.

'What?' She rubbed her eyes.

'Look.'

'It's expanding,' said Sam.

They watched as the cube, originally five miles long on each side, spread to ten miles wide in just a few minutes. Either the distance between the pods was growing, or it was reforming its shape.

The CNSA feed moved to a split screen – one half showing the real-time images, and the other showing possible end-state configurations. It still showed a total Ankor pod count of 343, but their distribution was changing. The average distance between the pods did not seem to be changing – it remained at just over one thousand metres – but the craft was enlarging from Earth's perspective.

'It's unfolding,' said Sam.

Tim felt her hand reach out and take his. He gave a little squeeze in what he hoped would be taken for general reassurance. Sam was right. The Ankor craft, having arrived in orbit as a seven by seven by seven cubic array, was transforming its shape.

As they watched, the craft continued to unfold, growing both in width and height.

After about an hour the unpacking stopped. The Ankor craft was now twenty pods wide at its widest point, stretching fourteen miles from end to end. Its height was ten pods – seven miles at its tallest point – and the CNSA estimated between one and three pods thick.

'A giant oval,' said Sam.

Tim felt a chill run down his spine.

*More like a giant lens … looking down at us.*

# CHAPTER 12

At five in the morning London was calm as Martel's unmarked car ghosted its way through its streets. The quiet wasn't going to last once people found out what the Ankor were currently doing.

For the last three hours, internet traffic had been running at twenty times its previous peak.

Martel activated his secure radio and put a call in to his second-in-command, Captain Whaller, back at Porton Down – the special weapons facility where Martel's team were preparing a whole range of possible physical responses.

'What's the latest, Captain?'

'It does not look like a denial of service attack, sir. They're just sucking up data.'

'How?'

'Every data access point that has the capability of transmitting data into space is doing so. All other communication hubs are relaying data to those uplink hubs.'

For the next five minutes, Captain Whaller gave Martel the locations of the major access points and the current estimation of the volume of data being extracted.

'Anything on the new shape of the craft?' asked Martel.

'Nothing other than the obvious: that they are presenting a much greater surface area facing Earth. The temperatures of the individual pods have not changed,' replied Whaller.

'I'm going to tell the prime minister we are sure that it is not an attack,' said Martel. 'Do you concur?'

'Yes,' said Whaller. 'The Ankor may simply be unaware of the fear it would cause. Although admittedly they may be purposely trying to destabilise us. As a precursor to attack.'

'I may suggest taking back some semblance of control,' said Martel. 'How easy would it be to turn off the data flow?'

There was silence for a few seconds.

'I checked the numbers as asked. Physically, we could cut the power to all satellite-enabled uplinks within forty-eight hours.' said Whaller. 'There are a few thousand of them. But that could come across as an act of aggression.'

'I'll discuss it with the PM,' said Martel. 'What's the latest public news from Anglesey?'

'Nothing new,' said Whaller. 'The place is gearing up for a test launch in five days.'

Just as Martel was preparing to hang up, Whaller spoke again. 'Just coming through now, sir. China is claiming it's being attacked by the Ankor.'

'Attacked?'

'Cyber-attack,' said Whaller. 'I'm sending you the transcript, just seconds old.'

Martel's phone buzzed.

*People's Republic of China is grateful for the efforts that the Ankor appear to be expending on Earth's survival. However, the data extraction currently underway is not commensurate with our expectations of their data needs. It is too much. We have tried to bilaterally discuss this with the Ankor but they have not replied, or acknowledged the request. We will continue to support their efforts, and mobilise our workforce for the development of rockets, shelters, and shield materials. However, as of now, we have cut access to our communications network, and without paralysing our country, are actively stopping the data extraction.*

# CHAPTER 13

Sitting at his desk in Mission Control, MacKenzie had one eye on the hundreds of technicians scurrying around below him, and one eye on the screens covering the walls. The image that held most of his concentration was that of the Ankor craft itself.

Many people looking at the same image were wondering where the engines were, or the power supply. MacKenzie didn't know the answer, but those subjects were of little interest to him. He accepted that they had the required technology. He saw it in action as they approached Earth.

The way the Ankor craft had unfolded was much more interesting. Not only did it now have a much larger cross-section of pods facing directly towards Earth, but the internal connections between many of the Ankor pods had altered.

The new pod distribution was showing well-defined grouping of the two Ankor factions.

In every communication with Earth, and almost every communication with MacKenzie, the Ankor represented themselves as a single unit.

They were not, however, united.

*Division hasn't been a problem so far.*

It would be too much to say that the Ankor factions were vying for his allegiance – the main faction definitely saw itself as far too civilised for that – but both sides seemed keen to keep him as an ally.

Of course, he was under no illusion that it was in any way a judgement of his own personal attributes. He simply had what they both wanted.

MacKenzie's eyes drifted to the CNSA information covering the pod temperatures. Seventy-eight pods at 220 Kelvin that held Ankor life in a state of suspension. Fifty-two pods, hovering above absolute zero, were empty. The remaining two hundred and thirteen were operational.

The Chinese could protest all they wanted; the Ankor would take whatever data they needed. They didn't require information from MacKenzie – not any more. It was physical materials that they needed. The Ankor couldn't descend into Earth's gravity well. They would pay MacKenzie handsomely for his services.

*Immortality.*

Movement from the bottom of the stairs that led up to his office level drew MacKenzie's attention.

MacKenzie stared at Taylor for a moment, and then shook his head, denying him permission to come up. Taylor tried not to look disappointed as he stepped back off the bottom step and waited.

Looking back at the newsfeeds, MacKenzie absorbed the news covering the British army as it was deployed across all the major cities: London, Birmingham, Manchester, Glasgow … the list went on.

*Did the Ankor advise you on the perfect timing for rolling out the army?*

Too soon, and Joshua Timbers would have looked weak. Too late, and the crowds might have become unruly. As it was, the deployment appeared perfectly timed; the UK population had had a chance to let off some steam, but not much more.

MacKenzie smiled. The more army personnel that were deployed on crowd control, the less would be available to interfere with his plans. Not that Colonel Martel's liaison team had been a problem. He'd had them scurrying around SpaceOp, allowed to look everywhere.

Not quite everywhere, but everywhere that appeared on a plan or blueprint of the facility.

MacKenzie stood up and walked down the stairs.

Indicating for Taylor to follow him and with Juan at his side, MacKenzie headed underground, deep into one of those areas that didn't appear on any blueprints of SpaceOp.

'The Chinese announcement came as predicted,' said Taylor.

MacKenzie acknowledged the point with a nod and murmured agreement. The Chinese satellite uplink restrictions had come as the Ankor predicted. However, MacKenzie was still not sure that the Chinese launch capabilities weren't a back-up for the Ankor, or vice versa, that the Chinese were their primary contact and he himself was the back-up.

*It could be a bluff ... a double bluff.*

Until he was one hundred percent convinced that the Chinese were not secretly supporting the Ankor, he would continue with all his countermeasures and counter-surveillance. Nothing from his moles in the last few weeks had given any impression of a double-cross, although annoyingly a few packages from China had not arrived at the dead-drops yet. It could just be delays in the public postal service – obviously he could not use electronic transmissions and he avoided over-use of private couriers: the photos, if intercepted, would look suspicious purely based on courier costs, particularly being delivered to anonymous numbered post boxes.

As they continued downwards, MacKenzie noticed the old bandages sticking out from Taylor's sleeve. He had mixed feelings about Taylor's implants. He was interested to see if they worked, but he disliked Taylor's implied submission to the Ankor. 'When do you need the new ones?'

'Early next week is fine,' said Taylor. 'The main procedure will require a general anaesthetic.'

MacKenzie shuddered. He didn't even like falling asleep alone in a locked room. The thought of having a general anaesthetic with Xandra Kusr poised above him with a knife …

'Let's hope that Dr Kusr comes round to our way of thinking,' said MacKenzie. She'd been kept underground for almost ten days. Each day she begged to speak to her children or simply be let out. Each day she was told to get on with reproducing her last set of experiments from MedOp. Each day she refused. The Ankor analysis – both behavioural and DNA-based – was clear that extended torture would not work and worse, would degrade her ability to do her job to the extent that she would become worthless.

*An impasse that is about to be broken.*

The Ankor arrival gave MacKenzie another weapon in his armoury.

After passing through the final set of doors, now six floors below the Hot Zone, MacKenzie indicated for Juan to open the final door and lead them in.

As usual, Xandra Kusr was wearing a white laboratory coat, latex gloves, and had her long black hair tied up in a bun. As usual, she was sitting on the floor cross-legged, staring at the very visible internal CCTV camera.

As MacKenzie entered the room, she turned to face him.

'Dr Kusr,' said MacKenzie. 'Are you ready to start?'

'No,' replied Kusr, not moving.

Ten days – enough was enough – MacKenzie hadn't pushed her too hard before but now it was time to move; and now, he had access to the tools for the job.

'Run the feed,' said MacKenzie.

A screen opened on the wall. Kusr quickly recognised the picture: it was her own living room.

She screamed, leaping to her feet.

Taylor scrambled backwards, but Juan grabbed Kusr in a vice-like grip and forced her face towards the screen.

Two men dressed all in black with black balaclavas were holding one of Kusr's daughters, facing towards an unseen camera.

'Mummy!' screamed Amber, clearly seeing Kusr on a television monitor at her end.

A third man came into shot. His hunting knife was raised level with Amber's face.

MacKenzie turned to Kusr. 'I'm sorry that we have not been able to convince you of how serious we are before reaching this point. Which of her eyeballs would you prefer him to remove?'

The camera zoomed in on the knife, its blade now just inches away from Amber's tear-streaked face.

Kusr screamed and collapsed. Juan let her hit the floor.

Amber screamed.

As Kusr retched on the floor, she didn't take her gaze from the screen.

MacKenzie interposed himself between Kusr and the screen. 'Well?'

Kusr's expression softened. 'Please just make it stop!'

'Only you can stop it.'

Kusr took a breath, her eyes darting past MacKenzie to look back at the screen. 'Okay. I'll restart the tests. Do you have the new protein-enzyme mix?'

'No,' said MacKenzie. This was still yet to be delivered. 'Just get to the stage you were at before you left MedOp.'

'I want to see my children,' said Kusr.

'They are being cared for and reassured,' said MacKenzie.

'I want to see them,' Kusr repeated, a fire still lit in her eyes.

'Do you really want to bring them in here?' asked MacKenzie. 'What happens the next time you refuse to do something for me?'

The light in her eyes went out.

'Good,' said MacKenzie, pointing at the cages of mice. 'You'll have new data in a few days. Meanwhile, rerun what you had achieved in Leicester … just to get your eye back in, as it were.'

Leaving Juan to watch Kusr, he beckoned Taylor and they walked back to the staircase.

'Something on your mind?' asked MacKenzie.

Taylor indicated he wanted to go further below ground.

Heading down an additional floor, they entered their quiet room. MacKenzie secured the doors and activated the electromagnetic field – no one could overhear.

'The Ankor told me about the heroin murders,' said Taylor.

'And?'

'They told me it was you,' said Taylor.

'I arranged it for *them*,' said MacKenzie, deliberately being obtuse. It had been the minor Ankor faction that had asked MacKenzie to arrange the killings – not that he had thought for too long before agreeing. He needed that faction's support.

*Besides … one hundred thousand men and women die every day, most of them worthier than the fifty or so drug addicts.*

'This improves the Ankor calculations by a fraction of a millionth of a single percent,' said Taylor.

'Agreed,' said MacKenzie. The extra deaths, and subsequent analysis of the social media response, would have done nothing to notably improve the Ankor's calculations on population dynamics. 'But I can't really see your concern, given what's happening next week.'

'You cannot compare this with the Blessed,' said Taylor. 'The sanctity of life is a core tenet of the faith.'

'I think they will accept a certain amount of fallout,' said MacKenzie. 'If it delivers their materials.'

*I certainly have reconciled myself with the blood price for my countless millennia.*

'God has decreed on the matter.'

'Actually spoke to the Ankor, did he?' asked MacKenzie, knowing the Ankor's belief was as much an act of faith as that of any Earth religion. The Ankor god, rather conveniently like most others in the modern era, lived outside of the universe it had created.

*Not to mention that, coincidentally, the Ankor worship a God exactly in their own image.*

# CHAPTER 14

Having spent the night in the Butler Street offices watching the Ankor craft unfold whilst listening to occasional lone gunshots and police sirens, Tim and Sam ate a makeshift breakfast in the main office.

'All okay?' asked Sam, wheeling herself through from the breakout area with one hand, whilst checking her phone with the other and balancing a couple of bowls of breakfast cereal on her lap.

'Except for the ever-present dread of the looming Ankor, all good,' said Tim, staring at the smart screens.

'We're still going to Anglesey, right?'

'Yep,' he said, standing up from the table. 'I'd better make a start on unmounting the encryption servers.'

'I'll help,' said Sam. 'Give me five minutes.'

Tim was only halfway to the door when Sam called out. 'Tim!'

Tim turned to see her staring at a newly opened smart screen.

'The invasion has begun,' she said.

The display showed that the Arecibo Observatory in Puerto Rico had recorded new contacts near the Ankor's craft. The contacts were moving blisteringly fast and were heading from their current orbit at twenty thousand kilometres directly towards Earth.

A few moments later, the MIDAS scans of official newsfeeds cross-linked with social media and produced a summary.

*A-Gravs released.*

```
Destination unknown.
Selected governments have indicated they were
given five minutes' warning: China, Egypt,
France, Japan, Russia
```

'I'm guessing that those are only the governments who received a warning and told people about it, rather than the only governments to get a warning,' said Tim.

Within moments, the data started flooding in: opinions, radar tracks, spectral analysis. A few video feeds from optical telescopes.

'They're not coming straight down,' said Sam.

She was right. The A-Grav units were gradually adjusting their courses as they fell, diverting from a direct descent to a horizontal trajectory that would settle them into a lower orbit.

For the next hour Tim and Sam sat, spellbound, as they watched the ten thousand A-Grav units settle into a roughly equatorial orbit at a height of two thousand kilometres above sea level.

The Butler Street office wall continued to blaze with real-time updates – although, given the size and speed of the units, no telescope could resolve them as anything more than a pinprick of light.

Creating an evenly spaced ring around the Earth, each A-Grav unit was separated from its neighbours by roughly five kilometres. Each of them completed a full orbit of the Earth just over every two hours.

'They're moving fast,' said Tim.

'The speed's not unusual,' Sam replied, reading from her own screen. 'All Earth satellites in comparable orbits move at similar speeds. Too slow … and you fall to the ground. Too fast … and you disappear off into space.'

As the A-Gravs settled into their new orbits, ground-based optical telescopes managed to lock onto on them. All of the units were identical, metallic looking, spherical, and approximately ten metres in diameter.

'We should go outside and look,' said Sam. Not waiting for an answer, she hobbled across to her wheelchair.

'Let me just check local news for disturbances,' said Tim.

Sam's eyes narrowed. 'Only assuming you would also do such a check if you went alone.'

'Irrelevant,' said Tim, smiling. 'If I was alone, I'd be locked in the toilets.'

'Come on,' said Sam. 'This is once in a lifetime.'

Leaving his keyboard, Tim followed.

Outside, many people had congregated on the pavements, all of them looking directly upwards. Tim recognised most of them as locals.

No-one seemed to be able to see anything.

High above the equator did not mean high above London. Tim did a quick calculation in his head.

'Equatorial orbit,' said Tim to Sam, pointing south.

If the A-Gravs were in an equatorial orbit, then they would be rising above the southern horizon before dipping below again. If the orbit was too low, they wouldn't be visible due to the curvature of the Earth.

'Let's go to the park for a better look,' said Tim.

'Suits me,' said Sam, already setting off in the direction of the park.

Arriving at Mile End Park a few minutes later, Tim was pleased to see he'd made the right call. It afforded a much clearer view of the southern horizon.

A crowd of at least five hundred people had congregated there and were looking southwards. Some were gaping in silence; others were whispering to their neighbours. All looked awestruck.

Sunlight was reflecting strongly off the A-Gravs, illuminating them. The resulting ring of lights rose above the horizon in the south-east, soaring into the sky in a sparkling parabola, before sinking back down below tower blocks in the south-west.

Perhaps it was the calming effect of the nearby soldiers, but the mood in the park was of wonder, rather than fear. Physically separated from each other in orbit by only five kilometres, the A-Gravs appeared to be almost touching, giving the effect of a diamond bracelet encircling the Earth.

'Ten thousand mariners on their way to petition the gods,' whispered Sam.

Tim nodded, and in silence, they simply watched.

Fifteen minutes later, Tim noticed Sam shivering. 'Shall we head back in?' he asked.

'No chance,' said Sam.

'We can come back later.'

'Okay.'

Back in the office, the MIDAS feed focusing on the A-Gravs continued to produce updated reports every few minutes.

`10,000 units at 2,000 kilometres`
`Trending words: orbit, bomb, invasion, falling`

'There's the word "bomb" again,' said Tim, clicking through to judge its importance.

Click. Scan. Click. Scan.

Nothing obvious.

Tim instructed MIDAS to run the media hype checker. The results came back quickly. There was no hard evidence from any serious agencies that the A-Gravs might be bombs.

*How would anyone know?*

'Just got a text from Charlie,' said Sam. 'He's back in London this evening but also checking we're set for Tuesday. Are we?'

'All good,' said Tim. 'You could ask him what he knows about the A-Gravs.'

'I'd rather not,' she said. 'He'll just make some stupid excuse not to tell me and I'll feel hurt.'

'Fair enough.'

For a few hours, Tim worked on the plan for the data encryption server move. He kept one eye on the news.

At lunchtime, Sam called over. 'I suspect I've overdone it. I need to get back home.'

'Okay,' said Tim. 'I'll walk you back.'

'You don't need to,' said Sam. 'I've made the journey alone about five hundred times.'

'It's fine,' he said. 'And then I'll take the Tube home.' Tim didn't want to hang around Sam's flat if Charlie was due home. He knew that Charlie knew about his feelings for Sam – and he knew that Charlie knew that he knew. Being at Sam's when Charlie arrived would be weird.

They set off.

Looking southwards between the buildings, Tim continued to get glimpses of the glittering arc of diamonds spread across the sky.

*In stable orbit for now…*

They arrived at Sam's flat just in time to catch a public address by the prime minister.

Joshua Timbers stood at the now-familiar lectern in front of Number 10.

**'Firstly, I would like to thank you all – the whole population – for the calm approach with which you are dealing with the ongoing uncertainty. I urge you all to refrain from resorting to anger or violence when faced with difficulties in these trying times. The police and army are deployed to maintain order and to keep the peace. Our only motive, our only strategy, is to keep the innocent safe from the few troubled elements within our society.'**

Timbers paused.

'*Secondly, the British government has received short additional messaging from the Ankor. Eighty-six locations, simple grid references, are to be prepared for A-Grav unit installation. We will be implementing procedures to evacuate those locations, with exclusion zones of half a mile. Please be patient and comply with the instructions from local police teams. We will share any additional information that arrives. We have no indication of timing.*'

'What did you think?' asked Tim.

'Not a bad speech. A little patronising … but not bad,' said Sam.

*But will it keep the peace?*

# CHAPTER 15

An alarm woke Tim from deep sleep at 3 o'clock on Sunday morning. A new Ankor broadcast message.

> **A-Gravs**
> **Each unit has specific instructions**
> **Do not open units**
> **Do not populate the host structures**
> **Do not send anything above 5000km**

Tim skipped across the newsfeeds to observe the general reaction. There was little discussion on authenticity; humanity, after only two messages, was used to the way the Ankor easily overpowered Earth's communications systems.

As the prime minister had said the day before, the UK would be receiving eighty-six of these. Irrespective of whether the UK government broadcast the details, Tim was sure that social media would soon be picking up evidence of the police preparing locations.

For the next hour, he scanned the various channels. One was showing a live feed of the *Lincoln* sitting on its launch pad.

*I assume the Ankor meant you ...*

Tim searched the internet for theories about whether the *Lincoln* would be able to reach the Ankor. The results were inconclusive. No shuttle had ever been above one thousand kilometres; the Ankor were at twenty thousand. The main issue was fuel capacity, but it was conceivable the Americans had worked around the problem.

The other discussion that drew Tim's eye related to the Ankor's communication strategy. Why were they broadcasting this information to everyone? Theories were mixed, but the two receiving the most support were: 'to stop governments hiding the information' and 'to continue to underline their technological superiority'.

Aware that he had forty-eight hours of seriously hard work in front of him, including a trip to Anglesey, Tim went back to bed.

Some time later, his phone woke him.

'Why haven't you replied to my texts?' asked Sam.

'Asleep ...' said Tim, rubbing his eyes with his free hand.

'Remember how the government has been emptying prisons?'

'Yep.'

'Last night, the prime minister talked about the A-Grav location preparation.'

'Yep,' he said again.

'Well, they're setting up an exclusion zone around Kirkmail. I can just about see them from my kitchen window.'

'Shit!'

'So, put on some clothes and get over here.'

'On my way.'

Tim rolled out of bed and pulled on his clothes.

*Will Charlie be there?*

Tim's phone buzzed.

**Come on – tanks! – big ones with guns … xsam**

Failing to see why a heavily armoured presence should be any more reason to rush, or even to go, Tim headed for the Tube.

As he passed the small park at the end of his road, he did a double-take. At seven in the morning, there were people spreading blankets on the ground as if preparing for a picnic.

The park wasn't full, but it was certainly more than just the few local crazies. It appeared that a fair number of people felt sufficiently relaxed about the Ankor to create an informal 'alien watch' vibe.

Tim was jealous.

*Watch the universe in wonder … not fear.*

A slamming car door drew Tim's attention away from the park. There was clearly an opposing school of thought: up and down the street, cars were being packed. These people, eyeing the picnickers with disbelief, were getting out of London.

*It'll be worse near Kirkmail.*

Tim was right. As he walked out of Mile End Tube station, he noticed two things. On the plus side, law and order was holding; cars weren't mowing down pedestrians on the pavements. However, the volume of people leaving town was causing gridlock three times as bad as the worst Bank Holiday rush he had ever witnessed.

There was no sign of Charlie when Tim arrived at Sam's flat. He found her looking over a recent MIDAS report. As Tim had surmised, social media was reporting the preparation of all eighty-six sites across the UK. There were at least ten prisons and the rest were almost exclusively schools.

'These are the host structures,' said Sam, overlaying the locations on a map.

'Is Kirkmail empty?' asked Tim, straining to look from the kitchen window.

'I think so.'

For the next hour, they scanned newsfeeds and scientific opinion pieces selected by MIDAS based on peer review scores and citations.

Feeling in need of a caffeine hit, Tim went to the kitchen.

'Whilst you're there,' called Sam, 'look out of the window.'

Tim leaned out of the window. Far to the south, the string of glittering A-Gravs hung in the sky. This time the eastern edges were brighter, whilst the western ones had yet to be fully illuminated by the Sun.

'It all looks normal to me,' said Tim.

'You're an expert on orbiting alien artefacts, are you?' Sam pushed the laptop around so Tim could see the MIDAS report.

```
~3% units falling under gravity
Each with different north-south velocity
vector
Terminal velocity currently at 600kph
Units slowing as air resistance increases
Falling units are shedding exterior covers but
heating
64mins to impact
```

The word 'impact' sent a shiver down Tim's spine. 'Shit!'

He looked back out of the window. His view was not great, but it appeared that some of the A-Gravs were now emitting a reddish light, and were diverging from their previous positions in the ring.

'Can you access the CNSA's public website?' Tim called over his shoulder.

'It's down,' said Sam.

'NASA?'

'It's up.'

Tim returned to the kitchen table, where Sam had her laptop. 'How come you've got such good bandwidth?' he asked.

Sam tapped a USB stick. 'Charlie couriered me a priority access one.'

'Good that he has some benefits.'

*Wow!*

That was one of the most aggressive things Tim had ever said about Charlie – to Sam's face, at least. He was usually hyper-careful on the subject, for fear of coming across as petty.

It was hard to make out on the small screen, but real-time images collated by NASA showed almost three hundred A-Grav units that had fallen out of the chain.

The first impact was expected in New York, followed by Moscow.

It was entirely feasible that one of the countries, frustrated by a lack of communication, could shoot a missile at a descending A-Grav.

No news yet about London. However, the fact the prime minister had talked about preparations, and the deployment of military tanks around Kirkmail prison, gave a strong sense that London would be part of the first wave.

Five minutes later, the UK government confirmed that one of the A-Grav units was heading for Kirkmail.

Social media analysis indicated that lots of people were also rushing towards it.

Tim looked at Sam. 'What next?'

'I need your help to get onto the roof.'

'The roof?'

'Much better view from up there. My windows point the wrong way.'

Tim looked across to the television. A real-time video of the Kirkmail-bound A-Grav was now showing on all the main channels. It was a glowing ball, red-hot, and shedding external materials.

*Heat shielding?'*

'Just one so far for London?' asked Tim.

'And one for Birmingham,' said Sam. 'A little behind.'

The television channel flicked to a live shot of the roads around Kirkmail prison. In general, cars appeared to be heading away from the prison, whilst people were running towards it.

Another update came through.

```
UK government confirm
London Unit - Kirkmail prison
Birmingham Unit - BT Head Office
Velocity currently 325kph
18mins to impact - 105km height
External casing being shed appears to be
carbon based
Diameter down from 10m to 3m
```

'Come on,' said Sam, now on her crutches. 'It will take me that long to get to the roof.'

Tim turned to the front door.

Sam called him back. 'No,' she said, pointing with a crutch to the kitchen table. 'You need to do my injection, otherwise I'll never get up there.'

Tim walked over to the kitchen table and picked up the syringe Sam had prepared. It was not an entirely new situation: he'd injected Sam a few times over the years.

'Wash your hands,' said Sam with a smile.

'I was just about to.'

He scrubbed up and returned to the task.

Sam shuffled around to present her back to him and pulled her shirt up to reveal her lower spine.

With her jeans riding low on her hips, Tim was struck by the juxtaposition of perfect form and mangled torture. The top part of her left buttock was visible. From here a vicious scar ran twelve inches up past her left kidney and then all the way across her spine, finishing just under her right shoulder blade. On either side of the scar, which itself was an inch wide, lay a two-inch band of damaged tissue, unbroken but livid red, and wrinkled. He knew her spine was held together with metal plates and pins, which in many places could be seen as they came up to within millimetres of the surface of her skin.

And yet the top of her right buttock was perfect. He longed to kiss it. Obviously, he told himself, he'd be just as happy to kiss the scarred one.

'Stop perving at my arse, and stick it in me,' said Sam.

Knowing she was using the innuendo to alleviate the tension, Tim stammered out a response. 'I'm just preparing myself.'

He checked the needle, and a sympathetic pain shot down his right side. Obviously, he didn't mention it; Sam was about to get the real thing, and there were limits to showing one's empathy.

Tim injected.

'Jesus. Fuck. Shit,' said Sam through clenched teeth. She took Tim's hand and squeezed hard.

They waited for five minutes for the drugs to work fully, then Sam let go of his hand and they went to the staircase.

On the first step, Sam misplanted a crutch and it slipped fractionally. She steadied herself and took another breath.

'They numb the pain but don't help coordination,' she said defensively.

'It'll be fine.' Tim kept a few steps behind, ready to catch her.

It took twenty minutes to get up on to the roof, one slow step at a time.

Once Sam was safely on the roof, Tim immediately returned to the flat for her wheelchair.

As he carried it back up the stairs, he got a rare view of its underside. There were three compartments under her chair. One was filled with pill bottles. Another had two mobile phones. Tim couldn't see all of it, but sticking out of the third compartment was something that looked very much like the handle of a large military knife.

Sam was waiting on the roof with a few of her neighbours – all up there for the spectacle.

Above them, the skies were awash with military helicopters. Kirkmail prison was about a mile away to the east. Soldiers operating passive, well-meaning crowd control had set up a half-mile exclusion zone all around the prison.

The main road leading north-south past the prison was empty … except for the military.

'I told you there were tanks,' said Sam.

To the west, high in the sky, a glowing red ball shot towards them.

'What's the latest landing estimate?' asked Tim.

Sam checked the MIDAS feed on her phone. 'Five minutes.'

They waited.

Two minutes later one of the neighbours, looking through a pair of binoculars, broke the silence. 'Something's changed.'

Tim squinted.

Something large and jet-black had appeared behind the ball.

For a few moments, everyone's brains scrambled to process the new image.

'Parachute,' said Sam.

She was right.

An alarm on Tim's phone indicated a significant update from MIDAS, confirming Sam's assessment.

*Parachutes deployed.*
*5km height*
*Velocity 3kph*
*Diameter at 2m*
*Units entirely spherical and metallic*

A few more people came onto the roof. Everyone murmured greetings, but all eyes were on the glowing A-Grav unit, drifting just northwards of the rooftop.

'It's not going to land in Kirkmail,' said Sam.

Tim checked her logic. Judging by the current drift and its rate of descent, she was right: it was going to miss by about a mile.

Looking over the edge of the roof, Tim saw more congestion in the street. Given they were seven storeys high, they couldn't hear exactly what was happening, but they could see signs of panic everywhere. Crowds surged, and abruptly changed direction without warning.

Amazingly, people were still gravitating towards the new predicted landing site.

'Escape by car. Gawp on foot,' said Sam.

'It's a free bet for the escapees,' said Tim. 'If everything goes well then they just come back. If the A-Grav blows up, they're safely away … maybe we should get off the roof.'

'I'm staying for now,' said Sam. 'Although I'm tempted to head for the landing site.'

'Let's stay here,' said Tim, watching the glowing A-Grav unit drift down until it was lost behind some buildings to the north.

They waited.

No explosion came.

They waited for another ten minutes.

'Shall we go down?' asked Tim. 'It's not as if we can see anything more here.'

'Sure.'

Helping her manoeuvre down the fire escape, Tim flinched each time Sam flinched.

Once inside the flat, they both sat at the kitchen table and reviewed the news streams.

**2 UK landings**

```
London Birmingham
No explosions
Parachutes
London, Furtival Street
Spherical metallic 2m diameter
Etching
```

Tim clicked through on the word 'etching'. The
information had come from a live video stream from the
landing site, Furtival Street. After the A-Grav had landed, the
final pieces of sacrificial cladding had fallen away, and
someone had managed to take a picture of the ball just
before the army had erected a barrier around it.

On the video stream, a distinct metal plate was visible.
Unfortunately, the writing on it was not legible from the
video footage.

Social media was in uproar demanding the immediate
publication of any information on the metal plate.

Live news streams from the landing site now picked up a
continuous chant from the thousand people who had
convened there.

```
'What does it say?'
'What does it say?'
'What does it say?'
```

So far, there had been no response.

The live stream changed. A few people in white all-in-one
suits climbed out of a black van and disappeared behind the
screen surrounding the A-Grav unit.

'Hazmat suits,' said Sam.

Tim's laptop chimed. One of the news screens changed.

```
Rumour from London
Etching demands installation in Kirkmail
within one hour.
```

'Why only one hour?' Tim mused aloud.
*What's the rush?*
Sam shook her head. 'No idea … Closer look?'

'Will the injection last?'

'I've got another hour,' said Sam, a grim look in her eye.

'You *really* want to go down there?'

'Come on,' she said, looking at the video stream. 'We'll just join the crowd.'

'How about …' said Tim, feeling adrenaline start to build. 'We wait for them to move the A-Grav and look in a few hours. We're not going to be able to get anywhere near close.'

'It's happening right out there, Tim. Just outside the front door.'

'Look at the exclusion areas.' Tim pointed at the laptop feed which was showing an annotated map. 'We won't be able to see anything.'

Sam's face hardened. 'Do you mean that I won't, because I'm stuck in my wheelchair?' She paused. 'I'd thank you to let me make my own decisions in that regard.'

'No,' said Tim. 'You know what I'm like. I see the crowds, the army, the unknown alien artefact.' He paused. 'Then I see anger, pushing, rioting.'

'None of that has happened,' said Sam, leaning over in her chair and squeezing his arm. 'I'll keep you safe.'

Tim remembered the knife hilt under her chair.

*Maybe you will.*

'But,' said Sam, 'We don't have to go down now. Charlie arrives later. I'll go with him.'

Tim looked at Sam. Was she goading him? Or was it a genuine offer?

Standing up, Tim looked out of the kitchen window. The main road leading from the landing site to Kirkmail was now full of soldiers. With such a vast army and police presence, Tim was reasonably sure that public disturbances wouldn't turn dangerous. That said, even from a mile away, he could make out that many of them were wearing the hazmat suits. He hoped it was just a precaution.

He looked back at the video feed on Sam's laptop. A large military flatbed truck had just arrived at the landing site.

'Okay. I'll go with you now,' he said.

'I've changed my mind …' Sam smiled awkwardly and gave a gentle shrug. 'Sorry. The juice is wearing off quicker than I thought.'

'I'll head home and let you rest, then,' said Tim, disappointment mixing in equal measure with relief.

Just at that moment, the newsfeed switched to Downing Street, and Joshua Timbers walked out to the lectern.

'Both landing sites are secured with no
injuries: Birmingham and London. In each case,
we are using special hazardous material suits.
I must stress that so far, we have not had any
indication of unusual biological, chemical, or
radioactive activity, but we must allow our
emergency services as much precautionary
protection as possible. We do not, of course,
wish to cause offence to the Ankor, but the
safety of our public servants must be
paramount.
The etchings reported in the newsfeeds are
simply exact locations for each installation.
We have not been given any indication of how
the units work.'

He paused.

'I have also received clear instructions from
the Ankor that we must not open or tamper with
the devices in any way. No occupation of the
selected buildings can occur before a clear
instruction is given … As such, following
installation these buildings, and a
surrounding radius of up to two hundred
metres, will be entirely quarantined.'

With the address completed, the prime minister returned inside Number 10 without taking questions.

The newsfeed immediately switched to a studio panel of experts analysing the statement.

Sam turned the sound off and settled herself on the sofa. Raising an eyebrow, she patted the space next to her. 'You're welcome to stay.'

Tim considered it for a split second, but as his brain sifted through the possible consequences of such an action, too many of the decision trees ended with him embarrassingly slinking away five minutes after Charlie arrived.

'I need to get back, thanks.'

Double-checking he had everything for his journey home, Tim left.

# Chapter 16

With Tim gone, Sam managed a mid-afternoon doze but nothing more – truly satisfying sleep eluded her. Part of her understood Tim's reluctance to have a closer look at the A-Grav. The greater part of her, however, deeply wanted to see it in the flesh. She looked at the clock. Charlie had told her to expect him at six o'clock that evening.

*It will be getting dark by then.*

And she didn't expect Charlie to be any more likely than Tim to want to go and see the A-Grav.

She had almost three hours.

Outside on the street, the roads were busy but the pavements less so. Sam wheeled herself down a side road towards Kirkmail Prison. She knew the army had erected a large screen around the A-Grav and so she wouldn't actually get to see it, but she wanted to be there – to be in the moment.

*Mackler Street works best.*

Fifteen minutes later, travelling as quickly as she could, Sam reached the main road leading from the original landing site to Kirkmail. A few hundred metres up the road stood the main gates of the prison, but much closer – only twenty metres away – a hastily erected army barrier blocked the way, guarded by armed soldiers, some in hazmat suits.

It seemed she wasn't the only civilian who wanted to witness history being made; a crowd of about fifty people were pressed right up against the barrier all straining to see inside the prison.

Tim might have interpreted it differently, had he been with her, but the mood of the people did not appear to be angry and aggressive; it was interested and inquisitive.

*Perhaps with a touch of fear.*

Sam absorbed the atmosphere. The lack of anger on the streets of the UK, not universally mirrored in other countries, could possibly be attributed to the prime minister's daily public addresses. Although it also could be that, according to a MIDAS report, the police had rounded up the usual civil agitators over the last week.

To the side of the barrier, the large military flatbed truck that had moved the A-Grav into the prison now stood idle. Sam smiled to herself, and wheeled her chair around next to it. She held up her phone for a selfie, with the prison in the background.

Photo taken, she sent it to Tim.

*Damn — no signal.*

There was no coverage. Sighing to herself, realising the nearby masts had probably been deactivated in the name of national security, Sam turned her wheelchair around.

Movement nearer to the prison drew her eye.

Two soldiers were running towards the crowd of people, waving frantically. Their faces showed fear, not aggression.

'Run!'

Within a heartbeat, people were running past her.

Away from Kirkmail.

Sam followed, pushing her arms hard to keep up with the retreating crowd.

'What is it?' Sam called over to a middle-aged lady who was hobbling in heels next to her.

The lady shrugged. 'Everyone else said run.'

Sam looked for someone else to ask, but everyone else had far outstripped her. Racing wheelchairs and suitably

151

trained athletes could achieve impressive speeds. Medical wheelchairs were slower.

Turning off the main street, Sam decided to head home.

On her lap, her phone still registered zero signal.

*Fuck!*

If she died there, Tim would bury her, dig her up, revive her somehow, and kill her again – she'd taken an unacceptably unnecessary risk.

Not that she even knew what the danger was yet.

Sam pushed on, and although her arms were tiring, she made good progress – the exclusion zone around Kirkmail had ensured these streets were quiet.

She turned a corner.

The next street – just outside the original exclusion zone – was a different matter. Every house door was open and people were flooding out onto the pavements.

A man carrying a young child ran down the stairs from a house and, not seeing her below his eyeline, bumped into Sam.

'Sorry!' he shouted over his shoulder, whilst pulling open a car door and shoving his kid inside.

Sam couldn't answer. The impact had caused her muscles to tense – trying to stabilise her sideways movement – and it had sent a jolt of pain through her.

*Shit!*

Taking a deep breath to help contain the pain, Sam looked again and considered her options. The man with the kid in the car pulled out into the road, clipping the parked car in front of him. Moments later, he was gone.

Sam pushed on, swerving to avoid a pair of teenage kids who were also heading for a car under orders from their parents. This family also had bags – which must have been prepacked for such an eventuality – with them.

Sam couldn't move quickly enough, and was hit in the face with a duffle bag carried by the teenage son.

'Sorry, I didn't see you.'

*People never do …*

The pavement was clearly not a good option, and Sam looked to see if she could use any of the road. Unfortunately, it had become a demolition derby racetrack. Staying on the pavement, Sam picked her way through crowds of crying children and screaming parents as they clambered into cars and drove off.

In the near distance the blaring of a car horn preceded a screech of tyres and a sickening crash. Sam turned the corner just in time to see a man climb out of his car, take one look at the crumpled front end, kick the front left wheel, and then run – leaving his car blocking one lane of the road.

The car that had been hit appeared relatively mobile. Sam watched the driver – a mother – scream at her children in the back seat whilst executing a nine-point turn to free her car from the crash.

Behind the abandoned stationary car, the road – one of the main roads leading north out of east London – was now gridlocked.

*Fuck!*

Sam did a double-take. It had taken the drivers of the trapped cars all of five seconds to grasp the situation.

Now, cars flooded onto the pavements to get around the road blockage.

Pedestrians scattered and Sam knew she couldn't risk it. Many cars had decided to stay on the pavement to make up time.

She looked at her phone.

*One bar …*

Looking around, Sam saw she was close to a large block of council housing. She wheeled herself through the gate and into the lee of a big industrial waste bin.

Footsteps coming from the stairwell drew her attention.

Two Indian ladies in saris emerged, each pulling a suitcase, and hobbled past.

'What's happening?' called Sam.

One lady, seeing Sam, let go of her bag and rushed over. 'Darling, the alien craft is leaking radiation. You must come with us.'

The lady took hold of the handles on Sam's wheelchair.

*Radiation?*

Sam started to feel itchy all over.

The Indian lady, although trying to be helpful, had the same issues as Sam had on the pavements. There were simply too many people.

'Leave me,' said Sam. 'I'll be okay. I have friends nearby.'

The first lady looked like she would refuse, but her friend pulled her away. 'We should go.'

With a final apologetic look, both women disappeared into the heaving crowd.

Sam exhaled and, swinging her wheelchair back around, headed back for the council estate on the basis that she wouldn't get trampled or run over there.

*Fuck.*

'Sam!'

*Tim?*

It was Charlie, with a look of severe worry on his face.

Looking at her, whilst consulting his phone, Charlie made his way through the crowd. 'Sam!'

'Hi Charlie,' said Sam, not wanting to give any impression of the fear that had been building. 'I'm just getting some milk for tonight's dinner.'

An enormous man wearing military fatigues appeared at Charlie's side. Spanish-looking and severe, he bent down and picked Sam effortlessly out of her wheelchair.

'The radiation isn't too bad,' said Charlie, looking intently at Sam. 'But the crowds don't know that. How's your back?'

The relief that washed through Sam – she hadn't been looking forward to getting radiation sickness – even stopped her from making a caustic comment about being permanently physically impaired. 'Fine, thanks.'

Again, Charlie scanned Sam with his eyes. 'Okay.'

'You weren't due for an hour or so,' said Sam as she was carried by the six-and-a-half-foot commando while Charlie pushed her empty wheelchair.

'Lucky for you I came early,' said Charlie, his earlier fearful expression now replaced by his serene 'meditation' face.

'Are we safe? Do I need to take iodine pills?' asked Sam.

Charlie shook his head. 'This is low-level gamma radiation. Only three or four times the normal background radiation here. It's basically the same as going on holiday to Cornwall.' He paused. 'Anyway, iodine is for a totally different type of radiation poisoning.'

'So, what's happening?'

'From what I can see,' said Charlie, consulting his phone as they walked, 'a few of the first wave of A-Gravs are behaving similarly – very low-level leakage.'

Sam looked around. The crowds were still behaving as if Armageddon was arriving. She checked her own phone. News was flooding in about leakages all over the world. A spokesman for the United States' Senate said it was in closed session discussing potential military reprisals. The story went on to say that most Americans felt that Earth should never have allowed the Ankor to make orbit.

*What choice did we have?*

Sam clicked another link. Charlie was right: the radiation level by Kirkmail was similar to the natural levels in Cornwall.

*Unless you were really close.*

'I guess people are worried that something worse is coming,' she said, as they turned up the street that led to her flat.

The soldier carried Sam into the lift and into her flat. Then, after putting her down at the kitchen table, he left. She remembered herself and said, 'Thank you' as the door closed behind him.

Charlie fussed over her for a few moments.

'I'm fine,' said Sam, switching on the television.

The prime minister's sombre face gazed out from the screen. He began to speak.

'I have just come from a further meeting of the COBRA committee. We continue to monitor the situation closely. The Secretary of State for Defence has informed me that across the globe, less than one percent of all A-Gravs have shown radioactive emissions. One of these is at Kirkmail, where there is an ongoing minor gamma radiation leak; in response, we have increased the exclusion zone around Kirkmail to one mile. We do not believe that there has been any emission of radiation at Birmingham. However, as a precautionary measure, we have introduced a similar exclusion zone at this site also. The Health Secretary and the security agencies wish me to stress that the increased levels of radiation pose no risk to the general public outside of the exclusion zones.'

--------

**Later that evening**

Sam couldn't sleep. She was wired – shaken, if she allowed herself to admit it.

Easing herself onto her side, she looked across at Charlie. He was fast asleep.

*New bandages?*

No.

Charlie was wearing a long-sleeved t-shirt but, on closer inspection, it was just an old bandage visible on his left wrist.

The open curtains admitted enough moonlight for Sam to investigate. She shuffled over and looked more closely. There hadn't been any new bandages over the last week – but she'd seen three in the preceding month.

One of the recurring thoughts she'd had – based partly on her imagination, and partly on Charlie's over-attention to her own injuries – was that he could be self-harming.

*Could be …*

Of course, anyone *could be.*

Gingerly she reached out, thinking to pull his sleeve back a little.

*What the fuck?*

Sam fingers touched something hard under the bandage. It felt like a metal stud.

*A piercing?*

In the half-darkness it wasn't easy, but Sam took hold of the edge of the bandage, intending to pull it back an inch.

Charlie murmured in his sleep and rolled over, taking his arm out of reach.

*It was a stud of some type.*

Noticing the ache in her side, Sam rolled onto her back and stared at the ceiling.

An hour later, no closer to sleep, she decided to get up. She edged over to the side of the bed.

'Sam …' Charlie whispered in the semi-darkness.

'Yes,' said Sam.

'Take a pill,' said Charlie. 'You need to sleep.'

Sam tried to avoid taking sleeping pills, they made her … drowsy. She chuckled to herself. The fact was they made her sluggish for five hours after she woke up, but Charlie was probably right. She reached into her bedside table.

--------

**Sam's Flat, Monday 22nd April**

Waking up, Sam – drowsy as expected – looked over to find it was ten o'clock and Charlie had gone.

Reviewing what she remembered from the night before, she found it difficult to distinguish between reality and dreams. After taking the sleeping pill, she certainly remembered Charlie stroking her hair and whispering sweet nothings about how perfect she was – a bit weird, but it had definitely happened.

The second part was hazier. The theme was similar, but it involved Tim – not unheard of, but not usual, and also purely a figment of her imagination.

Sam rolled onto her side and started her morning stretches.

A hastily scribbled note lay on Charlie's pillow. He'd been summoned back to Anglesey and would see her on Tuesday.

Finishing her flexibility exercises, she hobbled through to the kitchen, switching on her laptop as she passed the living room table.

Moments after the laptop had warmed up, it displayed a new Ankor broadcast that had arrived a few hours earlier.

*GRB location*
*52:13:07 based off Polaris*
*212 Light Years*
*Impact in 151 days*

# CHAPTER 17

**Southern England, Monday 22ⁿᵈ April**

In a helicopter heading back to the base at Porton Down, Martel reviewed the weekend's activity. Whilst the A-Gravs had started to drop and be installed, Martel had argued with the prime minister for a far larger exclusion zone around each site. His suggestion had been refused due to the significant additional impact on policing – area having a square relationship to distance – and the prime minister's concern that it could be seen as fearmongering.

In the face of political expediency, Martel had lost the argument.

*Next time we may not be so lucky …*

Shaking his head, Martel moved on and looked at the information concerning the GRB location. There was a blue supergiant star at the given coordinates. Assuming it collapsed as other supernovae did, then a major flood of gamma radiation could be on its way to Earth.

Even if the most ferocious intensity of the burst lasted only a few minutes, the energy involved would kill everything that was unshielded. There would be little long-term benefit in being on the lee side of the Earth – facing away from the blast – as the ozone layer would be stripped away, leaving Earth to be sterilised by cosmic rays from the Sun.

After a handful of years, only a few tens of thousands of hardy, and well-prepared, humans would survive.

The scenario was plausible. Well-regarded scientists had linked a similar cosmic event with a mass extinction on Earth five hundred million years ago. This could be the next big one – and it made completing the shield humanity's number one priority.

*Assuming the Ankor are not lying.*

Relative to Earth time, of course, the event that had created this terrifying threat had already happened ... two hundred years ago. The Ankor claimed to have witnessed it and then travelled faster than light ahead of the blast to help humanity prepare.

There was no way to verify either claim. The soonest that scientists on Earth could independently verify the supernova would be about three weeks before the actual gamma ray impact, when light indicating imminent collapse of the star's core reached Earth.

*Why did they wait two hundred years before coming?*

Martel had no ready answer for that. The best theory that Captain Whaller and he could come up with, other than an Ankor fabrication, was that the Ankor had decided that humanity would pull together best if under pressure – tenuous, but just about plausible.

Whaller had added that it was reasonable to think that, if the Ankor did have some goal concerning minimising cultural pollution or minimising the amount of technology humanity could 'steal' by observation, then they would keep interaction timeframes as short as possible.

*Hopefully, they've included some contingency time ...*

Irrespective of why the Ankor had waited, humanity's experts agreed that any independent proof of the supernova would arrive long after Earth would have been forced to send the plutonium – if they decided to comply with the Ankor's instructions.

*Plutonium.*

It was certainly a word to instil fear.

Martel looked at the two handwritten notes the prime minister had given him. One was from MacKenzie to the prime minister.

> **Joshua**
> **I have been asked by our Ankor partners to**
> **plan a plutonium payload by the fourth launch,**
> **mid-May. I confirm that SpaceOp's two**
> **satellite arrays are being used by the Ankor**
> **for analysis of Earth's key data. It is**
> **critical we allow them to continue.**
> **Francis MacKenzie**

The second note was one the prime minister had personally transcribed from a message he'd received directly from the Ankor.

> **Plutonium delivery is mandatory. The shield**
> **will be built by self-replicating robots.**
> **Plutonium will provide the power. We have**
> **insufficient power ourselves.**

Martel digested the second message. It was hard to fathom. The Ankor had showed themselves capable of travelling at meaningful fractions of the speed of light. They also were able to utilise some type of faster-than-light travel. These had to be hugely energy intensive. How could it be they needed energy from Earth to build the shield?

As for the part about 'self-replicating', Martel's training as the MOD's expert in space warfare meant he had a decent understanding of spacecraft theory. John von Neumann, a Hungarian- American mathematician, had theorised about colonising space by creating an exploratory probe that would fly to a planet, create copies of itself, send those copies off ... each copy would find a planet, create a copy of itself ... etc.

*Exponential proliferation ...*

Martel looked out of the window as the English countryside passed under him. Of course, he could construct any number of semi-plausible reasons why the Ankor might be behaving as they were.

Unfortunately, the critical timeline in each case meant that humanity had to comply with the Ankor before the truth could be verified.

Not that the Americans were making similar noises. The attitude from the US military was wary and mildly rebellious and, if the media was to be believed, that attitude ran all the way through the US population. Some American students had tried bouncing a visible light laser off the Ankor craft. Within moments, the power to the entire college campus had been cut off, and had remained off for twelve hours.

'Arriving now, sir,' said the pilot.

Porton Down.

*Time to review countermeasures.*

--------

The Porton Down war room had been set up on the assumption that the UK was being deceived. It was filled with electronics and Martel knew the Ankor would be watching every move they made.

However, much of it was deliberate misdirection, because further down, under the emergency response room, was a hardened electronic-free room just like the one in Whitehall. It was there that Martel discussed the real plans with Captain Whaller and the rest of the team.

'What's the latest from here?' Martel asked of Whaller, who led the physical countermeasure team.

'The United Nations have just made their own statement,' said Whaller.

**The General Assembly of the United Nations**
**'We remind all members of the United Nations**
**that it is now an offence, as stated in**

'What's new from the PM?' asked Whaller.

'The home secretary has assured him that the Kirkmail A-Grav unit was not tampered with,' said Martel.

Whaller nodded. 'All countries are explicitly denying tampering, except the Americans. They haven't said anything.'

'I think the Americans are still pretty pissed off about the Security Council being closed down.'

'They weren't the only ones to lose influence,' said Whaller.

'They lost more than most,' said Martel.

Over the last week it had been the CNSA that had taken a lead on many aspects of the response. All of its pronouncements had been performed in front of a pair of flags: United Nations and People's Republic of China.

'How's countermeasure development going?' asked Martel.

'All our problems stem from a lack of delivery options. We have nuclear, chemical, and biological measures available. However, we have no way of force delivering any weapon into the Ankor's main craft.'

It was possible that with enough collaboration the Americans, or Russians, or Chinese, could adapt a nuclear weapon for a high Earth orbit rocket, but it felt unlikely they could coordinate in secret. Of course, the Americans had *Lincoln*, a possible delivery option with sufficient modifications, but they weren't really talking to anyone.

'Our best hope remains the rockets that Francis MacKenzie will be sending up,' said Whaller. 'What's the latest from SpaceOp?'

'Lieutenant Briars has produced detailed maps of the Assembly Zone,' said Martel. 'We know the process. However, there's no guarantee the rockets will go anywhere near the Ankor craft itself. The shield materials may be dumped in a lower orbit, ready for the self-replicating machines to work on.'

'Agreed,' said Whaller. 'The rockets may not go near to the Ankor craft, *if* they are building the shield. But if they are trying to trick us into giving them resources, to steal or use against us, then it is quite likely they will take them onto their main ship.'

'Good point. Anything else you need from me?' asked Martel.

'An update on Francis MacKenzie?' asked Captain Whaller.

'Nothing of note,' said Martel. 'MacKenzie appears entirely focused on getting the SpaceOp launches off the ground. Apparently, he's obsessed with being the first launch site to send materials up.'

Martel's on-site team – Briars, Jones and Hardy – were the only genuine space launch technology experts in the entire British army. Most of the others had been lured away by MacKenzie five years previously to work on SpaceOp.

'Readiness for plutonium?' asked Whaller.

'They have buildings set aside for plutonium storage, colloquially referred to as the Hot Zone,' said Martel. 'It's secure. Assuming British soldiers escort the plutonium onto the site, it will be straightforward to protect it before it is sent.'

'I suspect the problems really start once the Ankor get it,' said Whaller.

# CHAPTER 18

**London, Tuesday 23rd April**

Bumper to bumper on the motorway, Tim and Sam crawled along at five miles per hour with all the other cars heading out of the city. Given the increasing levels of unrest in London, MacKenzie had arranged a military escort – a single jeep with a couple of soldiers in it. It had been fun for a few minutes, but effectively all it had done was delay their departure by an hour.

'I was expecting them to provide a secret escape route,' said Sam. 'At least some sirens.'

Tim looked at the jeep in his rear-view mirror; the army sergeant assigned to them didn't seem too impressed with his job for the day either. 'I guess if we are attacked, then we'll see the benefit.'

They inched forward. Looking left and right, Tim saw a lot of families with their cars packed to the roof. Clearly, news of the radiation leaks – however small the government protested they were – had hit home. Whereas a week previously the number of people leaving town had been modest, now everyone seemed to be on the road.

An hour later, as they approached the ring road, Tim's phone rang. It was the sergeant behind them.

'We've been asked to peel off here,' said the sergeant. 'We're needed elsewhere.'

'No problem. Thanks.'

They both hung up.

Sam looked at her laptop. 'He's right. Violence is breaking out near my flat.'

Again, the traffic edged forward. The motorway, four lanes wide, was more akin to a giant parking lot than a road. To his right, in the fast lane, a red sports car inched forward. At the current rate it would overtake Tim by early evening. Tim smiled to himself. Although they were going to be horrendously late for Anglesey, there was something reassuring about being safely in an orderly queue.

'Come on, you fuckers!' shouted Sam from the passenger seat, not sharing Tim's Zen on the matter. She pointed to the junction a mile ahead. 'Hopefully people will leave at this exit.'

'I suspect most people will stick on this road as far as they can.'

Their road went from London, to Oxford, to Birmingham, and then they changed to smaller roads into Wales. It was likely most of the drivers didn't have a finish point in mind; they just wanted to be away from London. But where to go? There was another A-Grav in Birmingham, albeit not leaking yet, and an estimated further eighty-five A-Gravs currently in orbit that would land somewhere in the UK at some time.

*Is anywhere safe?*

'That guy,' said Sam, pointing to her left, 'just drove up the emergency access lane.'

'It's fine,' said Tim, making eye contact with Sam. She looked about to argue but returned her attention to her laptop.

'There's a quote from Dr Felicity Rackling at DeityForNow,' said Sam. 'You like her, right?'

'She's all right.'

DeityForNow was a newish pseudo-spiritual website that had been gaining traction amongst the softer believers of all religions. It provided a halfway house between science and religion; Dr Rackling bridged the gaps by offering spiritual immortality whilst explaining away every difficult religious tenet as a metaphor.

'She's just published an editorial piece called *I Want to Believe*.' Sam scanned the material for a few minutes. 'Basically, it says the Ankor treatment of humanity is like the monotheistic deity-believer relationship.'

'And?'

'She says we should submit entirely to the Ankor and not question a single thing … "let them have the scraps they're asking for and hope they save us",' said Sam. 'What do you like about her?'

'I researched MacKenzie quite thoroughly before taking the MIDAS job. Dr Rackling had a history with him. They fell out when she exposed him as giving a lot of money to religious organisations to suppress scientific advancement. It was a long time ago, and he's almost apologised for it. Certainly, he's changed his ways and had all electronic records of it erased from the internet.'

The traffic shuffled forward again.

Then came to a dead stop … for what seemed like ages.

Tim craned his neck to see what was happening. In four of the five cars around him, the driver and all the passengers were looking intently at their phones.

'Fuck!' exclaimed Sam, not looking up from her laptop. 'Social media just blew up.'

'What is it?' asked Tim.

'Hold on,' said Sam, typing. 'It seems that a few million people in the UK just got personalised messages from the Ankor. Examples coming through.'

*'Michael, apologies for confusion surrounding our arrival. Be assured we are working hard to ensure the space shield will protect Earth from the gamma rays. We need you to support the overall defence process. Please report to $CO_2$ Scrubber Production Line – Lyle Park*

*Industrial Estate, East London. Arrive*
*Wednesday 1st May. We understand your keen*
*hand-eye coordination will be invaluable to*
*the production line. You can expect to be*
*there for 2 weeks. Food, shelter and other*
*basics will be arranged.*
*Your neighbour, Karen, has been asked to feed*
*your cat.'*

'Pretty specific,' said Tim.

'They're all like this,' said Sam. 'Each one is personalised, identifying the recipient's skills and targeting their specific personal levers.'

'Have you got one?' asked Tim.

'Nope,' said Sam, taking Tim's phone from the cup holder between them. 'Neither have you.'

'I guess we already have relevant jobs to do.'

Again, Tim looked around. Most people were now having animated discussions with their fellow passengers.

Then traffic began to move.

At least half the cars around them were now filtering off the motorway, all heading down the emergency access lane.

Within a few minutes, Tim and Sam were past the junction and doing a steady seventy miles per hour.

'People just obeyed ...' said Sam. 'Even with the radiation leaks.'

'Wouldn't you have done the same?' asked Tim. 'A detailed personal message, beamed directly down to you from space?'

'A massive invasion of privacy,' said Sam. 'Evident manipulation.'

'Yes,' said Tim. 'But would you have obeyed?'

Sam shrugged.

They drove on.

A few hours later, they were past Birmingham and heading into north Wales.

'It's getting dark,' said Sam. 'Do you want to stop for the night?'

'We can't really. It's just a couple more hours,' said Tim, who did want to stop. Ever since the crash, he'd dreaded driving her – and driving at night was almost unbearable. Not that the crash had been his fault, as the police, the lawyers, the judge, and his therapist had all repeated many times. A lorry had run a red light and smashed into the side of his car.

*I should have reacted faster.*

Sam reached out and laid her hand over Tim's. 'You'll be fine.'

Without taking his eyes off the road, he smiled.

'Do you want to hear the latest on the mass messaging?' asked Sam.

'Sure.'

She read from the screen.

**Mass mobilisation of resources across the UK to support the shield development and other safety initiatives**
**Estimated two million UK residents contacted: five hundred thousand have been mobilised to work in a production capacity**
**Main locations: London, Liverpool, Sheffield, Manchester, Newcastle, Leeds, Bristol**
**Trending words: $CO_2$, scrubbers, shielding, lead, steel, pre-fab**

'Mobilised for the war effort,' said Tim. 'What's social media saying?'

Sam was quiet for a moment as she absorbed the news. 'Umm … it's a good thing.'

'Is it just the UK?'

'Nope. All countries with space launch facilities are being targeted.'

Tim's phone buzzed.

A text from Dexter Hadley.

*Hopefully see you in a few hours. Flat's ready but installation needs to start tonight.*

Dexter Hadley was the Mission Control administrative lead. He did everything from ordering new chairs to confirming launch schedules. He'd been Tim's main contact on the Anglesey site. He was a decent guy.

Tim asked Sam to reply on his behalf. She took his phone and wrote a polite response before signing it with a hug-kiss emoji. Then she turned to Tim. 'I have a favour to ask. I was hoping I could stay with you. You've two bedrooms.'

'Sure. You're not sharing with Charlie?'

'He needs to be on twenty-four-hour call for MacKenzie,' said Sam. 'It doesn't really work for me.'

'But things are okay?' Tim heard his voice change pitch.

Sam looked at him, then let out a long sigh. 'Who knows …'

Tim wasn't sure what to say, and let the silence stretch.

'Do you ever discuss me with him?' asked Sam.

Tim thought back to six months earlier when he was drinking with Charlie in a pub in Madwyn village. They'd had little to do, and drunk talk had ensued. For some reason, Tim had confessed to Charlie that he was infatuated with Sam. At the time, it had felt like a sensible idea.

But, even in his drunken stupor, Tim had seen the glint in Charlie's eye.

*What's mine is mine. Not yours.*

Outwardly, Charlie had laughed it off and said it was just Tim's guilt about the crash – an emotional transfer. He'd gone on to say that he was sure Tim was obsessed with healing Sam … but that was different from loving her the way he did.

*I can't repeat any of that to her.*

'Tim?' said Sam.

'No,' he said. 'He hasn't said anything about you. We're not that close any more.'

*Funnily enough.*

Sam remained silent and looked out of the window.

For the next hour, with minimal chat, they crawled the final twenty miles bumper to bumper with other cars and trucks, all heading to SpaceOp on the narrow roads.

It didn't help that they had to stop at security checkpoints every five miles.

'So,' said Sam, as they pulled away from yet another one, 'a fairly relaxed place.'

'It was pretty tight last time I was here,' said Tim. 'I guess MacKenzie has dialled it up a notch.'

Eventually they reached SpaceOp and, after more checks, were waved in.

At the crest of the hill overlooking the facility, the view of the infrastructure was largely the same as it had been on Tim's visit a week earlier: launch pad on the left, factories to the north, and warehouses to the east, with movement between zones restricted by chain-linked fences and security gates. All of it was floodlit to allow twenty-four-hour working.

What had changed was the sheer level of activity. SpaceOp was full to overflowing with people and vehicles.

'Look at all the cabling,' said Sam.

She was right. Clearly, hard-wiring was the order of the day. Thigh-thick bundles of cables ran along every road and pathway.

Another security guard waved them into the car park, where they were processed and provided with mobile phone tokens, keys, and maps. They were also given radiation monitoring badges.

'Shall we snoop around a little before we meet Dexter?' asked Sam, fixing her badge to the belt loop on her jeans.

Tim looked around at the warren of chain-linked fences and electronic security gates. They couldn't physically snoop anywhere.

'Tim! Sam!' Dexter had driven down from the admin building in a four-seater electric buggy to meet them. 'You got here!' he said, storing their bags and Sam's wheelchair on the back of the buggy.

'No,' said Sam, with an innocent smile. 'We're performing astral projection from a lovely pub just outside Stratford.'

Dexter smiled. 'Hang onto that good humour. You're going to need it.'

'Tense, is it?' asked Tim.

Dexter whistled through his teeth. 'Oh, yes. I thought he was focused when he was just chasing his dreams … Now he's saving humanity it's a whole new level.'

Tim didn't need to ask who 'he' was.

'Can we freshen up first?' asked Sam.

Dexter turned. 'As long as you don't tell anyone. I'll take you to your flat and give you fifteen minutes.'

'Thanks,' said Sam, grabbing her crutches.

Their flat, a one-story concrete prefab monstrosity, was a five-minute drive away through similarly functional, hastily built accommodation.

Inside, Tim placed his bag on the sofa and then opened it. He took out a handheld Geiger counter he'd kept from his laboratory days and showed it to Sam. 'It doesn't do alpha particles. But if they move plutonium into SpaceOp and it isn't safe, then we'll know.'

'Could be useful,' said Sam, 'but we have these.' She tapped the radiation badge on her belt.

'Back-up doesn't hurt,' said Tim. 'Obviously, don't tell anyone about it.'

'Understood.'

Sam went into her bedroom to change and Tim joined Dexter outside the flat.

'Did you guys get the mass message thing?' asked Tim.

'My wife's sister was sent a long personal email imploring her to report to a $CO_2$ Scrubber Production Line,' said Dexter, pausing for a drag on his cigarette. 'I heard of a guy in Madwyn village receiving a printed letter that was waiting for him at the pub when he went for his lunch.'

'Wow.'

'It does imply total control of our communications systems,' said Dexter, throwing the cigarette butt onto the floor before conscientiously grinding it out with the toe of his shoe.

'Anything else unusual?'

'Of the set that contains everything in the known universe, the circle containing *usual* is very small,' said Dexter with a shrug.

'Probably means we have to redefine the set of *usual*,' said Tim with a smile. 'Anything more on the GRB?'

'Nope,' said Dexter, now nervously checking his watch. 'Will Sam be long? MacKenzie is expecting us soon.'

'She'll be here,' said Tim.

A few minutes later, Sam emerged on her crutches in a fresh set of clothes. 'For fuck's sake, Tim,' she said. 'I'm disabled but I still managed to have a wash and change my clothes.'

'I was catching up on gossip.'

'I have to share a server room with your smelly being for a few hours,' said Sam, shaking her head. 'You just dumped your bag on the sofa – a disgusting suitcase, regularly dragged through grim city puddles.'

'Sorry, I …' Tim started to go through the dramatic mea culpa routine.

Dexter, unaware that Sam was joking, showed signs of discomfort.

'That's where I'm going to have to put my bare arse later,' she continued, hobbling on her crutches over to the electric buggy and getting in the back seat.

Dexter's eyes widened.

'She just winding me up,' said Tim. 'She thinks I live like a slob. I think she does. We have different areas of focus.'

'We did the online survey,' said Sam, turning and checking her wheelchair was safely stowed. 'Tim is twice as likely as me to be eaten by cats.'

'I don't even have cats,' said Tim, as the buggy set off.

'Yet,' said Sam, opening her eyes wide. 'You don't have cats … *yet.*'

As Dexter drove towards Mission Control, he pointed out some of the newer developments. 'That constant stream of headlights,' he said, pointing east, 'is a convoy bringing in material for the Hot Zone. The nuclear materials … stay clear.'

'So, it's arriving?' asked Sam.

'I'm not sure. MacKenzie has it all wrapped up in secrecy,' said Dexter. 'It's the one area where I have no access, and no oversight.'

'Understood,' said Tim. 'Anything else to worry about?'

'Everything?' said Dexter.

As the lights of Mission Control came into sight, a gunshot echoed from the east.

'What the fuck!' shouted Sam.

Dexter didn't slow the buggy, but continued to head north towards Mission Control. 'We have over a thousand security personnel across the whole of SpaceOp. Most of them are unarmed and work for Tosh.'

'But …' said Tim, noting the dearth of information in Dexter's reply.

Dexter continued. 'The Hot Zone and some parts of Mission Control have MacKenzie's private security force. The Leafers. The ones near the Hot Zone are armed and occasionally fire warning shots to keep people away.'

'That's allowed?' asked Sam.

Dexter shrugged. 'There are a couple of British army liaison officers around. They seem to accept the Leafers ...' He paused. 'It's not a subject to bring up with MacKenzie.'

'Just warning shots?' asked Tim.

Dexter turned in his seat. 'There have been ... misunderstandings.'

'I haven't seen anything on the news,' said Sam.

Clearly concentrating hard on not saying anything inflammatory, Dexter slowed as they approached the main doors of Mission Control. 'Just don't go anywhere near the Hot Zone.'

# Chapter 19

Inside Mission Control, the security was just as serious. They passed through a series of checks, although the guards – who appeared to be ordinary security personnel, like Tosh – didn't make Sam get out of her wheelchair. They just waved their detectors over her.

The room was busy – double the number of people than on Tim's previous visit, all huddling around screens, watching the big boards, or walking purposefully.

Overlooking the whole scene was Francis MacKenzie, up in his open-plan mezzanine office. The office area had a large desk, a big executive chair which he was sitting in, and a workstation to the side. He was currently bawling out the four people standing in front of him.

At the top of the single open staircase which led from the main floor to the mezzanine stood two enormous guards – Juan and another equally imposing guard Tim hadn't seen before.

Tim looked back at the screens. One of them showed Kennedy Space Center. It was night-time in Florida, but the video images confirmed the *Lincoln* was fully assembled on its launch pad. Engineers, tiny in the video feed, were scurrying all over it.

'Apologies for the lack of a formal welcome,' said Dexter, winding them between desks and thick bundles of cabling that disappeared through drilled-out holes in the walls. 'MacKenzie is too busy to see you. The kit from your car has been unpacked and moved downstairs, ready to be plugged in.'

'We can get on with it now,' said Tim.

'Sounds good. I'll try to rustle you up some food,' said Dexter, noticing Sam struggling with her wheelchair over a particularly large clump of wires that ran across the corridor. 'Would you like a helping push?'

'No, thanks,' said Sam. 'Some junk food would be good, though.'

Tim smiled – the rucksack hanging from the back of her wheelchair was packed full of sugar.

Dexter took them to the double doors that Tim knew led to the server rooms. In common with the other changes in Mission Control, the downward-sloping concrete corridor was also now lined with significant additional cabling.

'Cheery, isn't it?' said Sam, nodding at the pale white neon strips.

At the end of the corridor they reached the anteroom with the four server rooms and the armoured doors.

Dexter stopped. 'Your phones open the server room doors.'

Tim stepped forward and swiped his phone over the security panel for the MIDAS server room. The door swung open.

'Good luck. See you in a few hours,' said Dexter.

'With junk food,' said Sam.

'As promised,' said Dexter, leaving. 'Remember not to go near the armoured doors.'

'We won't leave our room,' Tim called after Dexter's retreating back.

'Let's just start plugging in,' said Sam, wheeling herself over to the new stack of encryption servers that Dexter's team had brought from the car.

It took them twenty minutes to connect everything, and a further twenty minutes to boot up the servers. Once they were all active, Tim and Sam verified that the formats and sizes of the executable files were exactly as they expected.

*All good.*

'Sam,' said Tim, 'can you run the security layer install, please?'

She wheeled herself over to the relevant workstation. 'Ready.'

There was a physical element to the encryption server harmonisation. It had been designed specifically to stop anyone hacking into MIDAS. For each of the twenty encryption servers, Tim had to physically push a button on the server itself whilst Sam created a new one-time key exchange which she used to securely connect the encryption server and the main MIDAS application.

'Those armoured doors outside look ominous,' said Sam.

'They're electrified. A failed security clearance results in a taser-like experience,' said Tim. 'And one of us has to go through them later to reset the passive data sniffers.'

'I'd love to go and have a snoop,' said Sam. 'What else is in there?'

'Past the door?' said Tim. 'More dark corridors and cables.'

At four in the morning, Dexter returned with sandwiches. 'Just to let you know … all the other A-Gravs have now started their descent.'

'All ten thousand?' asked Tim.

'Yep, a similar pattern as before, all countries broadly getting an allotment relative to their population' said Dexter. 'Are you done here yet?'

'Basically,' said Tim. 'But I was hoping to get a bit of sleep before we switch it all on.'

Dexter looked uncomfortable.

'If we head back to the flat, will he have us dragged back?' asked Sam.

'Probably not,' said Dexter. 'You've got specialist skills that he needs. But I'll probably be strapped to the nose cone of the next launch.'

Sam wheeled herself towards to the door. 'What are we waiting for, then?'

Tim ignored her. 'Five minutes and we're done here. Then I'll reconnect MacKenzie's workstation.'

'Come up to the main floor when you're ready,' said Dexter.

'And then we'll need to do the data sniffer reset,' said Tim.

'Okay, but I don't have access down to the sniffers any more,' said Dexter. 'We'll need to get Juan.'

Dexter disappeared back up the corridor and Sam ran the final connection test before booting up the system.

It's all good,' she said, displaying a test run of MIDAS.

```
'full A-Grav deployment'
All ten thousand A-Grav units descending
No gamma ray emissions detected
Trending words: selection procedures,
lifeboat, Japan, bombs
```

Sam clicked through and scanned. 'It appears to be running smoothly – some have already landed. A fairly even distribution across the globe based mostly on population density, but also partially on ensuring maximum tribal diversity.'

'Tribal diversity?' asked Tim.

'Yes. There's basically one A-Grav unit for every seven hundred thousand people, but areas of large 'tribal' diversity – be that genetics, religious affiliations, or just customs handed down the generations, have relatively more units assigned.'

'A good time to be one of the last remaining Indonesian head-hunters,' said Tim.

179

'Or an Inuit.'

However, knowing the distribution of the A-Gravs didn't answer the questions on everyone's lips. *Who would do the selection? Who would be selected?*

The current rumour was that the Ankor would select people individually based on their own criteria, but Tim had not found any substantiation for the claim. Certainly, none of the world leaders had admitted to having been told the selection process.

Some type of selection process would be needed, with strict security and management around it. Otherwise, millions of people would descend on each of the A-Grav sites and try to secure a place by force.

'Women and children first,' Tim said.

'Survival instinct,' said Sam, clicking through.

'You look,' said Tim. 'I'd better go to MacKenzie.'

He headed back up the corridors. In the main room, Juan led him up the internal staircase to the mezzanine.

'So,' said MacKenzie, looking up from his workstation. 'Is it working?'

'Yes,' said Tim. 'I can do the repoint on your workstation now.'

'Good,' said MacKenzie, positioning himself ready at the keyboard. 'So, start explaining.'

For the next twenty minutes, Tim talked MacKenzie through the process. When it was done, MacKenzie turned to Tim. 'The MedOp applicants give me their personal data, they expect it to be safe. Is it safe?'

'From anyone on Earth, yes,' said Tim.

MacKenzie nodded – he understood. 'If anyone else touched the data, would they leave fingerprints?'

'I think so. The passive sniffers are entirely unnetworked but it's probably worth resetting them,' said Tim, simultaneously running science fiction scenarios in which the Ankor could hack into the unnetworked system.

*They could use miniature drones, or 'effector beams' …*

Tim left it unsaid. He didn't want to be the one to design and implement countermeasures. In any case Francis MacKenzie, albeit not particularly vocal, had been a cheerleader for the Ankor since they arrived.

'I'll arrange for the sniffer reset but I'd like you to stay for a few days to ensure MIDAS is working,' said MacKenzie. 'I'd also like you to install a basic workstation somewhere near Dexter's desk. I want one of his team to run public opinion searches for me. I don't have time to monitor it all myself.'

'Understood,' said Tim. When MacKenzie asked for something, the answer was always yes. Charlie had intimated that, as well as the bonus payment, Tim would be allowed to reuse the code if he completed the MedOp-MIDAS work in good standing. He had to keep MacKenzie in a generous frame of mind.

*Assuming the Ankor don't destroy all life on the planet …*

'Filter it to stick to good news,' said MacKenzie. 'And strip out all the commentary about data sources.'

'Okay,' said Tim, leaving the mezzanine.

Returning to the server room, he found Sam working hard on MIDAS.

'We need to set up a news service on Dexter's desk upstairs,' said Tim.

'Can we do it tomorrow?' asked Sam.

Tim looked at his watch. It was six in the morning. 'Can we compromise on later today?'

Sam smiled. 'I found out about "Japan" and "Lifeboat".'

She went on to explain that the Japanese government had said each A-Grav unit created a sphere two hundred metres in diameter that shielded everything inside from the outside world, including gravity. Apparently, once active, the A-Grav formed a bubble which would float upwards. Inside it, inhabitants would live for as long as they had provisions. The Ankor's requirements became more clearly understood: carbon dioxide scrubbers, water purifiers, waste containment, food, food storage, airtight containment, and heating insulation. All the things that people across Earth had been mobilised to produce. They would all support the A-Grav function.

None of which changed the fact that, if the shield could not be built, the A-Gravs would be able to contain no more than a fraction of a single percent of the Earth's population; nor the fact that the Earth would be uninhabitable if the GRB did the damage that some scientists were predicting.

'The indication from Japan,' said Sam, 'is that the Ankor craft will collect all the A-Grav units on a tether and drag them into the lee side of the Earth, well inside the Earth's magnetosphere, but facing away from the incoming gamma ray burst.'

At that moment, Dexter returned. 'Do you guys want a lift back to the flat? I'm off shift for eight hours.'

They headed back up the ramps. This time, Sam accepted Dexter's offer of a push.

'So, now I'm running a news service,' said Dexter, leading them through the corridors. 'Is there a three-month residential training class I can attend?'

'We heard you weren't that busy,' said Tim, smiling. 'A few hours' training and then on-the-job experience. You'll be fine.'

They emerged into the buzz of the main floor – there were still two hundred people working purposefully – and headed straight for the exit.

'What do you make of the A-Gravs?' asked Tim as they walked.

'There's no SpaceOp official line. It's seen as disloyalty here in Anglesey to approve of them in any way,' said Dexter.

'I read something that said the UN is demanding guidance on how to select people,' said Sam.

'Probably not a good idea,' said Tim. 'People who weren't selected would be less inclined to support the fit out.'

'Yes, idiot,' said Sam, reaching over and giving his arm a gentle squeeze. 'That would create just under seven billion people highly incentivised to get the shield working.'

'Fair point,' said Tim.

As they reached the main doors leading out of Mission Control, a ripple of silence ran across the floor.

Behind them, five armed soldiers in combat fatigues had appeared from the doors that led down to the server rooms. Armed with assault rifles and blank stares – each of them could have been Juan's brother – they walked across the main floor and straight up the staircase.

'Security,' whispered Dexter, turning. 'Plutonium division.'

'Leafers?' asked Sam.

Dexter nodded. 'We rarely see them. They are all in the caverns.'

'Caverns? Is that the Hot Zone?' Tim asked.

'Yes,' said Dexter, leading them outside. 'They were originally for general storage, but they've been repurposed over the last three weeks for plutonium handling. At least five floors below ground level, maybe more.'

'So … the plutonium?'

'MacKenzie just keeps saying that the UK government will eventually roll over and we need to be ready,' said Dexter.

# CHAPTER 20

**SpaceOp, Anglesey, Wednesday 24th April**
In the relative calm of the pre-dawn, MacKenzie looked at the ceiling. He needed sleep. What little he'd managed to get had been troubled. Turning onto his side, he saw the bottle of diazepam sitting invitingly on his bedside table. From taking one pill per week a year ago, he was now taking two every day.

China was – constantly, of late – on his mind. One of his moles had confirmed significant build-up of army resources near to the Chinese main launch site. Of course, it didn't necessarily mean anything, but China was the threat. Additionally, China had been asked to provide plutonium and was preparing accordingly.

*Am I the only game in town?*

Until he knew the answer, MacKenzie would remain uncertain of his leverage over the Ankor. They had been taking liberties since the arrangement started: they'd obviously hacked his systems and were stealing data; they were giving orders to Taylor without consultation.

He couldn't confront them. It would simply underline the overpowering technological advantage they had over him. One thing MacKenzie prided himself on was his ability to pick his battles.

Getting out of bed and dressing, MacKenzie looked at his computer tablet. A news item had come in. The CNSA had confirmed the blue supergiant star at location 52:13:07 was a possible supernova.

MacKenzie smiled to himself. Of course, the Chinese making such a proclamation was not in any way evidence that they were not in league with the Ankor. It was entirely in keeping with their behaviour towards the Ankor since the first broadcast – a reserved acquiescence to their demands, but with a passive-aggressive tone.

*Bluff? Double bluff? Two internal powers within China unaware of each other?*

MacKenzie put it out of his mind and made the short walk through the corridors to the main floor of Mission Control.

Even so early in the morning, it was full.

Nodding greetings to a few people – those who he knew would be particularly motivated by his attention – MacKenzie climbed the stairs to the mezzanine level. A moment later, Juan and another Leafer soldier appeared and stationed themselves at the top of his staircase.

His workstation displayed summary information related to the GRB, extracted and analysed by MIDAS. The other launch sites were saying they noted the CNSA position but were being instructed by their governments not to change their launch approach.

Opening the latest humanity sentiment survey on his workstation, MacKenzie checked how much trust there currently was in the Ankor's motives. It was just above fifty percent – as it had been since their arrival. Delicately poised but, as he had expected, short of the levels of mistrust that would impact his plans.

Next, he opened the latest report from the MOD on-site lead, Lieutenant Briars. It had been intercepted and decrypted by the Ankor.

*No issues, heightened security visible – particularly in Assembly Zone (last stage before launch) and Hot Zone (which has almost completed preparation for plutonium); close inspection of Hot Zone has verified there are three levels underground; currently empty of*

```
materials but containing heavy duty cages,
safes, and one-way secure pass-doors.
```

*Close, but not too close.*

The Ankor had designed the Hot Zone such that many
empty rooms could be shown whilst the working ones
remained hidden.

MacKenzie went to the back wall and plugged his tablet
into one of the many dedicated hard-wired ports to check on
the prisoner transfers.

Ten prisons had been emptied for the A-Grav installation.
Over the last week, over two hundred coaches had moved
prisoners to other prisons and to release centres. Four of
those coaches had been diverted, lost, reassigned … and two
hundred prisoners were now waiting five levels below the
Hot Zone. No-one even suspected they had been lost from
the system: every computer record and email clearly showed
they were exactly where they needed to be. If a relative
turned up for a visit, a new process would kick in to find that
only that prisoner had been lost in the system, and they
would be pinpointed at the most unhelpful location. If the
relative called, they would speak to a warden who'd confirm
he'd seen the missing prisoner.

The Ankor were in utter control over communications:
email interception, falsifying records, and impersonating
prison staff on the telephone.

A real-time image opened showing one of the holding
cells. Everything looked as it should. Cages of prisoners all
awaiting transfer and processing. They had no idea where
they were but were all expecting early release as a result of
the Ankor's need for prison space for the A-Grav units.

These were the so-called 'wolves'. Ankor analysis of the
brain tissue in the Jupiter Probe had identified a certain DNA
variant that bestowed heightened survival instincts. It was

rare in humans, and of specific interest to the Ankor – particularly to the minority Transcender faction.

MacKenzie switched his tablet's connection to a different port and opened the internal cameras on Kusr. The Transcenders had been instrumental in securing an earlier release of the enzyme data – now due any moment.

Kusr needed to be ready.

The scene that greeted MacKenzie both encouraged and worried him.

On the plus side, the laboratory equipment was all well-ordered and it appeared that experiments to replicate earlier neural bridge successes were underway.

*On the down side…*

There were three people in the room: Kusr, Taylor, and one of Juan's lieutenants.

Taylor was seated whilst Kusr performed a minor surgical routine on him. Obviously only under a local anaesthetic, Taylor could be seen chatting amicably with her.

MacKenzie reached for the earpiece that would give him an audio feed.

'*I'm sorry for the way we manipulated you.*'

The CCTV image did not have fantastic resolution, but Kusr appeared to give a small smile whilst still concentrating on the silver wire she was feeding into Taylor's right bicep.

*Manipulated? What has he already told her?*

MacKenzie desperately needed Kusr to run new tests when the last set of enzyme and protein data was provided. If Taylor had told her that the Ankor had helped them to fake her daughter's torture scene then they'd lose all leverage.

'*I will honour my side of the deal.*'

Kusr spoke quietly whilst continuing to work on Taylor, now making a small incision where his collar bone met his neck – perilously close to the carotid artery.

Perhaps sensing the same, the soldier that Taylor had brought with him took half a step closer.

Kusr ignored the gesture.

*What deal?*

For the next few minutes, both Taylor and Kusr were silent, leaving MacKenzie to stew.

Then he took a breath and relaxed. Of course, the Ankor would be monitoring all the conversations too. If Taylor had said anything meaningful, the Transcenders would have alerted him.

*Two more days …*

Assuming the new data came through, in two days he would have proof that the Ankor had the capability to deliver their half of the bargain.

A murmur fluttered across the main floor. MacKenzie looked up to the screen that was drawing everyone's attention.

The UN General Assembly had announced a new binding resolution – ES-15/3 – categorically stating that the USA were forbidden from launching *Lincoln*, and they were required to meet their payload distribution via normal two-stage rockets.

MacKenzie looked across to the large display showing a live feed from Kennedy Space Center. The *Lincoln* was being prepared for launch.

The Americans did not concern MacKenzie one bit. Although it was possible the *Lincoln* could be fitted out in some type of attack configuration, the Ankor had hundreds of ways to ensure it would never be successful.

MacKenzie returned his attention to his workstation, checking and double-checking all the various activities that had to be completed in the next week.

A little while later Taylor, with a new bandage poking out from his shirt's neckline, arrived in the main room and MacKenzie signalled to Juan to escort him up the stairs.

'What did Kusr have to say to you?' asked MacKenzie.

'Nothing of note,' said Taylor. 'She just progressed my implants.'

'Were the other experiments running correctly?'

'All one hundred percent successful,' said Taylor. 'But you should have more faith.'

'I do,' replied MacKenzie. 'In science. Those seventy-eight pods will remain dormant until Kusr has verified the new mix.'

'I understand,' said Taylor, his eyes flitting around the room. 'I was wondering about her future after that.'

'Released once I'm gone. Just like everyone in here.'

'She could become one of the Blessed.'

'Murdered?' MacKenzie had only said it to unbalance Taylor; the look on Taylor's face indicated he'd hit home.

A fervour burned in Taylor's eyes. He lowered his voice to a forced whisper. 'The Blessed—'

'The answer is no.' MacKenzie wanted to ensure that the very minimum number of his own associates were included in the special programme.

Taylor stared, his face thunderous.

'And,' said MacKenzie, looking briefly up at the ceiling, 'I apologise for my poor choice of words.'

For a few more seconds, Taylor remain motionless … then he nodded in acquiescence.

MacKenzie leant back in his chair.

*The Blessed … I shouldn't have poked that one.*

In fact, he had been deliberately antagonistic with Taylor. The Blessed weren't murdered but to him it felt like a type of death sentence.

*Not the route I will be taking.*

It didn't help that Taylor wanted everyone he'd ever known to become one of the Blessed with him. Top of the list – and the only one approved by MacKenzie himself – was Samantha Turner.

MacKenzie could see why Taylor was interested. Turner was sometimes spikey and abrasive but had an undoubted strength of character.

Not that Taylor would have scooped her had it not been for Ankor support.

Their behavioural algorithms had coached Taylor in his seduction of Turner, and little pieces of Ankor viral code – aim-bots – had ensured that he'd made a good impression on her during their courting rituals on 'OrcTalk' or 'FighterShooter' or whatever computer trash Turner had made him play.

Assuming that Taylor abided by the 'Turner Only' rule, then nothing would need to escalate. If, however, he tried to recruit a few more Blessed then Juan could be called into action to remove him.

*Would the Ankor call the whole deal off if I simply killed Taylor?*

The Ankor managed to maintain an unbalanced morality that MacKenzie couldn't bring himself to work through.

*Perhaps it could look like an accident?*

Unfortunately, in order to achieve the levels of efficiency required, MacKenzie had permitted the two hundred Leafers running the Hot Zone to have earpieces that allowed the Ankor to speak directly to them. The Leafers had no idea they were being spoken to by aliens. They thought the voices were their team leaders in a hidden chain of command.

*The Ankor would know.*

MacKenzie did have a few loyal killers in his team who were entirely unconnected to the Ankor. Conceivably, they could ambush Taylor somewhere deep below the Hot Zone where there were no cameras.

No. The Ankor would work it out in a heartbeat.

Taking a deep breath, MacKenzie put the thought out of his mind. Reasonable levels of death and destruction, where appropriate for the potential gains, were acceptable. He couldn't kill Taylor simply because the man sometimes annoyed him.

Of course, if Taylor broke his agreements, then it would be different.

# CHAPTER 21

**SpaceOp, Thursday 25ᵗʰ April**

Down in the server room below Mission Control, Tim sat glued to his favourite feed. The Chinese National Space Agency streamed a real-time image of the alien craft with superimposed colouring to indicate pod temperatures. There were warm pods, cold pods, and exceptionally cold pods.

```
343  Pods
213  Operating at an average 305K
78   Operating at an average 220K
52   Operating at an average 4K
```

There had been little change in the actual pods since arrival. However, there had been changes around the Ankor craft since the unfolding. The oval of pods only occupied the central portion of the screen, and there was a warmer area stretching out one hundred kilometres in all directions.

'Do you think it's the initial stages of the deflector shield?' asked Sam, who noticed Tim's attention drawn to the screen.

'We haven't sent them any materials yet,' said Tim.

'Maybe they brought some basic construction materials with them,' said Sam, typing.

```
Analysis Override: Alien Craft Heat Perimeter
Extension
```

Within seconds a few low-grade hits returned with unsubstantiated commentary. Most of it agreed with Sam – it was probably the start of the deflector shield.

Sam switched back to the summary searches.

The word 'invasion' was trending again. There had always been groups on Earth who disbelieved the gamma ray burst threat. But most of the pragmatic members of each country's leadership held onto a few salient facts: humanity was not currently being asked for anything meaningful except plutonium, and humanity had no meaningful defence against the Ankor should they turn out to be hostile.

*Any alien race with the capability for faster-than-light travel must be able to squash us without any difficulty …*

'We could reprogram an ICBM,' said Sam.

Tim disagreed. 'Missiles – even intercontinental ones – can't get anywhere near their craft.'

'What about the plutonium?' asked Sam.

'I don't think it can be mined from asteroids.'

'Surely they'd have a way of synthesising it,' said Sam.

Tim shrugged; he knew very little about the manufacture of heavy elements in space.

'At least they didn't ask for tungsten rods,' said Sam. 'Large tungsten rods would only be used for dropping back onto us.'

'How do you know that?' asked Tim.

Sam smiled. 'I got to level thirty on StarEliteCo.'

Tim smiled. Another of Sam's computer games.

A knock on the door preceded its opening by a split second.

Charlie.

'Are you coming?' asked Charlie.

'Where?' asked Sam.

'To watch the test launch,' said Charlie. 'On the roof.'

'We're allowed?' asked Tim.

'Yes,' said Charlie. 'Come on.'

Charlie led them back through the main floor. With only thirty minutes to go before the test launch, the main room was a scene straight out of the movies. Bespectacled scientists pored over banks of screens, whilst others ran around with clipboards and tablets, checking and rechecking.

Overseeing all of it, Francis MacKenzie sat at his desk flanked by four Leafer security guards – the Hispanic ones.

*Heavily armed.*

Tim shared a glance with Sam as they followed Charlie without pausing across the main floor.

Dexter intercepted Tim halfway and gave him a computer tablet. 'This is for remote MIDAS access,' he said. 'I may be unable to do the news. MacKenzie has got me on other stuff.'

'Do I need to decide what news items to display?' asked Tim, looking up on the main wall where a screen was displaying the news summary. It felt like an opportunity to annoy MacKenzie without doing much wrong.

'No,' said Dexter. 'Don't post anything unless MacKenzie or I tell you. But, from what he's said to me, it will just be summary motivational stuff. Just to remind people they're part of an Earth-wide response.'

'Okay.' Tim put the tablet in his inside pocket and hurried after Charlie and Sam, who had not slowed for him.

Just inside the main entrance, Charlie led them through a doorway into a dingy corridor that seemed to run just inside the main wall.

'No cameras down here?' said Tim.

'There aren't any,' said Charlie. 'Francis MacKenzie is very sensitive about being hacked.'

To Tim, it seemed that Charlie disapproved of MacKenzie's decision; his unusual use of MacKenzie's full name registered as odd.

'Which also explains the cabling,' said Tim; hard-wired cables were significantly harder to hack than wireless signals.

Turning a corner, Charlie led them into a service elevator.

Emerging onto the roof of the Control Centre, Tim took stock. The rooftop was large and flat, the size of a football pitch, with a one metre high ledge all around. Twenty parabolic dishes adorned the centre of the roof.

'Is this all the satellite comms stuff?' asked Sam.

'Only a fraction of it.' Charlie pointed northwards. 'Most is set below ground level over there. This close to the launch pad, everything needs protection.'

'How far is it?' Tim looked towards the rocket.

'Two thousand, six hundred and thirty metres.'

Over by the launch pad, the final checks were ongoing. 'What's in the payload today?'

'I don't know.' Charlie shook his head. 'I know it was loaded successfully.'

'You don't know,' said Sam, 'or you won't tell us?'

'No-one does compartmentalisation better than Francis,' said Charlie.

'Do you know what they're making in there?' asked Tim, pointing towards the factories in the north.

'Most of the prefabricated parts are being made at sites around the country, but those factories are making elements of the deflector shield.'

Sam pointed eastwards. 'What about the Hot Zone?'

'Plutonium,' said Charlie.

A mile away to the east, four concrete warehouses sat amidst three layers of razor wire fencing. As usual, a train of lorries was slowly being admitted into the first warehouse. From here it appeared that a ramp led straight down underground. There were no obvious connections between the buildings. But the easterly warehouse, with a large letter 'C' painted on its roof, also had an exit ramp on which lorries occasionally appeared and headed back towards the Welsh mainland. Even from this distance, Tim could see it was swarming with soldiers.

'Is there plutonium yet?' asked Sam.

'No,' said Charlie. 'It will only come with the army.'

Sam rummaged in her shoulder bag. She pulled out the Geiger counter and scanned. Starting with it pointing at the launch pad, she moved it around in an arc, past the factories and over towards the Hot Zone.

Charlie wrested it from her grasp.

'Fuck!' Charlie looked at them both in amazement, his eyes wide. 'These are totally forbidden!'

'Why?' asked Sam.

'First, they could be used by terrorists to locate and steal the plutonium. Any Leafer that saw you with this would shoot without hesitation.' Charlie took a breath. 'Second, possession of one is interpreted by Francis as a direct challenge of his ability to run a safe facility.'

'Well, it's mine.' Sam snatched the Geiger counter back.

For a second, it looked like Charlie would follow up with another attempt, but Sam put it on her lap and wheeled herself away, her face thunderous.

Tim followed. Keeping his voice to a whisper so Charlie couldn't hear, he said, 'It was just a misunderstanding.'

'He grabbed it,' said Sam.

'On instinct,' said Tim. 'To protect you from being shot.'

'I'm not apologising,' said Sam, adrenaline clearly still pumping.

'In a sense, he took a big risk. He could've been shot.' said Tim, trying to lighten the mood.

Sam did not see the funny side. 'So as usual you want me to apologise, to keep Charlie sweet … to maximise the MIDAS contract pay-out.'

'Ah, come on Sam …'

'Maybe that's why you pimped me out to him in the first place?'

Tim felt like he'd been punched in the stomach.

Sam raised her eyebrows.

'I …' Words failed Tim. The day she'd got together with Charlie had been one of the hardest of his life. 'For fuck's sake, Sam.'

He walked away.

Now all three of them were standing apart, and all three of them were avoiding eye contact.

Tim leant on the low barrier that ringed the roof. The tension of the situation was getting to everyone. At breakfast, Tim and Sam had witnessed an altercation caused by one person using too much tomato ketchup. The initial argument had escalated so fast. A few half punches had been thrown, none had landed, and a member of security had intervened.

Tim smiled.

Sam had said '*saucy*'.

Taking a few calming breaths, Tim reflected. No-one knew what the Ankor were up to. It was a powder keg, particularly to people who were used to having some control over their own destiny.

Tim turned back to Sam. She was now looking at him with a contrite expression.

He walked back towards her.

'Sorry,' said Sam. 'I'll give the Geiger to Charlie.'

'No need to be hasty,' whispered Tim. 'Just don't wave it around in public.'

A loudspeaker set in the front of Mission Control whined and crackled for a moment. Given the roof was only one storey up, they could hear perfectly.

It was Francis MacKenzie's voice.

*'We are the first stage of a strong response from humanity. Assuming we all do our jobs correctly, I have no doubts the Ankor will produce the required protection.'*

They returned to Charlie who was waiting quietly, looking out towards the launch pad, which was now devoid of people and vehicles – except for the rocket.

Charlie passed out visors with special tinted glass.

A little while later, the fifteen-minute siren blew.

They waited.

Primary ignition.

Even from almost two miles away, the roar filled the sky.

Tim expected smoke and flames everywhere, but initially it was just noise.

Smoke started billowing out of a vent from under the ground, a little way removed from the launch pad. Tim guessed there was an underground part of the launch pad that diverted the exhaust gases.

The rocket lifted.

Just a few metres … less than a millimetre, from his perspective.

Now Tim could see the furnace of the rocket fuel in action.

Flames consumed the space between the rocket and the launch pad.

White hot.

The rocket started to rise.

The gap between the rocket and the launch pad grew.

Five metres.

Twenty metres.

The whole building was now shaking. Instinctively, Tim reached out and grabbed Sam's arm.

'Is that for your benefit or mine?' she asked with a smile.

'Both,' said Tim.

For the next few minutes, they watched the rocket rise higher and higher, until it finally became a prick of light.

'Success,' said Charlie.

'How do you know?' asked Tim.

'There are no bits of rocket dropping down on us,' said Sam.

'There are bits dropping,' said Charlie. 'You just can't see them. Both Stage 1 and Stage 2 of the rocket are being retrieved from the Irish Sea for recycling.'

Sam grunted acknowledgement of the fact and returned her attention to the ever-fading pinprick of light.

'I need to go back down,' said Charlie.

'Can we stay up here?' asked Sam.

'Sorry, not without me,' said Charlie.

Returning to the main floor, Tim looked around. The atmosphere in Mission Control was happy but wary. The main screen showed the telemetry of the flight path. Tim was not an expert on ballistics but the fact that all the numbers were green gave him peace of mind.

'Good view?' asked Dexter, as Tim and Sam found a little space next to him.

'Great, thanks,' said Tim. 'When's the next one?'

'Exact hour to be finalised, but within three days.' Dexter turned his attention back to his screen. 'Can you find a summary of the launch, please?'

MacKenzie had given explicit standing instructions that all gossip and supposition was to be stripped away before anything was projected onto the main wall. Opening the MIDAS interface, Tim modified the news aggregation parameters and pointed MIDAS to look for comment from contemporaries of SpaceOp – other launch sites. Just to be safe, he also set parameters to triple check any quotes for positivity and factual support; given the overall nervous mood that permeated humanity, even well-respected academics were now prone to making unsubstantiated shock-jock comments.

*And they may be right.*

A moment later, the summary appeared. Almost exclusively positive, although a few repeated comments came through from other launch sites demanding exact payload information.

'No-one here knows the payload,' said Sam. 'I chatted with a bunch of the technicians. The ballistics team know the weight and packing density, but that's it.'

Tim released the news item to the main wall and surreptitiously watched MacKenzie's face for signs of approval, whilst also kicking himself for being too obsequious.

'Can we go back to the flat?' asked Sam. 'I'm tired.'

Neither of them had slept well for a few days. 'Sure.'

Tim and Sam made their way to one of the pathways through the crowded main floor.

Outside, Tim grabbed a buggy and they headed for the flat.

A few minutes later, Tim's tablet pinged. The test launch had reached the correct orbit – three thousand kilometres high.

Three minutes later, every siren in SpaceOp blared at full volume.

Tim saw security guards swarming out of the Administration Zone.

# CHAPTER 22

**SpaceOp, Thursday 25th April**

Stuck in the open, halfway between the Administration Zone and Mission Control, Tim looked at Sam, and then looked around.

Nothing physically obvious had changed, but the sirens weren't stopping.

'What do you think?' asked Sam.

In the distance, the security guards from the Administration Zone were speeding off in all directions. Two were heading their way.

As the jeeps rushed towards them – or towards Mission Control, Tim couldn't tell which – he pulled the electric cart over to the side.

His tablet pinged.

```
Nuclear Explosion Reported
Delhi, India
Trending words: A-Grav, Dirty Bomb, Nuclear
***
Release to Main Board Y/N?
***
```

A rush of adrenaline blurred his vision. He couldn't release something of this magnitude without express permission from MacKenzie. Could he? Should he?

*Nuclear explosion?*

Sam leant over and read it. 'Shit …'

Absorbed in the screen, Tim was brought back to the present by the screech of tyres as a jeep stopped next to him.

It was Tosh. 'Your cart works?'

'Yes,' said Sam.

'Please head back into Mission Control,' said Tosh, speeding away.

Back inside, urgent whispering filled Mission Control. On the mezzanine, MacKenzie stared directly into his workstation, his face betraying a mixture of anguish and anger.

Up on the wall, two screens were showing international news services; both were providing early pictures from Delhi. The picture was grainy. A large fire could be discerned and some damaged buildings. The explosion seemed to have been in a suburb rather than the densely packed centre.

Dexter was staring at the MIDAS news service screen; he'd already released the India news.

On their arrival, Dexter shifted over to his own desk. 'Welcome back,' he said, his face grave.

Tim wasn't sure if he really wanted to know the details. He hesitated … and then clicked through the item *dirty bomb*. *How much radiation?*

Feeling Sam take his hand in hers and give it a gentle squeeze, Tim stared at the screen as MIDAS searched through recent analysis to display the source of the 'dirty bomb' return.

Before the results were displayed, a second critical alert came through.

```
Nuclear Explosion Reported
Madrid, Spain
Trending words: A-Grav, Dirty Bomb, Nuclear
***
Release to Main Board Y/N?
***
```

'Madrid!' said Sam in an urgent whisper.

Tim turned to Dexter, who nodded in the direction of the mezzanine. His eyes locked with Francis MacKenzie's.

MacKenzie gave a small nod.

Tim released the news item to the main wall.

A new screen opened on the main wall, live-streaming video of the Spanish explosion. Another blast in the suburbs.

The murmuring that had accompanied the India news in Mission Control rose to animated conversation as people noticed Madrid.

One of the large screens showing the news cut to a wide shot of central New York. People were streaming out of buildings. The picture split into four. Each quadrant showed a different city: New York, London, Moscow, Beijing.

They all showed the same.

*Panic.*

'I don't blame them,' said Sam.

Watching the live pictures of people running through the streets of London – past landmarks he knew well – Tim fought to keep his mind under control.

There were ten thousand A-Grav units around the world. Of those, eighty-five had been assigned to the UK.

*Fuck … are they all going to explode? What if the next one is in a city centre?*

Adrenaline coursed through Tim. His hands, which had simply been clammy, now started to shake. 'Poor bastards.'

'We may be next,' said Dexter, leaning over. 'A large army flatbed truck arrived last night.'

'Could be the plutonium,' said Sam.

Dexter shook his head. 'I don't think so. There's been no political statement.'

Tim considered the probabilities. MacKenzie had been adamantly against the A-Gravs, but if he'd changed his mind … SpaceOp was huge. There would be hundreds of places to hide one. According to Tosh, Mission Control had four storeys underground.

Up on the mezzanine level, MacKenzie continued to stare at his workstation, concentration etched on his face.

Five minutes passed, and Tim felt every single one of the three hundred ticks. The public perception was that these were not accidents.

*Is this the first act of aggression from the Ankor? Are we at war?*

Tim couldn't believe it.

MIDAS pinged again.

```
Explosion Reported
Liverpool, United Kingdom
Trending words: A-Grav, Dirty Bomb, War
***
Release to Main Board Y/N?
***
```

This time, Tim didn't look to MacKenzie for approval. He simply released it.

Mission Control erupted.

Of the three hundred people working on the main floor, at least forty surged towards the main doors.

Barely holding onto the situation, Tosh's security team waved them back and Tim could see Tosh himself speaking earnestly to the crowd.

On the screens, large fires swept through a suburb of Madrid.

Up on the mezzanine, MacKenzie and his armed soldiers had still not moved.

'How bad is it in Liverpool?' asked Sam.

New information was already hitting the internet.

```
A-Grav Yield
1   kiloton - estimates
Significant physical destruction up to 1 mile
radius
Radiation levels variable
Fissile material unknown
Trending words: Dirty Bomb, Panic, Cloud
```

Tim clicked through the word 'cloud', simultaneously looking for video streams.

The explosion had been three to four times the size of the Madrid blast in terms of yield. Although it had not been a full nuclear blast, the news services were already reporting that a large cloud of radioactive dust had been created.

More news screens opened on the walls of Mission Control. Now there were twelve scenes from across the UK, showing people streaming away from known A-Grav sites.

'*Known* sites,' said Tim under his breath.

MIDAS pinged again.

```
Explosion Reported
Washington, USA
Radioactive source
Trending words: War, Invasion
***
Release to Main Board Y/N?
***
```

Having sat almost motionless at his desk for the previous alerts, Francis MacKenzie stood abruptly and paced around the mezzanine level. Three hundred people below him fell silent. One by one people looked up towards him.

A minute later, he took a few deep breaths and walked to the top of the staircase.

'I am assuming we are *not* at war. However, this is a serious situation. For the next thirty minutes, I will lift all restrictions on personal communications. Call your families, agree a plan of action. Do not assume you can leave the base. We may give permission for the most pressing cases.'

Murmuring built on the floor.

MacKenzie raised his hands for silence. 'If the explosions are the precursor to an attack, then we will respond. However, if they aren't, then I can assure you the damage they have caused will be insignificant compared to the gamma ray burst heading our way. Make your calls – then get back to work.'

The crowd at the main door had taken MacKenzie's words to heart and people were dispersing back to their desks as they dialled on their mobile phones.

The lights in the Control Centre flashed briefly.

Alien broadcast. All channels. The main screens displayed multiple copies.

**Test launch success**
**Orbit accessible**
**A-Grav decays due to**
**unexpected gravitational**
**flux**
**Others are safe**

'They would say that, even if it was to precede an attack,' said Sam, reaching over to the keyboard and typing.

Tim was not so sure. If the Ankor were playing humanity for fools, would they have done this? Dirty bombs, killing a handful of thousands of people instantly, with a further hundred thousand critically ill from radiation poisoning? What did it gain them?

*What do they want?*

An hour passed. Tim and Sam spent it scouring news services and local media feeds for updates on the situation in Liverpool.

Fortunately, as part of the installation, a one-mile exclusion zone had already been in force, so estimated direct deaths were numbered in the thousands rather than in the tens of thousands. However, the explosion had not simply been a dirty bomb, and the detonation had created a cloud of radioactive dust that would have a more insidious effect.

Liverpool was being evacuated, but no-one was sure where to send people. Other large cities had A-Gravs of their own.

Tim looked around the room, trying to gauge how close people were to melting down.

'You okay?' asked Sam.

'Yes,' he lied.

A soldier came over and called Dexter away for a meeting up on the mezzanine.

At that moment, a newsfeed switched to a live address from the Secretary-General of the United Nations.

'**The United Nations General Assembly has issued the following binding resolution ES-15/4. The A-Grav explosions were an accident. All members are ordered to continue as planned. Failure to adhere will incur sanctions, suspension and reprisals from the General Assembly.**'

Moments later, almost all countries broadcast a variation of the message, 'we accept these were accidents and will adhere in full to binding resolution ES-15/4.'

There were exceptions.

China, speaking through the CNSA, responded more contrarily. 'The PRC notes ES-15/4 but is proposing a delay of launches pending additional dialogue with the Ankor.'

Italy stated a delay was unavoidable: their launch site was close to an A-Grav unit and they had evacuated the area.

A little while later, Dexter returned briefly to grab some stuff from his desk.

'Anything new?' Tim asked.

'The dust from the Liverpool explosion is heading our way.' Dexter left again.

Sam typed into the workstation. Within a few moments, she'd found maps showing the projected track of the radioactive cloud. At current speeds, it would miss the southern edge of Anglesey by five miles, and SpaceOp by more than ten.

Things could change.

Tim checked to see what people were saying about the Ankor.

> *Reaction to Ankor Response*
> *Ankor don't provide explanation but indicate accidental releases*
> *Still no bilateral discussions*
> *Trending words: hard to know, invasion, pointless to resist*

'Boston!'

Tim looked up. Francis MacKenzie had shouted for him. Tim ran up the stairs to the mezzanine, the guards parting as he reached the top.

'Tim,' he said, moderating his tone, concern etched on his face. 'I'm shutting the bridges and offering the caverns in the Hot Zone as a nuclear radiation shelter for Anglesey residents. You're the only technology expert that I can spare. I want you to set up MIDAS to track the arrival of the Anglesey population. Speak to Dexter about accessing mobile phone mast data.' He paused. 'Some won't come. That's fine. There will be space for those that do.'

'Understood,' said Tim, waiting to see if there was any more instruction.

There wasn't. MacKenzie turned back to his workstation.

Returning to Sam, Tim gave the update.

Moments later, Dexter arrived with access codes, message configuration files, and admin IP addresses for the three mobile operators who maintained masts across Anglesey. He went through the information with Tim and then ensured that he had the right contact details if anything came up.

'Where are you going now?' Sam asked Dexter.

'Organising refugee processing and associated tasks,' said Dexter. 'Stripping supermarkets for food, looting hotels for beds, and moving fifty to sixty thousand people.'

'Good luck,' said Sam to Dexter's retreating back.

At that moment, MacKenzie stood and addressed the room. 'Everyone in this room must ignore SpaceOp's parallel efforts to support the Anglesey refugees. There remains one goal. Rocket Launch One, at ten o'clock Sunday morning, will take up the first components of the deflector shield.' He paused. 'Start the countdown.'

On one of the main screens, the countdown was projected in numbers eight feet high.

**61 hours: 12 minutes**

MacKenzie and two of his soldiers left the building via the main doors. Juan, plus one other, remained on the mezzanine level.

Tim handed Sam the notepad containing the codes and passwords. 'Can you create a new set of host data files and encryption routines? Then we'll suck the data out of the mobile operators and match names, locations.'

'On it,' said Sam. 'I'll go to the server room.'

'Great,' said Tim. 'I'll be down in a bit.'

Sam departed, and Tim started writing a small piece of custom matching code.

If there was a radioactive cloud of dust coming, then it would be unfair to abandon any refugees who wanted rescuing, but it would also be unfair on the support team to be driving coaches around Anglesey – through clouds of radioactive dust – trying to pick up people who had no intention of coming to SpaceOp.

It wasn't complicated, but it wouldn't be an exact science. There would be plenty of people whose phones were off, or had dead batteries, or were simply unused. However, Tim was sure that by refreshing the data every fifteen minutes, or so, they'd be able to track most of Anglesey's population. The major requirement was accessing the mobile operator data: customer names, addresses, and mobile phone numbers; that would then be cross-referenced with the infrastructure mast data to determine users' current whereabouts – which could be used to infer movement.

*And I can analyse social media reporting of the refugees themselves ... selfies and map pinning*

After twenty minutes, with the matching code written, Tim returned to the server room, where Sam was ready.

There was no reason to wait, so they accessed each of the mobile operators and sucked out the data. Once completed, Tim ran a series of viral checks which confirmed the files only held simple data.

Sam ran her encryption routines to incorporate the newly loaded data files into the system.

A knock on the door drew their attention. Dexter.

'All okay?' asked Dexter.

'Yes, no problem,' replied Tim.

'Okay, the caverns are being prepared now,' said Dexter. 'We just need to get people to the SpaceOp front gates.'

'What's the score with the bridges?' asked Tim.

'MacKenzie is adamant,' replied Dexter. 'The bridges are closed. Anyone on the mainland can look after themselves ... his exact words were, "they've plenty of coal mines".'

Moments later, MIDAS churned out the first set of results. They'd managed to get positive matches on close to fifty thousand mobile phones. Tim packaged up the information and sent copies to Tosh, who was managing the retrievals.

Fifteen minutes later they reran the tracking.

By comparing the first and second cell registrations for each mobile phone, it was possible to see how people were moving.

Most of Anglesey's population was heading for SpaceOp.

Tim checked his watch – almost midnight.

--------

## SpaceOp, Anglesey, Friday 26th April

Tim woke up in the server room at six o'clock. He'd shared the tracking activity through the night with Sam, each of them taking turns to ensure MIDAS was working whilst the other slept.

It had not been a comfortable place to sleep.

*God knows how Sam managed.*

Getting out of the chair and stretching, Tim wandered over to her. 'You were supposed to wake me at five. What's new?'

'I couldn't sleep anyway,' said Sam. 'Radiation damage in Liverpool is severe. The wind has apparently shifted and a heavy dose of radioactive dust will hit Wales.'

Tim looked at the tracking function. Three thousand more Anglesey refugees had arrived in the last few hours. 'How's it looking at the Hot Zone?'

'No idea,' said Sam. 'But I can show you this.'

She accessed the only two webcams that MacKenzie had authorised in SpaceOp. One was a long-distance shot of the launch pad – empty. The second was an external shot of Mission Control.

MacKenzie clearly wasn't taking any chances. Work teams in hazmat suits were everywhere with rolls of tape, sealing the cracks in the windows and doors.

'Shall we go up?' asked Tim. 'See if we've got any new instructions?'

'I'll stay here,' said Sam, kneading life into her legs.

'Sure.'

Tim walked back up the sloping corridors onto the main floor. One of the screens was displaying a new United Nations broadcast.

*Four launches scheduled for Sunday*

211

```
(RL1) SpaceOp - UK
(Test) European Space Agency - French Guiana
(Test) San Marco - Kenya
(Test) Esrange - Sweden
Our Ankor allies are entirely supportive of
the efforts. UN population must seek to remain
calm in light of the recent accidents
```

Dexter was at his desk, looking like he hadn't slept at all.

'So, we're first,' said Tim, nodding towards the screen.

'Never in doubt, given MacKenzie's ability to focus all his resources,' said Dexter.

'How are the refugee arrivals going?' asked Tim, sliding into the seat next to him. 'Is the tracking working?'

'Like a dream amongst nightmares,' said Dexter. 'At three-ish we had crowds forming at the main gate. The Leafers were very slow to shuttle people into the Hot Zone – they were searching everyone extremely thoroughly before letting them in. Luckily, MacKenzie made a personal trip to the gate and now it's flowing smoothly.'

'Has anyone gone over to the Hot Zone to help?' asked Tim.

'No-one is allowed near there. You can imagine how Tosh feels about that,' said Dexter, opening a new screen. 'I've got this, though.'

Tim looked at the screen. It was a grainy long-distance shot of the Hot Zone.

'It's a webcam on our internal network,' said Dexter. 'MacKenzie allowed it for fire safety purposes.'

'Are there more of these?' Tim thought that CCTV and webcams were forbidden.

'Hardly any.'

The camera was most likely fixed on the roof, or upper wall, of Mission Control. It showed the main receiving Hot Zone warehouse surrounded by a morass of chain-linked fences and gates. People were arriving by SpaceOp shuttle bus into a holding area about one hundred metres from the warehouse, and forming a queue.

They watched for five minutes as two shuttle buses emptied, and the people were led inside by Leafers in hazmat suits.

A large eighteen-wheeler truck arrived via the eastern perimeter road and drove up to the second warehouse.

'Food and bedding,' said Dexter.

The MIDAS news server pinged.

A new breaking story opened, with a video feed. The screen showed Chinese soldiers surrounding a large telecommunications installation outside the city of Xian. The news ticker at the bottom of the picture indicated that all private enterprises providing internet services were being nationalised to help the Chinese government control the flow of data.

'They're switching the power off,' said Dexter. 'No more internet for the Chinese.'

*Good news for Sam's Triple-Bs … the Fiery Fuyang Fatales, not so much.*

Tim couldn't help thinking about all the times Sam's team had lost to their Chinese rivals.

Would she play again? Tim wasn't sure. Doubts that had been gnawing at him, and the rest of the world, persisted. It seemed likely that the Ankor would not be operating in the way they were if it was a 'simple' invasion or annihilation. But equally, if the Ankor had arrived for their stated – purely benevolent – reasons, then their communication policy was appalling.

Poor communication was the only hard evidence of wrongdoing. The A-Grav explosions could be part of a planned destabilisation process, but equally could be accidents.

'How are the warehouses in the Hot Zone connected?' Tim asked Dexter.

'Some tunnels,' said Dexter. 'Some trenches.'

A new MIDAS alert screen opened.

```
Liverpool Radiation
Initial calculations imply fissile material is
Uranium
Radiation levels at ground zero less than 3
Sieverts
Minimal risk of excess Nitrogen-14
Cloud drift yielding 0.001Sv
```

Tim checked the internet. At those levels, anyone with a few inches of concrete over their heads would probably be safe.

Assuming nothing worse happened.

One thing was certain. The bridges were shut. Neither he nor Sam would be leaving Anglesey any time soon.

# CHAPTER 23

Military discipline allowed Martel to exude an air of calm whilst internally he seethed. Vital minutes were ticking away. An hour previously, he'd requested that the prime minister give him permission to land ten helicopters full of armed British soldiers to secure the launch capability at SpaceOp. By now, he was meant to be back at Porton Down with Captain Whaller finalising the plan.

Unfortunately, the standing rules regarding engagement with the Ankor meant he needed face-to-face confirmation from the prime minister.

'Sorry to keep you,' said Timbers, entering the room. 'I've had a meeting with the other party leaders, the cabinet secretary, the home secretary, and the minister of defence. The final decision is that we do not send the helicopters.'

*Wrong decision …*

'There's simply not sufficient evidence of wrongdoing. Fanatical compartmentalisation is not a crime,' said the prime minister, referring back to Martel's recent report on the prevailing operating conditions in SpaceOp.

'Given the stakes, Prime Minister,' said Martel, 'it feels prudent to add a level of control.'

'Politically,' said the prime minister. 'An invasion of SpaceOp will not play well with a public who already mistrust the government's ability to protect them.'

Martel stopped himself from reminding Timbers that he'd wanted far larger exclusion zones around the A-Gravs.

'Simply put, they trust MacKenzie more,' said the prime minister. 'The people want a working shield and they trust MacKenzie to deliver it.'

'Is it a question of there being insufficient excuse to land?' asked Martel.

At this clearly pointed question, Timbers raised an eyebrow. '*Casus belli?*'

'Within the next few hours, I will have undercover operatives inside SpaceOp posing as refugees from Anglesey. They can be instructed to cause enough disturbance that the British army would have a good reason to intervene.'

The prime minister paused to consider the offer.

'It can all be done in twelve hours,' said Martel.

The prime minister shook his head. 'No. The decision remains. You cannot send the army onto SpaceOp property without my explicit permission.'

Martel was used to taking orders, but, in twenty years, he'd never been given one he'd disagreed with so fundamentally. He accepted that his team had not found any evidence of the Ankor, or MacKenzie, doing anything wrong, but his instinct was to halt the launches until a full inventory of all payloads had been analysed. Currently, his team only had time to spot check a sample of payloads and SpaceOp was such a convoluted warren he could not be sure those containers weren't being switched.

It shouldn't have come as so much of a surprise; the prime minister had made remarks on the radio a few hours earlier endorsing MacKenzie's position. It was just that Martel was used to politicians saying one thing in public and then being more … pragmatic behind closed doors.

'Final decision?' asked Martel.

'Yes,' said Timbers.

They shook hands and Martel left the room, his mind whirring. He needed a way to protect the British population in spite of the prime minister's intransigence.

--------

**Later that day**

Approaching the Liverpool ground zero by helicopter, having picked up Captain Whaller, Martel reviewed the situation.

Only moments before, the prime minister had given one of his twice daily public broadcasts. The salient bit underlined Timbers's resolve in the matter of MacKenzie and SpaceOp.

> '... *I know the sorrow I personally feel for those killed or injured in the Liverpool blast reflects the sorrow felt by the whole country. It has made me more determined to deliver on the shield – working closely with the Ankor and with Francis MacKenzie.'*

Martel leant in close to Whaller, raising his voice over the whine of the helicopter's rotor blades. 'What happened to Jones?'

Whaller had been working in Porton Down on weaponry options for four days straight, but had also taken the recent report from Lieutenant Briars – the on-site lead at SpaceOp.

Corporal Jones, one of Briars's on-site liaison team, had been sent to the Royal Liverpool Infirmary.

'Last night he complained of severe stomach pains. This morning, the doctor sent him to the hospital,' said Whaller.

'Any suspicions?'

'He'd been in the Hot Zone all of yesterday,' said Whaller. 'He said he didn't eat or drink anything there, neither was there any unexpected radiation.'

'What's the latest status of the Hot Zone?' asked Martel. The liaison team had been shown around it twice now. There were at least three floors below ground level with huge empty rooms.

'The preparation for plutonium storage is accelerating: giant safes, internal gates, and a conveyor system linking to the monorail that feeds the Storage and Assembly Zones,' said Whaller.

Martel consulted his mental map of SpaceOp. The Assembly Zone was the last stage before launch, where the rocket was put together. The Storage Zone was where all the underlying shield materials were held and sorted. Crates from production centres all over the UK were sent to Storage where they were transferred into standardised containers.

'Still just as busy?'

'Briars says it doesn't stop – all day and all night.'

'Seems like a lot of materials,' said Martel.

'The Storage Zone is also being used as one of the secure locations for A-Grav fit-out materials.'

'A-Gravs? On MacKenzie's precious SpaceOp soil?'

Whaller shrugged. 'Obviously there are lots of shield components too.'

Martel kicked himself. He should have been more forceful with the prime minister. The continuing issue remained, however. There were very few facts: the Ankor refused to communicate in a useful bilateral way – with some human apologists mumbling about cultural contamination, the devices deployed by the Ankor had killed tens of thousands of people across the globe. The remaining A-Grav units – if they were bombs – were well positioned to kill a few billion more.

Beneath him, cars streamed along the motorways leading out of Liverpool, with the British army was overseeing the exodus. Tanks and armoured personnel carriers deployed at major road junctions ensured a systematic process. Not that there hadn't been some escalations. Since the explosion, forty people had died from causes not directly related to the nuclear blast: rioting, looting, settling scores …

The country was perhaps only one more shock away from total anarchy.

*It will take more than a set of personal emails from the Ankor to calm people if another A-Grav blows.*

As they approached the blast site, Martel turned to Private Hunter, shouting over the noise of the helicopter's rotors. 'Where's Captain Ulfsater?'

'At the two-mile perimeter, sir,' said Hunter.

'Great, please take us in.'

Regarding the installation in Liverpool, Martel had already spoken to the army team several times by radio. Their stories were consistent and plausible. They had followed the installation instructions to the letter, and no-one had been allowed close. However, given the Ankor could be intercepting and faking all those radio conversations, Martel had decided to make the trip.

Of course, his true line of investigation was with Francis MacKenzie in Anglesey. Martel checked his watch. Whether the Ankor were culpable or not, the Liverpool tragedy had afforded Martel the opportunity to send in his undercover team posing as refugees – they would be arriving soon.

As the helicopter landed, Martel was met by Captain Ulfsater from the Royal Engineers who gave him a face-to-face – albeit behind hazmat suit masks – briefing of the situation in Liverpool.

The A-Grav itself had been entirely vaporised in the explosion, but Ulfsater showed video footage of the installation. Again, this could be faked, but in Martel's mind it provided confirmation the A-Grav had been installed correctly.

Looking around, Martel could see the emergency response team had deployed incredibly effectively and quickly. 'How did you get it all in place so soon?'

'I'm told the Ankor provided emergency supply chain assistance,' said Ulfsater.

*Maybe they have a guilty conscience?*

Martel switched subjects. 'Do you have analysis of the projected radioactive cloud?'

'Yes, sir,' said Ulfsater. He opened a window on his tablet and showed the predicted track of the radioactive cloud with speed, bearings, and radioactivity levels. 'We have real-time verification: there are three aircraft tracking the extremities of the cloud and sending us continuous readings.'

The cloud was drifting westwards across north Wales. Evacuation of a ten-mile corridor running south-west from the Liverpool explosion site was ongoing.

'We've been lucky,' said the captain. 'Prevailing winds could have taken the cloud over densely populated urban areas.'

Martel looked around. The army cordon here, at the two-mile perimeter and upwind of the explosion site, also held one of the decontamination units and it was still processing civilians.

A line of about one hundred people stood waiting at the hastily erected Portakabins that housed the various scrubbing, sluicing, and garment-burning equipment.

On one side of the main Portakabin was a line of nervous looking people, scratching at their arms, reassuring their children, and pulling at the scarves that they'd tied over their faces.

On the other side was a series of shuttle buses loading 'clean' people for resettlement. These people were all wearing standard issue grey tracksuits and were wrapped in silver foil blankets. In most cases, they were holding tightly on to young children, who, between sobs, were asking questions that couldn't easily be answered.

Martel knew one thing. His team in Porton Down would be halving their efforts in looking for proof of wrongdoing by MacKenzie and the Ankor, and doubling their efforts investigating potential counter-measures.

*Guilty until proven innocent.*

# CHAPTER 24

**SpaceOp, Saturday 27th April**

With Juan escorting him, MacKenzie descended from his office to the main floor and then through the security doors. Next, he took a staircase down to the laboratory occupied by Kusr.

*Decision time.*

There were just under twenty hours before Rocket Launch One and it was time to select one of two metaphorical buttons to push. Start the processing to support the Ankor, or cleanse all traces of collusion and *uncover* evidence of Ankor ill will towards humanity ... perhaps even send them an unwelcome gift in RL1.

It was not clear-cut.

The Ankor had hit four cities with 'accidental' A-Grav releases. The only plan they'd ever discussed had been for three. Washington had been an extra. It went directly against the 'sanctity of life' tenet the Ankor continuously preached.

Every single death they caused was meticulously calculated towards their goals.

*Why did you hit Washington?*

It was possible that the radiation leak could be a warning to the USA, who were being generally surly and uncommunicative.

*Or it could be a gift to China.*

If China was in collusion with the Ankor, then his own negotiating position would be gone. Recent news items concerning the Chinese shutting down the internet hadn't altered his opinion at all: bluff, counter-bluff, and misdirection – these were all standard tools the Ankor wielded with ease.

Reaching into his pocket, MacKenzie fingered the packet of diazepam. He'd taken two the night before to get to sleep, and one more that morning to get out of bed.

MacKenzie entered Kusr's laboratory and indicated for Juan to stand to one side.

'Good afternoon, Dr Kusr,' he said, looking around the benches for signs of progress.

'Mr MacKenzie,' said Kusr, flinching as her gaze flicked past Juan.

The neon strip lighting gave a harsh blue-white glare to everything. The confined space was oppressive. 'Anything to report?' he asked.

Kusr looked over towards a sealed chamber with a glass front. 'It's stable.'

'Completely?' asked MacKenzie, trying to keep the hope out of his voice.

Kusr nodded and indicated for MacKenzie to inspect the chamber. 'I have all four configurations of neural link working. They've been stable for over ten hours of continuous information exchange.'

Behind the glass, two rats were strapped down on a wooden board, comatose. Each one had a series of ten fine wires coming out the base of its neck. In each case, the wires led into a small computer in the corner of the sealed chamber.

MacKenzie smiled – a hybrid of biological and non-biological. 'It's all unnetworked.'

'Completely,' said Kusr.

'What are they using the computer for?'

Kusr forced a thin smile. 'That's another fifteen years of work, not that I am volunteering.'

'Good work,' said MacKenzie. 'I recognise you didn't enter the bargain willingly, but I will keep my side of it.'

The pieces were in place. Walking to the door, MacKenzie felt growing hope. He had enough now to confirm the Ankor could deliver their part of the bargain and give him a true hybrid existence – TechMeld.

MacKenzie headed back towards the main floor with Juan.

Just before the armoured doors he met Taylor, who was clearly looking for him.

'Liverpool was four times the original planned yield,' said Taylor, falling into step beside him. 'Did you know?'

*Really?*

MacKenzie, taken aback for a moment, shook his head.

Although, given that Washington had been added to the list of initial explosions, it shouldn't have surprised him. There were clearly machinations and forces beyond his control at work.

'It was them,' said Taylor. He didn't mention them by name. The flash of hate in his eyes told the story clearly enough.

*The Transcender faction.*

MacKenzie doubted it would have been the main Ankor group. Most of the work he'd done with MIDAS to collate and send population dynamics data had been to strictly minimise the deaths required for the Ankor plan. Almost everything they did was with an ultimate reverence for life. The Transcenders, however, were a different story.

'I assume they had their reasons,' said MacKenzie.

'What about Martel's spies?' asked Taylor, the tone of his voice sharp. 'That was you.'

True. The spies – the ones Martel had slipped into Anglesey as part of the refugee groups – had been killed. The filtering systems within the first stage of the Hot Zone had easily identified them as British special forces.

'They were combatants,' said MacKenzie.

'They could have been locked up,' said Taylor.

'I suspect it may be the additional deaths in Liverpool that are bothering you,' said MacKenzie, unwilling to be lectured by Taylor. 'Why don't you take it up directly with the Transcender faction? They are, after all, members of your church.'

Taylor opened and shut his mouth a few times before turning and disappearing up the corridor.

MacKenzie reflected as he continued on his way up to the main floor.

When the Ankor had explained their beliefs – the so-called Simulation Theory – MacKenzie had researched it. Several credible Earth academics had already postulated the theory and devised potential experiments to verify it.

Taylor had been dispatched to Chile to determine whether it was possible that Earth, humanity, the Ankor, the Sun, the stars, were all part of an enormous simulation being run on a computer in another universe by the god that the Ankor worshipped.

The experimental results had been inconclusive. Taylor had returned partially chastened, mumbling jargon about how it was impossible to irrefutably prove the entirety of a system from within that same system. He'd also returned thoroughly converted to that same religion.

The ease with which Taylor converted to the Ankor religion had been noteworthy, although perhaps not so improbable. Taylor had already devoted his life to programming lifelike human characteristics into computer simulations of people; full Simulation Theory was a logical extension.

*It offers an alternative*, Taylor had said. *An eternal soul without the need for a rich old white man with a beard throwing lightning bolts.*

At that first meeting, MacKenzie had been mildly respectful to Taylor. Now, having had to put up with his nonsense for ten years, he was scathing.

The Ankor had clearly discovered – *constructed* – a god in their own image.

Just the fact that they somehow had a need for a god unnerved MacKenzie.

*God and Man: only one can live forever.*

After his own failed relationships with Earth's religious groups, MacKenzie had reconciled himself with that phrase.

He believed the final defeat of death – gaining physical immortality for all members of humanity – would render 'God' unnecessary. People would no longer have to debase themselves, scrape, and worship just for the chance of everlasting life in Heaven.

MacKenzie grimaced, remembering a particularly annoying exchange with a Jesuit Cardinal *Francois something* who said *Only God with Man can live forever*, implying a necessary symbiosis. Of course, God needed Man … after all, faith lends substance. But Man did not need God.

It was unsettling that the Ankor – as close to immortal as possible – appeared to need a god.

*There's always the chance they're right.*

Arriving at the main floor, MacKenzie climbed the stairs and walked over to the back wall. He plugged his tablet into the requisite port and opened the camera system.

A picture appeared of the holding area with the wolves … *the Blessed.*

The wolves appeared to be taking their new housing in their stride. Not surprising, given they lived in a prison and had been moved into a series of holding cells that looked remarkably like a prison.

MacKenzie opened a hatch below the port. Inside was a series of multiple mechanical dials and switches. Carefully selecting the correct ones – failure would have serious repercussions – he set the system to be operational.

Now, most of the wolves would be processed.

*Wolves …*

The DNA sequence that led to brains developing with enhanced survival instincts was present in about one percent of the general population. Within the prison system, that percentage rose to eight. A happy circumstance for Francis MacKenzie, as it made collecting the requisite number of wolves easier.

MacKenzie smiled. His own DNA had shown the wolf sequence too. That hadn't surprised him; his will to survive ran deep. It was interesting, however, that the Ankor needed that specific trait. It hinted of weakness.

*Weakness …*

His own DNA analysis had also shown a predisposition to asthma, which was most likely why he was in this current situation. His earliest memories as a six-year-old boy were of struggling for breath with lungs that wouldn't work. Four times before his tenth birthday he'd passed out, felt his consciousness slip away.

On the first occasion, waking up in hospital had been more frightening than the event itself – which he hadn't understood. By the third time, he knew enough to be scared.

*Am I frightened of death, or am I just being reasonable?*

On his actual deathbed, MacKenzie knew, if an angel appeared and offered him another ten years for the lives of ten strangers, he'd take it.

*A hundred? A thousand? Fifty thousand?*

A sliding scale, and everyone was somewhere on it. Many people wouldn't take life to extend their own, but they'd take a hand, or a finger. You'd have to look pretty hard for someone who'd refuse to slap a stranger in order to be allocated another three months of life.

The Ankor seemed to have similar moral conundrums. In fact, Earth was lucky that the current configuration of the Ankor had a tendency towards minimising collateral damage.

*Two factions.*

The two hundred and thirteen operational pods were all 'the Ankor', but of them, fifty-eight were aligned within a small faction that did not see themselves as part of the whole. Referred to by the majority as: 'those-who-do-not-submit', 'the-sterile', and 'the-breakers', the smaller faction accepted the premise of Simulation Theory and believed their universe was running on a computer. However, they had wildly different goals – *creation is not ownership,* they'd said.

MacKenzie called them 'Transcenders' and their influence over the Ankor majority – who were always trying to rehabilitate them into the whole – couldn't be understated.

*Prodigal sons.*

From the earliest negotiations the main body of the Ankor had allowed Transcender representatives to be involved.

They'd been openly hostile towards MacKenzie, but he'd eventually brought them around, mostly by committing to provide them with special favours at the expense of the main faction.

Once he'd gained a measure of the Transcenders' trust, he'd engaged them in discussion about their own beliefs and goals. He'd tried to be empathetic, but every conversation had filled him with dread.

*If they get their way, they'll nail the doors shut and set fire to the place.*

# CHAPTER 25

**SpaceOp, Sunday 28th April**

A sense of relief passed through the main floor as the rocket cleared the launch pad, and ninety minutes later entered a stable orbit two thousand kilometres above Earth. Rocket Launch One – RL1 – had gone without a hitch.

SpaceOp had needed that success. Even though significant radiation from Liverpool had not yet materialised and there had been no more A-Grav malfunctions, gloom was weighing on everyone.

Tim, resigning himself to staying in Anglesey for at least another week, sat with Dexter helping with the news feeds – a job he shared with Sam.

MIDAS reported the reaction to RL1. Generally positive, alongside the usual moaning about lack of transparency, distrust of the Ankor's motives, and general hype about plutonium.

An alert sounded on his monitoring screen. The director of the CNSA, Director Qin, was about to make a formal statement.

> *'We call upon our colleagues across the globe to significantly increase the level of transparency with regards payloads. We recognise that most launch sites have been told by the Ankor to keep payload information secret. We suggest that humanity disregards that requirement. Furthermore, we would like the UK Space Agency to submit to a physical inspection. In anticipation of a positive response, People's Republic of China is sending an inspection team to Anglesey.'*

From what Tim had gleaned from canteen and corridor discussions, the Chinese request was justified. Although some people knew roughly what was arriving into the Storage Zone, no-one had sight of what was assembled in the final rocket inventory. The people who worked in Assembly even lived in different accommodation on the northern coast.

Tim kicked off a private search. The results came back in moments.

*SpaceOp CNSA Disagreement*
*CNSA worried about SpaceOp cargo*
*Trending words: Ballistics, Flight Path*

Clicking through, there was nothing official from the CNSA. They had only broadcast the request for an inspection. On the generic science chat boards a rumour was trending that the flight path of the RL1 launch was unusual and that the payload may not be simple 'nuts and bolts'.

Aware that Mission Control was unnaturally quiet, Tim glanced up.

MacKenzie, now under a semblance of control, had walked to the edge of the mezzanine level and addressed the room.

'My orders are agreed with both the prime minister and the Ankor. We will not invite any inspection teams from anywhere, be they Chinese, Russian, American, or United Nations. Rocket Launch One has been a success. We have nine more to go.'

MacKenzie returned to his desk.

'What do you think?' asked Dexter, who had slid his chair over.

'No idea. Have you heard anything?'

'No,' said Dexter. 'It's hard to see who could claim something was unusual about the flight path, given almost no-one would know what the payload was supposed to be.'

Movement in the corner of his eye drew Tim's attention to the door that led down to the MIDAS server room.

*Charlie.*

Had he just been with Sam? Or had he been in one of the other server rooms? Or had he been through the armoured door?

As Charlie walked towards the staircase, Tim tried to catch his eye.

Success. Charlie started veering towards him.

MacKenzie descended and intercepted Charlie.

Tim couldn't hear what was said, but Charlie was sent towards the main doors.

'Follow me, Boston,' said MacKenzie, now focusing on Tim.

Leading Tim through the rear doors, past the MIDAS server room and towards the armoured door, MacKenzie studiously avoided eye contact and small talk.

Once through the armoured doors, they followed the corridor as it descended with a shallow slope, turning left and right. The only light came from the thin strip lights on the roof, and their footsteps echoed.

They passed the room with all the network connections and the passive data sniffers.

They didn't stop.

A few minutes later, after Tim had judged they had descended three floors, they arrived at another set of closed doors. On the left was a bare table and an old-fashioned lift.

Juan stepped forward and opened the lift manually, simply sliding a metal grid door the side.

MacKenzie pointed at the table. 'Do you have anything electronic on you?'

Tim showed him his phone. Juan took it and put it on the table before taking out a handheld scanner and using it to frisk Tim thoroughly.

Once it was clear Tim was clean, MacKenzie pointed into the lift.

Tim entered, MacKenzie next, and finally Juan, who shut the doors behind them.

Juan turned what looked like a steering wheel from an old sailing ship.

*The lift is operated manually!*

They descended.

Inside the lift, Tim could hear Juan's breathing as he turned the wheel.

*I'm going to be murdered*

After a descent of perhaps two storeys, Juan stopped turning the wheel and opened the doors manually. A further set of doors, heavily reinforced, stood closed in front of them. Juan opened them.

MacKenzie entered, ushering Tim to follow him. Remaining on the outside, Juan closed the doors behind them, locking them in.

The floors and walls of the new room were covered in a series of metal meshes. MacKenzie indicated for Tim to stand on a two-metre-square concrete plate in the middle of the room which held nothing but a couple of plain wooden chairs.

MacKenzie operated some switches on the wall.

Nothing appeared to happen.

'I assume the Ankor can read every transmission, listen into every conversation, and probably mimic any electronic communication,' said MacKenzie. 'But this is a secure Faraday room. You know what they do?'

Tim nodded. A Faraday room blocked all electromagnetic radiation. There was no chance of the Ankor eavesdropping electronically.

*Unless they have incredibly advanced technology, like anti-gravity or faster-than-light travel …*

'I don't entirely trust the Ankor … or the Chinese,' said MacKenzie. 'I want to know what the Chinese payloads are.'

Tim remained silent. Outwardly, MacKenzie was doing everything he could to please the Ankor.

'What do you need from me?' asked Tim.

'I have obtained passwords for the main server room at the Chinese National Space Agency,' said MacKenzie.

'Haven't they closed down the internet?'

'I have a route in.'

Knowing that MacKenzie was technically literate, Tim didn't bother to bring up all the issues about firewalls and network controls. He had to assume that MacKenzie would have considered the basics. 'They'll notice the activity and close us down in a few seconds. Maybe trace us.'

'I assume it would only take MIDAS a few seconds to find the information if it knew what to look for.'

Tim thought about it. A few seconds was a long time for a computer – but searching petabytes of arbitrary data still took longer than that. 'Do you know what you're looking for?'

For a moment, MacKenzie stared at Tim. 'I can give you a file that holds the search data: key words, basic images.'

Tim looked towards MacKenzie's hands, expecting to be passed a zip drive.

'Juan has it,' said MacKenzie. 'He will give it to you five minutes before you run the incursion.'

*So, I can't be trusted to see it now …*

'They'll trace us,' said Tim. 'It won't look good.'

'I have a hard-wired network pipe running from the coast just north of us across the Irish Sea and into a school just outside Dublin,' said MacKenzie. 'Once the results come through, cut the connection.'

*That should work. The trail will go cold in a school in Ireland. It may look like a student.*

'Where's the access point?'

'In the room that holds the network security,' said MacKenzie. 'You can hook up MIDAS manually to the Dublin network from there.'

Tim had been in the room before, when installing various upgrades of MIDAS. Even six months ago, it had been thick with cabling, physical breakers, and data sniffers.

'Actually,' said Tim, 'if I'm just using MIDAS to search, I can load a copy onto a laptop and plug it in directly at the access point. That way, it won't be so easily traceable back to us.'

'You can get a full copy of MIDAS onto a laptop?' MacKenzie sounded incredulous.

'If it's used simply for basic search, yes. You use it here for complex analysis. That takes up almost all the processing and data space. By loading a clean copy onto a laptop, we can be sure it starts without Ankor viruses.'

'Okay.'

'In fact,' said Tim, now warming to the task, 'we could use MIDAS Production as a diversion. Have Sam run a hack at the same time, draw attention away from Dublin.'

'Can you do it now?' asked MacKenzie.

'It will take a couple of hours to prepare.'

MacKenzie nodded, turned to the box of switches on the wall, and deactivated the electric circuits. A moment later they were back in the elevator.

--------

'He's not asking for much, then,' said Sam, sitting in her wheelchair at the MIDAS server room admin workstation.

Tim shrugged. Carefully not saying anything remotely contentious, and using scraps of paper to write notes on, he'd given Sam the summary of his conversation with MacKenzie

234

which, although only forty minutes old, was already feeling like a dream sequence.

'How long will it take you to write the code?' asked Sam.

'Just over an hour,' said Tim. He hoped to be ready by midnight.

A few minutes later, Juan entered the server room silently, gave Tim a new laptop and left without saying a word.

With Sam next to him, Tim booted up the laptop, disabled all its wireless capability, ran virus searches, and using a zip drive copy of MIDAS, started editing the code.

The hack would not need to be complex – assuming the passwords provided by MacKenzie worked – but Tim knew the Chinese, or the Ankor, would shut him down quickly. He needed to buy some time to run the search.

The MIDAS search would run from the laptop, but at the same time, Tim would introduce a small piece of code into the servers of the CNSA systems. That piece of code would be a diversion. It would look like a search algorithm.

Tim wrote on the pad of paper.

**TWT**

'Twat?' she said, raising an eyebrow.

Tim wrote it in long hand.

**Time Wasting Trojan**

Sam gently squeezed his arm and leant in closer. 'Infinite loop?' she whispered.

'Yes,' whispered Tim.

Software development folklore held that it was incredibly difficult for a calculation engine, be it human or electronic, to tell whether a piece of logic would execute to completion or get stuck in an infinite loop.

Tim wrote a piece of code that was so recursive and convoluted that the most powerful computer would take a solid half-minute to validate its purpose. Granted, he imagined that the Ankor, if they were all over CNSA systems, would do it in seconds, but that was all MIDAS needed. In fact, three seconds would be enough for MIDAS to search fifty gigabytes of relevant data and return any matches related to MacKenzie's file. What MacKenzie would do with that information, Tim had no idea.

A little while later, Tim shut the laptop lid and pointed at the MIDAS access workstation. 'Let's call Juan?'

'I just need to stretch,' said Sam. She had been sitting immobile next to Tim the whole time. Her job had been to read the code as he wrote it, identify bugs, and suggest improvements. She'd done the job brilliantly, but at a personal cost.

Leaning heavily on Tim for support, Sam stood up and moved around the room on her crutches, stretching out her spine as much as she could.

'Is it bad?' asked Tim.

Settling back at the workstation, Sam sighed gently. 'I've been skipping the painkillers, trying to keep sharp.'

'You're the sharpest person I know,' said Tim. 'Even when thoroughly dosed up.'

Sam smiled. 'Once we get the money, I'll do the Korean thing.'

'Really?' said Tim, feeling a surge of joy. 'Really?'

Sam smiled too. 'Yes. Assuming all this works.'

Tim looked at her again. 'If you'd prefer to do the cauterisation, I'll fully support you.'

'Nice of you to finally say it,' said Sam, her face hardening just a fraction, 'what with it being not your body at all.'

'I'm sorry,' said Tim. 'I know it's your choice.'

It was the first time, as far as Tim could remember, that he'd wanted Sam to be pain-free even if it meant she would never walk again.

'It's going to be fine, dummy,' said Sam, looking at the MIDAS screen. 'Hold on … There are rumours circulating that we sent up passengers in RL1 … That's rubbish, isn't it? SpaceOp rockets accelerate far too fast for people to handle it.'

'Could experts get information on a rocket payload just from its flight path?' asked Tim.

'Let's ask the expert,' Sam said, typing. She read off the screen. 'Blah … blah … the flight path is based on the mass, the centre of mass, and the engine thrust. You can't reverse engineer the contents. But … this article confirms RL1 accelerated too fast for *comfortable* human flight.'

'Anything else?' said Tim, suddenly aware of how hard he was gripping his laptop.

'The alien retrieval of RL1 was a success. They sent down a craft to scoop it up,' said Sam. 'The CNSA reported that moments before RL1 was delivered to the main craft, twenty of the Ankor pods realigned in order to create a docking zone.'

Wanting to discuss the potential implications but, more critically, mindful of MacKenzie, Tim stood. 'I'd better get onto it.'

'Give Mac a kiss from me,' said Sam.

--------

Returning to the main floor of Mission Control which, even at the dead of night, was humming with purposeful activity, Tim noticed MacKenzie in deep conversation with four Leafer soldiers on the mezzanine level.

He walked over to the foot of the staircase but Juan waved him away. Tim joined Dexter at his desk instead.

'What's new?' asked Tim.

Dexter grimaced. 'We have two hundred people at the front gates of SpaceOp, demanding to see relatives who've been housed inside the Hot Zone.'

'In the middle of the night? And?'

'And MacKenzie is adamant that we remain in lockdown until after RL2,' said Dexter. 'He said … any one of them could be a saboteur.'

Tim turned his attention to the MIDAS news service. The standard reports showed the populations of the UK and elsewhere had calmed slightly. There was now a general acceptance that the radioactive A-Grav explosions had been accidents. This, however, had not stopped the general migration of people away from the known A-Grav locations. Tim noted a positive point, in that the exodus was a steady line of cars, not people fleeing on foot.

The next moment, Juan appeared at Tim's side. 'Now.'

'Okay,' said Tim, following Juan as he strode across the main floor and down towards the server rooms, not a flicker of emotion on his face.

As they passed the MIDAS server room, Tim stopped to tell Sam – via a written message on a notepad – to be ready to run the decoy hack.

Sam acknowledged the warning.

Tim and Juan continued through the armoured doors and to the network room. It was just as Tim had remembered it, a morass of cables and passive data sniffers.

Juan pointed out the network port that led to the Irish secondary school.

Tim plugged in his laptop and ran a series of tests to ensure the connection functioned and operated at sufficiently high speeds.

It took twenty minutes for Tim to be one hundred percent sure he was ready, then he asked Juan to tell Sam to perform the decoy hack.

The moment that Juan left, Tim sprang into action.

*I have five minutes.*

As far as Tim knew, he was in the most sensitive, and technically vulnerable, part of SpaceOp – and he'd decided to take the opportunity to find out how MacKenzie had used BinCubes created from individual name indexes.

He wanted to know where they were going and, here, in the bowels of MacKenzie's technology empire, was where he could find out.

*A quick look … prove to Sam I'm not totally under MacKenzie's spell.*

A data traffic monitor controlled the routing of the major network outputs: Anglesey Internal, Anglesey Data Uplink, and Internet Public. He checked its logs. They showed massive amounts of traffic in all directions since Wednesday, but readings from before then were blank. That was to be expected – MacKenzie had said he would clean it down after the earlier reinstall.

Of course, what MacKenzie probably knew – but had possibly forgotten – was that each of the major network outputs had their own independent passive data trackers which sent their own data movement information to the main data traffic monitor for reconciliation.

Those independent passive data trackers could not be remotely deleted.

So, Tim plugged the laptop into the admin port of the network box for the Internet Public route. It took a few seconds to burrow inside. The volumes arriving into SpaceOp were enormous – but the volumes sent out were small fractions of that. Tim searched the history – which went back for months. There was no record of MacKenzie having sent any BinCubes of data out.

*MacKenzie could have used a different delivery method.*

Conceptually, the MIDAS data outputs could be put on a series of disk drives and physically delivered.

*It couldn't have been sent by satellite, could it?*

Next, Tim queried the Anglesey Data Uplink.

As, he expected there were hundreds of petabytes streaming upwards – Anglesey was clearly being used as an aggregation point for the Ankor data suck.

He checked the timestamps of the active send periods. It looked very much like over the previous few weeks – since arrival – there had been a four-hour-long burst every time the Ankor mother ship was over Anglesey.

That didn't tell him anything about what MacKenzie had been doing with the files created on individual names. Obviously, they could be going to the Ankor along with everything else.

*Shit!*

Hands suddenly trembling, Tim double-checked the readings. The enormous volumes were not only in the last few weeks. As he scrolled down, more timestamps with large volumes of data appeared.

**22.02.2016**
**22.08.2016**
**12.02.2017**
**26.04.2017**
**13.05.2017**

The list went on. Of course, MacKenzie could have been sending this up to his own satellite. But that satellite was not in a geosynchronous orbit – it was in a medium altitude orbit – and so was only visible to the SpaceOp uplink for perhaps an hour at a time.

These two- and three-year-old data transmissions included hundreds of petabytes of data, and were being burst over six hour periods. The implication was they were being sent much further than Earth's orbit.

*Neptune?*

# CHAPTER 26

As he quickly refastened the plates on the data sniffer modules, Tim's mind raced. It was not necessarily the case that MacKenzie was a traitor. It could all be part of a benevolent plan. This could be the Ankor's way of getting things done. It could be that they felt some level of deceit was required to ensure humanity met the requirements to build the deflector shield.

That was plausible.

It was also possible Francis MacKenzie had simply been pumping data into space in an arbitrary way.

*Shit.*

*Fuck.*

*Shit.*

Tim didn't believe a word of his terrified mind's attempts to rationalise what he'd discovered.

*I have to tell someone.*

The problem was that if the Ankor and MacKenzie were in league, Tim would never get a message out via the internet. The Ankor were too strong.

*Although …*

An idea started to form.

The door opened.

Juan entered the small room and handed over the zip drive containing the search files. 'Decoy in two minutes.'

Tim opened the local search copy of the MIDAS application on the laptop and plugged in Juan's zip drive.

'Ready.'

Next, Juan passed Tim a piece of paper with the passwords and network address for the CNSA datacentre.

His mouth dry, Tim reached for the keyboard.

Juan grabbed Tim's hand, holding up one finger.

Tim checked the time; Juan was correct, they had one minute before Sam was going to run the decoy.

'Sorry,' said Tim, taking a moment to reflect. His goal was to ensure that the Chinese understood MacKenzie's relationship with the Ankor. Specifically, that MacKenzie had probably been in contact with them for over a few years – in direct contrast to the story that MacKenzie and the Ankor were pushing.

Tim couldn't be sure that China, or any other country with launch facilities, didn't have a similar relationship with the Ankor. The Ankor could have been secretly preparing Earth for years through secret communications with any number of countries.

Warning the Chinese could have fatal consequences if they were also in league with the Ankor, and overall the Ankor's motives were bad for humanity.

*Then again …*

On the basis that Tim had been instructed to spy on the Chinese, it was likely MacKenzie had a toxic relationship with them. That made it a little less likely they were all in league together. Plus, the Chinese had been publicly critical of the Ankor.

It was worth the risk.

His plan hinged on accepting that, although the Ankor were massively overpowered in terms of computing ability, they remained limited by the speed of light. So, unless they'd managed to install thousands of sentient computing resources, each with permission to make unilateral decisions, they would have to observe, decide, and act, from their orbit. Messages to and from the CNSA datacentre would take fractions of a second. It should be a large enough window for what he planned.

Hopefully, the Chinese were just as worried as everyone else about alien interference and would be watching all their data access points for unusual behaviour.

Juan shook Tim's shoulder. It was time.

Tim navigated to the correct network address and was prompted for a password.

'Could I get a little more light please?' asked Tim, nodding towards the switch on the wall.

Juan walked over to the light switch and Tim quickly entered the password: 26A 18D 1D7 2AF.

The password was rejected, as Tim knew it would be.

A rush of adrenaline flooded through him. His hair felt like it was standing on end, and he could feel the blood pumping across his skull.

Juan was coming back.

Tim entered a different password: 508 4BF 414 4EC.

This password was also rejected. Of course.

Tim dared not look around.

Finally, he entered the correct password that MacKenzie had given him: ZZ3 8QB TP7 9XA.

This final password worked. He was inside the CNSA data centre.

He ran the macro on his laptop. It simultaneously loaded the diversionary trojan and triggered the local copy of MIDAS to search for files, words, images, anything that correlated to the materials on the zip drive MacKenzie had provided.

Within two seconds, the initial results were back.

No matches – the search was giving null returns.

With Juan now watching him carefully, Tim checked manually.

The connection was holding. They were inside the CNSA datacentre. Tim could see listings of files, servers and databases.

Tim selected one at random and looked more closely.

It was empty.

He checked another.

Empty.

A few seconds later the connection was broken.

Tim turned to Juan. 'We'd better report to Mr MacKenzie.'

Juan pulled out the connection cord and took the laptop in one of his massive hands.

Tim followed, his plan hinged on someone in China noticing the first two failed password attempts and wondering what had happened. If they did that, then a Chinese data security man would hopefully notice that the first two passwords, unlike the real one, had been submitted in hexadecimal format.

If they then ran the code through a simple brute force decoding algorithm, they'd receive a plaintext comment that Francis MacKenzie had been in contact with the Ankor at least a year before their first global broadcast.

*Just the accusation. Not the proof.*

*Shit!*

As Tim followed Juan back up to the main floor, he desperately wanted to run. His hands were shaking. If he could reach back in time ten minutes, he'd stop himself from doing the hack. The Ankor, if they'd seen it, would have already decoded it and told MacKenzie.

*Stop it …*

Tim knew his thoughts were only self-preservation. This was bigger than him.

--------

Back in their flat, Tim sat with Sam sat in the bathroom with all the taps running at full power, hoping the noise and steam would be enough to confuse any covert surveillance.

Using their notepad method of scribbling notes under folded paper, Tim told Sam how it went.

Sam approved.

Now, sitting close, whispering into each other's ears and using oblique language where required, they discussed the wider parts.

'What did MacKenzie say about the empty files?' asked Sam.

'Nothing, other than perhaps we'd try again in a day or so.'

'But he took the laptop away,' said Sam. 'We don't have any idea what the search was.'

'When I was watching it, I saw some of the single word references,' said Tim. 'But it was all predictable stuff: plutonium, tungsten …' He paused. 'There was a bunch of chemical formulae.'

'Remember any of them?'

Tim thought back; most of them had been very long, but one short one had stood out. '$CH_2O$.'

Sam took the computer tablet they had to access the MIDAS news service and ran the search. 'Formaldehyde … disinfectant.'

Sam reverted to the written note technique.

**Briars?**

Tim replied by written note.

**Not seen for a few days … can't trust anyone but Martel.**

Sam wrote again.

**Leave SpaceOp. During RL2 pre-launch? Raise the alarm.**

He nodded. They needed to tell Martel the latest.

'I have an idea …' said Sam, reaching for her own laptop.

She opened the MIDAS software Tim had written to track Anglesey residents' arrival. It produced an accurate map of SpaceOp on the tablet screen, with indication of where people were bunching.

As Dexter had said, there were a few hundred people at the front gate.

'They're demanding to have their family returned, but refusing to enter,' said Sam, and then mouthed the words 'good cover'.

'Yes.' If Tim and Sam could get to the main gate it should be easy to slip away. But the main gate was a good two miles away, with a multitude of electronic gates and razor wire.

They would need their car.

> I can try to get to the car park. If stopped,
> I'll say that you need additional medication.

'Now?' asked Sam.

'No time like the present.'

Sam took the notepad.

> Avoid Hot Zone

He nodded.

Sam continued to write.

> Rumour of a shooting yesterday

'Understood,' said Tim, standing.

'Good luck', mouthed Sam with an encouraging smile.

Tim left the flat and walked towards the car park. All the roads were lit with powerful floodlights but anything more than a few metres off the road was pitch black.

Adopting a confident air that was far from the reality, Tim walked purposefully along the main road, as if he knew exactly where he was going and he had the right to be doing so.

Not that anyone else was around to challenge him: it was four o'clock in the morning.

After a five-minute walk, he reached the entrance to the car park. Unfortunately, a locked steel gate barred his way.

Tim tentatively reached out to the gate, for a moment considering climbing it.

*No chance.*

It was four metres high, had anti-climbing paint, and was topped with razor wire.

Tim could see his car, not more than twenty metres away.

He scanned the area.

There was another route into the car park. An entrance to the east appeared to be open; all Tim had to do was approach the car park from the other side.

The road followed the fence along the northern edge of the car park. Tim headed east along it.

In the distance to the north, he could see the lights of Mission Control. Only dry-stone walls separated him from it. Unfortunately, the way he wanted to go was south, and that was entirely closed off with chain-linked fences.

After another few minutes of walking, it became clear that he was now twenty times further away from his car, and …

*I'm walking into the fucking Hot Zone.*

He had a choice: continue on the road; walk in near-total darkness north of the road but closer to the Hot Zone; or walk on the scrub between the road and the fence, semi-lit by the car park lights.

Instinctively, Tim chose the scrub by the fence.

It was a good choice. The terrain was slightly undulating, meaning that low hills – a few metres high – surrounded him at times.

A few hundred metres away to the north-east, just outside the Hot Zone main gates, two Leafers in full hazmat suits and armed with assault rifles were patrolling.

Through those gates to the north, Tim could see the lights of Warehouse C – the arrival warehouse.

To his south, the chain-linked fence ran unbroken for only fifty metres before turning south.

Tim wondered if he dared continue.

Just as he decided to press on, to try to sneak around that corner, one of the soldiers looked directly at him.

*Shit!*

The Leafer hefted his rifle up into the aim position.

Acting on instinct Tim threw himself down and, on his hands and knees, scurried into a small depression by the fence.

The low hill blocked the view of the Leafers.

Peeking out from the hollow, Tim looked.

They had not left the main gates but were looking his way.

*Gotta get out of the light …*

Mouth suddenly dry, he searched for cover. On the north side of the road there was a low dry-stone wall and beyond that the pitch darkness of the fields that separated the Administration Zone from Mission Control.

Keeping low, Tim scurried over the road and launched himself into the fields, clipping his shin on the wall in the process.

Looking over his shoulder, he saw to his relief the Leafers had still not left their posts.

Unfortunately, it seemed a message had been relayed.

In the distance, he could make out urgent movement around the Hot Zone. The headlights of a jeep flared, and it was heading for the gates.

The flat was only a mile away across the fields.

Tim sprinted, judging the Leafers had a three-mile circuitous trip on the roads.

His guts were churning. Up ahead, heavy bushes marked the boundary between two fields. Tim didn't slow.

A sweep of headlights to his left, still half a mile away.

Tim's anger towards MacKenzie built rapidly, until he was overcome with an incandescent rage. Those Leafers were armed, and stories about severe adherence to curfews and off-limits areas were constantly being bandied around the canteen.

He was also angry with himself. His idea to simply walk up the main road had been ludicrous. Smart, he was. Street smart, not so much.

Looking around again, Tim could no longer see the headlights, but that didn't mean safety. All of SpaceOp was dotted with walls and small depressions. Additionally, he couldn't be sure they hadn't radioed for back-up in the Administration Zone itself. They could be waiting for him up ahead using infrared to track him in the darkness.

The perimeter of the accommodation blocks loomed. There was no-one in sight.

A low dry-stone wall was his last obstacle. He slowed to climb over it.

Once over, he looked around again to get his bearings.

At that moment, a man in a hazmat suit reared up from behind the wall, grabbed Tim in a tackle, and wrestled him to the ground.

For a moment he struggled, but the man was inconceivably stronger than he was. Within seconds Tim was locked in a pressure point hold with a shooting pain running down his left side.

'Stop struggling!' his assailant said, in strangely accented English. 'If they see us, we're dead.'

Tim stopped.

The person took off their protective hood. It was a middle-aged Chinese woman. Her face was incredulous. 'So, you just walked down the main road to the Hot Zone? People don't come out of there.'

'Who are you?'

'Major Chen,' she said. 'People's Republic of China. We got your message.'

'How did you know it was me?'

'Instinct … and observation,' replied Chen.

'How could you have got here in time?'

Major Chen laughed and loosened the pressure point grip. 'I've been here all the time. Cleaning lady.'

'What do you know?'

She looked forlorn. 'We haven't managed to get anyone inside yet. But we suspect …'

'What?'

'I cannot say.'

The noise of a jeep engine in the distance brought the conversation to an abrupt halt. Again, headlights, coming their way, were clearly visible on the main road.

'We go,' said Major Chen, releasing the hold she had on Tim and leading him into the outskirts of the Administration Zone.

Obviously knowing exactly where she was going, she led him into a small cleaning supplies hut and locked the door behind them.

Whilst Tim took a few deep breaths and tried to regain his composure, Chen looked out of the small window.

'They've turned back,' she said after a few minutes.

'Please, what do you know?' asked Tim.

Major Chen shook her head. 'I am not at liberty to say. I saved your life. Return to your flat.'

# CHAPTER 27

**SpaceOp, Monday 29th April**

Preparations for RL2 had run smoothly throughout the day, and at a little after nine in the evening Francis MacKenzie gave final authorisation for the launch to proceed.

This one, and another eight scheduled rockets, would provide the materials so desperately needed by the Ankor. It remained to be seen whether the Ankor would meet their commitments. At a minimum, the work Kusr had done indicated with a large degree of confidence that the Ankor were able to augment their biological brains with technology.

*Will they provide that augmentation for me?*

If they changed their minds and refused to accept him then his current life on Earth would be over; he'd have to work fast, and ruthlessly, to secure any life at all.

Originally, he'd demanded that they allow him to be launched in one of the first rockets. The Ankor had not agreed. '*Have faith*', they'd said. Their concern, quite reasonably, had been that subterfuge could not have been maintained if he'd been on an early launch. He could only come at the end, once he'd met all his commitments.

Of course, he'd pushed, and they'd called his bluff, saying they could always work with another party.

So he'd backed down.

Backed down – and introduced an immensely complicated set of fail-safes to ensure that he was critical for every single one of the launches. Any hint of a double-cross from the Ankor and he could pull the plug.

They knew it.

MacKenzie sighed. Activating the clean-up routine would ultimately mean the deaths of most people within SpaceOp. In some of his quieter moments he thought that if the time came, he may possibly decide not to push that button.

But, of course, he would. To be caught at this stage would be effectively to die.

A buzzer indicated half an hour to go. Now most people on the main floor of Mission Control had a spectating role.

Up on the wall, the dedicated SpaceOp channel displayed the pre-launch routines of RL2.

Movement at the foot of the stairs drew MacKenzie's attention.

Charles Taylor had arrived and was indicating he had something to discuss.

MacKenzie indicated to Juan to allow him up.

'They know about the wolf mix,' said Taylor, arriving by the desk and angling himself carefully to avoid anyone overhearing. 'They're not happy.'

MacKenzie smiled to himself. He hadn't expected his manipulation of the RL1 payload to go unnoticed for long. Quite simply, the plan was always for the whole of RL1 to be delivered to the Transcender faction – and, at their request, he'd added a significant number of extra wolves. Of course, he hadn't checked with the main Ankor group, or told them he was sucking up to the Transcenders. After all, they were the ones who had from the earliest discussions advocated orbital bombing Earth into submission.

'What's done is done.'

Taylor's eyes flashed. 'You're making them stronger.'

MacKenzie remained silent; he knew where Taylor's touch points were, and top of the list were the Transcenders. It was the only significant area Taylor's position diverged from the formal Ankor doctrine – the Ankor looked upon the Transcender faction like a prodigal son, only one epiphany away from full reunification.

*Albeit they've been waiting for a hundred thousand years.*

'The Transcenders are not to be trusted,' said Taylor.

'I trust the Ankor, all of them, to act in their own best interests,' replied MacKenzie, wondering as he spoke whether those best interests might include the Ankor having alternative arrangements with another launch site.

'You're judging them by your own values,' said Taylor, oblivious to MacKenzie's fears. 'They're guided by their faith – a faith underpinned by countless millennia of continuous reflection and reaffirmation.'

*Perhaps the very first Ankor could be given that accord all those countless millennia ago … but since then, I suspect it falls into the category of 'give me a boy until he's seven.'*

MacKenzie left the inflammatory words about religious brainwashing unsaid. He would soon be rid of Taylor. There was no benefit in having an argument.

'They're not to be trusted,' repeated Taylor, staring intently at MacKenzie.

MacKenzie shook his head and changed the subject. 'What did you find out about the disturbance near the Hot Zone yesterday?'

He could see Taylor thinking, but whether he was dwelling on their previous argument or trying to remember something about the disturbance, he didn't know. 'Well?'

'It was just a cleaner who wandered the wrong way.'

MacKenzie nodded and turned his attention back to the bank of screens on the main wall.

The countdown started.

Ignition happened at exactly the correct moment … and RL2 cleared the tower.

A small cheer went up around the main floor as the rocket kept to its designated flight path.

An Ankor message appeared on MacKenzie's private workstation.

## Lieutenant Hardy almost penetrated the payload for RL2. Remove him.

One of the two remaining members of Martel's liaison team, Lieutenant Hardy had been at the Payload Zone overseeing the final moments of RL2 preparation. He would be an easy ambush target on his way back through the trenches.

MacKenzie walked over to the back of the mezzanine. Whispering so that Taylor couldn't hear, but aware the Ankor would be able to, he spoke to Juan. 'Ensure that Lieutenant Hardy doesn't make it back.'

Without a word, Juan slipped away.

Juan was 'on the grid' in the sense that he had a radio the Ankor tracked and could use to communicate with him directly. However, his team of four ghosts – all battle-hardened knife fighters – were kept in the corridors below the Hot Zone with no electronics.

MacKenzie had developed the team a few years previously for special tasks that he wanted to keep secret from the Ankor. Once the Ankor had made orbit, and their technological prowess had become apparent, keeping the ghosts hidden had become futile; MacKenzie now used them on Ankor business.

*Another miscalculation … although hopefully with no harmful side effects.*

Ten minutes later, the rocket reached the correct orbital height and started manoeuvring into its retrieval orbit.

A short sharp siren sounded, followed by an automated announcement on the internal speakers. 'Contact lost.'

*Lost?*

MacKenzie took a breath, fingered the diazepam in his pocket, and counted to five.

Meanwhile, Taylor ran to the front of the mezzanine ledge and shouted down. 'Get a visual.'

It wasn't easy.

Cameras had been following the rocket, but RL2 had finished all its boost phases when contact was lost so was not now emitting much light from the exhaust. There hadn't been an obvious explosion.

The noise from the main floor rose, as technicians darted between desks trying to re-establish contact.

'Contact lost,' was repeated. The calmness of the automated voice contrasted sharply with the panic that MacKenzie could see on every face. He waved over to the communications team, signalling for them to utilise the auxiliary uplink on the roof. The technician indicated she was already doing so, and was receiving no response.

'What happened? What do we do?' Taylor asked in a low whisper, having returned to the workstation.

'Maybe a malfunction,' said MacKenzie. 'More likely sabotage.'

Rocket malfunctions happened. Most accidents occurred in the first few minutes of take-off when maximum power was being applied. However, RL2 had been under no power, just falling into its stable orbit when contact was lost.

Outside, sirens blared.

Taylor stood next to the desk, anguish etched all over his face. He appeared close to tears. 'Genocide,' he said, barely in control.

'Pull yourself together,' said MacKenzie, fighting his own demons.

For the next few minutes, the whole of Mission Control checked, rechecked, and double-checked.

RL2 had gone.

MacKenzie thought for a moment. Only the Chinese, the Russians or the Americans had the ability.

'It's genocide,' repeated Taylor, resting his shaking hands on the desk.

'Whoever did it,' said MacKenzie, 'we're lucky it wasn't the first launch.'

RL1 had contained the far rarer wolves, but the payload of the second launch could be replaced easily enough. The Ankor needed the volume, but the same materials would be loaded into all the other launches through to RL9.

'We probably won't even need a replacement launch,' said MacKenzie, his mind getting over the shock and starting to process the consequences. The RL2 explosion was an interesting data point. It meant a more forceful defence than they'd been expecting was being marshalled by some parts of humanity.

A new message had appeared on the main screen.

'People's Republic of China confirms it destroyed the Anglesey RL2. An orbiting electromagnetic railgun charge was used. We regret the loss of materials for the deflector shield. However, given our limited data, we assume this represented less than one percent of the total required materials. People's Republic of China expects full disclosure from all parties. We urge the UK SpaceOp to invite an independent team of inspectors from across the United Nations to verify and validate payloads.'

Forcing himself not to laugh out loud, MacKenzie made a big show of gravely rereading the message. The Chinese had committed an act of war against the Ankor.

*I am the only game in town!*

Had it been the Americans or the Russians, his position would not have changed notably. But it was the Chinese –

the only other group on Earth who could conceivably be working with the Ankor.

A news screen popped up on the main wall.

**People's Republic of China will now move all communications broadcast to long-wave radio 186 kHz**

The LW radio broadcast decision was a pragmatic choice: it would be difficult for the Ankor to intercept and manipulate.

A few minutes later, another screen started displaying the LW radio feed in text form as a news ticker.

**Russia and China agree full and continuous disclosure via long-wave radio. Furthermore, given that payload and ballistic information has not been disclosed by the UK SpaceOp, the president of the People's Republic of China has asked the UK prime minister for an emergency summit.**

A few moments later a United Nations broadcast message came through, duplicated on the usual internet channel and the more secure LW radio feed.

**The UN condemns the use of weapons in space by the PRC as a flagrant treaty violation. The General Assembly has confirmed the Ankor has its official support. Further use of weapons in this way will attract an immediate military response.**

There was still no response from the Ankor on the initial RL2 explosion.

MacKenzie stood slowly and walked to the edge of the mezzanine level.

Immediately the main floor went deathly still.

'The Chinese may have just condemned humanity to extinction,' said MacKenzie, addressing the whole room.

'There is time to send up replacement parts, but our ability to shield the Earth from gamma rays rests entirely on the goodwill of our visitors. What the Chinese did was criminally insane. Their reasoning equally so.' He paused. 'I had been in discussions with the prime minister to allow some level of international presence here. It seems, however, that it would merely be giving in to trigger-happy bully-boys. This facility is in full lockdown. No-one arrives, and no-one leaves.'

The screen covering global launch schedules updated. All launch facilities, except the Chinese who had already stood down, continued to report they were on track.

'Questions?' asked MacKenzie.

Voices murmured below him. One spoke up.

'Was there any plutonium in the RL2 payload?'

'No, the proposed plutonium has not yet arrived in SpaceOp,' he replied. 'It may never do so now we have the refugees. I believe one of the other launch sites can provide most of it.'

'How will the Ankor respond to China?'

MacKenzie shook his head. 'I don't know that.'

'Can we still make the shield?'

'As I said, we have the materials and the time to make the shield. Whether we have broken our relationship with the Ankor is another matter.'

Unwilling to take more questions, MacKenzie returned to his desk. The Chinese probably thought themselves very clever. If the RL2 payload was just a bunch of parts, then no-one could be too angry. The Ankor could make comments, but any retaliation by taking Chinese lives would be an unjustifiable escalation.

*We'll see …*

Back at his desk, MacKenzie pondered. Did he need to do anything more? Was the British army on its way?

MacKenzie typed out a short direct message to the Ankor.

*I assume no change to Anglesey plans. Please*
*confirm. Please tell me what you intend to do*
*about PRC violation.*

MacKenzie's workstation flashed briefly.

## *RL3 to go ahead. Increase*
## *wolf ratio to maximum.*

*Maximum* …

MacKenzie assumed this was the main Ankor response to the fact the Transcenders had manipulated him over RL1. He typed a quick response.

*Understood.*

At that point, Juan returned and gave a computer tablet to MacKenzie.

MacKenzie turned it on.

A video recording was queued ready to play.

Black and white footage showed Lieutenant Hardy being dragged into a small concrete room. There was no interrogation … or procrastination.

Juan, in centre shot, took three steps across the concrete floor and, drawing his knife, pushed it under Hardy's rib cage, angling it up into the heart. As Hardy slipped to the floor, already dead, Juan pulled his body upright. Two more Leafers – Juan's ghosts – entered the room carrying a body bag. In seconds, Hardy was stuffed into it and carried out of the room.

MacKenzie couldn't bring himself to feel much sympathy for Hardy. He'd been an enemy combatant, after all.

He turned his attention back to the main screens which were showing news item responses to the Chinese proclamation. There was a surprising amount of support for

259

the Chinese. Would the Ankor respond to China's act of aggression?

They couldn't do it openly. And, even if they could, they wouldn't if there was no risk to future deliveries – their faith constrained them to a moral structure which considered life sacred.

Of course, if the Transcenders got their way, a multitude of 'accidental' radiation releases would issue from A-Gravs across China.

The next twenty-four hours would give MacKenzie some insight into the balance of power between the Ankor and the Transcenders.

# CHAPTER 28

**SpaceOp, Monday 29th April**

Dawn approached, and without having slept at all, Sam looked out of the window of the flat. The whole of SpaceOp was in double lockdown: first for the radioactive cloud which had missed SpaceOp days before, and second to minimise the chances of an invasion of Chinese personnel demanding on-the-ground inspections.

Sam smiled. She'd done it a lot over the twenty-four hours since Tim had returned from his password deception and Hot Zone escapade. He'd been quite the questing hero, trying to find out about MacKenzie's 'n less than five' data shenanigans for her.

Her smile slipped. Of course, what they found out was worse. MacKenzie was a traitor.

*Not 'maybe a traitor' like Tim says … a genuine fucking traitor.*

Now all they did was watch the highly regulated news feeds, look out of the window, and wonder when the door would be kicked down.

Sam reached for the pencil and notepad.

*Go into Mission Control?*

Tim rubbed his left armpit, where Sam understood the massive bruise courtesy of Major Chen was turning purple, then replied.

*Let's wait until summoned.*

*If MacKenzie suspected anything, we'd be dead by now.*

Moving onto her crutches, Sam hobbled into the small kitchenette and prepared a sandwich, musing on the subject. It was convoluted, to say the least. If MacKenzie was part of a benevolent Ankor plan – which he wasn't – then he'd probably just keep Tim and Sam under a watchful eye.

Which could be what was happening now.

*Is he?*

Taking her sandwich back to the living room, she lowered herself onto the sofa and turned on the television. Most channels were blocked inside SpaceOp, but Tim had thoughtfully packed a small Blu-ray player and a bucket full of discs. He knew that she was often awake during the night.

*A bright spark in my dark night.*

Sam sighed, and shifted her weight around, trying to find a sitting position that was pain-free.

Flicking through the available channels on the television, she continued to think. There was plenty of outrage about the RL2 destruction, but much of it was mixed with more balanced arguments that said the Ankor should be more accommodating. The prevalent opinion on MacKenzie was that he was right to continue with the launches.

Notably, there was zero coverage on any of the channels of the protests by the Anglesey residents, and zero coverage of the fact that the Liverpool explosion had not deposited any significant radiation in the area. Nonetheless, all shots of SpaceOp included multiple scenes of people in radiation protection suits.

'Maybe they're still preparing for incoming plutonium,' said Tim, sitting down next to her and somehow reading her mind. 'But … MacKenzie has consistently said no plutonium yet.'

A jolt of pain shot up Sam's left side as she gingerly rotated to shift her weight. Taking a deep breath, she continued the movement.

'Take an elephant tranquiliser,' said Tim. 'I'll stay awake.'

Sam doubted it; Tim looked more tired than she was. He hadn't slept either.

'Go on,' said Tim.

Reaching for her bag, she took out one of her strongest painkillers; if past performance was anything to go by, then it would give her four hours' sleep.

Tim passed her a cup of water.

'Thanks,' she said, swallowing the pill.

'It'll be fine,' said Tim.

A few minutes later, the cool warmth spread over her, and Sam felt herself slipping into a doze.

*What if it isn't?*

--------

It was mid-afternoon when Sam woke, stiff but for once not in pain. Looking over, she saw Tim on the other side of the sofa, also asleep.

*You're supposed to be on watch!*

Sam smiled. She didn't blame him in the slightest.

Reaching for her crutches, she tried to get up without disturbing him. As she rose, a few snippets of her dreams came back to her. She'd dreamt about Tim. The details were blurred but they'd definitely been a couple. Her smile faded.

She knew he'd been about to ask her out on the night of the crash. Apparently, he'd planned the whole thing: gaming evening, pizza, and the start of an awesome relationship. He'd also prepared a speech about how the fact he was her boss didn't matter to him and he was happy to fire her – or resign himself – to make things simpler.

A knock at the door disturbed her thoughts.

It was Charlie's knock.

*Shit!*

Obviously, Charlie was better than a detachment of Leafer killers, but not by much.

Sam pushed open the door. 'Tim's asleep.'

'Leave him,' said Charlie. 'We need to talk.'

They hugged – Charlie holding on tightly and kissing her on the side of her face.

Charlie released her and turned to a carrier bag on the floor. 'Tea?' he asked.

Sam put a finger to her lips. She didn't want to wake Tim.

Nodding his understanding, Charlie went through into the kitchen and started brewing a pot of tea.

Sam followed. 'What's the latest?'

Charlie's brow furrowed. 'The Chinese aren't apologising for RL2.'

'I don't expect they will,' said Sam. 'They think they're in the right.'

Charlie didn't answer, but she could hear him muttering under his breath as he prepared the tea, occasionally reaching up and pulling gently at his shirt collar.

'All okay?' asked Sam, noticing a bandage poking out from his neckline.

Charlie remained silent. He finished making the tea and brought it over to the kitchen table.

They both sat. Finally he spoke.

'You know how experts on consciousness are generally divided on whether the human brain could feasibly be simulated by a computer?'

Sam knew, of course. It was something she and Charlie had discussed a good many times. The theory was an extension of the NPCs – non-player characters – who were unaware they were characters in a computer game. It wasn't a one-sided argument; there were many respected academics who claimed the human brain was more than the sum of its parts and could never be wholly simulated.

She nodded.

'The Ankor,' said Charlie, his eyes blazing for a second, 'believe we are all living in a simulation.'

'How do you know what they believe?'

Charlie's jaw clenched. 'They've told me.'

Sam searched for a crack in his argument. 'Just you?'

Charlie frowned. 'No, I think they've told a few people. They've certainly told Francis.'

'He believes them?' asked Sam. The question of whether Charlie believed was moot. The animation on his face was enough.

'Not yet,' said Charlie. 'I think he is still preparing himself to believe.'

'So we all live in a computer simulation?'

'Yes,' said Charlie. 'But not just us … everything in this universe …'

'And the Ankor?' asked Sam, wondering whether they were the programmers.

'Everything,' he said, nodding stiffly. 'The Ankor are flesh and blood like us – just part of the universe that has been constructed.'

'They're biological?' Sam had been sure the Ankor were rogue artificial intelligence computers.

Charlie paused. 'They … utilise technology to augment their biological capabilities.'

'And what does this universe simulation mean for us?'

'That's why I'm here now. I want to show you,' said Charlie, looking at his watch. 'Timing is critical. We have to leave in ten minutes.'

'Why?'

'I can't say any more. We have to go now,' said Charlie.

'Why so urgent?' The temperature in the room had suddenly dropped. Sam shivered.

Charlie refilled Sam's cup, and then his own.

'You don't have to be in pain any more,' he said.

Sam couldn't bring herself to voice the obvious follow-up questions.

*What does he mean? Healing? Neural cauterisation? … Death?*

A few months before the aliens had arrived, she and Tim had had a terrible argument about her plans to have her lower spinal nerves cauterised. She'd said some horrendous things to him. She'd accused him of allowing her continued suffering to keep his own hope alive.

```
Sam: It's my body. My choice
Tim: There are other options
Sam: Which require horse tranquilisers for me
to sleep at night
Tim: Just a few more months
Sam: So you can hold onto your dream of a
clear conscience
Tim: I feel responsible!
Sam: You fucking are responsible! And now you
want me all patched so I'm worth screwing
again
```

That outburst had been followed by a very quiet working environment in the office for a week. Sam had known she'd gone too far. On the Friday, she'd half-apologised and Tim had happily blamed the outburst on her medication – which was possibly true.

Charlie took a sip of tea, his expression flitting between bliss and fear. He checked his watch again. 'We need to go now.'

'Where?'

'The server room. I'll explain it all there.' Charlie indicated with a wave of his hands that he too was sure they were under surveillance. 'Tim needs to come as well.'

Sam gave Tim a gentle shake.

Tim woke and rubbed his eyes. 'What's going on?'

Charlie signalled for silence.

Sam smiled at Tim with a shrug.

'We have to go,' said Charlie, going on to repeat only the most salient points and not taking any questions as he hurried them all out of the flat.

Ten minutes later, when the three of them arrived at Mission Control, Charlie didn't take them through the main door. He led them around the northern side of the building. They came to a side door, almost invisible. Charlie took out a heavy iron key and unlocked it.

The room behind the door was tiny: it contained just a chair … and another door.

Without saying anything, Charlie opened the second door and Sam wheeled herself through into a narrow corridor, gently sloping downwards.

A few minutes later, they arrived at another door that led into the back of a dimly lit server room. It wasn't the MIDAS room, but another generic one.

'Do you want a push?' asked Charlie.

Sam shook her head. Of course she did; there was a crippling pain running up and down her left-hand side. 'No, thank you.'

Leaving the server room, Sam got her bearings. They were now in the antechamber holding the armoured door. Charlie swiped his card and they went through it.

Once the armoured door had closed behind them, Charlie stopped. 'I'll keep this brief. Francis is planning to kill both of you in the next few hours. He knows about Sam's hack a few weeks ago.' Charlie's eyes flashed with something that looked like anger. 'And he's pretty sure you were involved in some way with the Chinese blowing up RL2.'

Sam opened her mouth to speak.

Charlie held out his hand for silence. 'Follow me.'

They followed the corridor, sloping ever-downwards, for another five minutes until Charlie stopped them outside another unmarked side door.

'I don't have time to explain it all.' He turned to Tim. 'This door leads east, a long way, well past the SpaceOp perimeter. Once you're outside, about half a mile south-east is a farmyard. There's a car hidden in one of the sheds. Find it, take it, and go.'

A million questions jumped into Sam's head.

'Why can't we all go?' asked Tim, his eyes narrowing.

'There's more than one escape route,' replied Charlie. 'If we split up we have more chance to go undetected.'

'Thanks, I guess,' said Tim slowly. 'But I'm not leaving Sam.'

'She'll be safe with me,' said Charlie, bending down and inspecting the thick cabling that lined the corridor. 'I designed this place. I laid a lot of the cabling myself. We're hidden from everyone down here. Francis only has a few CCTVs …'

Selecting a few wires, Charlie took out a pair of pliers and cut through them. 'Now even he can't see us past this point.'

'I'm not leaving Sam,' said Tim.

Charlie held up a hand for silence. It held a gun.

Sam, well versed in online games, recognised the powerful handgun – a Glock 19.

*What the …?*

'I am doing my best to save you, Tim,' said Charlie.

'Fuck's sake, Charlie!' said Sam. 'What's this about?'

'We don't have time for this,' said Charlie, keeping his gun trained on Tim but also checking his watch. 'We have to go.'

'I'm not leaving Sam,' repeated Tim, not taking his eyes off Charlie.

'Have I ever done anything but love and protect her?' said Charlie. 'More than that: with me she'll be pain-free. Have you ever managed to give her that, Tim?' He paused. 'She's better off with me.'

Sam looked at Charlie. What did he mean 'pain-free'? A suicide pact?

Palms sweating, Sam considered her options. Charlie's gun was pointing directly at Tim's chest. He couldn't miss from that range. Sam could see the situation escalating horribly. She wanted to stay with Tim, but she couldn't face seeing him shot in the name of chivalry … or love.

'I'll go with Charlie,' said Sam, deciding on *play-dead* mode.

'If you can't come with me then I'm staying here,' said Tim. His eyes burned into Sam's. He didn't believe she was safe with Charlie. He wasn't going to let it go.

Sam couldn't allow him to be hurt. 'Let's tie him up, Charlie. MacKenzie may see him as the victim.'

'Unlikely,' Charlie grunted. 'He'll be shot on sight.'

Cutting a length of electric cabling from the thick bundle running along the corridor, Charlie tied Tim up. He pretended to trust Sam not to jump him, whilst obviously thinking she was about to attack him at any moment.

Once Tim was tied up, Charlie took him just through the side door and laid him face down on the floor.

Before leaving, he clubbed Tim on the back of the head with his pistol.

Sam gasped involuntarily.

'His only chance is to take the corridor under the fences,' said Charlie, shutting the door as he came back into the main corridor. 'He may do that if he thinks we're long gone.'

'Does MacKenzie know we're here?'

'Maybe,' said Charlie. 'But I'm often down here on his business. We'll be okay if we meet anyone.'

At least three storeys below ground, in a dimly lit concrete corridor, Sam shuddered at the thought of meeting anyone.

'Can you push me, please?' she asked, feigning shaking hands.

Charlie walked up behind the wheelchair, and they carried on down the corridor.

After fifteen minutes a set of red lights flared as they reached the end of the corridor, and another door.

This one had a simple handle and no obvious lock, mechanical or electronic. People clearly only got this far if they were meant to.

Charlie opened the door, again using a half-shuffle to keep an eye on Sam.

The room had simple concrete walls, a few chairs, and no windows. There were narrow horizontal slits high up the walls on three sides. Plus two doors: a closed one in front of them and an open one to the left, revealing another long narrow corridor beyond.

'I glad you didn't kill Tim,' said Sam.

'Life is sacred,' said Charlie.

Sam wasn't sure. 'What's your plan for us, Charlie?'

Charlie didn't answer. He'd put a chair next to the closed door and climbed up on it so that he could see through one of the horizontal slits.

'*Charlie?*'

Charlie turned and shushed Sam.

A noise emanated from one of the horizontal slits.

Sam surmised some type of machinery had started in the next room.

Voices, urgent and scared, drifted through.

*Computerised voice: enter decontamination area*
*Male Welsh accent: I've been scanned already*
*Spanish accent: repeat measurement needed*
*Male Welsh accent: but my wife is missing*
*A pause*
*Spanish accent: Mr Brewer, she is already in the secure environment*
*Male Welsh accent: Are you sure?*
*Spanish accent: Rachele Maxine Brewer, processed one hour ago*

The rest of the exchange was mumbling and incoherent.

'Charlie!' whispered Sam. He continued to ignore her.

She wheeled herself towards the closed door.

As she did, the noise of the machinery behind it got louder for a few seconds and then was quiet again.

Charlie jumped down and grabbed one of her chair handles. 'We live in a computer simulation.'

'That's your belief,' said Sam. 'I believe in a real God.'

'Our creator is a machine,' said Charlie. 'You can still keep your God, or whoever made the first sentient being that made that first computer. But we're deep inside the cycle.'

'You have proof?' asked Sam.

Charlie's eyes blazed. 'I have faith.'

Sam took a breath. 'You want us to join the Ankor?'

'Yes,' said Charlie. 'You'll be free of pain.'

There was the phrase again. Alluring, and yet historically only ever used before another disappointment. She'd had three major operations, and so many minor procedures. She'd never reached anywhere close to pain-free.

'When it's done,' said Charlie. 'You'll love me as much as I love you.'

When she'd initially hooked up with Charlie eighteen months previously, it had been entirely unplanned. She'd just recovered from one of her more successful operations and was feeling confident. Early in the evening of her welcome back party, she'd made a move on Tim – not always easy from a wheelchair. He'd gently knocked her back. She was sure she'd seen a *yes* in his eyes. But the words that came out of his mouth had been *I can't*.

So she'd accepted Charlie, and been treated well by him, and convinced herself it was mutual love. But it was all a one-way street. He loved her. Not bad, but not enough.

Charlie reached out and gently stroked her face. 'You're perfect.'

271

Sam noticed the path of his hand traced the faint scar where she'd gone headfirst through the windscreen.

Sam slapped his hand away. 'Fuck off, Charlie.'

Charlie flinched and took a step backwards and returned his attention to the door that concealed the rumbling machinery.

*What do the Ankor want?*

Again, Sam knew she should ask outright, but the dread forming in her stomach stopped her. She was to be some type of sacrifice.

After listening for a few moments, Charlie opened the door.

The first thing to hit Sam was the stench – a mixture of disinfectant and dead flesh. The second thing she noticed were the six industrial units that dominated the room. Each had the start of a conveyor belt which led into the machinery and, probably, through into the next room.

Charlie went to a large box at the side of the room and pulled out two neck-braces.

He took off his shirt and Sam saw the entirety of the bandage around his neck.

He unwound it before removing the other two from his arms.

Faint scarring ran up his arms, and around his neck.

Looking more closely, Sam could see that he had wires implanted under the skin. 'What's that for?'

'They're electromagnetic inductors,' said Charlie. 'They're helping to prepare my brain for transition, and, if you're with me, they'll protect yours too.'

Charlie clipped the neck brace on, handing the second one to Sam.

She took it but made no effort to put it on. 'I'm not doing anything, Charlie, until you explain what the hell happens in there.'

Charlie looked at peace. 'We each lie on a slab. The conveyor takes us into the machinery which sedates us. When we wake, we are joined with the Ankor.'

'Why do the Ankor want us to join them?'

'They need us,' said Charlie. 'They're flesh and blood like us. But they are not operating at full potential. Many of their pods have been put into suspension until the coming of the Blessed can reawaken them.'

Sam remained silent.

'Have faith. We're the Blessed. We'll join with the Ankor – be part of them and help them grow.' Charlie paused. 'They're magnificent creatures: biological brains melded with technology to give them every conceivable advantage. No pain. No deprivation. Enormously long lives.'

'What about those people we heard before? Are they the Blessed too? Haven't they died?'

'The Blessed don't die,' said Charlie. 'The brain is removed from a fragile human body and transferred into an Ankor pod where it is assimilated and becomes part of the whole.'

*Brain removed … What the fuck?*

'Do individuals remember who they are?' asked Sam.

Charlie's brows furrowed and his fingers traced the wire implants in his neck. 'These will help me, and for those with true strength of character, some sense of self does remain.' He passed. 'But, mostly one gives oneself to the Ankor.'

A slight blast of warm air carrying an unpleasant smell emanated from one of the machines. Instinctively, Sam wheeled herself a little way back from the opening.

'As for the Blessed before us,' said Charlie. 'I do regret that they did not have it all explained to them. I couldn't convince MacKenzie to allow me to do it. We were forced to use chemical means to calm them.'

Charlie took a few pills out of his pocket. 'Being at peace will greatly improve the journey.'

'Are you taking one?' she asked.

'I have my faith,' said Charlie. 'I don't need anything.'

*Pity.*

Another blast of warm air from the machine doused Sam in the smell again. Dead flesh.

Relaxing her shoulders, Sam took the pill and pretended to swallow it – something she was very practised at from her stays in certain hospitals that believed patients should be seen and not heard.

'Free from pain,' she said, reaching out for a hug.

Charlie, now smiling, bent down, and embraced her.

Holding Charlie with her left arm, Sam reached under her chair with her right. 'I need my stronger pills,' she said, caressing Charlie's ear with her lips. 'I want to start the journey totally relaxed.'

'I understand,' he whispered back.

If Charlie registered a slight tension in her body, Sam assumed he would put it down to her muscles stabilising her body when twisting, to minimise the pain.

In a sense it was pain; phantom pain she felt in advance of the act.

Sam drove the eight-inch hunting knife up and under Charlie's ribs.

At the last moment, Charlie sensed something. He moved sideways and the knife, which should have gone deep under the rib cage, was deflected, and simply lodged in his abdomen.

Still, the wound went deep.

Charlie slipped backwards and fell on the floor, his hands reflexively grabbing hold of the handle – unable to let it go, but also unable to draw it out.

Sam looked around the room for cameras. Had she been seen?

Either way, it didn't matter. She still had no time to lose.

Ignoring Charlie's groans, Sam wheeled herself back towards the door they'd come through. If she could get back to Tim, perhaps they could both escape.

Halfway to the door, Sam heard a louder groan and a shuffle of movement behind her.

She turned, imagining Charlie stumbling towards her with the knife … or the gun.

*Fuck! I forgot the gun!*

Charlie, on his hands and knees, was attempting to climb up onto the conveyor. The knife still protruded from his stomach.

Sam watched as he clawed at the side of the machinery, and fell back down, only turning at the last second to take the fall on his back and not drive the knife deeper into his stomach.

His eyes locked onto Sam.

The door clicked open.

# CHAPTER 29

**SpaceOp**

Tim had no idea how long he'd been unconscious.

He stifled a groan as he rolled onto his side, terrified that he would attract undue attention from Leafers. He clearly remembered being tied up and led into the corridor, then as far as he could surmise Charlie had smashed him on the back of the head.

With his head throbbing, and his hands firmly tied behind his back, Tim manoeuvred himself onto his knees by pushing his head and neck against the wall.

After wriggling his hands for a few minutes, he managed to get free of Charlie's inexpertly tied knots.

The corridor, like others in MacKenzie's underground network, was lined with dim red lighting. Tim checked his watch. He'd been out of action a little under thirty minutes.

Taking off his shoes to muffle his footsteps, Tim slipped back through the side door into the main corridor. His assumption was that Charlie was going deeper into the complex, so Tim followed.

He inched forward, listening carefully as he went.

*I'll save you, Sam.*

The thought had jumped up unbidden, and Tim almost stopped in embarrassment at its presumptuousness: she may save herself, she may not need saving, or she may not want saving.

*No ... she was kidnapped ... for fuck's sake ... another thing to feel guilty about.*

Tim could see no more than twenty metres down the corridor into the gloom, but it was enough to see each successive set of faint red lights.

As he passed the lights, they flared gently, but nothing more.

He kept going.

At the end of the corridor was another door. Tim went through it into a room with two exits. Looking through the open left door, Tim simply saw a long corridor. In front of him was a closed door. Tim put his ear to it. Rescue mission this may be, but there was no point charging into the barrel of a gun. He could hear a faint rumbling.

*Could just be the bang on my head?*

Opening the door just a crack, he looked through.

'Tim!' gasped Sam.

Charlie lay on the floor, a knife hilt protruding from his stomach. His eyes were open. He was alive, but he was clearly in a bad way. Tim checked that Charlie wasn't holding the gun. He wasn't.

'Sam!' cried Tim and took a step towards her.

Whether he threw himself to the ground or his legs buckled, he wasn't sure, but a moment later they were hugging. Sam took Tim's face in her hands and pulled him gently away. 'We have to go!'

'Tim,' croaked Charlie.

Moving over to Charlie, Tim settled himself close by on the ground. It could be a trap, but the chances of Charlie pulling a knife out of his stomach and stabbing Tim with it were slim.

*Although, technically, neither have I ever been in a situation where it was more likely …*

'Please,' said Charlie. 'Let me go.' He eyed the conveyor belt.

'The machines here remove people's heads,' said Sam, wheeling herself towards Tim. 'And their brains are sent to the Ankor.

'The Blessed don't die,' said Charlie. 'They join with the Ankor, the pains and troubles of their corporeal burdens all taken away.'

'You were going to do this to Sam?' said Tim. 'Sacrifice her?'

'I was going *with* her. Our heads would be removed together and almost instantly flooded with a chemical that stops brain cell degeneration. Then, we would be cooled, and sent to join with the Ankor.' Charlie removed one hand from the knife hilt and pointed to the neck brace he was wearing which had wires attached leading under his skin. 'Plus, as Sam was going to be pair-bonded with me, she would have additional protection from cellular degeneration.'

Tim looked at Sam. Her face showed a mixture of disgust and sadness. He turned back to Charlie. 'Why do the Ankor need human brains?'

Charlie laboured for breath and a dribble of blood leaked from the corner of his mouth. 'They struggle … to reproduce brain material … So, they take it.'

'If they needed brain power,' said Sam, 'why not just build artificial intelligence and merge with that?'

'They can't. They tried,' said Charlie. 'They're hundreds of thousands of years old, but they can't program true individual consciousness.'

Tim remembered the difficulty he and Charlie had had ten years ago when they'd tried to write the high-level specification for a program that could mimic consciousness. It was very hard to define abstract feelings. 'Strength of will …'

'When they tried to create artificial intelligence with the computational complexity and power to sustain consciousness …' Again, Charlie's strength started to fade. 'There was always one of two outcomes. Either the machine

turned psychotic and tried to attack them, or it simply …
turned itself off.'

Tim could understand that. 'Existential angst.'

'The biological will to survive is so hard to replicate whilst
maintaining sociability,' said Charlie. 'Killing machines or
suicidal maniacs.'

'Okay,' said Tim. 'So, why do they need any type of
additional brain power.'

'Their goal is to amass sufficient processing power to
launch their own full universe simulation,' said Charlie. 'In
this way they can fully worship our own Creators.'

'Creators?' asked Tim.

'The Ankor believe in Simulation Theory,' said Sam.

Charlie didn't respond. He was struggling to move his
weight onto his left-hand side to relieve some internal
pressure on the knife wound.

Tim bent down and helped him.

'Thank you,' said Charlie. 'Creators. The beings that wrote
the program we live inside.'

'But that would mean these Creators *do* know how to
program a fully functioning brain,' said Sam.

'No,' said Charlie, shaking his head. 'It's not intelligent
design. They set up the correct parameters and launch a Big
Bang, then wait for stars and planets to form. Then watch as
molecules are synthesised. And then life …'

'So, the Ankor will do the same and then just watch static
for billions of years,' said Sam.

Tim interjected. 'I guess they can jack up the frame rate
and skip to the interesting bits?'

Charlie, clearly severely weakening, simply nodded.

'The Ankor steal brains to get enough processing power
to make their own universe,' said Tim. 'How close are they to
having this capability?'

'Tens of thousands of years away. First … they need all three hundred and forty-three pods hot, running at full power. That's just to work out the initial maths to build the computer required to run the simulation.'

Tim could see that Charlie was unlikely to remain conscious for much longer. 'Is this it for Earth? Or are they coming back?'

'Five more similar trips over the next hundred years. Each trip, they source and absorb the Blessed, assimilate them over a twenty-year period, and then come back for more.'

Sam bristled. 'They won't find Earth so accommodating next time.'

Charlie shook his head. 'The Ankor can bombard Earth with nuclear charges and remain untouchable. They chose subterfuge to keep collateral damage to a minimum. Next time …' He drifted to silence.

Tim understood the fundamental equation.

*Fifty thousand heads or one hundred million disintegrations.*

'You said life is sacred,' said Sam.

'That is part of the Ankor faith,' said Charlie, his expression hardening.

'Some people really died,' said Tim, frowning. 'The radiation and the bombs.'

'Tragically,' said Charlie. 'The Ankor did all they could to minimise the fatalities. Most of the deaths were unavoidable and necessary.'

'Most?' asked Tim.

'There is a small faction within the Ankor that is … not so pure.'

'The Transcenders advocated nuclear bombardment from the first day.' Charlie paused, a look of distaste mixing with pain. 'That's why I decided to leave now. There were new plans created after the Chinese blew up RL2. The Transcenders don't get any Blessed in this launch. I couldn't face becoming part of them.' Charlie coughed, and a spasm of pain swept over his face. 'Please put me in the machine. Please … you've nothing to lose.'

Tim took a step forward and leant over him.

'Put me onto the conveyor. Then turn that dial clockwise and pull that lever,' said Charlie, pointing at the control panel. 'Once I'm gone, turn it back as far as it will go. That will disengage the drive system. It's all mechanical.'

Tim nodded. 'I will.'

Charlie's shoulders relaxed and he turned his head towards Sam. Now, his face was a picture of religious rapture – it seemed as if his eyes actually shone. 'Please come with me. We would become the Blessed, transformed into the purest form possible in our universe. Free from the prisons of our bodies. Made anew in the image of our Creator.'

'You go, Charlie,' said Sam, shaking her head. Then her face softened. 'Good luck. I hope you find peace.'

'MacKenzie will get a warning. He'll send Leafers. You'll need to get onto the conveyor and crawl five metres. From there, an exhaust vent above you will take you out of the system.'

Without looking to Sam for agreement, Tim lifted Charlie onto the conveyor belt.

There was a look of beatification on Charlie's face as he lay flat on the conveyor. 'Thank you.'

Tim turned the dial and pulled the lever.

An engine whirred briefly and Charlie disappeared into the bowels of the machine. The engines within the conveyor system continued to whine for thirty seconds, then the lever reset itself to the neutral position.

Tim turned the dial all the way back. 'Shall we crawl down the conveyor and up an exhaust vent, then?'

'Before or after the swinging blades take off our heads?' said Sam, now holding Charlie's gun. 'You don't think it's a trap?'

'If the belts aren't running, the blades don't swing. It's all mechanical,' said Tim, deliberately checking the operating lever and the dial again.

'Yes,' she said. 'But the blades are probably triggered on pressure mechanism, or a switch.'

'I'm sure the first set of vents are well before the blades,' said Tim, looking down the conveyor tube. He couldn't see anything; the conveyor belt disappeared into darkness only a few metres in. The decision was an easy one. There was almost no scenario in which being caught would not result in their deaths … and most scenarios also included their brains being launched into space.

Sam looked at Tim for a few seconds. 'Okay,' she said. 'My arms are strong, but I may need some help. Pull is better than pushing for me.'

'Me first, then.'

'If I hear you gurgling,' said Sam. 'I'll know you've lost your head.'

After helping Sam onto the conveyor belt, Tim clambered over the top of her and into the depths of the machinery.

For five metres the conveyor angled gently downwards.

Critically for Tim's peace of mind, the belt wasn't moving of its own accord.

'You okay?' he whispered over his shoulder.

'Not really. But I'm still moving.'

Tim looked back towards her. She was dragging herself along, her face set in a rictus of pain. There was no point taking any painkillers; she needed all the feeling she could get to allow her legs to help the tiny amount they could manage.

'You're doing great,' whispered Tim.

'Yeah,' said Sam. 'I'm a real fucking trooper. Can you see anything?'

He couldn't see much. What little light had filtered in from the main room had now almost petered out.

He crawled forward.

A minute later, his left hand brushed the vent.

Tim listened at it for a few minutes. Nothing.

The vent covering didn't seem to be screwed into place. There were simple clips that Tim soon opened.

With the cover unattached, Tim pushed it into the vent and climbed after it.

'Are you okay?' Tim whispered over his shoulder.

'Shhh!'

The narrow space was just wide enough for Tim to wriggle into.

Sam followed.

Tim moved slowly.

Silently.

The vent was pitch black, heightening all their other sensations. Tim could feel the smooth metal of the vent under his hand. He could hear every creak as they crawled. And almost every breath included the stench of dead flesh or disinfectant.

They crawled on.

A minute later, they heard the machinery behind them starting up, and the conveyors starting to run. Tim and Sam stopped and listened, but there was no sound of pursuit.

*Hopefully, they think we went through the process.*

They continued, the vent now bending around to the right.

'You okay?' Tim whispered over his shoulder. The vent was narrow. He couldn't turn around, or even look around.

A hand grabbed his ankle and gave a gentle squeeze. 'I'll survive … stop asking!'

Up ahead, a small amount of light now filtered from a grill on the right-hand side.

Tim continued to crawl and peered through it. Whatever the underground configuration of the Hot Zone was, they were now at ground level of this new room he was looking into.

The room was empty. More than empty: it looked as if it had never been used. The floor was bare concrete, and there were small lights in the ceiling.

They could get out here, but they'd still be trapped deep inside the Hot Zone.

Tim kept going.

Ten minutes of crawling brought them to a point where the vent widened and split into two directions, left and right.

With a bit of grunting and shuffling, Sam brought herself alongside Tim.

Their heads were inches apart. 'There's a little light coming from that way,' whispered Sam, indicating to the right. 'And some noise. Should we look?'

Charlie hadn't mentioned the fork in the vents. Instinctively, it felt like the left-hand branch would lead out under the fields, whereas the right-hand would stay inside the Hot Zone. But there was a little light from the right. It may give them some information.

'I'll slip down the right-hand tunnel for ten metres. You wait here,' said Tim.

'Just a quick look,' said Sam. 'Then wriggle back to me.'

He crawled back down the tunnel.

Now it felt as if the vent was angling downwards.

After a few more minutes of silent slow crawling, he reached the source of the light. Another grill led into a new room, this time at ceiling height.

Tim looked through. There were ten chutes emerging from the far wall. Coming out of each chute was a steady stream of blood emptying into its own shallow steel vat.

The fetid smell made Tim gag. He suppressed it. He had to, because amongst the vats were at least thirty people, ten Leafers and the rest workers – dressed head-to-toe in blood-covered overalls.

The workers were doing exactly what he'd been dreading. A couple of metres away, Tim watched as one of them reached into the steel vat and picked up a severed head that was resting on the central drainage grill. The mouth was wide open, fixed in an eternal scream. One eye was missing, and a trail of ligaments and arteries dangled from what remained of its neck.

Thankfully, Tim did not recognise the face.

Feeling bile rise in his throat, he desperately wanted to crawl back down the tunnel, but he knew he had a job to do.

The worker used a hose to spray the face and head with water, and then rolled it over so that the neck cavity was pointing upwards. Next the worker took a thin hose that was attached to his belt and fiddled inside the victim's neck, obviously hunting for something.

*Carotid artery …*

The worker slid the tube into the artery and pressed a button on its nozzle. From such a close distance Tim could hear a pump start up next to the vat; this was clearly the chemical flushing stage. A white vapour started emanating around the head.

After a few minutes the worker, apparently satisfied, now placed the head into another plastic drum which was standing nearby.

Where the headless bodies were, he didn't know. Tim assumed they were siphoned off the conveyor belt at some point.

The process clearly wasn't perfect as a few severed torsos lay on the floor of the room.

His nausea rising, Tim took out his phone and, checking the camera function was set to silent with no flash, he took photos and video footage through the grill.

He wriggled backwards to Sam and gave her the news.

'I didn't expect anything different,' she said. 'We have to stop this.'

They took the other fork. The smell got worse, and they were forced to crawl over a series of holes where up-vents joined into the one they were following.

After more crawling, they reached a shaft which led vertically upwards.

A ladder led three metres up to a heavy metal grill, through which Tim could see the starry sky.

He climbed.

Unfortunately, the grill was not only an industrial-strength grid of vertical and horizontal steel bars, it was also securely locked.

They were trapped.

# CHAPTER 30

**SpaceOp**

For a few moments, Tim hung onto the ladder in silence, absorbing the situation. He checked his phone. The photos were clear and damning, but there was no signal, neither mobile nor Wi-Fi. He couldn't tell anyone, but people needed to know.

Tim whispered over his shoulder. 'The exit is welded shut.'

'Back?' asked Sam, who'd climbed, without much strength in her legs, halfway up the ladder on arm strength and willpower.

Through the steel grill, Tim could see the tops of some of the small surrounding hills and the stars twinkling in the night sky. 'I don't know.'

Sam reached up and gave his calf a gentle squeeze. 'Let's get our breath back, and then head back.'

The words gave Tim equal measures of strength and shame. He knew she would have been in agony for the last thirty minutes; her spinal injury did not allow easy movement. He even wondered whether she regretted not joining Charlie in his pain-free nirvana.

*No. If she'd gone with Charlie, she'd be dead.*

Tim knew that Transhumanism did push ideas of cryosuspension, but the thought that one's self, one's ego, survived decapitation was … a long shot.

Tim shook his head clear. If he didn't find a way out they'd soon be dead anyway. The Leafers would find them stuck in the pipe and shoot them. Tim squeezed his hands open and shut three times, whilst breathing slowly and deeply. 'I love you, Sam,' he whispered.

'I know,' she said. 'Nice time to bring it up.' Again, she squeezed his ankle, and he felt her shuffle up towards him. She kissed him gently on the ankle. 'Now get on with saving my life.'

Tim pulled himself closer to the steel cross-bars and looked. Was there any way of getting through or past them?

No.

'Perhaps I can be of assistance.'

The sudden voice caused Tim to freeze.

Were they talking to him? Had he stumbled upon a midnight meeting?

A pair of shabby dark trainers came into view. 'Mr Boston?'

The voice was muffled but vaguely recognisable.

A pistol came into view … and then a face.

*Major Chen!*

'Move back down the vent as far as you can, Mr Boston.'

Tim called over his shoulder. 'Shuffle back. Shuffle back.' He started climbing downwards.

'Careful, you just kicked me in the face,' said Sam.

'Sorry.' He slowed his retreat.

They climbed back down, and around the first corner, back towards the stench.

From above came a forced whisper. 'Shut your eyes.'

They did. There was a loud hissing sound and the acrid smell of burning.

'You'll have to wait for it to cool,' Major Chen said down the vent.

A few minutes later, Chen climbed in and dragged first Tim, and then Sam, back up into the open air.

'You need to see these,' said Tim, holding his phone outstretched, displaying the photos.

Having given the phone to Chen, he crawled over to Sam and helped her into a sitting position. He saw pain etched all over her face.

'You okay?'

'Yes,' said Sam. 'But I'll take an aspirin if you have one.'

Chen squatted down and swiped through the pictures, then let out a low hiss.

From the darkness, Tim heard a shuffle and a member of Chen's team appeared, carrying a large radio backpack. Chen spoke to the man in what Tim assumed was Mandarin. The man spoke into his mouthpiece.

'What will happen now?' Tim asked.

'Now, the British army will come,' said Chen.

'The Leafers may attack us before they get here,' Tim said.

As he spoke, the whole Hot Zone lit up. Floodlights blazed to life along all four warehouses.

Deep in the fields, Tim and the team remained hidden in shadow, but Tim didn't know for how long. If the Ankor actively supported a search, then they would be found immediately. Tim looked upwards. They were there, and they knew what he'd done.

'The army is coming based on you telling them about my photos?' asked Tim.

'We had doubts. Now we have proof. We're uploading the photos.' Chen turned to the radio operator and spoke again.

Tim looked over towards Mission Control. Unlike the Hot Zone, nothing material appeared to have changed; only the standard external lights shone.

What was Francis MacKenzie doing now? How would he respond?

Sam spoke up. 'From what Charlie said, the … processing for RL3 is complete.'

289

'Are you sure?' asked Chen.

'As much as I am about anything,' said Sam.

Chen gave a small nod to indicate her understanding and spoke rapidly to the radio operator.

'Are we staying here?' Tim whispered to Chen.

'No. An attack is imminent.'

With the Ankor sitting in orbit above them, Tim felt exposed – and judging from Chen's vigilant behaviour, she was similarly unconvinced that the shadow from the small hillock would be any use to them.

One of Chen's team scurried over and reported. Chen looked around. 'We have to move now!'

Tim turned to Sam. 'Need help?'

'Depends,' she said. 'I can crawl another two metres … is it further than that?'

'I'll carry you,' said Tim, not really expecting to be able to. He was utterly exhausted.

Sam smiled and batted away his outstretched hand. 'I'd have more chance lifting you.'

Seconds later, a Chinese commando had helped Tim to his feet, whilst Major Chen, all five foot nothing of her, had gently picked Sam up without apparently noticing the effort.

Tim stumbled after Chen, moving away from the Hot Zone, towards the Administration Zone. A few minutes after they started walking, machine-gun fire erupted behind them for a few seconds and then silenced.

Before the firing had stopped, Chen had put Sam down, pushed Tim down also, and scurried towards the gunfire with three of her team.

Not long after they left, more firing started.

Tim looked at Sam.

As one, they looked at the lone radio operator, who'd stayed behind. The radio operator, a middle-aged, balding man, had his service revolver out and a grim set to his face.

# CHAPTER 31

**Porton Down Army Base**

Martel stood in silence, absorbing the information from the Chinese radio transmission. To his left, Captain Whaller was already tapping out messages to trigger the team of helicopters that had been on constant standby. The transmissions were distributed using a laser semaphore line-of-sight relay – highly skilled specialist soldiers from the Royal Signal Corps were distributed in tree tops, hill tops, and church steeples all across England.

Martel picked up his hot line to the prime minister, knowing the conversation would be intercepted by the Ankor.

'Prime Minister,' said Martel. 'Orders?'

'Contingency Two, courier with paper confirmation has been dispatched.'

Contingency Two was one of four different planned scenarios. The basic premise was that it authorised Martel to take control of SpaceOp with live weapons and, critically, to stop the current launch – securing the launch facility if possible, destroying it if not.

'Understood.'

Click.

Grabbing his combat pack, Martel hurried out to the helicopters.

This was what the previous weeks of preparation – and the years of hypothetical planning – had been leading up to. As he'd briefed the prime minister a number of times, the British army had nuclear, chemical, and biological options but, even if they secured the facility, they still didn't have a

291

method of delivering the attack into the Ankor craft twenty thousand kilometres above Earth.

*Even if we can't win, hopefully we can force a negotiation.*

The Ankor had options too, in the shape of ten thousand potential nuclear bombs they'd smuggled into some of Earth's most densely populated areas. Exactly how many of the A-Gravs were bombs was not yet clear, but even if it was just a few percent, they would still spell doom.

There were three helicopters from Porton Down, all carrying specialist teams and equipment. A further seven carrying SAS personnel were also heading in from other bases.

Each member of his team had multiple skills, and it was Lieutenant Richardson piloting the helicopter Martel clambered into.

As the blades started to whir, Captain Whaller sat down next to Martel. 'All loaded, sir.'

Private Hunter, Martel's personal guard, sat opposite, studiously checking and rechecking the workings of his assault rifle.

Martel took out a handwritten note he'd received from James Piper earlier that day.

**Apologies. Washington has stood me down. WF**

The note had been written about ten hours previously, when there was no explicit proof of the Ankor's wrongdoing. However, 'WF', was shorthand for 'war footing', which meant that core elements of the American leadership had already decided the Ankor were hostile. The pressure of the Ankor's arrival, and their subsequent behaviour, had caused significant fear spikes within America – more than in most countries.

*What does war footing mean for the Americans?*

Quite how the Americans would fight a war with the Ankor, who appeared conventionally untouchable, remained to be seen. However, Martel knew each member of the American armed forces would be stripping the electronics out of every piece of equipment that could be kept operational without them.

That was what the British forces had been doing.

Martel's helicopter had the barest amount of electronics, and only one-way communication equipment. Every few seconds the co-pilot, Corporal Edwards, was tracking their position using dead reckoning with a compass and a paper map, whilst Captain Whaller listened to the long-wave radio on a basic receive-only radio.

Specifically, Whaller was listening out for any signals from the three on-site liaison team members.

'Anything?' mouthed Martel to Whaller.

Whaller shook his head.

They flew onwards, Martel reviewing the plan of action. There were no magic answers. No solutions. The decision, led by the prime minister, was based on the assumption that even if the British army staged an assault on the Hot Zone, the Ankor would not explode all of the eighty-plus A-Gravs across the UK.

They'd discussed how many the Ankor would detonate. It could be none; the actions of the Ankor so far indicated an elaborate bluff, a level of misdirection they may not have wasted their energies on if they were intent on genocide.

There was also the possibility that only a very few of the A-Gravs were capable of exploding or leaking significant radiation.

*But we just don't know.*

A calculation had been drawn up, barbaric and cold-blooded. The prime minister was prepared to risk one million people in order to save the remaining people in the Hot Zone. The remaining … current estimates were that forty thousand were still alive.

Martel was on his way to rescue the hostages and shut down SpaceOp. One serious issue being that the innocent civilians were incarcerated in a set of buildings specifically modified to be impenetrable. MacKenzie had armoured the Hot Zone to keep the plutonium safe.

They flew on, Martel reviewing and re-reviewing the plan.

As they crossed over the final part of Snowdonia National Park and over the Irish Sea, a flash to the north broke Martel's train of thought.

*Nuke!*

The signs had been unmistakable. A bright flash over the horizon had been followed a split second later by a blast wave that shook the helicopter.

The helicopter dropped vertically as Richardson fought to control the descent.

Martel grabbed his harness. 'Brace! Brace! Brace!'

Judging from the intensity and direction of the flash, the nuclear blast had centred on the Menai Strait.

His stomach lurching from the drop, Martel reviewed the flight paths of the other inbound helicopters. They would have been widely spaced, but only compared to conventional weapons.

*How many will get through?*

Martel looked at Richardson who was still fighting for control.

An acrid smell indicated some of the remaining electronics had not survived.

Martel felt pressure on his chest, a good sign; the helicopter was slowing its descent as Richardson regained control.

Beckoning to Private Hunter, Martel shouted above the whine of the struggling rotors. 'Try to contact the others.'

'Yes, sir.'

Martel was not hopeful. The timing of the blast had not been a coincidence. The SAS would have been passing into Anglesey as it happened.

Captain Whaller held up a small radiation counter. It showed a gamma pulse had passed through them, not in itself large, but confirming that it had been a nuclear blast.

It didn't fundamentally change the basis for their decision. The Ankor had obviously already caused the limited nuclear explosion in Liverpool which had driven the Anglesey residents into SpaceOp. So Martel knew they were prepared to play the nuclear card to some extent.

*How bad will it get?*

The helicopter, now listing to the left, continued to whine at a much higher pitch than Martel knew was operationally normal.

'Can we get there?' Martel leant forward and shouted into Richardson's ear.

Richardson, wrestling with the controls, nodded.

Martel turned back to Private Hunter. The nuclear blast would have created an electromagnetic pulse that could have fried all the electronics. However, it appeared Hunter's radio was working.

The helicopter limped on, Richardson heading further west than the original flight plan to avoid the blast radius and unnecessary radiation.

'Nothing from the others, sir,' said Private Hunter, confirming Martel's fears. Each helicopter was stripped of most electronics; every piece of communication equipment could only either send or receive. It had been set up that way, to make it harder for the Ankor to subvert them.

Five minutes later, they passed south over the Irish Sea, making a large detour before coming back in towards SpaceOp.

A little while later, SpaceOp came into view. As per the original briefing, Richardson headed for Mission Control.

Martel strained to look. From two hundred metres up, Martel could see that, to the north, the Hot Zone was lit up with floodlights.

Mission Control had minimal external lights.

From the ground came a flash of gunfire.

The windscreen of the helicopter cracked. Heavy machine-gun fire was coming from the Hot Zone.

Richardson took evasive action and pushed the helicopter steeply downwards, aiming to land with Mission Control between the Hot Zone and the helicopter.

Another hail of bullets hit the cockpit.

A splash of blood indicated someone had been hit.

Corporal Edwards.

With ten metres to go, the engine took a hit and gave out; the helicopter started to spin.

They hit the ground hard, but Richardson had done his job. Mission Control was blocking the line of sight from the Hot Zone.

Military training took over.

Whaller helped Edwards from his seat, whilst Richardson and Hunter readied weapons and formed a perimeter.

Martel took stock. Out of the darkness, to the west, a party of soldiers could be seen making their way towards him.

'Contact,' said Martel to the team, pointing.

As one, the remnants of the British force sighted up their assault rifles.

'They're not Leafers,' said Whaller. 'Orders?'

'Wait,' said Martel.

It was the Chinese team … with Tim Boston and Sam Turner.

To the north, the Leafers had stopped firing and did not appear to be pushing.

*Probably under orders to hold the Hot Zone.*

Martel turned to get a report on Edwards, but the look on Whaller's face, although professional, said it all. Edwards was dead.

'I'm Colonel Martel,' Martel called out to the approaching Chinese soldiers. 'Is one of you Major Chen?'

A soldier, carrying Sam Turner, came forward at a trot. 'Major Chen.'

Martel stared past Chen; behind her were a few more Chinese commandos.

'We need to get inside,' said Chen. 'The fallout.'

'Agreed,' said Martel, indicating for the British contingent to follow. 'Your forces?'

'We have three companies of commando, just off-shore,' said Chen. 'Subject to your orders.'

'Thank you,' said Whaller. They walked around to the main entrance of Mission Control. At ground level, because of the undulation of the land, the Leafers would not be able to shoot them from the Hot Zone.

The doors were shut.

Assuming that entering Mission Control would initiate a firefight with armed Leafers inside, Martel decided to take stock for a few moments.

A set of headlights approached from the direction of the Administration Zone. Richardson and Hunter readied their assault rifles, but it was Tosh driving the jeep.

Martel had met Tosh a few times and trusted him. He signalled for the soldiers to lower their weapons.

The main doors to Mission Control opened and Francis MacKenzie, flanked by two heavily armed Leafers, came out.

Martel indicated for his team not to raise their weapons.

The Leafers held their own rifle barrels pointing at the ground, albeit closer to the horizontal than those of the British forces.

'I suspect you understand just how unwelcome you are,' said MacKenzie. 'Any moment now the Chinese population will be paying for their role in this.'

Martel did not flinch. 'We are here on the orders of Her Majesty's Government, of which you are a subject. Lay down your weapons and submit to a full search.'

Francis MacKenzie looked to his left, towards the Hot Zone. 'I've just ordered four jeeps full of Leafers. They are heading to the ring road. They will open fire on arrival. You have three minutes to lay down your weapons.'

Martel would not surrender without explicit orders from the prime minister.

He'd planned to land with ten helicopters full of special forces, sufficient to take and hold Mission Control. As it was, with a handful, he could not hope to survive a firefight against the full Leafer force.

But right now, it was he who had the numerical advantage. He could take MacKenzie hostage and negotiate.

He had three minutes.

# CHAPTER 32

**SpaceOp**

Tim held his breath as Martel, with an icy calm expression on his face, walked to the foot of the steps leading up to the main door. There, he took off his beret and pocketed it. Then, very deliberately, he ran his hands through his hair and looked around before focusing his gaze back onto Francis MacKenzie.

'Mr MacKenzie, until I receive direct orders to the contrary from the prime minister, I will not be surrendering. I am here to negotiate your surrender.'

MacKenzie whispered something to the Leafer on his right, who appeared to be receiving information through an earpiece. He turned back to Martel. 'You've now got two minutes before my reinforcements arrive. If your weapons are on the ground at that time, they will not shoot.'

MacKenzie turned his attention to other members of the group.

Tim's heart lurched as MacKenzie singled him out. 'Mr Boston, I see you've become embroiled in some way. That is unfortunate. You can expect reprisals.'

Tim was intrigued. It sounded as though MacKenzie didn't know exactly what his role had been.

*How much do you know?*

MacKenzie's attention skipped onwards. 'Tosh, if you don't go now, then you will share the fate of the soldiers here.'

Tosh stared straight at MacKenzie. 'Suits me.'

MacKenzie looked out towards the ring road. The Leafer jeeps were now less than a minute away. 'I don't even need the extra soldiers. A detonation in central London will suffice … perhaps fifty kilotons, and the prime minister will call you himself to surrender.'

Whether from pure hope or not, Tim wasn't convinced that MacKenzie believed the threat he was making.

*Bravado?*

Martel turned to face the oncoming Leafers. He had less than one minute to give the order to fire.

Tim looked at the British soldiers. Even with their consummate training, they were all gripping their rifles nervously … just like the Leafers behind MacKenzie, who were now holding the barrels almost at the horizontal, rather than pointing to the floor as they had been.

*Twenty seconds.*

After coming around the final bend in the road, the jeeps stopped a few hundred metres away. Given the general darkness, and the fact the jeeps had strong headlights on full beam, Tim couldn't see what was happening.

A few seconds passed.

Tim noticed that Sam, leaning heavily on him with one hand, now had Charlie's pistol in her other.

Did they have any more time?

Probably; the Leafers would not open fire from the distance at which they had stopped. There was too much risk of them hitting MacKenzie and his own guards.

*Maybe?*

The headlights of the front jeep flared slightly and veered to the left. The next moment, the headlights were pointing away from them, and the Leafer jeeps were heading back towards the Hot Zone.

MacKenzie turned to his closest Leafer and talked urgently.

Again, the Leafer appeared to be taking orders from his earpiece.

The Leafer lifted his rifle, ejected the magazine, and laid it down on the ground. The other Leafer followed suit. Both knelt and put their hands on their heads.

*Surrendering. What the …?*

'What are you doing?' said MacKenzie, his face a picture of incomprehension.

Martel took three quick steps, drew a pistol from his belt, and hit Francis MacKenzie on the side of his head.

MacKenzie fell to his knees, clutching his head.

'Lieutenant Richardson,' said Martel, 'secure the prisoners.'

Richardson stepped forward and applied hand-ties to the Leafers on the ground. He dragged MacKenzie off his knees and put him into a restraining arm-lock.

'Tosh, would you put these two inside somewhere,' said Martel, indicating the Leafers.

'Yes, sir,' said Tosh. 'I can lock them up.'

Martel looked back at MacKenzie, stepping in close. 'Where are Hardy and Briars?'

'I have no idea,' said MacKenzie, suddenly looking contrite.

'We have Hardy marked down as in the Assembly Zone,' said Major Chen, stepping forward. 'We haven't logged Briars for over a day.'

'Thank you,' said Martel. 'Do you have layout information about the Hot Zone?'

Chen shook her head. 'None of my team have got close.'

Martel walked over to Tim and Sam, addressing them both. 'I understand you provided us with a critical service. I'll need some more from you. Are you up to it?'

'Yes, sir,' said Tim and Sam in unison.

Martel turned to Private Hunter. 'Please help Miss Turner inside.'

Making quick introductions as they walked, the group entered Mission Control.

As they entered the main floor with MacKenzie clearly injured and restrained, there was uproar. No-one left their place, but frantic conversations sprung up on all sides.

There were no Leafers obviously present, but Martel still detailed Whaller and Tosh to search the main floor to check none were hiding amongst the technicians.

None of the news feeds on the walls were displaying the recent escalations. A few feeds were covering images of the Lincoln space shuttle, but most were dedicated to RL3.

RL3 was due to launch in nine hours.

--------

During the minutes that it took for Tim to follow Martel across the main floor and up to the mezzanine level, the noise quietened. Whaller and Richardson led MacKenzie over to his desk, whilst Martel pulled Tim and Sam to the back of the mezzanine.

'I'm sorry to ask you two to give more, but I must,' said Martel.

Tim, holding hard onto Sam's hand, tried to stand a little straighter. 'What do you need?'

'I need to get MacKenzie to tell us the secrets of his systems,' said Martel. 'You'll know considerably more than I do.'

'We'll need Sam's crutches, and painkillers. They're in the server room,' said Tim.

'I'll send Tosh in a moment,' said Martel. 'Sam, why don't you take a breather until they've retrieved your gear, and then you can join us.'

Sam shook her head. 'I can help with MacKenzie.'

'Thank you,' said Martel, now turning his attention to the large screens streaming news.

'It can't be trusted,' said Tim. 'Anything could be faked.'

'Agreed,' said Martel. 'But I suspect they're not faking the mass panics.'

As Martel spoke, new screens opened. Broadcasts from most city centres were showing chaotic scenes as people swarmed away from the A-Gravs.

Sam tugged at Tim's arm and pointed. A screen was showing a transcript of the long-wave radio channel – which the Ankor could not block. It was the full accusation from the People's Republic of China, detailing murder, human trafficking, and obvious deceptions by the Ankor.

Moments later, an Ankor broadcast came through.

**Continue with delivery of RL3.**
**China to receive punishment for interference.**

Mission Control held its breath.

It didn't take long for the Ankor response.

An explosion in China.

Shenyang received a thirty-kiloton blast.

Initial estimates indicated that four million died instantly, with millions more likely to die from radiation sickness within a few months.

Nausea washed over Tim. China had been punished for broadcasting the pictures from the Hot Zone, and yet it had been he who had taken them.

Tim looked over towards Major Chen, who was now speaking rapidly with her communication lead, who in turn was speaking on the field radio.

Tim's brain raced. How did this change things? Would the prime minister surrender?

The Ankor clearly placed less value on human life than Charlie had implied – or was this the Transcenders seizing their moment?

Tim looked at Francis MacKenzie.

MacKenzie's face was ashen. For all his previous bluster, he had clearly not been expecting this.

Major Chen finished her own conversation on the long-wave radio. She approached Martel. 'I have been ordered to lay down my weapons,' she said, her eyes cast downwards. 'I am sorry. The companies of commandos are also stood down.' Turning to her own soldiers arrayed behind her, she gave the order.

The four of them unslung their assault rifles, removed the magazines, and cleared the chambers. They laid their weapons on the ground and removed their berets.

Chen turned back to Martel. 'We will return to our rooms in the accommodation blocks under self-imposed house arrest.'

A moment later they'd left.

Colonel Martel walked to the edge of the mezzanine and turned to face the room.

The room went silent.

'Until you hear differently from me, you will all remain here. There is no question of anyone leaving this building. The radioactive fallout from the explosion on the Menai Strait will reach here any minute. This building, fully sealed, will give us some protection.'

'What about the Anglesey hostages?' said a voice from the floor.

Tim suspected that Martel did not want to answer that question, since the Ankor would be listening. 'We do not have the resources to storm the Hot Zone,' said Martel.

'They're being slaughtered,' shouted someone else.

'Not at the moment,' said Martel.

'How do you know?' Another pained voice.

'I'm sorry, but I cannot say,' said Martel. 'But I am sure.'

There were no more questions. Hundreds of pairs of dead eyes looked at each other in mutual impotence.

'You are all innocent victims,' said Martel. 'We will do what we can to help the hostages.'

Tim shared a look with Sam. There were forty thousand souls stuffed into the Hot Zone caverns. Maybe not being slaughtered now, but the machinery would soon be restarting.

More calculations sprang up in Tim's head. If Martel did stop the slaughter by storming the Hot Zone, or in some other way, how many innocents would the Ankor kill in reprisals? Perhaps Martel and the prime minister had originally assumed a relatively low number. The China explosion turned all that on its head.

'MacKenzie must have been planning this for years,' whispered Sam.

'The bastard,' said Tim. It had always been about delivery of human brain tissue – from the so-called Blessed. The plutonium angle was clearly a decoy, just an excuse to build a secure underground processing area. The Hot Zone had been designed from the start as a death camp, with the rest of SpaceOp developed as the delivery mechanism.

'MedOp was built up to give him credibility,' he continued. 'MIDAS was feeding the Ankor data.'

A scuffle drew Tim's attention. Whaller had forced MacKenzie into his chair in front of the workstation.

'Unlock it,' said Martel.

MacKenzie hesitated.

'Hurt him,' said Martel to Captain Whaller.

Whaller wrenched MacKenzie's arm.

MacKenzie screamed.

A few pairs of eyes from the main floor looked up before returning to their own business.

'Unlock it,' repeated Martel.

MacKenzie gave the password.

'Show me what's happening,' ordered Martel.

Still in obvious pain, MacKenzie opened a file. 'Status …'

```
Status Report at 7pm
RL-Sent-Packed-Available-Status
1-4540-0-0
2-4812-0-0
3-0-1235-3421-Green
4-0-0-0-Green

Status Report at 11pm
RL-Sent-Packed-Available-Status
1-4540-0-0
2-4812-0-0
3-0-4656-0-Green
4-0-0-0-Green
```

'What does it mean?' asked Martel.

'The 4656 number. They've just finished packing the heads for RL3,' said MacKenzie.

'When are the next batch killed?'

'Not until sixteen hours before RL4. Tissue degradation. It has to be done at the last minute.'

'Show me all your communications with the Ankor.'

MacKenzie navigated his file directory for a few seconds. It soon became clear all the folders were empty. Everything except those recent status reports had been wiped. It made sense; the Ankor would have the ability to delete whatever they wanted.

'They didn't delete the status reports,' said Martel.

Tim spoke quietly. 'Maybe they're trying to dissuade an immediate frontal assault by implying the current hostages are not in immediate danger.'

Martel acknowledged Tim's point with a nod, then turned back to MacKenzie. 'Where are Hardy and Briars?'

MacKenzie answered immediately – changing his story from minutes earlier. 'Hardy is dead. They ordered the Leafers to kill him. I don't know about Briars.'

'Show me the Hot Zone,' said Martel.

'The cameras are all hard-wired,' said MacKenzie, pointing to the back wall.

Gesturing for Tim and Sam to follow, Martel led MacKenzie over.

The first few wires MacKenzie plugged in resulted in nothing but blank screens.

'Charlie cut some wires,' said Sam.

MacKenzie raised an eyebrow. With Martel's pistol still trained on his head, he selected another wire from the back wall. This one gave a picture.

The low-resolution image was of a large underground room with holding pens made from chain-linked wire. The ones MacKenzie had told people were ready for secure plutonium processing.

These underground cages were not empty.

Although not crammed, they all held people. Whether for some pseudo-humane reason, or simply to perpetuate the façade to stop them from rioting, the cells had bedding and basic household furniture: tables, chairs, sofas.

'How many rooms are there like this?' asked Martel.

'Each cell holds twenty people,' said MacKenzie. 'Each room has forty cells.'

To Tim's untrained eye, the security down in the Hot Zone caverns looked formidable. Leafers in hazmat suits patrolled the pathways that led between the cells.

'What type of locks are on those cells, and the interconnecting doors?' asked Martel.

'A mixture of electronic and physical,' said MacKenzie. 'But all of the electronic locks are on their own closed circuit. They can't be accessed from here.'

Martel turned to Private Hunter. 'Can you get me point-to-point with the prime minister?'

'He's already on his way here, sir,' said Hunter.

'Good,' said Martel. He clearly approved of the prime minister's decision.

An alarm from a new screen opening in the corner of the room drew everyone's attention.

It showed the current radiation levels outside the Control Centre.

**0.1 millisieverts per hour**

*Two months' allowance in every hour.*

Clearly the radioactive material from the Menai Strait blast was now settling and causing levels far in excess of what would be regarded as safe background.

'What else happens back here?' Martel asked MacKenzie, indicating to the other hatches on the back wall.

'Control points,' said MacKenzie. 'I have manual overrides for the launch processes.'

'The Ankor can't launch RL3 remotely?' asked Martel.

'No,' said MacKenzie.

'Can they initiate the Hot Zone processing?'

'No.'

That made sense; everything Tim knew about MacKenzie pointed towards the man being highly prepared. MacKenzie would want ongoing leverage.

Of course, the Ankor had plenty of leverage over the prime minister and the UK population.

Tim looked at MacKenzie.

*What leverage do they have over you?*

'How do you communicate with them?' asked Martel.

MacKenzie pointed to the keyboard. 'I just type,' he said. 'Or, on these floors, I can speak into the air. They're listening.'

Martel pulled the keyboard towards himself.

*We need to talk. Your actions threaten all-out war between us but it is not too late to step back.*

The reply came quickly.

*Continue with delivery of RL3 and then we will talk. We will detonate more bombs if you disobey.*

Tim wondered what Martel had already agreed with the prime minister as contingency. Had they decided that a certain number of the hostages could be given in settlement? Tim knew it would not be acceptable to most of Earth's population, and, in particular, the US president had explicitly warned the prime minister against it.

Was there a middle ground that avoided moral bankruptcy, nuclear oblivion, and reprisals from fundamentalists on Earth?

Tim didn't have to wait long to see the opening gambit from the British government.

Martel typed again.

*In the light of your military superiority, we are prepared to allow human volunteers to replace existing prisoners such that you get something of your wishes met. Any hostages not replaced must be set free.*

The rest of the world would cry shame, with perhaps worse from some quarters.

*Continue with delivery of*
*RL3 and then we will talk.*
*We will detonate more*
*bombs if you disobey.*

The message had simply repeated.

Tim wondered if any volunteer programme could possibly deliver another forty thousand people in time.

At that moment Lieutenant Richardson came up the stairs carrying two large holdalls. 'Still no sign of Hardy, sir.'

Martel walked to the front of the mezzanine level and addressed the three hundred people waiting below.

'Stop the RL3 countdown.'

# CHAPTER 33

**SpaceOp**

The screens covering the walls of Mission Control continued to show constant images of people rioting in the streets of London. Although little coordinated activity was apparent, there seemed to be three broad groups: *give them what they want*, *never surrender*, and *we're all going to die*. The army were on the streets trying to keep the peace, but inevitably they were mostly making targets of themselves.

As terrifying as the breakdown of law and order in the British capital was, it was the live stream videos of the Shenyang firestorms in China that held Tim's attention.

*How many million people did I just kill?*

Breathing slowly and deeply to counteract the adrenaline coursing through his body, Tim took Sam's hand.

She squeezed it gently. 'Those deaths are not on us.'

'We took the photos.'

Sam shrugged. 'The Ankor pressed the button. They're the murderers. We just exposed the crime.'

'MIDAS has been collating large oceans of data for the Ankor to analyse,' said Tim. 'We've helped them.'

'Yes,' said Sam. 'But from what Charlie said, they used the data for detailed behavioural analysis explicitly to minimise the number of deaths.'

*That seems to have gone out the window.*

'What else did Charlie say?' asked Tim.

'He said that initial Ankor calculations showed that a simple deal – either, heads for cash, or heads to avoid nuclear obliteration – could not be struck. That's why they went for subterfuge.'

'If I'd known about the reprisals …'

Sam pointed at the main floor. 'They all feel responsible too.'

Small groups of people stood huddled beneath them, quietly talking and consoling each other. The collective sigh of relief had been palpable when Martel had delayed RL3.

Tim looked over towards Martel, who was surreptitiously exchanging handwritten notes with the other members of his team.

Tim joined the group, and after signalling for a pencil, wrote his own and gave it to Martel.

> **Much of infrastructure here is designed around**
> **MacKenzie keeping leverage over the Ankor.**
> **There's a room below they cannot see or hear.**

Martel nodded and then spoke on his radio.

Less than a minute later, Tosh and Hunter returned with Sam's crutches and medicines from the MIDAS server room.

Martel gathered the small group together and addressed them. 'Private Hunter will stay up here with me. Tosh, guard the main doors. No-one leaves.' He paused. 'Sam, can you find any data remaining on the workstation?'

'No problem,' said Sam.

'Captain Whaller,' said Martel, beckoning him over. 'You know what to do. Tim will take you down. Send Richardson back if you need additional support.'

Richardson grabbed MacKenzie. Whaller picked up the large holdalls and Tim led them down to the Faraday room in absolute silence.

Tim used MacKenzie's security pass to access the mechanical lift that took them down the last stage. Stopping outside the Faraday room, Tim gestured that they should leave all electronic items on the table outside.

Inside, he activated the electromagnetic shielding, then turned to Whaller. 'This is as secure as we can hope to be. I know of at least one dangerous person unaccounted for: Juan, the head Leafer and MacKenzie's personal bodyguard. He may be down here somewhere.'

MacKenzie shrugged. 'I suspect he's gone to ground somewhere, under orders from above.'

Whaller ignored MacKenzie and led Richardson into a corner where they had a hushed discussion.

Appearing to reach an agreement, Whaller turned to Tim. 'I'm not going to mislead you,' he said. 'We are going to torture Mr MacKenzie. It will not be pleasant, but I would prefer you stayed to validate his answers.'

'You don't need to torture me,' said MacKenzie. 'I can tell you everything I know and still no power on Earth can possibly hurt the Ankor. The worst you could do would be to utterly self-destruct rather than send the materials.' He paused. 'I suspect the chances of that happening unilaterally across every nation on Earth are infinitesimally low.'

Tim turned to Whaller, wondering if the warning had been for his benefit, or as an extra incitement for MacKenzie. 'I'll stay.'

Whaller turned to Richardson. 'Relieve Mr MacKenzie of his clothes.'

*Fuck … that moved fast.*

MacKenzie flinched as Richardson took out a razor-sharp combat knife and cut his clothes away, leaving him entirely naked.

Tim shuffled to the back of the room. Still only three metres away.

MacKenzie, his hands tied behind his back, was pushed into a kneeling position on the floor.

'Where are our liaison officers?' asked Whaller, meaningfully wielding a short truncheon.

'I already told you Hardy is dead,' said MacKenzie. 'And, I don't know about Briars.'

Whaller hit MacKenzie on the side of the head with the truncheon. MacKenzie, his hands still secured behind his back, fell sideways and landed on his face.

Richardson pulled him back up into a kneeling position. A livid bruise was blooming, and blood seeped from the corner of his mouth.

'When do the decapitations for RL4 start?' asked Whaller.

'I already told you that too,' said MacKenzie, drawing a breath. 'Sixteen hours before launch.'

'Where are the heads for RL3?' asked Whaller, turning back to MacKenzie.

'The heads for RL3 are immersed in freezing gel and will soon be shipped out to the Assembly Zone,' replied MacKenzie. 'Look … You don't need to hit me.'

Without appearing to consider it further, Captain Whaller kicked MacKenzie right between his legs. 'I don't need to, but I want to. The current deal is … you answer every question entirely accurately and I will not physically detach your bollocks with my boot.'

Whether MacKenzie registered Whaller's threat, Tim was not sure. After the kick, he had rolled onto his side and was retching on the floor.

Richardson eased MacKenzie back up into the kneeling position once more.

MacKenzie whispered something through pain-pursed lips about the Geneva Convention.

Whaller took Richardson's knife, addressing MacKenzie with the tip held only an inch from his left eyeball. 'You are not human. You will not be treated humanely. You will not benefit from Geneva. If I don't like your answers, or your attitude, then you will be tortured in a way that inflicts permanent damage.'

Involuntarily, Tim retched. He clamped his mouth shut and swallowed the vomit back down.

Whaller reached into his pocket and took out a small roll of masking tape. He pulled out a line and then wound it around the little finger of MacKenzie's left hand. 'I need to make sure you don't doubt my resolve.'

MacKenzie's eyes bulged. Whaller had his attention.

Whaller laid the knife on the floor a metre from MacKenzie. 'How does the Hot Zone work?'

For the next few minutes MacKenzie, hardly stopping for breath, explained how the process ran. It was entirely devoid of electronics, except for a few entirely closed-circuit pieces – certainly there was no network connectivity. MacKenzie had designed it to be unhackable.

'The Ankor didn't mind this?' asked Whaller. 'All the processing being hidden from them?'

A small part of MacKenzie's self-belief returned. 'They had no choice but to accept.'

At Whaller's prompting, MacKenzie went on to describe the service corridor layout and the various timings.

Whaller turned to Tim. 'Consistent with what you know?'

'Yes,' said Tim.

'So, they can't start or stop the processing?' asked Whaller, confirming.

MacKenzie shook his head. 'Only I can start or stop it. All the controls are on the back wall of the mezzanine level. Only I know how to use them. Any wrong input causes catastrophic cleansing of the whole area.'

'Catastrophic?'

'The Hot Zone is sitting on top of a series of conventional, but very large, phosphorus bombs.'

Whaller paused to consider MacKenzie's information. 'Do the Ankor know about them?'

'Yes,' said MacKenzie, although a flicker of his eyes indicated to Tim that he could be lying.

MacKenzie's confidence was building. 'Forty thousand more heads for the price of not detonating A-Gravs across the UK. It's not even a real choice. You saw what they did to China.'

'What about the physiology of the Ankor themselves?' asked Whaller. 'What do you know about them?'

'They have computing power beyond your imagination. Each of those pods is a two-thousand-kilogram biological brain. They've analysed us. They've experimented on us. They know the world's governments will cave in.' MacKenzie paused and looked directly at Tim. 'The Ankor have ten thousand nuclear bombs strategically placed across Earth.'

'How many do you think the Ankor are prepared to kill?' asked Whaller.

'I don't know. The original plan was devised to minimise casualties and, once they had what they wanted, they were going to provide detailed information on how to effectively counteract radiation damage for those who'd been caught in the crossfire.' MacKenzie looked uncertain. 'Now, however, my guess is the main body of Ankor will be prepared to kill a few tens of millions to secure their fifty thousand brains.'

'Main body?' asked Whaller.

'There's a radical minority faction,' said Tim, giving Whaller a quick summary of what Charlie had already told him. 'The Transcenders.'

'Yes,' said MacKenzie. 'The Transcenders – they'd be happy to kill all seven billion minus the fifty thousand … to get their fifty thousand.'

'They're psychos,' said Tim.

'Perhaps, by our standards,' said MacKenzie. 'But every year you spend a few thousand pounds going on holiday. That same money could save the lives of three hundred children currently drinking contaminated water somewhere in the Sub-Sahara. It's just a matter of scale.'

'You can't be serious,' said Tim. 'Scale is everything.'

'On that we agree,' said MacKenzie. 'You know, I died three times as a child. I had asthma attacks that stopped my breathing. Luckily on each occasion I was brought round before permanent brain damage occurred.' He paused. 'I know that on my deathbed, if I was offered the chance to live another five years in exchange for the deaths of fifty thousand strangers … I would take it without hesitation.'

'Maybe not if you felt you'd have a fulfilled life,' said Tim.

MacKenzie scowled. 'It is never enough – not for me – and you'd have your price, too. Perhaps you'd do it for the death of one very old stranger … or three paedophiles … or five mass murderers … there's always a price.'

'I can't believe anyone would do that,' said Tim, feeling a need to defend the moral position even though he could, in fact, believe that a small minority would do it readily.

'I can't believe everyone wouldn't,' said MacKenzie, deadpan.

'What's the basis for the Ankor's … ethics?' asked Whaller, obviously still trying to gauge how many innocent people might be at risk if they staged a fight-back on behalf of humanity.

'I know a bit there,' said Tim. He outlined the basics of Simulation Theory. 'As MacKenzie says, they probably do have a moral code, of sorts.'

'Mr Boston is correct,' said MacKenzie. 'As I said before, they're trying to get the brain material while causing minimal suffering on Earth, but they won't leave without it.'

'Do you believe we're living in a simulation?' asked Tim.

'I am prepared to be convinced that it is the reality,' said MacKenzie. 'But that doesn't mean I worship whoever encoded our universe. Creation doesn't automatically confer ownership.'

Whaller looked at Tim. 'Do you believe it?'

'No,' said Tim with a smile. 'The Ankor are giant brains, enormous biological computational creatures. I suspect they've simply created their god in their own image ... a computer, for them, is the natural choice. Early human civilisations had gods of hunting, more recent ones had gods of laws.'

'My reservations entirely,' said MacKenzie. 'Well done, Mr Boston.'

Whaller turned to MacKenzie. 'Did you plan to be decapitated like Charles Taylor?'

'No; mine is planned to be a live merge,' said MacKenzie. 'Retaining my own conscious thoughts and ego.'

'You still think you're going?'

'Who knows?' said MacKenzie. 'Obviously, you could kill me now. But it took the Ankor five hundred years to get here; they're not likely to leave without the brain material. And I have all the codes.'

'Which you will tell us,' said Whaller.

'Your problem is,' said MacKenzie, 'that if I give you the wrong codes then the whole place goes up in flames ... and here, with you, I am staring certain death in the face.'

Whaller remained silent.

'Do they just plug the brains in and reformat them ... like a hard drive?' asked Tim.

'I ensured that every resident of Anglesey was enrolled in MedOp. We have sequenced their DNA and provided the Ankor with that information,' said MacKenzie. 'The Ankor will distribute each brain to where its appropriate skills are needed.'

'Skills?' asked Whaller.

'Some people are more adept at data crunching, others to intuition. Some have well-developed memory,' said MacKenzie. 'Most of these skills are nature not nurture.'

'What sense of self survives?' asked Tim.

MacKenzie shrugged, making a face to indicate he didn't know.

A knock on the door drew their attention.

Colonel Martel.

Tim went through the process of demagnetising the room, and then reactivating once Martel was inside.

Whaller took Martel aside and gave him a whispered update.

'Five hundred years,' said Martel, turning to MacKenzie. 'That means no hyperspace technology.'

'I'm afraid not,' said MacKenzie. 'It makes their position a little more desperate.'

Martel, his face grim, addressed Captain Whaller. 'Do you have what you need?'

'I could do with some more time, sir,' said Whaller.

'We don't have it. They just blew a nuclear charge in Birmingham.' Martel paused. 'The countdown to RL3 is back on. The prime minister gave me the order verbally via point-to-point, but he'll be here soon.'

'In that case, sir,' said Whaller, 'we have to go with Chimera.'

Martel turned to MacKenzie. 'Do I need codes from you for the launch?'

'No, RL3 is already primed.'

'Can the A-Gravs be deactivated?'

'Not by me or you,' said MacKenzie. 'Any tampering will cause them to explode.'

Martel looked at Tim. 'Are you up for a trip back into the Hot Zone?'

'I wouldn't be much use in a fight, but I can help,' said Tim. 'I've been down there. I can … be a lookout.'

Whaller and Martel exchanged a look. Whaller clearly had reservations about Tim accompanying him.

'Good, we need all the support we can get,' said Martel, overruling the unspoken opinion. 'Sam also volunteered.'

'Shall I get her?' asked Tim.

'Yes, please,' said Martel, before turning back to MacKenzie. 'The pod temperatures ... what do they mean?'

MacKenzie shrugged. 'It's pretty basic. Those at a temperature of 4K are empty. 305K are operational. 220K are in suspension but contain material. They have to be at 305K to accept new materials.'

--------

Entering the main floor, Tim looked up at the screens. The external radiation levels across the SpaceOp facility had risen again.

```
External
0.2 millisieverts per hour
```

People probably wouldn't leave the building, but whether they performed their jobs correctly was another matter.

Tim looked at the screens showing launch sites across the globe. They were all inactive. Only Anglesey remained operational to provide payloads. Clearly, the gamma ray burst had been one big fabrication.

A MIDAS newsfeed reported on Birmingham.

```
Birmingham reported explosion
Western suburb
Two kilotons
```

A reminder from the Ankor to obey. Tim fervently hoped they would consider one explosion a sufficient reminder. It was a small one, by nuclear standards. The Ankor did seem to be shepherding the UK.

Looking around, Tim saw Tosh consoling a man who was sobbing at his desk.

Tim climbed up to the mezzanine level.

Sitting on a chair, kneading her left thigh to work blood into it, Sam looked troubled. 'About half the people here say we should just give them what they want. They say it's a tragedy, but no more than the poor souls living without clean water, or living under a high voltage electricity pylon, or being sent to an avoidable war.'

'And the other half?' asked Tim, disturbed by how much Sam's words echoed what MacKenzie had said.

'The other half say *come and have a go if you think you're hard enough*,' said Sam with a forced smile.

He didn't answer. The fact remained that an additional forty thousand souls to save seven billion was a no-brainer …

*As long as you don't have to push the button yourself.*

Was it seven billion at risk? Would the Ankor blow all the nukes if humanity stood firm? Would that consign humanity to extinction? Could the fact the Ankor appeared to have some moral code mean they could have their bluff called? What power did the so-called Transcenders have over the main Ankor group?

Sam had read his mind. 'And will they just keep coming back indefinitely?'

*Charlie said five more trips … but he may not be party to their innermost plans.*

'I guess Martel is assuming so,' said Tim.

Sam nodded. 'He told me that much when you were downstairs.'

They looked up at the newsfeeds. Most of them were showing mass panic as people tried to get as much distance as possible between themselves and their closest A-Grav units.

*Not that anyone can get that far away on an island …*

The sick feeling in the pit of his stomach turned to churning nausea as Tim focused on another newsfeed.

This one was showing pictures of the detonation in China. Fires raged through Shenyang.

*I did that.*

Tim stepped forward to help Sam into her crutches, but she waved him away.

'Don't worry, I'm fully juiced up,' she said.

'The sleepy ones?'

'No, the little red ones.'

She didn't fool him for a moment; the red pills did nothing more than take the edge off the pain.

Tim's attention was drawn to a screen displaying the Ankor pod configuration and temperature status. Constructed from infrared pictures taken every hour by a satellite at the Lagrange Two point, the display showed that significantly more of the 343 pods were now warm. Martel's question to MacKenzie now had context.

```
Ankor Mother ship - Pod Temperature
Distributions:
343 Pods
232 Operating at an average 305K
86  Operating at an average 220K
25  Operating at an average 4K
```

Twenty-one more pods operating at 305K. From what Tim understood, that was the required temperature for activation of empty pods, or simple brain material augmentation of existing pods.

*More pods on the Ankor ship are waking up.*

Was this the RL1 material being utilised? Or were they just preparing for new material?

Moments later, the United Nations put out a broadcast.

*Notwithstanding the final word on this matter from the UK government, to whom we cede the*

> ultimate decision making, it is the position
> of the United Nations General Assembly that it
> is prepared to countenance the transport of
> the existing material.

The message was met with silence in the Control Centre.
'We have to go back down,' said Tim.

Before they'd opened the door, the USA had added its
own broadcast.

> It is the position of the United States of
> America that any transport of material is an
> affront to God and will not be countenanced.

# CHAPTER 34

**SpaceOp**

After double-checking the magnetisation on the Faraday room was functioning, Tim gave Whaller, Richardson and Martel an update about the UN message and the USA's subsequent response.

'The hard-line military are making the calls,' said Martel.

'With friends like these ...' added Whaller, before turning to Richardson. 'Ready?'

'Yes, sir.' Richardson now had two rucksacks, presumably taken from inside the holdalls he'd brought with them.

Martel spoke directly to Tim. 'If you encounter Leafers, you run. If one of my men is shot, you run. No heroics. Understand?'

'Yes, sir.'

'Come back safe,' said Sam, settling on the single wooden chair in the room, her eyes not leaving MacKenzie who was slumped in the corner.

Moments later, leaving Martel, Sam, and MacKenzie, they were on their way.

Whaller and Tim walked side by side along the corridors, down past the data rooms, and onwards.

As before, the corridor was lit with faint red lighting, each light just enough to see the next.

Whaller and Richardson wore high-tech low light vision gear, and both carried silenced snub-nosed machine guns.

No-one spoke. As he walked, a hundred questions leapt into Tim's brain. Was there a bomb in the rucksack? Did Whaller intend for them to destroy the crates? How would the Ankor respond?

After a few minutes, Whaller abruptly put up a hand for them to stop. He spent a few minutes adjusting his vision gear whilst looking intently down the long straight corridor.

A further hand gesture started them walking again.

They reached the door where Charlie had clubbed him. Tim put his hand on Whaller's arm and indicated it was the one he'd already told Whaller and Martel about, showing them where Charlie had cut out flex from the cabling.

It could be used as an escape route, or an incursion route if there were more soldiers available.

Whaller looked for a few moments and then, apparently satisfied, indicated for them all to walk on.

Now the end of the corridor came into sight, or rather didn't. It was pitch black: the corridor lights stopped five metres short.

Whaller crept forward, with Richardson holding up his machine gun.

Within a few metres of the door a set of red lights flared, giving them a half-view of the final door, which was shut.

Whaller slowly turned the handle and went through, followed closely by Richardson.

They were in the anteroom. From here Tim knew the door straight in front of them led to the decapitation room. The left-hand door, he assumed, followed on a parallel track to the production line, broadly running underneath the vent that he and Sam had crawled along.

Whaller passed a note.

**Packing crates?**

Tim nodded as Whaller pointed to the left-hand door. Richardson went first.

The door opened onto another corridor, lit with more dim red lights.

This corridor also had thick cabling running along the floor.

Tim followed Richardson, with Whaller taking the back position. As they walked, Tim made a mental map of where he'd crawled in the vents. The processing room would be about fifty metres further on.

He was right. After a minute of slowly creeping forward, they reached a door leading off to the right. Tim hung back whilst Whaller and Richardson examined the door.

Whaller took out a short length of flex, attached one end to his low light goggles, and pushed the other end under the door.

The door opened.

Blinding light flooded into the corridor and a man pushed into Richardson and Whaller, knocking them over and advancing on Tim.

Instinctively, Tim stumbled backwards.

His attacker was silhouetted against the bright light, but Tim recognised him based on size only.

*Juan.*

Light glinted off Juan's knife as it slashed towards him.

Tim scrambled backwards, losing his footing. He fell.

The knife sliced past the point where Tim's neck would have been.

*Phft. Phft. Phft.*

Knife raised, Juan advanced.

*Phft. Phft. Phft.*

This time it was Juan who stumbled and fell, his head whacking into Tim's left foot.

Dead.

Whaller shuffled forward, his machine gun held ready, unwaveringly pointing at Juan's head.

All the bullets from Whaller's gun had taken Juan in the back – he was dead.

Richardson grunted in pain.

Tim climbed to his feet and joined Whaller at Richardson's side.

Richardson tried to reassure Tim with a smile, but pain was clearly etched on his face. He'd been stabbed in the shoulder as Juan had come through the door.

'What can I do?' Tim mouthed, hoping Whaller could make it out in the semi-darkness.

Whaller indicated for Tim to keep lookout whilst he administered first aid to Richardson.

'Shall I stay here or make my way back?' whispered Richardson, easing himself up to find a comfortable position.

Whaller took Richardson's backpack. 'Try to get back.'

Looking at the blood seeping through the makeshift field dressing Whaller had applied, Tim felt that simply returning to the Faraday room would be both a stretch and perhaps a mistake.

Whaller took a look through the open doorway, then closed the door. 'That's the room from your photos. It's empty,' he whispered. 'We need to go to the next one.'

Leaving Richardson, they continued.

About fifty metres later, the corridor ended in another door, with another concrete anteroom behind it. This room only had one door leading onwards. They listened for a minute and Whaller used the fibre optic surveillance wire again.

Silence.

Whaller handed Richardson's rucksack to Tim and eased his machine gun into position.

Weapon ready, Whaller opened the door a crack.

Light flooded out.

Tim squinted his eyes to adjust.

This room was large but devoid of Leafers.

He checked again.

No Leafers.

They went in.

The room was over twenty metres long with a high ceiling, but relatively narrow. A rail track ran down the centre of it. At each end of the room was a set of hatches that controlled entry and exit of the flatbed trolleys that ran on the rails.

There were eight separate cylinder segments, each standing on its own flatbed trolley. Each segment was a quarter wedge of a cylinder about two metres high and wide. The full payload would obviously consist of two full cylinders, one on top of the other. Unable to stop his instinct to 'do the maths', Tim calculated each segment would hold between five and eight hundred heads.

'Okay?' asked Whaller, shutting the door behind them.

'Yes.'

'We can talk quietly now,' said Whaller. 'MacKenzie was adamant the Ankor had no eyes or ears down here, and the risk of us miscommunicating is far greater than the risk of being found.'

'Okay,' said Tim, not really understanding. He'd assumed the rucksacks held some high-powered bombs that they would hide.

*Is there more to it?*

'What do you need from me?' asked Tim.

'We've got less than an hour before the crates are sent for loading,' said Whaller. 'You're off sentry duty and on injection duty.'

*Injections?*

Tim acknowledged with a nod.

Whaller shifted his body slightly to bring the rucksack off his shoulder.

He opened it. 'We developed a few options in Porton Down and chose this one,' he said. 'It is the synthetic

Chimera virus, embedded in biodegradable host nerve cells. The whole package makes Ebola look like a tickly cough.'

He took out a wooden case, inside which was a glass case containing a line of five large syringes with hypodermic needles attached.

'The plan is to inject the heads bound for RL3. As many as possible. Hopefully, the Ankor are so intent on assimilating the brain matter that they'll overlook it. It certainly wouldn't come up on any tests we could do on Earth.' Whaller paused. 'Once the virus reaches body temperature, it will start to multiply exponentially.'

'Will it infect Ankor tissue?' Tim asked.

'MacKenzie said the Ankor confirmed human brains could be assimilated. So, our viruses may be able to thrive too. But even if the viruses only reach maximum infection density inside the human skulls, Phase 2 should still work.'

'Phase 2?'

'The virus has two modes. Replication first, and then chemical synthesis. The virus will enter a suicide state where it generates a nerve agent. Even if the virus hasn't spread widely, the nerve agent will.'

'What about reprisals?' asked Tim. It was crunch time. If they succeeded in stopping the Ankor, okay. But if they failed, then at a minimum the remaining forty thousand hostages would die – the prime minister wouldn't risk ordering a new invasion of the Hot Zone now the Ankor had nuked both China and Birmingham. How far would the Ankor punish the UK for a failed attempt at stopping them? Would more cities be obliterated by nuclear blasts to deter further insurgency?

Whaller acknowledged Tim's question. 'We haven't taken this decision lightly. We suspect only a small proportion of the A-Grav units are viable bombs. Each of the ones that have blown up has had a particular pattern of radioactive emissions since installation … low tick neutrons. Across the globe about five percent are showing that pattern.'

*That's still five hundred nuclear bombs …*

Tim let it go unsaid. He simply nodded and reached for the first syringe.

Whaller held out his hand in warning. 'Don't accidentally get any on yourself.'

'How does it work?' Tim asked, pointing to a syringe.

'Each syringe has ten doses; the plunger will click to let you know when you've delivered a full dose.' Whaller pointed at one of the packing cases. 'Take a head. Push the needle through the eyeball and inject one dose. Inject as many heads as you can in ten minutes, and then move onto the next packing case. I'll start at the other end.'

'Okay,' said Tim, nervously looking around. MacKenzie's obsession with security meant if there was a camera, which there appeared not to be, then it would probably only be accessible from the mezzanine. With a bit of luck, it would also be linked to one of the wires that Charlie had cut.

The packing cases did not look easy to access. They were too tall for Tim to see over them, plus they were already on the trolleys.

Tim looked for a way to climb up the side of the one nearest the exit hatch.

'Ladder,' whispered Whaller, pointing to a stepladder in the corner of the room.

*Good news and bad news.*

The good news was that Tim now had a means by which to climb up. The bad news was that someone might have put the stepladder there for a final set of checks that some heavily armed Leafers were on their way to perform.

Whaller had thought the same thing. He took a small package out of his rucksack and fixed it onto the door that the Leafers would likely come through.

Whether it was a bomb or an alarm, Tim didn't know. He took the stepladder and, putting it up carefully next to one of the cylinders, climbed to the top. He laid the syringe case on the top step and inspected the lid.

It had been bolted shut. Whaller had foreseen this and the rucksack also held tools. Tim took a spanner and unscrewed the first bolt of five that secured the lid.

Then the next.

Along the line, Whaller was doing the same, having found a crate to stand on.

Once Tim had undone all the bolts, he levered open the lid. Inside, the space was much smaller than he'd expected from the outside. The cylinder seemed to have extensive insulation.

Tim peered inside. As explained by MacKenzie, the heads were suspended in a freezing gel. Tim poked it with the spanner. It was highly viscous but hadn't set hard. There was no way of knowing if it would. However, given it was at least forty degrees below freezing, he had to avoid putting his bare hands inside.

Searching back inside the rucksack whilst balancing on the top step of the ladder, it appeared that Captain Whaller had prepared well. There was a pair of thick leather gloves in a top compartment. Whether they were intended to protect from the cold or the killer pathogen, Tim wasn't sure.

He put them on and picked up the first syringe.

Usually, on commencing an unpleasant or gory task – such as unblocking a shower drain – Tim would flinch, and possibly shut his eyes. With a needle full of killer virus and a tank full of severed heads, he kept his hands steady and his eyes wide open.

The gel was sticky. Tim reached in and pulled out the first head by its hair. He turned it and rested it on the edge of the packaging case. It was a middle-aged man.

*Not Charlie …*

Gulping, Tim pushed the needle into the right eyeball. It slid in without resistance. Tim pushed the plunger down one unit, click, delivering the Chimera virus deep into the brain.

*Shit!*

Tim hadn't thought this through. He had nowhere to put the head. If he put it back, he might mix it up and reinject it. The efficacy of the plan depended on as wide a distribution of brain material across the Ankor craft as possible. The hope was that, of the four thousand brains being sent, on average each pod would get twelve of them. In this way, the chemicals would get a chance to attack all of them. In any case, double injection into one brain was a waste.

At the same time as this thought hit his brain, the cold hit Tim's hand. The gloves had not been as effective as he'd have liked. One slip and Tim would get serious burns from the gel, probably rendering further injections impossible.

*Fuck!*

It hurt.

'Double speed,' hissed Whaller from the next cylinder. 'The gel is setting. We've no more than ten minutes.'

'Come on,' Tim whispered to himself.

On the next injection, Tim noticed that Whaller was correct: the gel was getting more viscous. If it set fully, then he would not be able to get the heads back in. Tim pushed the head back into the gel, angling towards his left-hand side. He took another head near the surface and injected again.

The process continued.

Each time, Tim took a few seconds to try to memorise the facial features of the head, to mitigate against double injections, and he continued to push injected heads down on the left and pull them up from the right.

After twenty injections and two empty syringes, Tim began to lose feeling in his left hand. He tried to switch hands and scoop with his right and inject with his left. That failed.

Rubbing life back into his hands, Tim looked towards Whaller.

Whaller was hard at work, but also scanning the room every five seconds or so.

*Will they come?*

Judging that he was unlikely to get uninjected heads due to his inability to reach more deeply into the current packing case, Tim moved on.

After securing the bolts back on the cylinder, he climbed down.

The injections continued.

Eight minutes later, and with half of the final syringe still full, sirens started.

Tim looked over to Whaller again.

He had finished and was packing up.

Tim quickly grabbed for another head.

As he pulled it out, a sound from the end of the room indicated the exit hatch was opening.

'Let's go,' said Whaller, now standing under Tim.

Pushing the head back into the near-set gel, Tim secured the packing case, and then carefully put everything back into the rucksack.

Quietly opening the door, Tim and Whaller slipped back into the secret corridor.

After the relatively well-lit transport room, the corridor seemed even more dim, and Tim could not see more than a few metres ahead.

Richardson was not where they'd left him.

They reached the first anteroom to find him slumped against a wall; he was still alive but his breathing was laboured. His hand still pressed a blood-soaked cloth to his shoulder.

'Can we move you?' asked Whaller.

'Just drag me into the corridor, and leave me there,' said Richardson, 'there's more chance of discovery here.'

'I have an idea,' said Tim. He reached up to the observation slit and looked into the decapitation room.

In the half-light, he scanned the room.

*Empty.*

'One moment,' he said.

Whaller raised an eyebrow, but Tim had earned a modicum of trust by now and was allowed to carry on.

He cracked open the door and crept through.

There, in the corner: Sam's wheelchair.

Whaller and Tim gently lifted Richardson into it, and then set off back up the corridor.

On the journey, now using sign language and lipreading, they'd decided they didn't want MacKenzie to see Richardson hurt. Not only would it give him satisfaction, but also he would have known where Juan had been stationed. They'd prefer for MacKenzie to think they were still planning a Hot Zone assault.

At the top of the corridor, Tim left Whaller and Richardson in the MIDAS server room, before heading back to the Faraday room.

--------

Tim found Sam sitting on a wooden chair outside the Faraday room. After a brief hug, he gave her a thumbs-up to indicate success, then mimed that Richardson was injured.

Sam knocked quietly on the door.

It opened, and Martel came out. His eyes widened when he saw Tim. There was blood on his hands. He indicated for them both to come inside.

MacKenzie was lying half-conscious on the floor, blood oozing from a bandaged hand and from his mouth. His hands were still tied, but now in front of him.

Once the door was firmly shut behind them, Martel turned to Sam and Tim. 'Apologies, but there have been developments on the RL3 launch. MacKenzie had not been entirely honest with us. He did have some codes that locked down the launch.'

'Has he told you them?' asked Sam.

'He told them to me when I first asked,' said Martel. 'What you see here is a punishment for his original misdirection.' He paused. 'All good?'

Tim looked towards MacKenzie, wondering what he could hear. He kept it brief. 'Captain Whaller is in the server room. It's fine.'

'I'll go and look in on him,' said Martel. 'One of you should get some sleep, and I'd like the other on the mezzanine with me.'

'Who will guard MacKenzie?' asked Sam.

'I'll ask Whaller to do it once I've spoken to him,' said Martel, turning for the door.

Once Martel had closed the door behind him, MacKenzie stirred and manoeuvred himself into a sitting position against the wall.

'So, what's new with you?' Tim asked Sam, one eye on MacKenzie who was stifling groans in the corner.

Sam smiled at him, seemingly finding it easy to ignore MacKenzie. 'The US have noticed we've restarted RL3. Apparently, the prime minister had assured the president it would not happen. They're angry.'

'They weren't swayed by what happened in Birmingham?'

'Could not give a shit,' said Sam.

'Nice to have one more thing to worry about,' said Tim. The US had the most capable military on Earth and appeared to be spending an inordinate amount of time judgementally eying those countries taking an insufficiently hard line with the Ankor.

Uncomfortable with MacKenzie's nudity, Tim took off his jacket and draped it over him.

MacKenzie said nothing, but Tim saw a flicker of appreciation flit across his face. He was obviously in extreme pain.

'I have an aspirin somewhere, if you'd like?' said Tim.

MacKenzie's eyes registered the gesture. 'Anything stronger?'

'I've got Tramadol,' said Sam, reaching into her pocket for her medium strength painkillers.

'Thanks,' said MacKenzie, swallowing the pills that Tim pushed directly into his mouth.

Realising that he and Sam were now alone with MacKenzie, Tim decided to dig. 'Did MedOp ever work?' he asked.

MacKenzie, clearly addled with pain, took a few moments to process the question. 'Yes. The technology was child's play for the Ankor.'

'You're planning to join them in a live meld.' said Sam.

'Yes,' said MacKenzie, gingerly touching his heavily bruised face. 'Hopefully, they'll demand my release soon.'

'Do you really think they'll still ask for you?' asked Tim. He could have asked it in an aggressive way, but it came out quite softly.

'They need me,' said MacKenzie.

'Charlie said you supported the Transcender faction,' said Sam.

'The Transcenders …' said MacKenzie, grimacing through the pain as he moved his weight. Tramadol could only do so much. 'They're the ones humanity needs to worry about. As the Ankor are slowly becoming starved of brain material, more pods are getting desperate and turning to the Transcender methods, if not their end-game.'

'Methods?' asked Sam.

'It must have been they who demanded the detonation in China. Actual full nuclear explosions were never in the original plans.' He shifted himself again to find a more comfortable position. 'Obviously, talk is cheap.'

'What did you do to support the Transcenders?' asked Sam.

'Nothing much,' said MacKenzie, looking a little unsure of himself. 'I listened to them rage for the last fifteen years. And, more recently, I tweaked the contents of RL1 for them.'

'So, their end-game?' asked Tim, wondering if a weakness could be divined from their goals.

MacKenzie nodded. 'They want to create a critical mass of computational ability, with an information density limit so great that they break the simulation they consider us all to be part of.'

'Can they do it?'

'They say that what's black holes are – local informational densities so great they cause a computational node overflow in the Creator universe. They think they can reproduce them with massive computational systems that are impossible to simulate. They think that if they cause enough then all the Creator's back-ups and recovery systems will crash and the whole system goes down.'

'But a total system crash would mean oblivion,' said Tim. 'If a computer fatally crashes then the programs running on it die too. Do they think they can somehow escape into the programming substrate … into its operating system?'

'I'm not sure what they expect,' said MacKenzie. 'I think they hope to be taken out of the simulation and join the higher reality. But I suspect they'd be equally happy with oblivion for this reality.'

'They're not worried about dying?' asked Sam.

MacKenzie shook his head. 'Neither do they spare a thought about all the life created and ended in the fourteen billion years before they were born.'

'So they're simply psychotic,' she said.

'It's the reason Taylor changed his original plans ran for RL3. He couldn't stand the thought of his brain being allocated to a Transcender-aligned pod,' said MacKenzie.

'But you're supporting the Transcenders,' said Tim. 'If they win and meet the information density requirements, you'll die along with all of us.'

'Firstly, I'm not convinced the Creators, if they exist, running this universe would allow that to happen,' said MacKenzie. 'Secondly, the current calculations suggest a requirement for trillions of times more processing capability than the Transcenders have access to. By the time they get anywhere near it, I will have unhooked and be living inside a terraformed gas giant, from where I will make it one of my goals to stop them.'

'Unhooked?' asked Tim, wanting to hear the technicalities.

'By joining with the Ankor, my life will initially be extended by a factor of one thousand.' He paused. 'I will work towards creating a computer capable of electronically housing my entire consciousness and then I will unhook myself from biology altogether.'

'But you said even the Ankor couldn't manage that,' said Tim.

'No, I said they couldn't create electronic artificial intelligence from scratch,' said MacKenzie. 'I don't know what they've achieved in terms of sequential replacement of biology with tech. It may be their belief system is hindering them in some way … a prohibition against idolatry, perhaps.'

'Then what?' asked Sam.

'After I've thwarted the Transcenders and safeguarded the universe,' said MacKenzie, 'then I will create my own universe-sized simulation to hook into.'

Tim felt himself being swept along. 'But you said—'

MacKenzie cut him off. 'What I said was that I didn't necessarily believe that this reality is hosted on a computer in another dimension. I am very prepared to believe that, building from the Ankor's base knowledge, I can build a full simulation that my real self can interact with.' He paused. 'Once complete, I can jack up the frame rate to maximum – extending my life by another factor of a hundred million.'

'A single person simulation,' said Tim. 'With NPCs that think they're real.'

'As real as you or me,' said MacKenzie.

'And your immortal soul?' asked Sam.

'Died at the age of eight clawing at his own throat,' said MacKenzie.

'It all seems so reasonable,' said Sam. 'Except for the fifty thousand people being decapitated.'

For a moment, MacKenzie looked unsure of himself, then his resolve hardened. 'I am reconciled with the price.'

Sam snorted in derision.

MacKenzie turned and stared at her. 'Don't you want to live forever?'

Tim shuddered. He remembered himself asking Sam the same question at the MedOp launch.

Whether Sam remembered, Tim didn't know, she simply shook her head at MacKenzie in disbelief.

# CHAPTER 35

**SpaceOp**

Once Whaller had relieved them, Tim headed back up to the main floor of Mission Control, while Sam returned to the server room to get some sleep.

Up on the mezzanine level, Martel was urgently typing on a small handheld tablet. Tosh and another security guard were circulating around the floor areas, but mostly keeping close to the main doors. Private Hunter shadowed Martel whilst constantly listening to his radio set.

Tim climbed the internal stairs and reviewed the key screens. RL3 countdown was nine hours away and internal radiation was up, now matching the external readings from earlier.

```
Internal
0.1 millisieverts per hour
```

Whoever stayed in Mission Control for the next eight days, to oversee all the launches, had a twenty percent chance of being dead within a year.

*Assuming no further increase in intensity.*

The insidious presence of the radiation played on Tim's mind. Even knowing the feeling was psychosomatic, he scratched his tingling arms. He was not the only one, either. All around the room, people were doing the same.

A screen drew Tim's attention – the space shuttle *Lincoln*.

The image was dark – it was just before midnight at the Kennedy Space Center – but floodlights provided enough evidence to show imminent launch was possible.

Would the Ankor allow it to take off?

A separate screen, ten feet wide, showed a composite image of thirty-six prominent cities that had A-Gravs installed. Tim's eyes flicked between New York, Washington, and Los Angeles.

'Tim,' said Martel, who'd walked over. 'What are people saying about the *Lincoln*?'

'I'll check,' said Tim reaching for the workstation keyboard. 'Although I'm not sure how unbiased it will be.'

As far as Tim was concerned, the Ankor had total electronic control everywhere except the Faraday room. He wasn't sure what they would like to make Martel believe about the *Lincoln*, but if they had an agenda any search would be worthless.

'I understand,' replied Martel, returning his attention to his tablet.

Tim launched a series of searches.

*Lincoln* was dominating the newsfeeds.

'Most people situated near to an A-Grav are unsympathetic towards the Americans. Most people far away from an A-Grav are sympathetic towards them.' Tim paused. 'Irrespective, generally people think it's a counter-attack of some type.'

'It helps that their country is so big,' said Martel.

Martel was spot on. In America, it was considerably easier to get twenty kilometres away from the nearest A-Grav without getting close to another one.

Tim searched. There was no information on potential launch times, or on the purpose of the mission.

'What else can I help you with?' asked Tim.

'I'm still trying to get the Ankor to confirm a delay to the RL4 launch schedule to allow us to get momentum on the volunteer programme.'

'How's it going?' asked Tim.

*Will this be jail clean-out?*

'We're hoping to get enough terminally sick, remarkably brave, or entirely mad people to go ahead with the exchange. The prime minister got agreement from the Cabinet and is going to launch the scheme now. I want you to track responses. We need to understand our chances. We've got just over twenty-four hours before the Ankor demand RL4 preparation starts.'

'I guess,' said Tim, 'if we could give the Ankor sufficient assurances that the replacements would be healthy brains. Particularly if their ethical position is one that minimises unnecessary suffering.'

Martel looked down towards the main floor but didn't reply.

'If we don't make the numbers, will the prime minister agree to killing Anglesey hostages?' asked Tim, aware the Ankor would hear him voice the question.

'He may not have a choice,' said Martel. 'Given the locations of the A-Gravs, we have about sixty million actual hostages. The whole of the UK.'

Tim noted that Martel didn't repeat the point Whaller had voiced earlier that perhaps only a few of the UK's A-Gravs were viable bombs. His assumption was that Martel was continuing to look beaten so that the Ankor were less vigilant and missed the Chimera virus currently being loaded into RL3.

A moment later, the whole of Mission Control listened to the prime minister as he broadcast the request for volunteers on long-wave radio.

Timbers, speaking from a helicopter on his way to Anglesey, stated the case simply. The Ankor were not prepared to leave without the brain materials they needed, but they were prepared to allow substitutions if done in a timely manner. The prime minister went on to state that, in times of national crisis, moral sacrifices, as well as physical ones, sometimes had to be made, and that this was the least bad option in the face of overwhelming military might. He finished his briefing by giving locations where volunteers could meet transport helicopters.

Murmuring rose across Mission Control, not least because the prime minister had reaffirmed his belief that each of the eighty remaining A-Gravs across the country was a functioning nuclear bomb.

## *RL4 delay predicated on RL3 clearing tower by 10am. No exceptions.*

The Ankor broadcast was clear. Tim looked at the countdown clock on the wall. It was now three o'clock. Seven hours to go. It would be a serious challenge to the meet the launch window, and probably even harder to get four thousand volunteers into the Hot Zone in whatever timeframe the Ankor allowed them – the length of the RL4 delay had not been stated.

*How will the Leafers deal with swapping hostages for volunteers?*

It seemed more likely to Tim that the volunteers would simply disappear into the caverns, never to be seen again.

Turning to the main floor, Martel waved for Dexter Hadley to come up to the mezzanine.

All eyes in Mission Control tracked him as he climbed the stairs.

When he arrived, Martel addressed him directly. 'Can it be done?'

Dexter thought for a few moments. 'Bringing forward RL3 … yes, if the Ankor are prepared to accept additional launch risks. We'll have to pump the tanks at a higher flow rate than we'd generally like, and we'll have to halve the time gaps between filling the separate tanks.'

Instantly, a message was displayed on one of the large Mission Control screens.

## *We accept these risks.*

Martel waited for Dexter to nod his assent, and then addressed the floor. 'Bring the launch forward. Set the clock for ten.'

The noise levels on the main floor tripled as people set to work whilst also sharing urgent conversations with their neighbours.

Martel turned to Dexter. 'Thank you.'

It was a polite dismissal, but Dexter didn't leave. He spoke quietly, such that only Martel and Tim could hear. 'It's not a foregone conclusion that the launch teams will support RL4 if there is any hint that existing hostages will be killed.'

'I understand,' said Martel.

As Dexter descended back to his desk, an alarm sounded. The external radiation levels were up again.

**External**
**0.7 millisieverts per hour**

Some members of the launch teams may not want to support RL4 – but they weren't going anywhere else any time soon.

*Should I warn the Ankor?*

The thought came unbidden and unwanted, deep from Tim's unconscious.

A rush of shame spread through him. Somewhere in his brain, his survival instinct was considering telling the Ankor about the Chimera virus.

Assuming the virus instantly disabled the Ankor, then all was well. All other outcomes would lead to retaliation, and just about any retaliation would result in more than forty thousand deaths.

Tim pushed the thought down.

A second later it came back in a different form.

What if Charlie was right? What if the Ankor were right? What if the whole of reality was running on an extra-dimensional computer, and the programmers of that computer had created a set of moral imperatives that they expected humanity – all sentient life – to adhere to?

If those moral imperatives assigned a higher value to 'units of life' than to 'honour' … then what?

*Am I breaking some universal moral law by potentially condemning millions of lives to save forty thousand?*

Taking a deep breath, Tim loosened the collar on his shirt. After the relatively cool temperatures of the underground tunnels, the main floor felt like a furnace. Martel had ordered all the air-conditioning turned off to reduce the spread of radioactive dust.

Clearing all notions of betrayal out of his mind, Tim looked at the screens around the room, his eyes drawn to the one showing the alien craft composite. Over the previous day, even more Ankor pods had risen to the operational temperature of 305K.

Tim checked the details coming from the CNSA feed. The data may be being hacked by the Ankor but the CNSA assured anyone logging onto the system that there were over one hundred independent infrared telescopes concurrently analysing the pod temperatures and sharing readings via long-wave radio.

*Ankor Mother ship – Pod Temperature Distributions:*
*343 Pods*
*276 Operating at an average 305K*
*42 Operating at an average 220K*
*25 Operating at an average 4K*

More pods were waking up.

Given the immense changes in pod temperature from just the single payload of brains delivered by RL1, Tim wondered if the Ankor really needed the ten launches that had been originally scheduled for SpaceOp. Had they put redundancy into their plans?

*Maybe they only need three or four rocket-loads?*

If they had, it gave the volunteer programme a bit more breathing space.

'You're able to track response to the volunteer programme?' asked Martel, appearing at his shoulder.

'Yes, sir,' said Tim.

Within minutes the information started to drip through MIDAS. Analysis of social media feeds indicated thousands of people were already considering volunteering – although there was a big step from social media bravado to physically turning up at the processing station having said goodbye to your loved ones.

Kicking off a quick aggregation routine, Tim turned his attention back to Mission Control. Down on the main floor, the teams focusing on RL3 continued to run checklists. Everyone else watched the screens: internal radiation rising, external radiation critical, panic in the streets.

Obviously, there was ongoing panic, but had anything meaningful changed?

MIDAS pinged its response – not optimistic. A meme was already spreading quickly concerning the expectation that the number of actual volunteers would fall well short of the Ankor's needs.

Would the prime minister take any shortfall from the existing hostages?

Would vigilante mobs start to volunteer people?

'Hey, champ.'

*Sam!*

Tim leapt up from the chair and gave Sam a hug.

'It's your turn to get some rest,' she said. 'You need some sleep.'

'I think I'll keep you company for a bit,' he said.

'No,' said Sam. 'You haven't slept for ages. Go.'

--------

**9am**

Tim felt like he'd only just shut his eyes when he was roused from sleep in the server room by Tosh.

'Anything new?' asked Tim, as he followed Tosh up the corridor to the main floor.

'The prime minister arrived. Apart from that, RL3 is on track. An hour to go.'

Tim climbed to the mezzanine level whilst taking in the latest information from the screens.

Internal radiation was up again. Eight days' exposure would now kill over half the people in the room, and they knew it – almost everyone had scarves wound around their faces.

'Trying to filter out the radioactive dust?' Tim asked Sam, giving her a hug.

Sam shrugged. 'Some of them. The others are hiding their faces in shame.'

'Surely they know the Ankor would murder millions,' said Tim.

'What they really know is that they are complicit in murdering thousands,' said Sam.

'The latest on volunteers?'

Sam shook her head. 'Not good, but Martel asked us to be optimistic in any dealings in here.'

Tim looked at the screens. Although numbers, or projections, were not being given, headlines indicated that momentum for the volunteer scheme was strong.

*Ankor propaganda to keep the SpaceOp workers motivated.*

At that moment Martel, Whaller, and the prime minister emerged from the back door – having most likely been down in the Faraday room. Huddled together, they went over to Dexter.

An internal siren announced the formal pre-launch routine for RL3: payload lockdown, fuelling, and final checks.

The ten-minute countdown started.

*Tick, tick, tick, tick …*

The whole of Mission Control watched the ticking down of every one of the six hundred seconds.

When RL3 eventually took off, it did so to total silence on the main floor.

As it established a two-thousand-kilometre-high orbit without any issues, the teams responded again with silence.

The CNSA screen flashed briefly. The Ankor craft was rearranging its pod configuration – as it had done for RL1, though the CNSA feed stated that it was a different set of pods that were preparing themselves for receipt of RL3.

*An additional worry …*

Tim now knew that the RL3 cargo would be absorbed solely by the main Ankor faction. If the Chimera worked, but only partially, then the Transcender faction may have an opportunity to gain ascendancy.

The CNSA feed updated. More pods were rearranging. Ones that had been involved in the RL1 docking.

*The Transcenders?*

Likely, the Transcenders would want as much material as they could get; were they prepared to fight for it?

Tim watched as a second docking zone was prepared.

*Shit!*

The worst case would be a stand-off between the two factions that meant the material was not integrated into any of the pods.

The prime minister walked to the front of the mezzanine level and addressed the main floor. 'None of us like this. But it has to be done.'

Tim and Sam shared a look. The prime minister was right; the brain materials sent up in RL3 were from people who had died before the full picture had become known. They could not have been saved.

Sam leant in. 'What else will *have* to be done?' she whispered.

Unless the volunteers started to flood in, the Ankor would flex their nuclear muscles in just under a day's time, and then someone would make the decision whether another five thousand poor souls would be murdered.

A news broadcast screen flared to life.

**The United States of America restates that transport of material is an affront to God and will not be countenanced. The fleet has been dispatched to neutralise the SpaceOp launch capability.**

'What do they mean by neutralise?' Tim had to believe that the prime minister would have tried to reason with his counterpart in the US. However, the tone of recent US proclamations had had a fundamentalist tinge.

'We'll find out soon enough,' said Sam.

# CHAPTER 36

**SpaceOp**

It didn't take long for the Americans to follow up their words with action.

The whole of Mission Control turned to watch the live feed as the *Lincoln* fired its initiation motors in Florida. The image of the shuttle on the screen bloomed white as the camera struggled to adjust to the intense light.

It rose.

It cleared the tower.

'Every system must be hard-wired,' said Sam. 'Nothing for the aliens to hook into.'

A new screen opened showing a live broadcast from the US president.

> `'The people of the United States of America`
> `cannot and will not accept the launch of the`
> `British tribute. It is a violation of God's`
> `commandments and as the leader of a Christian`
> `nation – one nation under God, indivisible – I`
> `have no option but to take action.'`

The shuttle continued to climb.

'Come on,' whispered Sam.

*Nothing good can come of this.*

Actually, Tim reflected, that wasn't true. The Americans could destroy the Ankor craft and save the day, but anything less than that would likely lead to disaster.

If the shuttle only managed to intercept and destroy the RL3 payload then surely the Ankor would retaliate. With over two hundred A-Gravs across the US mainland, the price would be too high.

*Plus it would end the chances of the Chimera working, and put the*

*Ankor on their guard.*

Tim felt hypocritical. Hadn't he just helped launch an attack on the Ankor himself? The Ankor would quite easily work out where the Chimera virus came from.

'Now we know why the Ankor asked for RL3 to be brought forward,' said Dexter, who had appeared at the top of the mezzanine steps and was obviously waiting to speak to Martel.

'Why?' asked Sam.

'To prevent the US from destroying it. Their delta-vees are all mismatched now,' said Dexter. 'The shuttle can't intercept.'

'Could the shuttle get up to the Ankor mother ship?' asked Sam.

Dexter paused for a moment. 'Not unless there have been crazily radical changes to the shuttle internals. Its usual configuration wouldn't carry anywhere near enough fuel. The cargo bay would have to be full of fuel, and they would have had to remove thirty percent of its overall weight. Theoretically achievable with new compound materials … but unlikely as hell.'

'But possible?' asked Sam.

'In the same way it's *possible* you could toss a coin, and have it land on its edge three times in a row,' said Dexter.

They watched as the *Lincoln* continued upwards.

'How's the volunteer programme going?' Dexter asked Tim.

Tim turned in his seat and forced a smile. 'People are assembling at the transport sites, but numbers are not clear yet.'

'Will we get to four thousand?'

'Hopefully,' said Tim, one eye still on the shuttle.

*Although, even more hopefully, Chimera will work and volunteers won't be needed.*

Dexter's unconvinced expression said it all.

Tim's stomach cramped. It would be grim for the volunteers and all their friends and family. They had no idea about the Chimera attack. They genuinely thought they were going to Anglesey to die.

*And they still might.*

Martel, noticing Dexter hanging around, left the prime minister and came over. 'Everything okay?'

Dexter flicked his eyes back at Tim before speaking. 'The orbit is stable at two thousand kilometres. It's all in the Ankor's hands now. They should send a craft to descend from their orbit at twenty thousand, and scoop RL3 any moment.' Dexter paused and indicated towards the main floor. 'Most people here have little to do for the next ten hours except worry. We need some direction.'

'Things haven't changed,' said Martel. 'We prepare for RL4 on the basis that the volunteers will come. The first helicopter is due soon.'

Dexter opened his mouth to speak, but changed his mind.

Martel returned to the prime minister, whilst Sam and Tim continued to watch the shuttle climb.

Without warning, an Ankor broadcast flashed on the screens.

### Disobedience has consequences

*The Americans or us?*
*How many reprisals? Where?*
Less than a minute later the news service erupted.

```
Detonations
Mainland USA
New York, San Francisco
```

'Fuck!' Sam grabbed Tim's arm.

At the back of the mezzanine level, Martel and the prime minister had hushed conversations.

Everyone else simply gaped at the horrific images on the main screens. Times Square was in flames and the Golden Gate bridge had been vaporised.

Seconds drew out into minutes.

Still, everyone waited.

Would there be more explosions?

On the main floor the scientists, technicians and support staff all watched as the report ticker continued to give updates on the two explosions.

The death toll was in the millions.

*So much for Martel's price of one million.*

'Ankor bastards,' said Sam.

Tim's instinct was to tell her the Americans had brought it upon themselves, but he held his tongue. Clearly, the poor bastards in the nuked cities had done nothing to deserve it.

*Like the people across Britain who didn't inject the Chimera …*

Joshua Timbers walked to the front of the mezzanine level, and the whole room went silent. 'We pray to God that he receives those poor souls with his infinite grace and kindness.'

Murmured responses of support echoed up from the main floor and the prime minister turned away. There was nothing more to be said.

At two o'clock, the radar tracks indicated that the Ankor had scooped RL3 and that it was less than thirty minutes away from docking with the mother ship.

The configuration of the Ankor receiving zones had not changed. There were still two 'harbours' created by the arrangements of pods. Tim assumed one was for the main faction and one for the Transcenders.

Which way would the Ankor scoop craft take the RL3 module?

The screen showing the CNSA's composite image indicated that more pods had come up to the operational temperature of 305K.

```
Ankor Mother ship - Pod Temperature
Distributions:
343 Pods
276 Operating at an average 305K
42  Operating at an average 220K
25  Operating at an average 4K
```

Based on the information MacKenzie had given to Whaller while Tim had been present, he couldn't quite reconcile MacKenzie's comments about the size of the Ankor brains and their expectations with regards to how much human material they'd need.

Fifty thousand people would provide about fifty tons of brain materials, but empty pods – of which there had been 52 initially – would need two tons each.

*So we're already fifty tons short … plus however much the other three hundred plus pods need to top up.*

Dexter opened a news screen on the main wall – the first helicopter full of volunteers had arrived.

The prime minister, to his credit, had tried to get permission from the Ankor to meet the volunteers, but it was denied. He was confined to Mission Control with everyone else.

Everyone stopped what they were doing and watched on the screens as the twenty volunteers, naked except for their underwear, disembarked from a helicopter outside the Hot Zone. They were met by four Leafers in hazmat suits and had their hands zip-tied behind their backs.

They were led inside.

The helicopter remained where it was, its rotors turning on half power.

The return of twenty hostages was insignificant compared with the Ankor raining nuclear hell down upon all of humanity, but the world still held its breath to see if the Ankor would meet their half of the deal.

A minute passed.

And another.

Twenty people ran from the Hot Zone, and into the helicopter. A wave of relief passed through the main floor.

'Twenty down,' said Sam.

Tim nodded. The volunteers who'd just arrived would be murdered tomorrow. It was hardly a victory – and the current projected volunteer numbers arriving at the transport sites would cover maybe twenty percent of the Ankor's demands for RL4. The rest would have to be made from the existing hostages.

'Current projections?' asked Martel quietly, hunching over the workstation.

'We'll get five hundred in total,' Tim said. 'To meet the RL4 payload and timeframes, existing hostages will need to start being processed just after five tomorrow morning.'

Martel walked back over to the prime minister. After a brief discussion, Timbers left the mezzanine and headed through the back doors.

'You okay?' asked Sam.

'Yes,' replied Tim. 'You?'

Sam shifted in her seat. 'Sore.'

'Do you need painkillers?'

Sam smiled, taking Tim's hand. 'Right now, you could sell my blood for two hundred quid an ounce.'

Once more, Tim's thoughts drifted back to the concept of warning the Ankor about the Chimera. Ultimately, he had no idea whether the level of catastrophic response from the Ankor would be any different if he told them now than if he kept his nerve, the virus didn't incapacitate them, and then they retaliated.

*Stick with the plan.*

In any case, he reflected, if he warned them and then was found out, he'd have had a bullet in the back of the head from Martel, and eternal damnation from Sam.

He squeezed Sam's hand.

The screens didn't have real-time visuals on the alien craft, but the radar arrays pointing that way tracked the RL3 payload as it was taken to the Ankor ship.

It appeared to be docking with the main Ankor faction.

For the next few hours, everyone not involved in preparing for RL4 was glued to the screens: *Lincoln* updates, Ankor craft changes, and volunteer arrivals by helicopter.

Martel, Tim and Sam were particularly focused on the composite CNSA image of the Ankor craft.

There were no further updates on the *Lincoln,* which seemed to have settled into a low Earth orbit, well away from the Ankor craft and the staging area height of the RL modules.

An hour passed.

An alarm drew everyone's attention.

Internal radiation levels had risen another tick.

The minority of people who didn't yet have pieces of cloth tied over their mouths now changed their minds.

Tosh started making more frequent visits up to the mezzanine for furtive whispered conversations with Martel.

Each time Tosh came up the stairs, Sam widened her eyes conspiratorially at Tim.

Martel must have known the Ankor would be able to hear even the slightest whisper outside of the Faraday room. Tim hoped they were keeping the communication oblique.

Another hour passed.

```
Ankor Mother ship - Pod Temperature
Distributions:
343 Pods
32  Operating at an average 310K
218 Operating at an average 305K
```

**42   Operating at an average 220K**
**51   Operating at an average 4K**

'RL3?' asked Sam, pointing to the CNSA feed.

The pod temperatures of the Ankor mother ship were increasing above 305K. 'Seems likely,' said Tim.

*A good thing, or a bad one?*

Another hour passed.

Now, Martel left the mezzanine and through the back doors in the direction of the Faraday room.

The composite infrared image of the Ankor craft blinked out.

Information on the pod temperatures was gone. Tim dared not submit a search into MIDAS. He looked around the mezzanine level for Private Hunter.

*He'll have radio information.*

Hunter was crouched at the back of the mezzanine level, listening to the radio set.

Tim scurried over.

As Tim approached, Hunter gave him a knowing look and indicated for him to wait whilst he continued to listen.

Hunter stood and, beckoning Tim to follow, headed for the Faraday room.

Tim walked back over to Sam and grabbed her crutches. 'Come on.'

'Are you sure I should come as well?' asked Sam.

'We're a team,' said Tim.

Together they followed Hunter down to the Faraday room, where Martel, Whaller and the prime minister were already in conversation.

Also in the corner of the room, closely guarding Francis MacKenzie, was Lieutenant Briars – the last remaining member of the liaison team. Tim smiled a greeting at Briars, who returned it.

357

'I evaded capture,' said Briars, grinning. He prodded MacKenzie. 'Unlike this one.'

MacKenzie opened one eye but didn't speak.

Martel ignored the exchange, signalled to Whaller to confirm the electronic seals were in place, then turned to the group. 'Good news. Three separate measurements from the Ankor mother ship in the last ten minutes indicate that at least eighty of their pods, after showing initial signs of overheating, are now cooling rapidly.'

# CHAPTER 37

**SpaceOp**

Tim looked at Sam, not quite daring to allow the hope to rise … eighty pods were cooling.

*Frankly, that means at least eighty. We don't know what's happened in the last ten minutes … it could be more …*

'Do you have an update, Hunter?' asked Martel.

'There are explosions in some of the cross-strut connectors between the pods,' said Hunter.

'Possibly isolating the infections,' said Martel. 'Do you have a sense of how many?'

'Almost a third of the pods are being isolated to some extent,' replied Hunter.

Martel turned to Tim and Sam. 'Can you quietly try to assess the status of the Ankor's control of Earth's technology?'

'Of course,' said Sam. 'We'll get straight onto it.'

'Also,' said Martel, 'I'm planning evacuations of SpaceOp with Tosh. The Americans have diverted their Atlantic fleet this way. I'm not sure how far they're going to take it.'

*All the way … if their rhetoric so far is any guide.*

'Captain Whaller said you showed him an escape tunnel?'

'Yes,' said Tim. 'It runs all the way to the coast.'

Martel turned to Francis MacKenzie who, half-forgotten, was slumped in the corner of the room, drowsing. 'Is this true?'

MacKenzie didn't even try to open his eyes, which were bruised and swollen shut. 'True. One of my contingency options.'

Whaller crossed the room and grabbed MacKenzie by the ear. Twisting hard, he pulled his head up. 'Are there any traps?'

'No!' MacKenzie squirmed, levering himself up onto his right knee to avoid more pain.

Apparently satisfied, Whaller allowed him to drop to the ground. 'If the Ankor are beaten, then all we have to do is storm the Hot Zone. The Leafers may even surrender.' As an afterthought, he turned back to MacKenzie. 'Are the Leafers believers or hired guns?'

'Hired guns,' said MacKenzie. 'They have no idea what's going on.'

'Okay,' said Martel, absorbing the information. 'Sam, would you please look in on Richardson on your way up?'

Sam nodded.

Leaving Whaller and Briars guarding MacKenzie in the Faraday room, and dropping Sam off in the MIDAS server room, the rest of them returned to the Mission Control mezzanine.

On arrival, with Martel next to him, the prime minister started talking urgently on Private Hunter's radio. He was trying to convince the Americans not to fire on SpaceOp, on the basis that the volunteers were coming.

Tim strained to listen. The conversation didn't appear to be going well.

Logging on to the workstation, Tim considered how to check the current state of the Ankor capability.

No sooner had he touched the keyboard than they made it clear themselves.

Screens opened on the main wall to show two giant detonations had hit China. Two one-hundred kiloton blasts – city-busters – had hit Beijing and Tianjin, vaporising vast swathes of each city.

*Thirty million people … Is this the last act of a trapped dying beast?*

Tim scanned the news feeds playing across the screens on the main floor, trying to ascertain if China was the only target.

*Why China?*

Down on the main floor, people shared worried glances but continued to go about their business.

*They probably think it's more payback for China's previous rebellions.*

Tim looked at the composite radar image of the Ankor craft. The craft, once oval, was now looking ragged. Large gaps were appearing where pods were being jettisoned – possibly just for quarantine purposes, but potentially permanently.

The minutes ticked by.

Another screen opened.

Another two large blasts.

Sao Paulo and Mexico City.

*Thirty million more … so much for their belief in the sanctity of life.*

Utter silence descended on Mission Control as people simply stopped whatever they'd been doing.

Before that moment, people could rationalise that China had been punished. This was different. Brazil and Mexico had done nothing wrong. It was true they both had space launch capability, but neither had even been selected to send shield materials.

Screens opened on the wall showing that news of the blasts was spreading quickly.

The most immediate reactions came from people who happened to be in their cars when the reports came through. Tim watched screens of people acting similarly in every major city, be it Tokyo, Sydney, Moscow … everywhere.

Disregarding traffic signals and pedestrian safety, drivers scrambled to get distance from their respective A-Grav sites.

The Ankor had other plans for them.

Having taken control of the electronic transport infrastructure, the Ankor raised bridges leading out of cities, lowered automated barriers, and jammed traffic signals – all the actions required to create gridlock.

People were being bottled in, the way that old time cowboys used to corral cattle.

Fires. Deaths. Panic.

Again, the minutes ticked by.

A screen opened on Tim's workstation.

> **Mr Boston, it's time to deal**

Tim looked around. The Ankor message appeared to have been sent only to his workstation. Only sent to him.

*Shit.*

He didn't bother typing his response; he simply whispered aloud, knowing the Ankor would be able to hear. 'What?'

> **The Ankor are barely holding on. The latest explosions are the result of the-sterile circumventing our controls. We stopped them and they are listening but they will not hold forever.**

'What do you want from me?'

> **The volunteers are not coming. The Americans will**

*be with you in three days.*
*They will destroy SpaceOp*
*and everyone in it.*

'And?'

*Help us get RL4 and we*
*will stop the Americans*
*and leave Earth alone.*

'If I refuse?'

*We will leave SpaceOp to*
*the mercy of the Americans*
*and leave the rest of the*
*UK to the mercy of the-*
*sterile.*

There was a chance they were bluffing. Charlie had been explicit that the main faction of the Ankor considered life sacred. Now, the Ankor themselves had admitted the recent explosions had been caused by the-sterile: the Transcenders.

*If you refuse, the-sterile*
*will blow A-Grav units*
*across the UK, wiping out*
*most of the population …*
*we estimate 40 million*
*deaths within two months.*
*And we will simply start*
*again with another*
*country.*

'No-one will comply.'

*They will. We may be forced to wait a few months … we will get our Blessed.*

'They'll all say the same. No.'

*Will they? Because we'll be offering a global dictatorship underpinned by our nuclear arsenal to the leader who helps us.*

Tim stayed silent. He could think of a few countries that would accept that deal.

*Do you see now?*

'What would you need me to do?' Tim was still sure he was going to refuse, or at least refer the request to Martel, but he wanted to understand the whole picture.

*Save 40 million lives. With your help we can take control of the Hot Zone mechanics. Head to the back of the mezzanine, open the hatch furthest left and closest to the floor. There will be seven wires lined up vertically. Cut the third and the sixth counting from the*

**left. Then close the hatch.**

'And?'

**Once you have done this, we will be able to trigger the processing of the RL4 Blessed. Once the Blessed are prepared there will be little purpose in your government sacrificing more people to stop them being delivered. Then we will leave – just this one launch.**

Tim was unsure if they would leave, but the Ankor were right. Once the hostages were dead, the prime minister would look himself in the mirror and give the order to launch RL4.

Tim looked down at the staff on the main floor.

*Would they all obey the order?*

'If I was seen, Martel would shoot me.'

**You'd be saving 40 million lives. And, we'll give you something to soothe your injured morals.**

'The launch technicians will mutiny.'

**We can control them.**

Tim wanted to walk away but found himself unable to.

Perhaps sensing this, the Ankor continued.

**You're not going to get any money from MacKenzie.**

Tim knew that the money was gone, and the impact on Sam's recovery had been dwelling in his conscience for the last few days – albeit, not getting much airtime up front due to the reasonably constant fear of imminent death.

**We'll send you detailed schematics and medical information to allow Sam to be cured. After a suitable time for an evacuation, we'll blow Anglesey and any evidence of your tampering will be destroyed … it will be our secret.**

'Why this way?' asked Tim.

**To use a human idiom … cards on the table. Taking control of the Hot Zone without evident human support makes us look powerful. That makes people less likely to resist us. That makes it less likely we will need to contravene our faith and blow nuclear charges.**

*But you said you'll accept just this one launch. What would it matter how people feel?*

The admission that they wanted to look powerful worried him. Were they vulnerable? Were they lying when they said that RL4 would be the last?

Tim's thoughts returned to his estimates of the brain material required to fill all the Ankor pods. They needed a minimum of two hundred and fifty launches. They couldn't travel faster than light. Why would they go anywhere else?

'Your faith doesn't allow you to take lives,' said Tim.

**Our faith allows us latitude to take lives when the cost is justified. The early China explosion was necessary. The radiation leaks to drive people to SpaceOp were acceptable. More recent blasts are unacceptable.**

Tim stood up. If he refused and the Ankor made good on their threat and blew the UK, he would have forty million deaths on his hands.

'Are we living in a simulation?'

**We have faith, not proof, although one often cited example is our inability to reconcile what you know as quantum mechanics and general relativity. This could be explained by many**

*things, of which one would
be that our simulated
universe simply uses
different algorithms at
different scales.*

'I need time to decide.'

**There is no time. Observe.**

Three screens opened on the main walls of Mission Control.

Each showed a cityscape: London, Manchester, Newcastle.

# CHAPTER 38

**SpaceOp**

As the screens opened showing the real-time feeds from London, Manchester, and Newcastle, a rumble of conversation built amongst the people working on the main floor.

A shiver of dread passed over Tim.

Were they showing the pictures specifically to him as a threat?

He rechecked the screens.

The first screen bloomed bright white, seemingly losing the picture to a technical fault.

A split second later, the screen adjusted. It had not been a glitch, but an explosion.

London.

'No!' Tim's scream had come involuntarily and, afraid his outburst had been noticed, he glanced around the main floor.

He needn't have worried. His voice had been lost in the tumult. Cries of despair filled the room but people remained at their stations – to some extent the blasts had just been the confirmation of an expectation.

*Our turn …*

The other two screens now bloomed white with explosions and live images of the stricken cities dominated the walls.

Nuclear firestorms raged in London, Manchester, and Newcastle.

How far would the Ankor go?

Sitting back down at the workstation, Tim whispered at the screen. 'I hadn't said no.'

Silence.

'I didn't say no,' Tim hissed urgently. 'You didn't give me any time.'

He felt his chest tighten.

The screens on the main walls, with their sound mercifully muted, continued to show tragedies unfolding. Giant fires raged unchecked. People scattered in all directions and abandoned their useless stationary cars on foot.

Amongst all the anger and pain on the main floor, the internal radiation counter ticked up another unit.

**Internal**
**0.3 millisieverts per hour**

Somehow, even with all the proofing that Tosh had done, the radiation was leaking into the building.

Martel, standing by Tim, stared at the screens. Every vein on his head and neck appeared to be attempting to break out through his skin. He stood stock still, slowly breathing in and out.

'Tim!'

Sam appeared at the top of the stairs on her crutches.

Tim ran over, lowering his voice to a hiss. 'Sam. Listen. They did this because of me. They asked me to hack into a system to start the Hot Zone processing people for RL4.'

For the next minute, Tim recounted the conversation he'd had with the Ankor.

'But you didn't say no?'

'Ten seconds after the final question, they blew the bombs,' said Tim, still struggling for breath.

'What were you going to say?' asked Sam.

'I was going to say no,' said Tim. 'Now I wish I could say yes. The consequences are too severe.'

Perversely, Tim's brain immediately constructed a scenario in which the long-term detrimental effects of succumbing to the Ankor outweighed the short-term gain.

The scenario depended on Earth getting a reputation for being blackmailable, and successive alien civilisations bleeding it dry. Tim pushed the thought away. 'I didn't realise ... Charlie's talk of moral code.'

'I'd have cut the wires,' said Sam. 'Just based on the fatality numbers ... and perhaps a bit for the cure.'

'I thought you'd hate me if I sacrificed all those people just to cure you.'

'You wouldn't have had to tell me,' said Sam, her eyes deadly serious.

Tim had no answer to that.

Noises of dissent intensified over by the front doors where a crowd of thirty people appeared to be begging Tosh to let them out.

Leaving Hunter and the prime minister, Martel walked over from the back of the mezzanine. 'Cambridge was hit too. Plus an army base in Wiltshire.'

Tim didn't know what to say. He suspected that coming clean might be the best option.

Standing at the edge of the mezzanine level, Martel shouted to get people's attention. Just as he was about to shout again, the word 'SIMULATION' superimposed itself across every screen.

'What the fuck?' said Sam.

The screens showing Newcastle city centre flickered. The pictures that returned were peaceful views. Newcastle untouched. The camera zoomed in on casual smokers standing outside a pub, oblivious to the apparent nuclear attack they'd just suffered. Then it panned across to a main road: a few cars were driving serenely through near-empty roads.

Down on the main floor, everyone knew they were being played in some way by the Ankor and angry mutterings mixed in equal measure with sighs of relief.

Wondering whether he should tell Martel about the Ankor offer, Tim looked over towards Martel, Hunter and Timbers who were talking quietly at the back of the mezzanine.

Martel looked over towards Tim. Their eyes locked.

*I'll tell him.*

Movement from the main floor drew Tim's attention before he could get to Martel. A group of about twelve technicians, arguing strongly with Dexter Hadley, were at the foot of the stairs and coming up.

Private Hunter replaced the radio receiver and readied his assault rifle, but Martel indicated for him to stand down and quickly walked over to address them.

Martel walked with such purpose and speed that he met Dexter halfway down the stairs; the technicians were forced to stay on the lower level.

His neutral expression giving nothing away, Martel addressed the group. 'How can I help you, Mr Hadley?'

Dexter, after looking over his shoulder briefly, took the lead. 'They're clearly trying to manipulate us. We'll not launch any forced decapitations.'

'Agreed on both counts,' said Martel. 'We are working hard to replace the hostages with volunteers.'

'Volunteers only?' asked Dexter.

'Yes,' said Martel.

Dexter nodded. 'Okay. We just wanted you to know the position. If you support activity in the slaughterhouse … there'll be open rebellion here. A few people here have close friends and family in there.'

*A few people have friends and family across the country too.*

The prime minister, who had not reacted to the incursion with the same speed as Martel, now joined the group, standing shoulder-to-shoulder with Martel. 'It will be volunteers only.'

'We've counted the helicopter rotors,' said Dexter. 'By my calculations, the Americans will blow us away before we get enough volunteers to fill RL4.'

'I have been speaking to the US president,' said the prime minister. 'He is considering our position. I expect him to call off any attack.'

*Liar ...*

Everything Tim had overheard during the previous few hours had implied that the US president was continuing to refuse all calls from Timbers for fear it was an Ankor trap.

Dexter also looked unconvinced; he turned and had a few whispered exchanges with the technicians, then he shepherded them back to their desks. None of them looked happy.

'Maybe they used simulations because they won't do it?' said Sam.

'They already really hit China and Mexico and Brazil,' said Tim. 'I suspect they're more worried about contaminating the cargo.'

'So,' said Sam. 'Do we do it?'

Tim looked around.

Martel, Hunter and Timbers were in huddled conversation back at the rear mezzanine wall. They were standing directly by the hatch that the Ankor had specified.

*Do they know?*

Tim stood up. 'Colonel?'

'Yes, Tim?' said Martel.

With Sam next to him on her crutches, Tim walked over and joined the group. This far back from the ledge, they were entirely hidden from the main floor. Tim pointed at the hatch. 'They just asked me to do this.'

'Just?' The understanding in Martel's eyes was unmistakable. 'You refused?'

'A few minutes ago. They didn't even give me a chance to think about it. They asked. I said I needed to think. I got up to talk to you, and the simulations started.'

'Perhaps they knew you wouldn't be swayed,' said the prime minister.

'I hadn't decided,' said Tim.

'I have been given five minutes to cut the wires,' said Martel, looking at his tablet. 'Five minutes – or it happens for real.' He looked at Timbers, who indicated his agreement.

Martel leant down and, checking he was hidden from the rest of the room, opened the hatch. Private Hunter took up a position guarding the top of the staircase.

*There will be seven wires, cut the third and the sixth …*

Inside the hatch were over fifteen multicoloured wires.

Martel checked the next hatch along. That one had no wires. He checked the next. None.

A message flashed up on Martel's tablet. He shared it with the group.

> **I hope you have not killed Francis MacKenzie. Only he will know the correct process. The Ankor assume that any wires cut incorrectly will result in the Hot Zone being rendered inoperable.**

--------

Leaving Private Hunter and the prime minister on the mezzanine, Martel indicated for Sam and Tim to follow him, saying he may need back-up. Tim would have been happier not to accompany Martel to 'see' MacKenzie. It was clear to him that torture would be used.

When they reached the MIDAS server room where Richardson was resting, Martel turned to Sam. 'Would you please check on Lieutenant Richardson?'

Sam nodded as Martel surreptitiously gave her a small folded piece of paper.

Tim and Martel walked on to the Faraday room, where they found Whaller and Briars sitting on the floor with an array of assault rifles laid out in front of them.

As they entered the room, they stood and saluted Martel.

Martel secured the door and activated the electrified barrier, then he turned to Tim. 'The Americans are coming. We have two, or at most three, days as they need to be in range for their naval artillery. They are under orders to flatten SpaceOp, together with anyone left inside. The prime minister has been unsuccessful in his efforts to deter them.'

'Understood.'

'If we try to leave without triggering RL4 decapitations,' continued Martel, 'the Ankor will blow up all the UK's major cities.'

Martel walked over and kicked MacKenzie. 'Which are the right wires to cut behind the hatch?'

MacKenzie had clearly been expecting the question. 'I can't remember. Too many blows to the head.'

Based on previous encounters, Tim expected Whaller to draw a knife and threaten to cut out MacKenzie's eye.

He didn't. Neither did Martel.

Martel squatted down next to MacKenzie. 'What do you want? We need your full cooperation.'

'Some clothes,' said MacKenzie.

Whaller took some clean clothes from one of the large holdalls and helped MacKenzie into a tracksuit.

'Water,' said MacKenzie.

Whaller took a canteen of water and, untying MacKenzie's hands, allowed him to drink as much as he wanted.

Within a few minutes, MacKenzie was ready to talk. 'You send *me* up in RL4. I have a modified pod equipped for my own transport – it was always going to be the tenth launch. Once I am there, I will give the required data.'

'What will stop the Ankor venting you into space once they have the data?' asked Tim.

MacKenzie smiled. 'Their faith.'

'And if the Transcenders are in control?' asked Tim, aware that the escalating violence was probably down to their increasing influence.

MacKenzie shrugged. 'I'll take my chances. My future down here is not exactly brimming with possibilities.'

'Wait,' said Tim. 'One more thing. Do we think they'll really stop after RL4? They need at least two hundred and fifty tons. If we do this one, won't they keep coming back until they have two hundred and fifty thousand brains?'

'If we don't do it,' said Martel, 'they'll kill one hundred million right now … and may still keep coming back, depending on how irradiated Earth is.'

'Two hundred and fifty thousand,' said MacKenzie slowly. 'You know that's less than three days' worth of natural deaths across the globe? It's a drop in the ocean.'

Tim focused on MacKenzie 'Do you think they could be convinced to stop after RL4?'

MacKenzie appeared to consider it. 'For what it's worth, I'll try to argue your case. Once the Americans are stopped, then time is of limited importance to them. A volunteer-only tribute system running over decades could be used to provide the materials.'

'They could have done that from the start,' said Whaller.

'No, they couldn't,' said MacKenzie. 'You can see how the Americans are – sanctity of life. Humanity would have never agreed and would have gone to war with itself.'

'Okay,' said Martel. 'For now, we take them at their word. RL4 will be the last.'

Opening the door to break the electronic seal, Martel relayed MacKenzie's demands to the Ankor. The reply came quickly.

**Launch RL10 by 10am. Retrieval completes by 2pm. HZ processing starts 3pm. RL4 launches final cargo 10am Friday.**

Tim looked at his watch. Two o'clock. They had eight hours to launch RL10 from a standing start.

Martel turned to MacKenzie and lifted his pistol. 'Deal. But timing is tight. I need to understand the RL10 location and the process for loading.'

'The Ankor will guide you step by step,' said MacKenzie. 'But a copy of all the information is on a zip drive hidden under my workstation.'

'I suspect that bringing you to the main floor will cause a riot,' said Martel. 'Tell me where to find it.'

MacKenzie gave the location. 'Dexter will know what to do with it.'

'Password?' asked Martel.

'No spaces. No capitals,' said MacKenzie. 'God and man only one can live forever.'

'That's a quote you made twenty years ago,' said Tim, remembering it coming up in one of his pre-employment due diligence searches.

'My favourite quote, and I stand by it,' said MacKenzie. 'Education will light the fire that burns back the darkness.'

'And yet you're not staying to help,' said Tim.

'I have another favourite expression … fit your own life jacket first,' said MacKenzie, now smiling. 'Immortality beckons.'

**Go now. USA attack sooner than expected.**

# CHAPTER 39

**SpaceOp**

Tim, Martel and Sam arrived on the mezzanine just as the prime minister stepped forward to address Mission Control.

'The Space Shuttle *Lincoln* is inbound,' said the prime minister, raising his voice to be heard across the room. 'On its present course it will hit SpaceOp in just under an hour.'

*The Lincoln is a flying bomb!*

Sam leant into Tim, whispering, 'I suspect their reasoning goes along the lines of *better dead than enslaved to the Ankor*.'

'Can we stop it?' asked someone from the floor.

The prime minister looked ashen and consulted his computer tablet. 'The Ankor will engage it with missiles from a Royal Navy destroyer stationed off the Outer Hebrides.'

The murmuring on the floor rose.

'We'll fire on our long-term allies?' Dexter Hadley had climbed halfway up the internal staircase.

'We must deliver RL4 to save millions of British lives,' replied the prime minister, as Martel shepherded Dexter up the stairs.

More murmuring echoed around the floor, but no-one called out.

'Complicated,' said Sam.

'You may not like this,' said Martel to Dexter as they arrived at MacKenzie's workstation. 'But the cost of getting extra time to find volunteers is releasing MacKenzie.'

'Where would he go?' asked Dexter.

'Assuming the Americans don't kill us all, MacKenzie will be on the next launch … at 10am.' Martel paused. 'Both the Cambridge explosion and the Wiltshire one were real … one hundred thousand dead. Larger targets will be hit if he is not released.'

'10am?' said Dexter. 'It's not possible.'

Martel retrieved the zip drive from the hidden compartment and opened the file that MacKenzie had indicated held the plans for RL10. 'Does this look right?'

Dexter skimmed the file's contents. 'Seven hours …'

As he spoke, the information on the screen changed. The Ankor were making updates and providing a detailed list of minute-by-minute activities for every person in SpaceOp. They did not mention the actual payload.

'It's a precondition of getting extra time to use volunteers instead of hostages,' said Martel.

Dexter checked. 'Possible … Is the payload a secret?'

'Keeping it a secret would be impossible,' said Martel. 'But we'll try to keep it quiet.'

Dexter nodded. 'I'll get to work.'

Five minutes later, Joshua Timbers live-streamed to the whole nation.

'There is no legal precedent for what I am about to say. I suspect that myself and everyone in the chain of command will be accused as war criminals in years to come … but the threat of further nuclear retaliation is too much to risk and I cannot delay this difficult decision any longer. I am hereby announcing the full surrender of the British government to the Ankor. Additionally, I have ordered the Royal Navy to work with the Ankor to bring down the United States Space Shuttle Lincoln, which we believe is on a suicide run aiming at the SpaceOp launch pad.'

Statement over, the prime minister returned to the back of the mezzanine, speaking on Private Hunter's radio.

Tim looked around the floor at the men and women, young and old, who were busily preparing for the launch. He turned to Martel. 'Could we evacuate non-critical personnel?'

Martel was not convinced. 'Where would they go? The radiation outside is critical.'

There was no answer to that.

A screen came to life. Whether it was a library shot or a live stream was not clear. However, all three hundred personnel within the main room watched a series of missiles being launched from a British ship.

The screen closed.

Sam typed into the workstation, looking for possible news services.

A tangential news item confirmed the strike.

The *Lincoln* was lost.

Moments later, the US government made a statement.

**The United States of America will not stand idly by while acts of aggression are committed against it. As a consequence of this unprecedented attack, the United States is now at war with the United Kingdom.**

Tim sat down next to Sam. 'I assume the Ankor will protect us.'

'Until they get their brains,' said Sam. 'And then we're on our own.'

A new commotion broke out at the foot of the internal staircase.

Martel headed down to address the twenty people who had congregated.

Listening from the top of the staircase, Tim picked up the thread of the conversation.

'You must unlock the doors,' said one man.

'The radiation levels outside are too dangerous,' replied Martel.

'It should be our decision whether to leave. Or are we all hostages too?'

'I'm sorry,' said Martel. 'But the answer is no.'

Tim saw Martel's hand drift towards the pistol at his belt.

Perhaps the ringleader noticed too, as he backed away from the stairs.

Martel came back up to the workstation. 'Tim, I need to take personal control of the RL10 set-up. I will be going over to the Assembly Zone. Obviously, the prime minister is in charge, but if anything unusual occurs please get Private Hunter to call me.' He paused. 'And take this.' Martel handed Tim Francis MacKenzie's computer tablet. 'See if you can get any of the video feeds of the Hot Zone working at the back wall.'

'Yes, sir,' said Tim.

A minute later, Martel left the mezzanine level.

'Shall we plug in?' asked Sam, wheeling herself towards the back wall.

'Sure,' said Tim. They might see something that could help.

--------

For a few hours, Tim and Sam checked video feeds of the Hot Zone by plugging into hard-wired network ports at the back of the mezzanine. Most feeds were either broken or showed empty rooms, although occasionally they came across a corridor shot that showed a Leafer patrol. However, as there were no reference points at all, they could not tell where the corridor was.

'Charlie probably cut all the interesting ones,' said Tim.

'What do you think happened to him?' asked Sam.

'I don't know,' said Tim, still skipping through the CCTV channels.

Sometime just before dawn, Tosh appeared with food. 'RL10 is almost ready for launch,' he said, handing out sandwiches.

'Thanks,' said Tim, taking one and looking at the main screens. 'They're early.'

'Martel has been cracking the whip,' said Tosh. 'RL10 won't actually go early, though.'

'Why?' asked Sam.

Tosh leant in conspiratorially. 'MacKenzie insisted on being able to check his retrieval unit thoroughly.'

Tosh went on to explain that the RL10 module was set up such that, even at 300km above the Earth, MacKenzie could abort and return safely to ground by a series of perishable parachutes.

'I don't think he'd be safe for long if he did return,' said Sam.

'Well, for now, we're all pretty incentivised to get him into orbit,' said Tim, feeling a little wretched that MacKenzie's safe arrival at the Ankor craft would not trigger – as people generally thought – a time extension for volunteers, but would trigger the Ankor overwhelming the Hot Zone controls leading to the deaths of approximately five thousand people.

*But saving millions more from reprisals …*

A few hours later, MacKenzie's checks completed, RL10 launched.

The screens in the main room tracked its ascent.

The climb went without a problem and it reached stable orbit.

Around Mission Control the feelings were mixed. People were angry that MacKenzie had escaped, but they were pleased that it would cause the Ankor to give the UK the time extension required to fill the RL4 payload with volunteers.

All that was required now was for the Ankor to retrieve the pod, rehouse MacKenzie, and for MacKenzie to give the required information to override the Hot Zone processes.

That part would have to be done very quietly.

*Maybe we should have been open with everyone in Mission Control.* Tim wasn't sure.

'Look!' Sam pointed to the feed showing the Ankor craft. 'That's the Transcenders, right?'

As with RL3, the Transcenders appeared to be preparing an arrangement of pods to receive MacKenzie. Of course, for RL3 they hadn't been successful.

*Maybe this time?*

'I wonder if the Transcenders are going to push a little harder this time,' said Tim.

Tim looked around. Martel was still gone, with just Private Hunter and the prime minister on the mezzanine with Sam and himself.

'Maybe they'll destroy each other,' said Sam.

Tim smiled but didn't answer. The Ankor would be listening to anything he said.

His eyes flicked to the main screens.

The transcription of long-wave radio confirmed the US fleet was two days away.

More pressingly, the main screen showed that the pod alignment on the Ankor craft had completed. Both factions had prepared docking areas.

Tim's smile faded. Nothing good could come of the Transcender faction getting MacKenzie.

*A few hours to go …*

# CHAPTER 40

**SpaceOp**

Sitting on the mezzanine level, monitoring the status of RL10, Tim dreaded the thought of MacKenzie successfully docking and then sending the instructions for restarting the Hot Zone decapitations.

*Although that is the goal we've been working towards …*

Next to him, Sam was also morose.

'They may just vent him,' said Tim, trying to cheer her up.

'I would if I was them,' said Sam, not sounding genuine.

Tim sighed; it was a clusterfuck of choices. MacKenzie had originally chosen to kill close to seventy thousand people across the world in order to give himself eternal life. The Ankor had chosen the same but, critically to their moral standards, only thought they were killing twenty thousand – the Blessed were not actually dying.

*Of course, that was just the original plan.*

Since then, the Ankor had killed fifty million across China, Brazil, Mexico, and the USA in a twisted programme made up of equal parts retribution and coercion.

On the main wall, a real-time feed of the Ankor craft covered five square metres. The temperature distribution of the pods hadn't altered since the Chimera virus had been contained. There appeared to be well under two hundred pods at operational temperatures.

*I hope Charlie made it.*

'How long do you think?' asked Sam.

Tim scanned the composite image. The Ankor craft still had two docking areas prepared, but he couldn't tell where MacKenzie was. The infrared telescopes could only focus on the Ankor craft. They couldn't track the recovery module.

The main screen went blank and a collective gasp emanated from the main floor technicians.

'What's going on?' asked Sam, reaching past Tim for the keyboard and starting to type.

At the back of the mezzanine, Hunter started talking urgently on the radio.

Sam nudged Tim and pointed to the workstation.

**Explosion reported.**

'Did the Chinese send up a rocket?' asked Tim, immediately feeling stupid. Obviously, a bomb had been smuggled inside RL10.

*Is MacKenzie dead?*

As Martel and Whaller climbed the stairs towards them, Tim wondered if he could ask.

As he approached, Martel gave a look that implied questions would not be welcome. 'Please can you two see what damage they've sustained and if they have lost any control of our systems?'

With Tim offering advice, Sam got sifting. Theories were hitting the internet at the rate of a thousand per second.

The most obvious change, if the data could be believed, was that in the past few moments data extraction from satellite uplinks across the globe, which had been running at terabytes every second, had slowed to a trickle.

It certainly looked like their hold on Earth's systems had loosened – but the severity of the damage they had sustained was critical. Would they retaliate?

*Plus ... who got hurt ... the Ankor or the Transcenders?*

'They're moving,' said Private Hunter, listening into his long-wave radio set.

'What about pod temperatures?' asked Martel.

Sam dug into the transcripts. 'We're not getting real-time temperature readings now they're moving.'

'They haven't blown us up yet,' Sam whispered to Tim. 'That's a good thing.'

Tim smiled at Sam's gallows humour.

'No!' The scream had emanated from the prime minister at the back of the mezzanine level. 'You cannot believe that!' he shouted into his own radio. He strode forward to Martel who was still standing next to Tim.

'The US have given us three hours to evacuate.'

'But they're two days away,' blurted out Sam.

'They have a stealth destroyer much closer,' replied Timbers. 'It has artillery with tactical shells.'

Tim looked at Sam. Tactical shells didn't sound so bad. 'Some type of precision bombing?' he asked quietly. Perhaps the Americans would just destroy the launch platform and leave.

Sam wiped his growing hope away. 'Tactical *nuclear* shells. It's cold war technology. Each one of them yields up to ten kilotons. They could flatten all of Anglesey in a five second barrage.'

'Three hours,' said Martel, looking at the prime minister. 'I suggest we evacuate.'

Timbers nodded.

Martel immediately went to the front of the mezzanine level, looking down on the three hundred technicians below.

'Full evacuation! Go directly to the car park. The keys will be in the cars.' He paused. 'Do not leave the car park unless your car is full. Head for the east coast. We have arranged a flotilla to pick us up.'

There was total silence.

'What about the radiation?' called someone from the floor.

'There is no significant radiation outside,' said Martel. 'The Ankor were manipulating the readings to keep people in here.'

387

*Fuck! Martel must have known all along.*

Tim widened his eyes at Sam, who had come to the same conclusion.

'And he didn't think to allay people's fears when he took over?' whispered Sam.

'I guess he was incentivised to keep people working effectively too,' replied Tim, aware that Martel was only a few metres away.

'Why are we evacuating?' asked the same person. Tim did not see their face.

'The Americans will start bombarding SpaceOp within a few hours.'

'Where do we go?' Another voice from the floor.

'Anywhere between Abbey Bay and Hunter's Point,' said Martel. 'We've been working on evacuation plans since even before the Ankor's true nature became clear. Tosh's team will be ensuring the keys are in the cars and all the barriers to the main gates are open.'

'What about the hostages?'

Martel stiffened at the question. 'I will lead a detachment of my soldiers to free them.'

*Shit!*

There were hundreds of fully armed Leafers. That was a suicide mission.

Tosh opened the main doors and shouted over the rumble of whispered conversations, 'No more questions! Go!'

Mission Control workers, accustomed to taking orders from Tosh, surged towards the doors.

Private Hunter, having been listening to his radio, walked forward and gave Martel an update. 'Sir. China have just destroyed all their space launch platforms and disabled all their long-range missiles.'

Tim understood their reasoning. If they had no capability to send materials into space, then they could not become the focus of any new Ankor efforts.

The door leading to the underground server rooms opened and Whaller came through, heavily armed. Martel took a step towards the staircase that led down to the main floor.

'Do you need help?' asked Tim.

'Ever fired a gun at another human?'

'No.'

Martel smiled. 'Thank you for the offer, but we're expecting a heavy firefight down there. I can't spare a man to watch your back.'

Tim indicated towards the back wall. 'I can provide video surveillance, what's left of it.'

'Thank you. That would be appreciated,' said Martel. 'As a last resort I may ask you to try to operate electronic locks from here. MacKenzie said all the electronic locks are on their own closed circuit and can't be accessed remotely, but I can't help thinking he'd have some control from here.'

Martel beckoned Private Hunter and took a radio from him, passing it to Sam. 'I can't imagine for one moment you're not staying for the dust up.'

'You bet your ass I'm staying,' said Sam, a glint in her eye.

'Good luck,' said Martel. 'In one hour, no matter what happens, head for Abbey Bay. Tosh will ensure your car is just outside.'

'MacKenzie?' asked Tim.

'We are ninety-nine percent sure he died in the explosion,' said Martel, heading down to the main floor with the prime minister in tow.

Dead at a shade over fifty years old. The irony was not lost on Tim. Francis MacKenzie had spent most of his life chasing immortality. His search for spiritual immortality early in his life through involvement with various religious groups had met with failure. Since then he'd focused his efforts on physical immortality through technological, and biological, engineering. Yet if the MedOp arterial cleansing had been MacKenzie's one and only venture, he'd have achieved cultural immortality through the legacy he'd left to the world.

*He'd probably have been able to replace the Nobel Prize with the MacKenzie Prize.*

As it was, the guy would be remembered – quite rightly – as a monster. An unempathetic entitled fuckwit who'd lived his life as if it was more valuable that anyone else's … a position from which, with fear chasing close behind you and unlimited resources at your disposal, evil is almost inevitable.

Walking over to the back wall, Tim plugged in the tablet. Having experimented with the feeds the previous night, he'd found some operational ones. He managed to find a camera showing the main corridor behind the decapitation rooms. The corridor that Tim suspected led to the holding cells.

Sam relayed the information to Martel. Given that Martel and his team were attempting their incursion via the underground route, the signal was very poor.

There were no Leafers to be seen.

'We have such limited coverage,' said Tim.

'Whatever we manage to find for Martel is a bonus,' replied Sam. 'He was expecting to go in blind. I wonder if Richardson is with them … and whether he has my chair.'

'There's nothing on the tablet that implies we can open gates from here,' said Tim. 'It must be some of these dials.' Tim pointed to them through one of the open hatches.

The feed of the main corridor showed Martel's team entering from the direction of the decapitation room: Martel, Whaller, Hunter, Briars, Tosh, and Richardson in Sam's wheelchair. All heavily armed and making their way stealthily down the corridor.

Managing to split the screen, Tim accessed the next video feed.

Now he could see the first holding room – forty cells, just as MacKenzie had originally claimed. Still no Leafers, but the cells were full of hostages.

Whaller was still working on the external door to get from the corridor into that first holding room.

Tim split the screen again and managed to find a camera on the far corridor. They'd be able to warn Martel if anyone was coming.

The radio squeaked. Sam listened.

'They think this door will be a ten-minute job,' said Sam, relaying Martel's concerns. 'They need automated cell release.'

The prime minister approached. 'Mr Boston, Miss Turner. The Americans won't speak to me. Can I help here?'

'Maybe open some of those far hatches,' said Sam, pointing. 'Can you see if there are any discernible markings inside? We're looking for switches, levers, and dials.'

The prime minister nodded.

Sam's radio buzzed again. She listened to a report from Whaller and relayed the information to Tim. 'The lock is military-grade titanium. It's totally unlike the locks that Briars was shown on the other levels. It's a thirty-minute job. They need another way of opening the doors.'

Tim turned to the prime minister. 'Are the US really going to fire on us?'

Timbers looked grave. 'I can't see why they won't. We have a viable launch platform and forty thousand hostages.'

Tim shuddered. They had an hour. Although football stadiums regularly emptied in those time frames, football stadiums didn't have potential Leafer firefights and titanium cell doors to contend with.

'What if we blew up the launch pad ourselves?' asked Sam. 'Would the US stop?'

'They simply don't trust us to do anything,' said the prime minister. 'We have to run.'

Leaving Sam and Timbers at the back wall, Tim walked back to MacKenzie's workstation and typed.

```
Help us. There is no advantage for the Ankor
in letting the Americans slaughter forty
thousand innocent souls
```

Tim waited.

A moment later he got a reply.

> **You poisoned us and then sent a nuclear bomb This is after you saw our limited needs … less than half humanity's average daily death rate … hardly genocide … but you almost destroyed our whole being.**

Tim considered his response.

```
You nuked us - fifty million dead
Now you have a chance to save lives
```

> **We tried to conserve lives We have killed less than one percent of the human population You have killed fifty percent of the Ankor.**

There was no point getting into a philosophical argument about the relative value of lives. They had no time.

*Will you help us or not?*

# CHAPTER 41

**SpaceOp**

Silence.

Looking over his shoulder, Tim called over to Sam. 'How's it going with you?'

Sam shook her head. 'They still haven't opened one. There's hundreds to do.'

The workstation chimed.

> *Middle row. Fifth hatch*
> *from left*
> *Third dial from the left*
> *inside hatch*
> *Turn full left and push*

Tim hesitated. Could it be a trap?

> *You contacted us Mr Boston*

Tim relayed the information over to Sam who opened the specified hatch, then turned the dial as instructed.

'They've all opened,' shouted Sam from the back wall.

> *Time for you to leave Mr*
> *Boston. Good luck*
> *The Americans will fire*
> *within the hour*

'Are you leaving?' asked Tim, knowing they could hear.

*To be decided. The-sterile*
*are in open war with us*
*and have captured key*
*communications points. If*
*they break into the A-Grav*
*circuits, it will not be*
*good for humanity*

'Can I help you?'

*Say a prayer for us*

'Is Charlie there?' asked Sam, hobbling over to the
workstation on her crutches.

*We are Ankor*
*You must leave now*

Beckoning to the prime minister, Tim led them out of the
building.

Outside, his own car was waiting. The keys were in the
ignition and it started first time.

'Abbey Bay,' said Sam, as she climbed into the passenger
seat whilst Joshua Timbers got into the back.

Sam pulled out her phone and launched the satellite
navigation function. 'It seems to be working,' she said.

'Or, the Ankor are going to lead us off a cliff face,' said
Tim.

Focusing on the road, Tim didn't see Sam's facial
response, but she said, 'Turn left out of the gates.'

On his left, Tim could see a passenger coach being loaded
outside the Hot Zone.

At the next junction they went straight on, and at the next
junction turned right.

'I hope Tosh makes it,' said Sam.

Tim took his eyes off the road for a moment to give her a reassuring smile.

A road sign indicated Abbey Bay was ahead.

Tim was desperate to get them away from the incoming barrage but he fought the urge to drive too fast.

*I'm not going to crash again with Sam in the passenger seat. Not to mention the bloody prime minister.*

'You're doing fine,' said Sam, laying her hand on his forearm. 'A minute won't make a difference.'

'Incoming nuclear shells?' said Tim. 'One minute may really matter.'

Sam rolled her eyes. 'Just drive.'

The road followed a valley that led directly down to the coast, but the contours of the land and the surrounding trees stopped any long-distance views.

In the back of the car, the prime minister was speaking to a senior member of the American administration. From what Tim could discern, the US president was unwilling to speak to 'the enemy'.

'Tell him we understand his need to neutralise the launch facilities, but we need a few more hours to get the innocent hostages out of the Hot Zone,' said the prime minister, hanging up.

With one mile to go, the valley opened out, and the small village of Abbey Bay appeared ahead. Directly in front of them was a car park, and beyond that, the granite sea wall.

The car park was rammed full.

'Go right,' said Sam. 'Ignore the car park. Drive onto the beach.'

Tim turned right at the sea wall, and fifty metres later a small slipway came into view. Turning left, Tim drove down the slipway and onto the beach.

Abbey Bay itself was a sandy beach, probably half a mile wide. The tide was low, and a few hundred metres of sand lay between them and the sea. Many SpaceOp personnel were on the beach. Not just the few hundred from Mission Control, but the administrative staff, the payload specialists ... Everyone.

At least two thousand people were crammed onto the sand.

Waiting.

A flash in the sky drew Tim's attention.

Just around the headland to the south, a single red flare shot vertically, framed by the blue-grey sky.

It was not alone.

Another.

Then another.

'Look!' said Sam, pointing.

A boat – gunmetal grey.

Heading their way?

Not just one boat.

From the far end of the bay, British Navy craft of all types appeared, ploughing through the waters accompanied by a flotilla of civilian boats.

Within minutes, Navy landing ribs were heading into the beach, ready to ferry people out to the larger waiting craft.

Turning the car wheel, Tim drove south across the beach.

The flotilla of civilian boats that rounded the headland were not just fishing boats. There were vessels of all types: small yachts, working trawlers, pleasure cruisers.

Tim picked out a small fishing boat that appeared to be venturing close in to the shore.

'Open the windows,' said Tim.

'We're doing this?' asked Sam.

Muted expletives came from the prime minister on the back seat, but he didn't tell Tim to stop.

397

Pushing the accelerator full down, Tim pointed the car directly at the ocean.

Hitting the water at well over forty miles an hour, the car ploughed in … and kept on going.

Water flooded through the open windows and a few moments later the engine spluttered and died.

Tim climbed out of his window and waded, chest deep, around the car.

Sam had already levered herself partially out of the window. Tim grabbed her and pulled. She yelped in pain and Tim felt phantom pain jolt through his own stomach and legs, but she managed to scramble onto the roof of the car as the small fishing boat approached them.

It had two occupants; Tim presumed they were father and son. Both looked like they'd lived on boats all their lives. The old man was at the bow, looking down through the waves to gauge depth.

When he was twenty metres away he called over. 'We can't come closer. The tide is dropping, and we'll get beached!'

'Okay,' Tim shouted back. 'Sam has mobility difficulties, we had to leave a wheelchair behind.'

'I can swim,' said Sam quietly.

'Take off your shoes, coats, and jumpers!' The old man mimed taking off his clothes. 'Or you'll sink.'

Tim, Sam, and Timbers started to strip.

Over on the boat, the old man took off his heavy coat, replaced his lifejacket, tied a rope around his waist, and jumped in.

After Sam had slid elegantly into the water, Tim tried to help her, but, as she had said, she was a good swimmer. Her shoulders and arms compensated well, if not fully, for her lack of leg movement.

The old man met the group halfway and led them towards the stern of the boat where there was a small ladder.

The cold was starting to seep into Tim as he manoeuvred himself around the back of the boat – adrenaline could only do so much.

'You first,' said Sam, now shivering violently.

Tim clambered up, took the proffered blanket, and immediately turned to help her.

Between himself, the old man, and his son, Sam was lifted into the boat and provided with a blanket.

'There's space for a few more,' said Timbers, climbing up last.

The old man did a double-take, realising who he'd just rescued, but recovered his composure quickly. 'You're right there, sir,' he said, waving one of the Navy ribs over.

Once its cargo of five was safely loaded, the son put the boat into reverse, and turned around before heading out to sea.

Collapsed on his back on the deck of the trawler, Tim wrapped the coarse blanket tightly around himself. Surrounded by coiled ropes and the smell of dead fish, he helped Sam lower herself down next to him.

'You know what kept me going?' Tim asked Sam.

'Love?' replied Sam, one arm reaching over him and pulling him closer.

'Well, that …' said Tim, 'and I was scared of what you'd think of me.'

'I reckon that's a good basis for an ongoing relationship,' Sam said, laughing.

Her levity was cut short a minute later when a flash high in the sky drew everyone's attention. Tim turned, internally begging the universe not to show him a mushroom cloud.

There was no cloud, and the flash was not repeated, but a low rumble lasted for a few heartbeats.

'What do you think it was?' asked Tim.

Timbers, sitting quietly next to them, replied, 'My best guess is that the Americans used a precision shell to destroy the launch pad. They'll give us time.'

'I hope you're right,' said Sam.

--------

Huddled in the small forward cabin of the trawler, Sam and Tim desperately skimmed the long-wave radio channels, trying to find news about Martel and the Hot Zone hostages. What little news there was gave cause for hope. The Americans had only fired on the launch pad.

Furthermore, many thousands of hostages had been seen climbing onto a procession of coaches and leaving SpaceOp.

'As long as they didn't meet the Leafers,' said Sam.

Tim nodded, continuing to listen intently.

More news came through about the coaches used for the evacuation. Some of them were UK Prison Service coaches. It appeared that during the A-Grav preparation period a week previously, some prisoners had been diverted to SpaceOp.

An hour later, they pulled into Rhyl harbour with about fifty other boats.

Sam and Tim were swept up with at least five hundred refugees being unloaded onto beaches, piers, and hastily constructed floating pontoons whilst the flotilla turned around to collect the next load of survivors.

On their journey to Rhyl, the radio had been clear that local residents were ordered to stay away from the harbour and the irradiated survivors.

But, of course, they had come.

Locals mingled, handing out food, drink, and blankets, consoling the grieving, and just giving a helping hand wherever needed.

'What's that noise?' asked Sam. They'd found a bench and were simply sitting gazing out to sea.

A low rumble was growing louder from the east.

The crowds had heard it too.

Someone screamed.

Everyone watched the sky, looking around wildly.

The rumble resolved into a slow whump-whump-whump of helicopter rotor blades.

Five large British Chinook helicopters swooped low over the town and landed.

Immediately they lowered their ramps and more relief teams swept out.

'Sam.' Dexter had found them. 'I saw you earlier. I got these for you.'

Sam took the crutches with a smile and laid them on the bench next to her. 'Thank you.'

Dexter turned and disappeared back into the crowd.

'He'll sleep well,' said Tim. Dexter had made a moral stand in Mission Control and had not given an inch with regards to the hostages … whereas Tim had been content to support Martel in cutting the wires to sacrifice the forty thousand.

'The Ankor could have blown the whole country to hell.'

'Dexter didn't make his stand based on weighing up the evidence,' said Tim. 'He just knew what was right.'

'No,' said Sam. 'He made a decision based on the avoidance of short-term guilt.'

'That doesn't seem fair,' said Tim. 'He knew what was right.'

Sam shrugged and turned to watch the ebb and flow of the crowd as army personnel started herding people towards hastily constructed decontamination units.

Helping Sam up from the bench, Tim looked for the unit with the shortest queue and they hobbled over.

# CHAPTER 42

**Tim's Flat, North London**

Looking out of the military jeep's window, Tim tried to piece together a plan of action. It was just before midnight and he hoped to get some sleep before dawn. The helicopter they'd clambered onto had taken them to a sprawling army base.

Tim smiled. As they'd landed, Sam had said she'd thought the journey time was probably too short for them to be in Guantanamo, but had given Tim advice on how to hold his breath.

As it was, until a few hours previously, they'd undergone extensive, but broadly sympathetic, debriefing.

*Deprogramming.*

Colonel Martel had been present to protect them from the more overzealous military intelligence investigators – and he had explicitly confirmed that MacKenzie had perished in the five kiloton nuclear charge they concealed aboard RL10.

Joined also by Captain Whaller towards the end, they'd talked about the Ankor's religious beliefs and how Simulation Theory might influence their behaviours. However, it had quickly descended into the equivalent of a late-night pub conversation which reached a dead end when someone asked, 'who made the people that wrote the first simulation?' Fundamentally, a bunch of army jocks and a few computer nerds were not the people to unpick the mysteries of the universe and – once they'd drained Tim of every actual word the Ankor had said – the whole investigation was turned over to a panel of religious experts, philosophers, and other academics.

Tim had been very happy to be off the hook.

During the debriefing – and, again, fully chaperoned by Martel – Tim had tried to contact the Ankor, but they'd remained resolutely silent. According to Martel, this had been the case with any attempted communications he was aware of.

The jeep turned into Tim's street. Lights were showing from just under half of the nearby buildings.

*Home sweet home.*

Tim smiled and kicked himself at the same time. As they'd been packing up from the debrief he'd considered fifty ways of asking Sam if they could perhaps spend the night together. Unfortunately, every phrase he'd considered had either sounded cheap or too oblique. Then, just as he'd turned to climb forlornly into his own jeep, Sam had squeezed his hand and said, '*Your place or mine?*'

It was possible that he'd thanked her – the memory was hazy – before explaining that, although her flat was far better set up for her mobility issues, it had too good a view of the Kirkmail A-Grav unit which was one of the thousand globally that was still ticking.

She smiled and simply said, '*Cool, your place then. I'll pack a bag and be over as soon as.*'

Tim opened the door to his flat, still thinking about the A-Gravs.

The ticking A-Gravs were emitting regular pulses of low-intensity gamma radiation. Additionally, they appeared to have anti-tampering mechanisms such that if anyone, or anything, approached within fifty metres then the emission intensity increased substantially. The remainder of the A-Gravs across the globe were silent and did not react, but the standing UN orders were that no-one was to approach them.

His phone buzzed. A text from Sam.

**Home safe thanks. Squaddies packing up my stuff. Be with you in two hours.**

The couple of soldiers who had accompanied Tim into his flat now checked it for extraneous surveillance devices. There were many. Tim stood by his kitchen table while the bugs were disposed of, and then the soldiers left.

*MacKenzie protecting his investments.*

Once alone, he turned on the news. Most countries were declaring themselves stable, even those that had suffered the most horrendous backlash: China, US, Brazil, and Mexico.

To Tim it seemed like each country had different proportions of three main groups: those who declared themselves entirely comfortable with providing the remaining forty thousand brains to avoid a nuclear massacre, and to be clear, they already had a list of names ready; those who would rather die than be party to blasphemy as all life was deemed sacred; and the final group who preferred not to think about it and rather hoped they'd never have to make the choice.

News pertaining to SpaceOp itself was greatly restricted, but during the debriefing Martel had informed Tim that a detailed sweep of the island confirmed the Leafers had gone. There was no information as to how they left, or where they went.

*Were they really just hired guns? Or something more?*

# CHAPTER 43

**A few days later, Tim's Flat, North London**

Still nothing from the Ankor. Their craft had retreated to the orbit of the moon and had reformed itself into a cubic lattice. Analysis of its composition indicated that it had been reduced to just under two hundred physical pods: some had been jettisoned in the Chimera attack, some had melted in the nuclear explosion, and others had been cut loose subsequently.

Only one hundred now appeared to be at operational temperature and there were none at the so-called suspended animation temperature of 220K. Neither Tim nor Sam had any indication of how the internal struggle between the Ankor's warring factions had progressed, but clearly no energy was being wasted on Ankor members who were 'asleep'.

Tim walked through to his living room.

'Sam,' he said, gently shaking her arm – she was wired into her VR headset.

Sam had had a large portion of the MIDAS kit from Butler Street moved into Tim's flat. The computing power at her disposal was ten thousand times more than she possibly needed to run OrcLore, or any of her other games.

Sam pushed the VR headset off her face. 'On my way.'

They were due to have lunch at a nearby restaurant.

'I heard a rumour,' said Tim.

'Whispers of a nameless fear,' said Sam.

'Unfortunately,' said Tim. 'Apparently the Ankor have done a deal.'

'When you say rumour … you don't mean they told you directly?' said Sam.

'No,' said Tim, speaking theatrically to the ceiling, where he was sure the British army had replaced MacKenzie's bugs with their own. 'The Ankor have not contacted me.'

*They really haven't. Honest.*

'So you got it off the internet,' said Sam.

'Toby sent me a link,' said Tim. 'He's still with his parents, who've made him swear never to come back to London.'

'I spoke to him yesterday. He's fine,' said Sam, smiling. 'So … this rumour?'

'The Indian launch facility is showing significant unusual activity,' said Tim. There was a lot of activity at other launch sites too, but they were all doing medium-term decommissioning.

'They won't launch,' said Sam.

'I hope not.' Smiling, Tim helped her up from the sofa – she let him do that now – and they headed out for lunch.

'Did you read about Kusr?' asked Tim as they walked.

Sam chuckled. Xandra Kusr had been found, alive – and incandescent with rage. Having been locked below ground for four days with little food and zero information, she was rescued from an alien invasion she knew nothing about and was immediately arrested for being complicit. Tim was sure it would be sorted in the end.

--------

**A few days later, Tim's Flat**

A scream of joy from Sam caused Tim to wake up and get out of bed in the same movement.

'Thank fuck for that!' she shouted at the television.

407

Sam, lying next to him on the bed was watching live stream feed on her laptop. It showed a burning launch pad … in India.

'What?' asked Tim. 'Did they launch?'

'No,' said Sam. 'Controlled demolition.'

'How many others?'

'About half the launch sites have done the same.'

Tim nodded. In a world that was still reeling from major atomic explosions in large cities across the globe, and with ticking A-Gravs still in place, every piece of good news was worth savouring.

'Any news on the A-Gravs?' asked Tim.

'Sort of,' said Sam. 'Investigation of their emission patterns implies that there are three categories of A-Grav. And …' Sam opened a new web page and scanned it. 'People think it could be only one type that are City Buster bombs.'

'How many of those?'

'Just under a hundred, but no-one is sure. The tests weren't performed on the A-Gravs that actually did explode. It could be many more, or less …'

'The bombs were only one lever,' said Tim. 'Given their technological superiority, they could have paralysed hospitals, power stations, airline flights, payroll systems … automated farming systems.'

'I guess you're right,' said Sam. 'Just as well we beat them!'

--------

**A few days later, Tim's Flat**

There was still nothing from the Ankor, who were now in orbit around the moon, constantly keeping it between themselves and the Sun.

The only new item of note was a 'tell-all' breakfast television interview from a Dr Xandra Kusr. Who, released from custody, had decided to attempt to clear her name by doing a series of 'tell all' interviews.

Tim and Sam watched in wonder. If Kusr was to be believed – and she seemed very credible – then she knew nothing about what MacKenzie had been trying to achieve.

On a much more sombre note, a global week of mourning had been announced to honour the memories of those murdered by the Ankor.

Still nothing on the location of MacKenzie's private army – the Leafers. It was fairly clear that MacKenzie had taken that secret to his grave.

# EPILOGUE

**Months later**

Bank Holiday Monday, the hottest day of the year. Sam hobbled into the flat on her crutches and slumped onto the sofa, reaching for the VR headset. She had sweat patches on her sweat patches and longed for a shower but had received a text from Tim that he was keen to play OrcLore, so she'd cut short her chores.

'Tim!' she called through to the bedroom. 'Are we going to play?'

'Yes,' said Tim from the doorway. 'I got your text.'

*I got yours …*

Booting up the game, Sam's customised load screen appeared, and she chose the rainforest start zone.

'Jungle start?' asked Sam, feeling Tim sit down on the sofa next to her. He'd be using the television monitor as his screen – noob.

'Sure.'

Their characters materialised in a jungle clearing. Instantly, Sam's VR headset started providing her with the sights and sounds of exotic fauna and flora. Somewhere high up in the trees, the OrcLore equivalent of baboons were cavorting. It was not beyond Sam to shoot a couple down in order to brew up a health potion, but this time she didn't.

In game, Sam turned to look at Tim. His character – a dwarven barbarian called DismemberLong – was pacing the clearing, inexpertly swinging a massively oversized axe like a scythe. 'Where do you want to go?'

'Don't mind,' said Tim.

'Something's out of place,' said Sam.

'What's wrong?' asked Tim.

'Not sure.'

With her headset on, she could hear Tim's voice and the jungle foliage sounds. It was normal gameplay but … a little off.

'What's that?' said Tim, looking towards a bush.

Sam looked.

From amongst the dense green bush an elven head was protruding, watching them.

Sam was using her Valkyrie Slayer. It was level eighty, had full dragon scale armour and a vorpal blade. No single elf could even cause her to break a sweat.

As they approached, the elf disappeared back into the bush. In fact, although it looked elfish, it wasn't quite that simple. Sam pushed through the bush. The elf, a little way ahead, did not turn but kept moving. It was beefier than a normal elf. Half-Elven.

*It also has a yew bow.*

'It's Eddie,' said Sam in a hushed whisper, watching the elf pushing through low bushes as it continued up the densely wooded hill.

'Who?' asked Tim

'It's not his usual skin,' said Sam. 'He usually wears Greenstone livery. But I recognise the bow.'

'Eddie?' asked Tim.

'Edward Mariner,' said Sam. 'Charlie's main character.'

As she spoke, the half-elf disappeared over the top of the hill.

Sam sprinted.

Over the hill, a small valley lay before her, with a river meandering along its base. Eddie disappeared into a cave halfway down the slope.

Sam turned to see Tim struggling along – dwarfs were not fast in OrcLore, albeit they had plenty of momentum.

'Into that cave,' said Sam.

The cave was pitch black.

Sam keyed her microphone. 'Hello?'

'Eddie? Charlie?'

The sound of her own voice echoed back at her through her headset. 'Eddie? Charlie?'

At that moment, a faint light started to shine a few metres ahead.

As the light got brighter, Sam could see it emanated from a necklace that Eddie was wearing.

On the floor at his feet was a chest. Eddie signalled for Sam to open it.

Sam waited for Tim to get to her side, then did so.

Inside the chest was a scroll.

The scroll had an IP address.

**231.12.3.43**

'On it!' shouted Tim, throwing down his game controller and getting up from the sofa.

Sam focused on Eddie. 'Are you okay?'

The half-elf simply stood there with the generic smile on its face.

'I need to know if you're okay?' she repeated. She felt something for this man. Not love, but … something.

'We've thirty seconds,' said Tim.

'Charlie?'

The generic smile on Eddie's face broadened a fraction and then the character blinked and faded out.

After waiting a few more seconds to be sure he was truly gone, Sam ripped off her headset.

Over at the table, Tim was scrolling through pages and pages of data on his laptop.

'Have you saved it locally?' asked Sam.

Tim turned his head. 'To three different drives, of which I have already isolated this one,' he said, waving a small zip drive in the air.

'And? What is it?' asked Sam.

'I'm no expert,' said Tim. 'But I think it is an exact DNA, biochemical and physiological analysis of you, Samantha Turner. With detailed genetic engineering schematics showing how the damage to your spine can be reversed.'

Sam looked over his shoulder.

The file was three hundred pages long and, skimming the contents page, Sam saw that four surgical procedures had already been mapped out. They appeared to be based on non-invasive chemical triggering of stem cells to stimulate neural regeneration.

'Want to find a doctor?' asked Tim.

'I guess we could ask Dr Hung to take a look,' said Sam.

'Was that Charlie?'

'I don't know.'

'Maybe all the Blessed retain some individual awareness when they join an Ankor pod.'

Sam shrugged. 'Seems unlikely ... would a brain work with so many conscious voices?'

'Maybe he was given MacKenzie's pod?'

'Or,' said Sam, with a sad look on her face. 'Maybe the Ankor just simulated him to make us more likely to trust the information.'

Tim remained silent, watching Sam as she appeared to process her thoughts.

'It was him,' she said, leaning over and kissing Tim on the cheek. 'That's what I choose to believe.'

# ABOUT THE AUTHOR

Nick M Lloyd

Independent author, living in London.

I hope you enjoyed the book.

Please leave a review with Amazon and Goodreads

I can be found…
Twitter              @nick_m_lloyd
Facebook          nickmlloyd.writer
www.nickmlloyd.com


Also By The Author

Emergence
www.amazon.com/gp/product/B00OAGX4L2

Disconnected
www.amazon.com/gp/product/B06XSQTG91

Printed in Great Britain
by Amazon